HEART OF VENGEANCE

Shane L. Coffey

BURN THE MAP PUBLISHING

I dedicate this book to the greatest cover artist in
the history of indie fiction

Other books by Shane L. Coffey

The Spirit of the Trees Series
Identity & Community
Calamity

The Winds of Vengeance Series
Hand of Vengeance

Table of Contents

PROLOGUE

𝔗he outlaw stirred in his sleep, disturbed by the sound of breaking wood to his right. He had no time for thought before a weight hit him from above like a stooping falcon, what felt like a knee hammering his sternum, driving the air out of him as his left arm was trapped beneath taut blankets. He tried to cry out, but a hand clamped his mouth shut, forcing his panicked breath through his nose in sharp hisses. Not a second later he felt the unmistakable cold of sharp steel against his throat.

"Any sound above a whisper, and you die," murmured a woman's voice against his ear. "Nod if you understand."

He nodded.

The woman pinning him shifted her weight, taking her hand from his mouth to find his right wrist in the dark and press it against the wall above his head. The lethal pressure of the blade didn't relent.

"Who's the other man in this room?" the voice quietly demanded.

"M-my partner," the highwayman quavered. For an instant he thought he saw an impossible flash in the woman's eyes, a spark of ruby and emerald that over-whelmed him with unnamable terror.

"You rode all the way north with him?" the woman asked.

The man gulped, his throat bulging against the steel. He nodded again. The hideous slicing of the blade was the last thing he would ever feel.

The merchant sat hunched over his ledger in the lamplight, muttering to himself, when he heard a thumping commotion from the room across the hall. He stood and approached his door. He hadn't much liked the look of his neighbors, but one of them had been ill. What if he had gone delirious with fever and needed help? He hesitated, then finally picked up his lamp and forced himself to open his door. The noises intensified, and he paused in the hallway, unnerved. Suddenly the facing door flew open, revealing a tall silhouette wearing a head scarf and holding a knife in each hand. "Who–?" he began. His eyes went wide as he realized the form's black, wool coat was soaked with blood. "Help!" he shouted. "Help! Murder! Help!"

The form lunged at him, and the merchant shrank back toward his room, but he continued to yell, unable to control his voice in his fear. The form turned away and fled down the stairs. He heard the inn's common room rousing to alarmed wakefulness as the front door boomed open, wind and snow howling through the opening. With trepidation he crossed the hallway, holding his lantern high, immediately overcome by the reek of blood.

Across the settlement, two men, one a human and the other an elf, stood in a small cottage lit by a fire in the hearth. "Where do you think she went?" the human asked.

The elf raised one eyebrow. "I take it you don't know her very well."

"Not overly. I mean, by reputation, I reckon I know as much as anyone, the stories of her slaying orcs and helping lift the siege on the Capital and all. Before that I rode with her as caravan guard for a couple months when she first came south. Happened the spring after some big to-do up north in Atlund, think their king led an army against an evil wizard in their western forests or some such. She said she was in it, but apart from that she wasn't much for talking. She was reckless as a mad badger back then, though, worse even than the minstrels tell it."

The elf nodded. "When I first met her wasn't much after that, and she was about the same as far as I saw. I only had eyes on her for a minute, after her new employer asked me to put an enchantment on this great, two-handed tree cleaver she calls a sword." He pointed to where the great sword lay on the cottage's table. "She'd wrecked it against the magical barriers of an orc sorcerer–"

"A zil'bast?" the man exclaimed. "I thought *sure* that tale was horse apples."

"No, she killed the thing alright. But the sword took a beating, so Lord Baraxis put his smith to work through the night to repair it. I'd come calling looking for a place to lodge. He asked for the magic in trade, and I did it, though I haggled him up a lot, I have to admit. The next morning when he handed the sword back to her, though, she was *not* appreciative. I'd meant to stay there a week or so, but one look in her eyes and I bowed my goodbyes and got out of there as fast as I could, believe me.

"I didn't see her again for over a year, when we broke the siege and scattered the orcs. She was different than her reputation, less arrogant than I'd seen her, but in some ways she was even worse. I've run with soldiers the best part of twenty years, and I don't think I'd seen anybody so cold and brutal."

"I heard one of her comrades got killed, a captain she was best friends with."

"That's what she told me, after. She lost at least one other friend that day, thanks to me, in part."

"I think we all did," the man replied, gazing into the fire.

The elf nodded. "She had business to do, settling the score for that first friend that died. We parted ways."

"So that was four months ago, thereabouts."

"Thereabouts," the elf agreed.

"So what got you mixed up in this mess now?"

"That's," the elf began, hesitating, "a longer story."

CHAPTER I

One month, a hundred leagues, and much blood before, Gwyn spurred the mighty, black steed, Thunderhead, a parting gift from her lord, to the top of a hill just east of Baraxis' castle gates. Her older horse, a sleek gray bred in the forests of Atlund, followed behind on loose reins. When Gwyn reached the hilltop, she turned back, and as the first rays of dawn's light crested the rise, she lifted her great sword high in salute to the Lord Major Baraxis, rearing Thunderhead onto his hind legs so his forehooves pawed the air, horse and rider bathed in the sun's golden fire. For a moment she held the form, sensing the balance of the superbly trained warhorse as Baraxis, framed in his open gates, returned her salute with a raised hand. Finally she allowed Thunderhead to set his feet back on the road. Lowering her sword with a last, lingering gaze, she turned away from Baraxis' keep, wondering if she would ever lay eyes on it or its people again. She wrapped the gray stallion's reins around her saddle horn and eased Thunderhead down the east side of the hill until she approached a footbridge that led over a slow, dirty stream at the slope's base, it's underside still untouched by the early dawn light. She came no closer than ten or twelve yards before a voice cried out from the shadows. "Gwyn? Gwyn the Savage, is that you?"

"Who's there?" she demanded, her sword still in her hand.

"I am!" the voice called again, its owner stepping out into the light.

Gwyn regarded the small stature, pale skin, and deep blue robes. Even having only a brief association, and that all of three months gone, there could be no mistaking the elven speaker. "Drax? What in all the hells are you doing here? And don't say you were just 'happening by' again," she concluded, referring to the circumstances of their last meeting back in the Capital.

"No, this time I *was* looking for you," the elf admitted.

"Why?" Her tone rang more aggravated than interested.

"Well," Drax answered, seemingly unperturbed, "with the war ended and the demand for my particular services greatly reduced as a result, I have decided to return home. I was here in the western fiefs anyway, and word was thick through the villages that you were coming back, so I hoped you might be heading north as well. The intervening wilds have grown even more dangerous, I'm told, and I thought our roads might run together for a time."

"Your road runs where it may, and if the end is along my path, that's no business of mine. If our roads are to run *together*, you must match my speed and earn your keep. You don't even have a mount."

"And yet I can't help noticing you seem to be flush with horseflesh."

"Yes, *I* am, of late. So you ask for my protection and now for my horse as well."

"Only the loan of him, and the protection would be

mutually traded, as would be the company, though you could gain unequal advantage on that point–"

Gwyn snorted.

"–so all that remains is to negotiate for the loan of one horse."

"Alright," Gwyn relented, curiosity finally overcoming frustration. "What can you possibly offer in security for the loan, or by way of a rental fee?"

"Knowledge," the elf answered, tapping a long, ringed finger expressively against his temple. "I know the lay of the land, the shortcuts, the warning winds that come before the big storms. While you've been hunting in the east and south, I've been traveling the west. I know which towns are safe, which keeps have enough supplies to accommodate travelers, which taverns serve the best ale. And when we come to it, I can secure safe passage through the Elven Forest, even off the major roads, provided we go first to my village."

This last, in particular, intrigued Gwyn. The Elven Forest was honeycombed with smaller trails, but only the main roads were safe for outsiders, and the nearest could take many wasted days to reach if the wilds forced her path east or west. An ally could prove useful on the journey as well, and Gwyn doubted she could waste time waiting for a northbound trade caravan with the Southern economy suffering as it was. Even if she could, it was likely to go out of her way and to travel more slowly than she dared. "Very well," she finally agreed. "Let me shorten the damn stirrups." She climbed down from Thunderhead and began making the adjustments on her gray's saddle. "I don't have a stepstool for you, though," she shot with a smirk.

"I needn't one." Drax walked up to the animal, rubbed his muzzle, and petted his mane as Gwyn worked. Then he whispered to the horse, which bowed down on his front legs so the short elf could easily climb up.

Gwyn stood back, astonished. "How did you get him to do that?"

"I asked."

"You talk to horses?" Gwyn raised a skeptical eyebrow.

"And other animals, at need. They aren't particularly stimulating for conversation, but most have a language of sorts that I can borrow with a little magic and elven sense. I overwintered in a wolf den one time. It was alright, once I convinced the family I wasn't food."

"Elf, I can't decide if you're mad or daft."

"Me either, but a moment ago I was afoot, and now I'm mounted, so mad, daft, or both, it seems to be working." He grinned at his own jest.

Gwyn sighed and took Thunderhead across the small bridge, praying silently that once they got underway, the elf would not talk so much.

As the day would show, Drax was an amiable enough companion. He spent most of his time quietly absorbed in his own thoughts but was quick with advice or observation when the time called for it. They passed a few wains traveling south with Baraxis' share of late harvest crops, but little else.

"You gave me reason to think the way would be more dangerous," Gwyn commented as the sun dipped behind trees to the southwest. So far the elf's help had been merely convenient, not transformative, perhaps not justification for the food she'd shared with him at midday or the wear on her horse, though both were light enough.

"Baraxis' lands fared better than most," Drax replied, betraying no offense at Gwyn's clear implication. "The Storn River bridge he defended allowed him to keep his levies at home much longer than most in the west, and to leave better subordinates behind when he was finally called. When we leave Sutherset altogether, you'll see things change quickly."

Knowing Shon's and Tira's ranch, where Gwyn was now bound on a final errand for Lord Major Baraxis, stood on the very edge of his holdings, Gwyn unconsciously quickened Thunderhead's pace as she wrapped her cloak more tightly against a sudden gust from the northeast. Nevertheless, less than an hour later Drax pointed toward an inn and recommended they halt for the night.

"We still have an hour of daylight," Gwyn protested.

"And nowhere else within that hour that's still taking boarders," Drax countered. "I don't mind sleeping on the ground any more than you do, but we can also eat here and save the storable rations. There won't be many more chances to get oats for the horses, either."

Gwyn looked up the road to the north, hesitating.

"I know you've traveled far," Drax insisted, "but a soldier travels well-supplied. I guess you haven't gone many miles with nothing to live on but your own kit. Or am I wrong?"

Gwyn sighed, loathe to admit a weakness. "You have the truth of it. We'll stop here," she relented.

An hour later Gwyn had seen to the horses and joined Drax in the common room. The prices of everything staggered her. On her way south a year and a half ago, her challenge had been the debatable value of her Atlund coins. Now, food and shelter were of more value than metal, no matter whose face was stamped on it. At least her back pay had added up substantially enough to fund such accommodations without concern, and if what she knew of wizards' service fees were true, Drax had no reason to scrimp either. She found the atmosphere of the dining hall just as unsettling as the boarding fees. Even during the harshest press of war, the country inns she'd visited had been boisterous with drinking and talk, offering respite from uncertain tomorrows. Now the Southerners had peace, but the privation that came along with it made them sullen and still.

Gwyn sought a small table where she could sit alone, but before she could pull out the chair, Drax joined her with a board of sippets, bowls, and tankards, which he sat before her. Too disinterested to complain at his company, she reached to her coin purse as she sat. "What do I owe you?"

"No need," Drax assured her, taking his own chair. "You paid to board both horses even though I'm riding one. We're even."

Gwyn nodded her thanks, still wary of Drax's mien and motives. The elf began wolfing down his supper with gusto, but Gwyn stirred the thin stew dubiously. She'd eaten better in the Capital under siege conditions, at least part of the time. She crumbled her portion of bread into the broth to soften the one and thicken the other, then began her repast just as Drax finished his and washed it down with weak ale. "Can I ask you a question?" he hazarded.

Gwyn shrugged her shoulders without commitment.

"Why are we tending easterly? We passed two forks that would have taken us more quickly north."

"I have a stop to make before returning home," Gwyn answered between swallows.

"Care to elaborate? I know, I know, you think it's none of my business, but I'm bound to find out when we get there, anyway."

Gwyn assented. "Sometime tomorrow, if we continue on this heading, we should come to a ranch. A friend's family lives there, and I need to make sure they're safe and relay that they're welcome at their lord's table."

"Because their man isn't coming home?"

Gwyn nodded.

"And because you still owe something to his memory?"

"No, I settled that score," Gwyn asserted. "This is a favor, not a debt."

"The man must have been quite the friend to earn any kind of favor from Gwyn the Savage."

"He was."

"Well, best get what rest you can. We'll need to be alert tomorrow; this road grows less and less safe in the direction we're going."

"Story of my life," Gwyn muttered, putting her feet on an empty chair and nursing her ale. Drax slid a warded lock key, adorned with a numbered strap of leather, across the table to her and took his leave, quipping something about his 'beauty sleep.' Gwyn was glad for the time to herself, a commodity she'd lost without warning upon encountering Drax after dawn, but in a short time the somber hush of the common room unnerved her. She retired to her own chamber immediately after finishing her ale.

The morning came on slowly through overcast skies. The pair set out shortly after dawn, and by midmorning the truth of Drax's warning became clear. Cast off possessions, broken cart pieces, even whole abandoned wagons littered the roadside. Most seemed to have been heading south, toward the safer lands nearer Baraxis' castle, but some had tried north or west. All testified that the region ahead was one people had fled as quickly as they could, and many had met with disaster in the attempt. Gwyn wondered briefly why Tira had not taken refuge with her lord when she could, but she just as quickly dismissed the notion. If the woman was even half as brave as her husband, she would never run. Though the heavy clouds held onto their burden, as Gwyn and Drax moved north the ground grew increasingly wet, giving proof that rain had swept through the night before.

The sun hung high but still invisible when Gwyn turned down a lane off the main road, following her instincts and a description Shon had given of the place as much as the Sutherese's directions she'd requested two nights before.

After a quarter mile the lane turned out of a cleft between two hills, and Gwyn suddenly spurred Thunderhead to a full gallop. Up ahead, smoke rose from what was left of a stable and barn, and the thatch of a long, low house was charred, still smoldering in places.

Gwyn flew off Thunderhead even before he stopped, freeing her blade as she hit the ground running. "Tira!" she shouted, sprinting across the long house's broad porch to the door. A trail of blood ran back out to the lane.

She burst through the door to find a scene of destruction. All the furniture in the main room was overturned or smashed, and four bodies lay scattered within, one pierced with crossbow bolts and others slashed or stabbed. In here, the reek of decay overpowered that of smoke. These men had been dead a full day, at least. Gwyn followed the trail of blood and damage to the back of the house, looking in larders and bedrooms. What appeared to be a child's room was likewise ransacked, but the other spaces had been left alone.

"Gwyn!" she heard Drax calling her from outside. She left the house of death and ran toward the elf's voice, following his shouts to the wreckage of the barn. As she went, she saw bodies littering the ground, another half dozen, whether ranch hands or raiders she couldn't tell. Probably some of both. Nearing the smoldering barn, she spotted Drax crouching, his blue robes clear and somehow shocking against the blackened timbers and pallid ash. "Help me," he asked when he knew she was close enough.

Gwyn stepped around Drax to see the focus of his labor. A slim body, moaning almost inaudibly, lay pinned beneath a fallen timber too large for the elf to shift away. Setting her sword down nearby, Gwyn took up the beam on the other side of the crushed survivor and heaved, making space enough for Drax to grab the body by the ankles and drag it free. Gwyn looked down once more to see a small woman, older than herself but still in the prime of her life, with deep brown eyes and black hair, her fine features bruised and caked with soot. Gwyn dropped to her knees and cradled the woman's head. "Tira? Tira, what happened?"

Tira's eyes worked open but didn't seem to see anything. "On us...too fast. Too many. After Baraxis' message. Distracted...getting ready to travel. Have to... No! The barn! Loose the horses! Shon's horses, don't let them burn!" Gwyn looked across the wreckage and saw no burnt or crushed animals it its midst. For all the horror that had befallen, at least that much had been saved. Tira began to flail, but though her hips twisted Gwyn saw her legs didn't move.

"Tira, Tira, wake up. Look at me, Tira," Gwyn ordered.

The woman calmed, and her eyes seemed at last to focus on Gwyn's face. Her words grew weak. "How do...my name?"

"I fought with your husband," Gwyn answered. "I'm–"

"Gwyn the Savage," Tira said, trying to sit up. The effort left her coughing and rasping as she sagged back on Gwyn's lap.

"Can't you help her?" Gwyn demanded, looking up at Drax.

The elf stood with his skull cap in his fist, crumpled over his heart. He shook his head in a tight, agonized denial.

"Gwyn!" Tira gasped, coming around once more. "Please, help. Karon! They took him. Threw him in a cart and rode off. West, I think. Please. Save our boy. Save..."

Gwyn felt for breath without hope, then reached up and closed the woman's staring eyes. She rose slowly, laying Tira's head down as gently as she could. For a moment she stood silent, looking at the dead woman. Then her rage exploded out of her. "Dammit! Damn them all! I swear I'll slaughter every murdering–" Her words were choked by her rage, but thunder shook the skies in answer. She kicked a dead outlaw behind her, she punched the timber posts, then Drax dodged out of the way as she flung a milking stool through an empty doorframe. She lifted her sword, but there was nothing to kill. Finally she rounded on Drax. "I'm going west as fast as Thunderhead will carry me. Our deal is off. Come with me, help me find the boy and put the sword to his mother's murderers, and you can *keep* the horse, for good. If not, you're on your own and on foot starting right now."

"Let our old deal stand. I'm with you anyway."

"Why?"

"What does it matter? There's no time to discuss it in any case."

"Fine," Gwyn consented. "I wish we could lay her to rest, but there's no time for digging graves."

"I can b– Would a cremation be acceptable?"

"Better than leaving her for the crows. Go ahead. No, wait." Gwyn leaned down and reverently slipped the wedding ring from Tira's finger. "Karon should have this," she stated. Gwyn reached into a pouch on her belt and removed a small bundle of cloth. Opening it, she placed Tira's ring inside next to Shon's, which she had rescued from his last killer's trophy pole, then returned both rings to safekeeping.

Drax nodded. "Ready? Stand clear, then."

Gwyn stepped back from the razed barn as the wizard waved his hands in intricate gestures and chanted a few guttural syllables. One of his rings sparked white, there was a flash, and Tira was gone, her ashes lost amidst the ruin of her world.

The pair mounted their horses and flew from the homestead.

~ * ~

The road west was even worse than the road northeast had been, for on it the broken wagons were joined by fresh bodies. Gwyn rode on at a gallop, begrudging every second. Tira hadn't been coherent enough to reckon time, but she'd implied she was awake when the attack fell, though marauders would likely have struck before it was fully light. Added to the state of the bodies she'd seen, that meant her quarry were a day and a half ahead of her, and every minute was precious. Her chest was tight; a tingling gripped the back of her neck. Shon's only child was in danger, an innocent boy of no more than five years, and she could have no peace until he was safe. The image of Tira's broken form and lifeless eyes clawed at her thoughts, the need to rain hellish fury upon the killers ripping a hole through her heart as real as her worst physical wounds. Silently, she repeated her vow of vengeance, and the lightning on the horizon was mirrored in her eyes.

Drax had said nothing and made no complaint. After several minutes of hard riding, though, Gwyn felt him slowing behind her. She looked over her shoulder, anger flashing over her face, but when she saw Drax's expression she slowed as well. The elf's forehead was creased with worry, but his eyes and the set of his jaw remained resolute. It wasn't the elf whose will had faltered; her gray stallion, bred for bursts of speed through broken, forested terrain, was better in the sprint than endurance. She realized it was foolish, even wasteful, to drive the horses so hard without a clear destination. Forcing herself to take a measured breath, she checked Thunderhead and allowed Drax to catch up. As they trotted along the road, Gwyn looked down at the elf and made an effort to swallow her pride. "I don't know where to go," she said.

Drax nodded. "I know, but I have some idea, and I wouldn't have advised any different direction. I figured to follow until Thunderhead got tired of your spurs, but my beast flagged first. He doesn't seem to like a long gallop."

Gwyn shook her head. "He's forest-bred, and I never had the chance to train him for distance and open ground. I don't know Thunderhead's limits yet; if he's much like his father, I'll be hard pressed to find them." Thunderhead was the last colt sired by Storm Cloud, the great charger that had carried Lord Major Baraxis into many battles, another casualty of the orc wars.

Drax came back to the pressing subject at hand. "I've been keeping eyes open for any tracks that might stand out, but nothing shows on this road. There's a crossroads we should make by nightfall, and a tavern that's still running, as far as I know. The patrons are cutthroats, and the owner is worse. Somebody there is bound to have information if we live long enough to collect it."

"Or they live long enough to give it." Gwyn had no fear of bandits. Some may even remember rumors of her passage south and give her a wide berth. On the other hand, if any wanted to try at her again when they felt the odds were better, she was more than ready to make an example of them. She pressed on urgently but now at a sustainable pace, knowing she could ill afford to overwork their mounts and be forced to go on foot to rest them. Still, it was a full hour before nightfall when Gwyn and Drax arrived at the tavern he had described, its dim windows looking from the right onto the north side of the half-frozen road. Just past the lit building loomed a stone structure, likely a meeting hall or temple but in disrepair, its doorway and window frames empty.

Opposite the two buildings stood a stable which Drax approached first. The long, low building was of logs, the front interrupted by three large doors. The central one stood open and was flanked by shuttered windows. A boy nearing his teens sat on a three-legged stool in the doorway; when he saw the riders headed in his direction he stood and disappeared from sight. A moment later a man emerged, bald and sun-toughened. His nose was bent from an old injury and his lip split from a fresher one. Gwyn noticed the shoeing hammer he held in a nervous grip, but Drax spoke first.

"All is well. Do you remember me, Orvix?"

The stablemaster squinted for a moment. "Drax, is that you? Who's the woman?"

"She's a friend. This is Gwyn."

Gwyn caught motion at the window to the right as the shutter cracked open, and she just made out the boy's head in silhouette.

"Gwyn," Orvix repeated. "*The* Gwyn?"

"The same," Drax confirmed, climbing down from the gray horse. Gwyn dismounted Thunderhead as well, then opened her saddlebags while she eyed a board marked with the prices for service. Summing quickly, she retrieved a small stack of coins and turned to the stablemaster.

"Two stalls, best feed," she explained, dropping the money into his open hand. "I'll settle them down myself, just come around and fill their troughs and bins in a bit."

Orvix nodded as Gwyn led the horses into the lantern-lit stable. She walked to two stalls at the far end as the boy gazed on, nearly unmoving. Drax and Orvix had entered behind her, and she listened to their conversation as she unburdened Thunderhead and her Atlund stallion, checked their feet, and rubbed them both down.

"It's good to have proper paying customers again," Orvix began to the elf. "These ruffians throw me some coin occasionally, but mostly they take what they want. It's even worse in the weeks since you were through."

"I'm sorry to hear that, friend," Drax replied, "and I wish we had more to give."

"Nah, nah, after your help last time, I'm indebted to you."

"Well, we could use some information about folks passing through here, if you have it."

Orvix nodded. "I'll help if I can."

"Any new faces in the tavern? Maybe a sizable mob yesterday, midday or after, likely with some riderless horses and a cart. You might have seen a young boy with them."

"Don't, Pa," the boy cried out from his place by the window, and Gwyn turned to look at him between tasks. His fear was real.

"See that?" Orvix remarked to Drax, his voice tight. "I can take the beatings and the disrespect, and I can swallow my pride to keep my family alive, but I'll not have my son learning to be a coward. You hear?" he called to the boy before turning back to Drax. "Yeah, there was a group like that yesterday, eight or nine men. Came through two or three hours after noon, had a couple extra saddled horses, and a few others with rope bridles I guess they'd gathered up someplace. Don't suppose they gave the market price, if you take my meaning. Didn't see a boy, but they did have a cart, a big one, which stood out. Most anybody with enough of anything to need a cart is long gone from here. This bunch rested their mounts until nearly dawn, made us water and feed them for nary a copper, then lit out before sunup. Headed west, like everybody else in these parts."

Gwyn considered the length of day for the season and figured the murderers were nine or ten hours ahead of her, so close she could feel it as tension in her chest and behind her eyes. She had to rescue Karon from banditry or slavery or whatever evils awaited him, but even more than that, to avenge Tira was a *need*, as fundamental to her existence as her next breath of air. She couldn't bear the thought the cutthroats might elude her, and as urgently as she needed to be in Atlund, for the moment it was far from her mind.

Drax and Orvix were still speaking. "Thank you," Drax answered the stablemaster. "Consider us even."

"There's more," Orvix interjected. "Late this morning, another man came here asking after those same robbers. Tall, wiry fellah with a cut on his face. Member of the bigger band but got separated going after a stray horse, he said. Didn't seem in too big a hurry to catch up, though. His riding horse and the other he was leading are in the far stalls, there." He pointed to the opposite end of the stable from Gwyn.

At last Gwyn walked back toward the central door and joined the conversation. Her sword was in her hand. "So this latecomer is still here, then."

Orvix nodded and led the pair to the other stalls. "That's the one, and there's the other he was leading in."

Gwyn took a lantern from the far wall and surveyed the unsaddled horse's left hip. The circle-and-diamond brand of Shon's ranch was plain there. "This is one of Shon's," she said. "No doubt now this man and the rest of his gang are the ones we're after."

"We could've figured out he was here on our own this way," Drax muttered to Orvix. "It won't lead back to you." Gwyn ignored them as she headed out of the stable and across the road to the tavern. She passed the boy in the doorway, his anxiety clear in his stance and expression.

"Hold, Gwyn," Drax called from behind her, hastening to catch up.

"Don't get in my way, Drax," she growled back, only barely slowing.

"I'm not. How far do you think you'll get, just barging in there and demanding answers?" He kept his voice low.

Gwyn ground her teeth. "I can be convincing."

"'Convincing' him to flee out the back as soon as he hears you're looking, maybe. I have a better idea." The elf motioned to the left, then moved to the front corner of the tavern, peering into the space between it and the stone building.

Gwyn followed but took a wider arc to crouch on the opposite side of the narrow alley. "Now what?" she demanded.

Still looking into the shadowy lane, Drax answered, "This may not come to a lady's mind immediately, but flowing ale, uncouth men, and a convenient side door always leads to one thing: frequent trips for relief." As if on cue, a creaking door some thirty feet down the side of the tavern opened, spilling firelight into the shadows, and a man staggered out, opening the front of his pants as he leaned with one arm against the abandoned stone structure. Gwyn tensed, but Drax shook his head even as she also realized this man was of average height and stocky.

Once the drunkard had gone back inside, Gwyn whispered, "Will you be able to see the cut on his face? Could be lots of tall, thin men in there."

"Not from here," Drax agreed. "Stay there." Before she could stop him, Drax slipped into the alley, hiding himself in the deepening shadows beside the tavern door. Gwyn gave an exasperated growl, hoping the bombastic elf could handle himself.

The best part of an hour went by, and Gwyn's hiding place grew darker and colder as she waited, neither of which troubled her. Her impatience, on the other hand, mounted greatly. Other drinkers came and went, and Drax must have hidden himself effectively as none showed any alarm. Gwyn had nearly decided to abandon the elf's plan and storm the main entrance when, at last, the side door opened to permit a lanky man into the chill night. Between the shadows and the distance, Gwyn couldn't make out his face. The door closed behind him as he moved into position against the stone wall. Even from thirty feet Gwyn could hear liquid splattering against the rock when a smaller shadow drew up behind the tall man, reaching a hand up to his neck. Gwyn saw, or thought she did, a quick flash of purple light, then the man abruptly turned, a strangled, rasping sound reaching her ears as he clutched at his throat. He lunged at Drax, but the elf moved to the side and touched the man's outstretched arm, who then turned toward the front of the tavern and bolted, working at the front of his pants with his other arm as he ran.

Gwyn very much doubted he ever saw it coming as he drew abreast of her and she swung her fist into his jaw, spinning his head around so hard the rest of his body seemed to follow as he heeled over onto the frozen mud of the road. Drax was a few steps behind the man's long-legged stride, and Orvix was moving across the road to the scene as well. "Get him inside," the stablemaster whispered, and between the three of them they managed to half-carry and half-drag the wiry, unconscious villain, all knees and elbows, into the stable. Orvix barred the doors while Gwyn and Drax shoved their captive into an empty stall.

The stablemaster's son looked up from measuring out fodder for Gwyn's horses. "Pa! What are you doing?"

"Quiet, boy," Orvix grunted. "I'm sick o' crawlin' for these curs."

The elf then turned away from the captive and peeked out a window. "Doesn't look like anybody heard anything, or if they did they weren't enough concerned by it to turn from their libations." He looked back over to Gwyn, standing in the open stall with her sword point against the bandit's chest. "Well?" he asked with a raised eyebrow.

"You did alright out there," Gwyn answered, "now stop that smug look before I stop it for you." Drax only snorted as Gwyn returned her attention to the man they'd apprehended. He was starting to come around but looked to need another minute before he could offer anything coherent. She noticed his neck was strangely thin and wrinkled, and his right shirt sleeve looked nearly empty. "What did you do to him?" she asked the elf.

Drax twisted one of the rings on his left hand, a small stone of amethyst in a silver setting. "It'll wear off presently."

"Good," Gwyn answered, remembering the gurgling sound the man had made in the alley. "I need him to talk."

"He can talk. Well enough. Just not scream, or breathe hard enough to fight or run for very long."

Gwyn could see the bandit's eyes now focused properly on the sword point in his chest. "You attacked a ranch about dawn yesterday," she accused. "Don't deny it. That act signed your death warrant, do you understand?"

The man's eyes went wide, and he whimpered as he tried to push himself back from Gwyn's blade. Drax's attack had interrupted his obligation in the alley, and fear now prompted it to completion.

"Maybe you should have asked some questions before you promised to kill him," Drax observed from the window. Gwyn pinned the elf with a withering stare. "Just commenting for future reference," he concluded.

"I can't let you live," Gwyn confirmed, turning back to the brigand, "but I can end it quick and clean…or I can hack off your hands and feet and let the wolves have you. They won't bother killing you before they start eating."

"Oh, in Terillah's name, have mercy, please," the brigand whimpered.

"You dare invoke the creator's name after a life of theft, rape, and murder? *This* is more mercy than you deserve." She leaned into her sword, just enough to pierce the skin. The man howled in terror.

"Get in the house, boy!" Gwyn heard Orvix command his son.

"But Pa–"

"Out the back, now!" The sound of squeaking hinges filled the stable as the boy obeyed.

"Some of the natives heard his yowling, Gwyn," Drax cautioned. "I can see people looking out the front windows. Best make it quick and quiet."

Gwyn could feel events accelerating around her. Her brain was forged for combat, not interrogations; the whole situation made her uneasy. "Where is your gang taking the ranch woman's son?"

"Ranch woman… Son? What are you talking about?"

"Don't lie to me," Gwyn growled, struggling to keep her voice low.

"He's telling the truth," Drax called from the window. Gwyn looked over to see the silver cuff high on the elf's left ear glowing with a spiderweb of blue lines, dim enough she doubted they would show in daylight. The elf continued, confirming, "He has no idea what you mean."

Gwyn's eyes narrowed. "Were you in the house when the boy was taken?"

"I don't know nothin' about the house. We fired the barn, then a woman came out of the house and grabbed one of the hands that wasn't fighting yet and ran toward it to turn the horses loose. I was hangin' back and rode out to start rounding 'em up."

Trusting Drax to warn her if the man spoke false, Gwyn continued. "That ranch has been there forever. Why attack it just now?"

"They had lots of sturdy hands still." The brigand seemed to be recovering some hope in his survival, leading to less mewling as he replied. "Some of us asked the boss why not go someplace with easier pickin's, but he only told us to shut up."

The timing of the attack, just a day after Baraxis returned to his demesne and shortly after his advance courier had delivered a message to Tira, had been nagging at Gwyn, but her prisoner didn't seem knowledgeable enough to shed any light. "Where were you going?" she pressed. "If you separated, where were you to meet up?"

"There's a town, what's left of one, twenty leagues west of here to another crossroads, then another ten miles or so to the north. We been collecting horses there until we had enough to drive to market in the spring. S'posed to be someplace way up north paying the best coin."

"Twenty leagues?" Gwyn responded. "Seems a long way to range for plunder."

The man shrugged. "Boss says 'Go,' we go."

Gwyn had all she needed. She looked the brigand in the eye. He started to speak, but she raised the point of her blade and ran it through his throat before any sound could emerge. Blood spurted to the roof before she wrenched the blade sideways and watched his life wink out. When she turned away, Drax's face was ashen.

"Why did you do that?" he demanded. "He didn't kill Tira, may never have killed anyone."

"Her blood was still on his hands, no less than any man in the gang. He knew where we're going. We couldn't risk turning him loose or taking him with us." Gwyn paused for a moment and pinned Drax with a hard stare. "Didn't you tell me once you're a killer by trade?"

The elf's eyes were downcast. "Not everyone enjoys their work as much as you."

"You asked to ride with the Hand of Vengeance, and there's bloody business to be done. If you can't stomach it, best we part ways."

Drax shook his head. "I'm with you, at least until we find the boy." He looked at the dead bandit, then closed his eyes for a moment. Finally he looked to Orvix. "Somebody is bound to come looking for this cur. I think it's time you and yours were gone from here, friend."

"This is our home," Orvix rebutted.

Gwyn nodded. "Seems like a fine enough place to die if that's what you're after. If not, take the horse this scum brought in and head south to the Storn, then east. You'll be in the lands of your neighbor, Lord Major Baraxis. Make your way to his manor and give my name to the guards to get an audience. Tell the Lord Major I sent you with the message that Tira is dead and Karon abducted. Give the directions to the meeting place you just heard."

"This is something necessary?" Orvix prodded.

"Yes," Gwyn confirmed. "Something worth a place in Baraxis' holdings if you succeed. Much better life for your family than this one."

"Alright," the stablemaster agreed. "We'll start packing our things."

"Only take what you need for a two or three day journey and anything you can't bear to part with," Gwyn urged. "Baraxis will see to your needs, and the lighter you travel, the better."

Orvix nodded and went out the back, the same way his son had gone.

CHAPTER II

$\mathfrak{D}$reams are made from the stuff of the sleeper's life, so when Gwyn dreamed, most of her experiences were tense and bloody. The real nightmares, though, leering orc faces, searching dark figures, and disembodied voices, had released their overwhelming grip the morning she decapitated the last of Shon's killers. Now they returned.

She ran through Shon's homestead, fire and carnage swirling around her. Men grappled on the ground or pitted pitchfork against bloody sword and spear. The *twang* of bowstrings and lower *thunk* of crossbow limbs perforated the prevailing noises of yells and roaring flame. A man limped out of the house, his left leg oozing blood from a gash above his knee, and in his arms he clutched a small, struggling boy. Horses whinnied and nickered in fear, but none screamed in pain as a small herd burst from the unbarred doors at one end of the barn just moments before a section of the roof collapsed. As Gwyn strained to mark the features of the villains, the images dissolved around her in a rushing, ghostly swirl, reconstituting into a line of ten men, their faces invisible in shadows save the one nearest her. A thin face with a fresh cut, it tipped backward in a sudden gout of blood, then the form crumpled down, disintegrating into black smoke. It's disappearance cleared a path in her vision to a dark-cloaked figure, his head turning side to side and at last resting in her direction, looking nearly at her, though she sensed her face remained as hidden to him as his was to her. A woman's voice, soft and familiar, intruded on her dreaming thoughts. "You are too reckless, Gwyn. You had little enough of time, and you've made that no better."

The impenetrable darkness beneath the cloaked figure's hood seemed to emanate outward, but before it could reach her, and with a final look at the line of doomed men, she opened her eyes.

Gwyn woke Drax well before dawn. "The horses are rested and *Aridan* is bright," she told him. "Let's make the most of it."

The elf nodded and rubbed the sleep from his face. Gwyn led Thunderhead from his stall, already saddled and with a large sack of oats hanging on either side. The gray stallion was likewise burdened with extra food, the forage growing scarce with the descending winter even in the warmer south. They walked into the chill, stars still bright over the hard shadow-line of the Tunari mountains in the west. The moon *Aridan*, the Faithful One, lit the road with his pallid light. *Bia Creg*, the Little Wanderer, the tiny glimmer of a moon that sailed backward through the sky on her own agenda, raced upward from the jagged peaks.

Gwyn set a relentless pace, and by sunset she and Drax had covered perhaps two-thirds of the twenty leagues to the crossroads. They passed inns; all were deserted save one. This final waystation they spurned as well, hours still to go before Gwyn would relent, and shelter of any kind was lacking as the shadows grew long. At least the water was adequate, with Drax remembering or locating occasional sources that were just out of sight from the road; above a bend in one of these streams stood a thicket where Gwyn and Drax could tether the horses and set camp for the night. Gwyn forbade a fire, but Drax gathered wood and did some gesturing with one of his rings, a band of blackened metal set with a small ruby. The stone glowed like a dying ember, and at that the tinder began to crackle and produce heat, but the flame was lightless and invisible. Gwyn smelled smoke, but the naked boughs overhead broke it up sufficiently not to be noticed in the moonlight, at least from afar. The elf was proving useful after all, Gwyn admitted to herself, if somewhat grudgingly.

They set out again at sunup, the day dawning gray and chill. Indeed, since their most recent meeting the days had been so overcast Gwyn had not seen Drax don the darkened lenses he sometimes wore in protection from the sun. As they went, he advised her of the road ahead. "At this pace, we should reach the crossroads by midday. There's nothing permanent there; local tradesmen would set up wagons to sell their wares when times were better, but I don't expect we'll see anyone."

"Any chance of an ambush?"

"No, it's open terrain all around, no place to hide."

"We'll trust speed then," Gwyn concluded, returning her focus to the road.

The heavy clouds thinned to a distant haze as the morning wore on, and they reached the crossroads with the pale, winter sun above them and tiring horses below. The area was indeed deserted, so they dismounted and surveyed the grounds. Gwyn arched her back, stretching the effects of the bone-jarring ride from her joints. Thunderhead was indeed a powerful and tireless animal, but his faster gaits were trained for war, not comfort. The road was too packed to make out individual tracks, but in general the wagon and cart ruts ran west, and the horse prints, mostly unshod, ran north. "Dammit!" Gwyn growled, kicking a rock. "All we can do is guess."

"The bandit wasn't lying," Drax reminded. "The gang meant to go north."

"But he didn't know his betters' plan for the boy, and the cart tracks go west. A light wagon could have gone north on this hard ground without leaving a sign, though, or they could have put the boy on a horse. We're probably going twice their speed, or near enough, so we could overtake them tonight or tomorrow if we keep pushing, but not if we go the completely wrong way."

"I might be able to improvise something, if we can spare the time," Drax hazarded.

"How long?"

"Couple of hours. I'll be spent when I'm done if I go that fast," he warned.

"The horses could use the break. I'll rig up an extra rope halter for your mount while you work. You can lash your arms down and rest while we ride."

Drax immediately began, removing the dark spectacles from one of his pouches and taking them some distance from the road, where he sat cross-legged with the object in his lap. Gwyn watched for a moment as he chanted and gestured, but she quickly lost interest and paced back to Thunderhead to retrieve some rope from her rig. In ten minutes she had a serviceable harness knotted together around her gray stallion that Drax could hook his arms through and, if not sleep, at least nod in the saddle without falling off. The horses were no longer breathing hard, so Gwyn led them to a ditch south of the main road and let them slurp from the small stream running down its bottom. With no fear of them drinking too quickly from such a small supply, she left them to it, surveying the horizon for trouble or anything else that might appear. Nothing did. She considered throwing down her bedroll and trying to catch a little sleep, but Drax seemed to have slipped into some kind of trance, so she thought it best to stay alert. She sat on the ground and leaned her back against the signpost marking the road, preparing to pass another hour or more in solitude.

In what felt like twenty minutes, Gwyn spied a lone figure walking down the road from the east. She rubbed her eyes, surprised to see anyone traveling alone through such dangerous territory, especially on foot. As she looked harder, the person seemed to be wearing a cloak and hood and walking with a tall staff, though he did not lean on it as an old or lame person might. Her chest felt suddenly tight, her breath quickening. She couldn't guess who this traveler was but remembered her dream of the prior night, and the thought of him reaching her filled Gwyn with dread. Suddenly she heard the same woman's voice from far to the north, crying out loudly but too faint with distance for Gwyn to make out the words. She turned her gaze to the northward road but saw nothing there, nor on the flat, scrubby plain stretching to either side. Gwyn shook herself with a start, peering again into the eastern distance, to see the road in that direction now empty as well. Her eyes felt heavy, and she realized she'd dozed off and dreamt while waiting for the elf. Chiding herself, she stood, stomping back to the ditch and the horses, checking her gear to ensure all stood ready for their departure as soon as Drax finished his enchantment. She begrudged every minute, but it wasn't only the horses that felt weary, she had to admit.

At last Drax stirred, wasting no words to explain his work to Gwyn before placing the glass lenses before his eyes and peering at the ground, whispering to himself all the while in a language Gwyn didn't recognize; whether simply elven speech or some secret language of magic she had no way of knowing. It only took a few moments for Drax to speak up in the Southern tongue. "Sometime late yesterday a gang of men came through, probably less than ten riders and a few extra, unshod horses." Drax paused, walking between the west and north roads. So intent was he on the ground that Gwyn had to shove him sideways to prevent him running into the signpost. He looked up at that intrusion to his search, but only briefly, then returned to the tracks. "The mob split then. Three men went north with the unshod horses and four, five, six…yes, six continued west with the cart, moving quickly."

"You can tell all that? Enough to be sure?"

"If there'd been more traffic, certainly not, but I'm sure these are the most recent tracks, and they match our knowledge too closely for coincidence," Drax answered.

Gwyn cursed. Until this moment she'd maintained a flicker of hope the enemy band would stay together, allowing her to save Karon and avenge all Tira's killers as well. Now that flicker winked out, leaving only the darkness of unanswered questions. The war had made so many orphans and slain so much livestock, a young boy had less value than even the least of the horses they'd taken. Any brigands sent into Tira's house to grab Karon would have been better spent rounding up stray mounts. Something about all this was too strange to ignore. "No time to lose, then," Gwyn concluded, walking to the stream and mounting Thunderhead, Drax only a few steps behind as he stowed his lenses and blinked his eyes, hard, several times. True to his prediction, his shoulders sagged with weariness, and for a moment Gwyn thought he would need her help, as well as the horse's, to get into the saddle. He managed with only a brief wobble though, and threw his bedroll over the saddle horn to pad it before twisting his arms through the rope halter and laying across the horse's neck. Gwyn thought she caught him whispering something to the animal as they started off, but she ignored it. They still had far to go and no time to get there. She turned to gaze one last time at the north road. Three of Tira's killers had gone that way, and she had no idea how, or if, she could reach them. The thought soured her stomach.

Less than an hour later they crossed a patch of burned ground with fresh horse leavings nearby, almost certainly the outlaws' campsite. While Gwyn couldn't know exactly when they'd set out, the confirmation they hadn't ridden through the night ensured they couldn't be too far ahead of her now, and at the pace she was driving the horses she must be closing the gap. She prepared to come upon them at every cutting and hill in the road. Around sunset, Drax recovered and sat his saddle properly, gnawing on some dried biscuit and jerky as he rode. There was ample moonlight from *Aridan*, full and long-risen, so Gwyn hastened on as *Bia Creg* fell in the east.

The Faithful One shone overhead and northerly, as high as it would rise that night, when Gwyn and Drax crested a rise and saw a large campfire below. Six armed men sat around it, eating and talking. Their horses were hobbled at the edge of the firelight near a wide, four-wheeled cart.

All but smelling Tira's blood on their hands, Gwyn spurred Thunderhead down the hill at full tilt. The men at the campfire stirred, and those on the near side jumped to their feet. The bandit nearest her turned to the sound of hoofbeats just in time to see the battle light flash in Gwyn's eyes and moonlight glint off her hammer before it crushed his skull in the darkness. Thunderhead leapt the fire with no trace of fear and trampled down another enemy as they sped by. His training was better than Gwyn dared hope. Lightning lanced from the hilltop as Gwyn wheeled for a returning pass, and another highwayman screamed and died, his clothes in flames as Drax's magic hit him. Gwyn charged a pair of them, smiting one, then rolling from the far side of the saddle to avoid a spear thrust by the second. She dropped her hammer as she fell and tore her sword from Thunderhead's trappings as he rode clear, then engaged the spearman, battering the thrusting point aside with a sweeping arc to step inside his reach and hack off his left hand. He dropped to the ground, screaming. The final man bolted, not even trying for his horse. "Follow?" Drax shouted as he cantered down the hill.

"Just kill!" Gwyn growled. Drax hesitated, so with a frustrated grunt Gwyn lifted the maimed bandit's spear and hurled it at the fleeing man's back. Her aim was true, and though he writhed and wheezed for a few moments, she knew he would not live to murder again. Less than a minute had passed, and the enemy was defeated, four dead and two crippled.

The cutthroat at Gwyn's feet cradled the stump of his arm against his chest and wept. "This is what happens to murderous curs when real warriors are about," Gwyn spat at him. She kicked him over onto his side. "Look!" she commanded.

The man turned panic-stricken eyes to Gwyn as she paced over to the fire and the unconscious man Thunderhead had trampled. As the conscious brigand watched, Gwyn plunged her sword into his compatriot's heart with barely a downward glance. The living bandit cried out in protest as Gwyn leaped back toward him, putting her sword point to his throat and pinning his maimed arm to the ground with her boot. "Drax, can you stop his bleeding, or shall I?" Drax gestured with his white-flashing ring, and the reek of burning flesh assailed Gwyn's nose as the bandit screamed again. Gwyn kicked him into silence. "Now," she began, "your dead friend over there was broken in a dozen places. Killing him was more mercy than he deserved. You need to decide quickly how much mercy you're willing to bargain for yourself."

"Please," he begged. "I don' wanna die."

"Stop whimpering," Gwyn ordered. "I'm running out of patience, and you're running out of hands. Are you ready to be useful?"

The bandit drew a shuddering breath and nodded.

"Why did you take the boy?"

"What boy? If there was a boy I never saw him."

"That's a damned lie," Drax called from where he had dismounted the gray horse next to the cart.

"I already know that," Gwyn answered. "There was a blood trail leading out of Tira's house, and this bastard is favoring a leg." She didn't mention how these observations confirmed what she'd seen in a dream two nights before, not fully understanding it herself. Instead she put her boot on the prostrate man's left thigh and leaned her weight into it, causing the outlaw to grunt with new pain, and watched fresh blood seep into his pants from a pad of bandages she could just feel under the leather of her sole.

Gwyn's eyes narrowed at the man, then she kicked him in the ribs. His shoulders came off the ground as he retched, and she slammed her right boot onto his chest to push him back down. Gwyn heard movement from the cart as Drax leaned over the side.

"Let's try again. Why did you take the boy?"

"Lots o' places to sell a kid," the man grunted.

"Not one too small for a man's work. There was a bigger boy at the stable you rode through, and you didn't grab him. Lie to me again and it'll cost you an eye."

Drax came to Gwyn's side. "The boy's in the cart, but he's scared witless. Do you want me to drag him out of there, or would you rather see to him yourself?"

Gwyn scowled. "Watch him," she ordered Drax, then

walked over to the small wagon. In the moonlight she could just make out the shadows of rumpled blankets, the dull glint of tarnished silver candlesticks and a large platter.

Gwyn's eyes were fixed, however, on two points of twinkling light amidst the gloom, points attached to a shadow that pressed back in sudden fear when Gwyn loomed over the side. Circumstances demanded this must be Karon, but more than that, she knew this was Shon's son, as surely as she knew anything in the world.

"It's alright," Gwyn said, her voice more flat than reassuring. She'd have made it gentler for his sake, but she didn't know how. "My name is Gwyn. I'm no marauder; I won't hurt you."

It might have been a woman's voice the boy responded to, or perhaps he could feel the same subtle bond weaving between them that she did. Whatever the reason, Karon relaxed from his cowering and leaned forward, holding up his bound wrists to be freed. Gwyn first pried the gag from his mouth, then pulled her belt knife and sawed through the tough cord wrapping his wrists, careful not to cut the child. The second his hands were loose, even before Gwyn could turn her attention to his ankles, Karon threw open his arms and pushed off from the floor of the cart, jumping at Gwyn and clutching onto her. She held him in turn with her free arm, then sheathed her knife and adjusted her grip on the shaking boy.

The moment they touched, something small and deep and powerful stirred within the being of Gwyn the Savage. Throughout her life she had fought for many things: for vengeance, for pride, for money, mostly for the love of battle and blood. Suddenly this child demanded her protection, compelling her to offer her sword to something more urgent even than bloodlust. These demands were answered by a sudden desire in Gwyn's heart, as certain as it was unlooked-for, that both elated and terrified her.

Something stranger yet was weaving through the chill of that dark night, for as Gwyn dropped her head instinctively to lay her cheek on Karon's hair, shielding him, a sudden rush surged through her body, coming to rest in her brain as a buzzing tension not unlike the frustration she'd felt when first she met Captain Shon. With the father, Gwyn had taken that strange, pulse-quickening anxiety for contempt and, later, attraction. For his son, however, this same stirring of the blood quickly manifested as a fierce and unquestioning fidelity, a bond she'd sometimes wondered if she would share with her younger brothers had they been Girahl's sons and not Adric's.

"Are you alright?" she finally asked.

Karon nodded.

"Were you afraid?"

He nodded again. "Mama told our men to look after me, but the robbers killed them all. They were my friends. Then they took me so far I don't know the way home."

"I'm sorry, Karon," Gwyn whispered, not knowing what else to say.

"How do you know my name?" His voice was muffled against Gwyn's shoulder.

"I was your father's friend, and I looked in on your mother. She was badly hurt by these same brigands, but before the end she asked me to find you."

"The end? Mama?"

"Yes."

Karon started to cry then, not the loud sobs of shock, but the silent weeping of incalculable loss, of hearing what he already knew to be true but was afraid to acknowledge. His lack of surprise unexpectedly grieved Gwyn, the notion that death had become such a foregone conclusion in so young a life.

Gwyn held him close and walked back to where Drax watched the maimed bandit. "He's not harmed," she said.

The bandit started to speak, then shut his mouth.

"What?" Drax demanded.

"Nothing," the robber replied.

"Last chance," Gwyn threatened. "Why him? Why now? Is this your own plot, or are you working for someone?"

The bandit looked away. "I know who you are," he muttered. "I know you'll kill me anyway. You won't get another word from me."

Gwyn looked to Drax, not sure what to do next, when suddenly the brigand screamed in agony as he pushed himself off the ground with his stump of a wrist, pulling a dagger from his boot with his remaining hand and leaping at Gwyn and Karon. Gwyn's eyes went wide as she found herself unable to make any defense with her arms full of the boy; she stepped back and turned her body to shield Karon, hoping her mail would turn the blade but knowing by the angle and desperation of the strike that it would not.

Drax shouted, and from the corner of her eye Gwyn saw the attacker sent flying as if struck by an invisible ram. He landed crookedly, and Gwyn set Karon down and ran to the stricken man, stepping on his knife hand as she felt for breath. He was dead, his stillness only confirming what the unhealthy angle of his neck made evident.

"I'm sorry," Drax said as he paced over. "I didn't want to kill him. I just reacted."

"It's alright," Gwyn sighed, frustrated. "It's my fault, getting that close unarmed, and with Karon. As it was, you may have saved my neck."

"It isn't *all* your fault; I let my guard down. I really thought the fight had gone out of him."

"Yes, and I believe it had, too, until," she paused, replaying the interrogation in her head. "Until I asked who he was working for." They both looked over at Karon where he sat on the ground, hugging his knees.

"What's going on here?" Drax asked. His voice was ominous.

"I don't know, but it makes me anxious to be away. The boy and the horses all need rest, but come first light we have to move fast, and I mean to leave the road and strike out cross-country."

"Going where?"

"South and east, back to Baraxis."

"That's a dangerous path, Gwyn," Drax cautioned. "The terrain goes to hills and woods that way, and no few outlaw bands are hiding in them. It's bad enough here where the pickings have gotten slim, but the closer we get to the river, the rougher things are. We're west of Sutherset now, where they've been without their fighting men for a lot longer and had even fewer come back."

"Baraxis will bring order," Gwyn asserted.

"In time, yes," Drax agreed, "but today, in that direction lies little hope and no safety. If you'll risk the road–"

Gwyn shook her head forcefully, remembering the cloaked figure coming up from that direction as she'd seen in her dream. She scowled. "Let me sleep on it. Douse that fire, and no magic one tonight. Without any cover, the smoke will show too much with the moon full. There's extra blankets in the cart, and we can turn it on its side for a windbreak."

As she removed as much extra weight from the horses as she dared, Gwyn remembered something and reached into her belt pouch. Finding a silver chain on one of the dead bandits, she took it and went to where Drax worked to free Karon's ankles and bundle him up in blankets.

"I have something for you," Gwyn told the boy, threading the chain through Shon and Tira's wedding rings. "These were your parents'," she said, holding them up so he could see. Then she hung the chain on his neck and dropped the rings under his travel-worn shirt. "Wear it close to your heart," she whispered as a tear ran silently down Karon's cheek, following the trail left by so many others. She turned to see Drax looking down at her with a bemused expression. "What?" she demanded. "I'm allowed to be human once in a while, aren't I? And don't think I've forgotten how selective you were with your lightning when that bandit was running off. If I say to kill something, you kill it!"

"I'm not one of your soldiers," Drax answered, turning his back.

"I'll say you're not," Gwyn snapped.

Having resettled Karon, Drax went about his own duties to secure their cold camp and enable a rapid departure in the morning. Gwyn began dragging bodies into a heap downwind from the cart. She was glad of a few minutes to think, realizing her snapping at Drax had more to do with her own weariness and unease than his actions. The fastest way back to Baraxis was to keep to the roads, but she knew retracing her steps was no option. Even setting aside her dream or vision or whatever it was, some other party had likely paid these cutthroats for their brutal services, and given that Gwyn knew nothing of the reach of that party or if the gang she'd now killed was only a part of some larger whole, the roads were simply too dangerous. Drax had been right at every turn so far, though; she had to believe the straight, overland route she'd suggested would be just as fraught with peril as the elf claimed. She would, indeed, sleep on it, but she had little hope the morning would provide any clarity.

As if her immediate dilemma wasn't enough, Gwyn realized she hadn't given a moment's thought to the trouble brewing in Atlund since finding Tira's home ransacked. She glanced involuntarily toward Thunderhead and her saddlebags in the full moonlight, considering the letter from her homeland stowed within. News of a poisoned king and threats of civil war buffeted her mind, and even the proof her family lived was no comfort as half a year had come and gone since the note was written.

Struggling to focus on the essential tasks before her, Gwyn moved to the cart and emptied it, then heaved it onto its side before doffing her armor and spreading out her bedroll next to Karon, who pressed into her for warmth. The cold was no great discomfort for her, but the boy was bred of Southern stock.

Drax approached after finishing his work. "I hoped to take at least a couple of the ruffians' horses, but there's no extra fodder for them. Either these men didn't know how much to pack–"

"Not likely for horse thieves," Gwyn ventured.

"Right. Meaning it's likely we're very close to where they were going."

"Wonderful," Gwyn replied wryly.

"Depending on which way you choose," Drax continued, "it may be better to just turn the extra horses loose and for Karon and I to ride double. Even together we're lighter than a big, Atlund warrior, so I doubt we'll be any great burden to Flamewind."

"To…? Did you name my horse?" Gwyn demanded.

"No, he had a perfectly good name already."

"And how did *you* find it out?"

Having already demonstrated his ability to speak with the animal, Drax's expression at Gwyn's query was dumbfounded. "I asked," he replied.

"And he just *told* you?"

"…Can you think of a compelling reason why he shouldn't?"

In her homeland's tradition, a horse's true name was a closely guarded secret, shared only with the worthiest of riders, not impudent elves, and never after a mere four days.

Gwyn shook her head. "The world's gone mad. Never mind. You rifled through the bandits' kit, then? Anything worth taking?"

"Some trail rations that will keep a few more days, a little silver. I already put anything useful in Flamewind's saddlebags."

Gwyn sighed at the repeated use of what was, apparently, her horse's name. "You want first watch or second?" she asked.

"Second, if it's all the same. That blast at the last highwayman was a bit of a panic, and I didn't control it well. It took the rest out of me."

"As you say." Gwyn assented.

Drax hunkered down in the lee of the cart as Gwyn moved Karon, already asleep in exhaustion, to the elf's warm side, then stood in the shadows and began her vigil.

The night was long and cold, though not so cold as even late autumn nights in Atlund. Toward the end of Gwyn's watch, a pack of feral dogs roamed by and dragged off a few of the bodies, but they didn't approach the makeshift shelter with such easy pickings nearby, so Gwyn let them be, only warning Drax they were about when she woke him.

A few hours later Gwyn opened her eyes to Drax shaking her shoulder. She batted his hand away in alarm and jolted back at the early dawn rays reflecting in a red glow from the elf's pupils, forgetting for a moment how she had seen the race's night-attuned eyes reflecting light like a cat's during her journey through the Elven Forest. Momentarily she recovered, throwing aside her covers onto Karon as she sat up. The sky was still black in the west.

"Trouble, Gwyn. I thought I'd have a look around before I woke you to strike camp. There are six riders coming down from foothills to the west, maybe a mile away now. I don't like the feel of them, and I can't be certain they're alone. They're heading right for us, stopping occasionally to look for tracks but moving with a purpose."

Gwyn bolted up. "Why didn't you say so?"

"I just did."

Karon protested in his sleep when Gwyn lifted him from the ground, but he didn't awaken. Drax held him as Gwyn mounted Thunderhead, then handed the boy up to her and climbed to Flamewind's back. "Where do we go?" the elf asked.

"There's no cover in any direction," she observed, sweeping her gaze about. "We go north."

"There's nothing there," Drax protested.

"That's my purpose," Gwyn answered as she started Thunderhead down the long, gentle slope north of the road. "If these men are another band after the boy, coming from the opposite direction, then what we're up against is at least as bad as I'd feared. They could have forces waiting to ambush us to the south, maybe even followed Orvix back to Baraxis. Our best chance is to leave the roads and get into the wilds. Unless you have a better idea?"

The tone of Gwyn's question was sincere, but Drax was forced to shake his head.

Thus resolved, the trio began riding hard to the north, hoping against hope to get out of sight before this new group of riders left the obscuring hills. Unfortunately there was scant cover to be had, and the wide, flat plain offered no ridges or defiles to the north to hide their position. Not even a stretch of bedrock where they could run without leaving prints was to be found. After another quarter of an hour the sun had risen, painting the distant Tunaris' eastern slopes with light. Gwyn hazarded a look back and saw the six men Drax had reported. Two, now dismounted, were sorting through the wreckage of bodies Gwyn and Drax had left behind. As Karon blinked himself awake on

Gwyn's saddlebow, she saw the others scanning the horizon, and even across the distance Gwyn was sure she saw one stop as his body was pointed toward them. "What do you see, Drax? Prove that elf eyes are as sharp as people say."

"One of them is looking right at us."

"No chance they're some proper authority?"

"No livery and generally unkempt. We're stuck for sure; best run for it."

"Just wait," Gwyn said. "There's a chance to learn something here. If, may Terillah will it, they *are* just ordinary highwaymen, they won't follow."

"Why not?"

"They have some spoils right there, free for the taking, and reason to think we just killed half a dozen men. If you were a simple robber, would *you* follow us?"

"I see your p– Damn!"

They had their answer. Four of the riders left the road and started thundering toward them while the other two hurried to remount. Gwyn swung Karon around behind her and ordered him to hold on tight as she spurred Thunderhead back into a gallop, Drax and Flamewind following hard on her heels.

"What are we going to do?" Drax shouted.

"They have crossbows, don't they?"

"Yes."

"So we can't risk charging them. What can your magic do?" Gwyn asked, yelling over the pounding hooves and wind in their ears.

"They'll shoot us down before I can get close enough. There's no time for anything too subtle. I've got an idea, though; you go on ahead."

"But–"

"Don't worry, Flamewind will catch up to you on his own in the event of my untimely demise. Now go!"

Gwyn did as she was instructed, if reluctantly. The elf knew his craft. Still, she kept Thunderhead to a canter, allowing Drax at least the chance to catch up when he was done with whatever he was doing, slow enough that she could feel it when the wind suddenly changed. She turned in the saddle to see Drax speeding toward her; behind him, the dry grass of the plain glowed with a rapidly spreading fire. The wind, now from the north, fanned the flames back toward their pursuers, but the flames spread east and west as well; the inferno became harder and harder to circumvent with every moment that passed.

Drax caught up quickly, then they kept a more sustainable pace, granting the horses a partial respite. "Interesting tactic," Gwyn remarked.

"When targets are too distant, you can usually find something closer to hand, with a little imagination."

"And you changed the wind?"

"Yes."

Gwyn was impressed. "I didn't realize you could do that."

"Neither did I, but it worked. Just don't ask me to do it again."

It was then Gwyn noticed the customary weariness in Drax's voice. For all the elf's unexpected competence, she couldn't afford to rely on him too heavily. She looked back again. Their pursuers were no longer visible through the flames, but the fire continued to spread. The enemy would be forced to wait out or go around the conflagration, and between that and their three-mile head start, Gwyn was confident she could elude capture until nightfall or the appearance of some terrain that would give them an edge over the enemy.

The land began to climb, slowly but steadily, and at the end of an hour Gwyn reined in Thunderhead and looked back along their uphill path. The flame still smoldered some five miles back, and only two of the riders still pursued them. This seemed a good turn on the surface, but the unknown whereabouts of the other four hunters made Gwyn uneasy. There was little chance the flames had surged quickly enough to engulf men on horseback, so to be completely out of sight they must have sped back to the south. Why? Every new development seemed to confirm the existence of some superior, some guiding hand behind the attacks, eager for news if Karon's capture or murder continued to prove impossible. With knowledge of their whereabouts flying into the hands of an unknown enemy, return to the south was now completely impossible, cutting Baraxis off for good and forcing Gwyn to care for Karon for the foreseeable future. She was more than willing, even felt compelled, but was she able?

More immediately pressing, if the enemies' first priority was to report on their location, why were these final two still in pursuit? They couldn't be sure of Drax's range, so why risk a conflict even after losing the advantage of numbers. Unless they had no intention of conflict, unless their only purpose was to ensure Gwyn and her little band kept running. On such a wide plain, though, and lagging by at least four miles, now, they couldn't hope to drive her into any specific point of ambush. Maybe they just wanted her worn down, weak. But why? What was the endgame? She didn't know, but she was struck by an overwhelming desire to change course. She didn't know where she was heading except to know she didn't like it.

Finally, after another mile of riding, a gully yawned open in the earth before them, and they ran to it like starving men to a banquet table. The horses managed the steep slope with surefooted ease, then Gwyn and Drax dismounted to give themselves and the mounts a much-needed rest. The defile was some eight feet deep and barely wide enough for the horses to turn around. A meager trickle of water ran down the middle; the horses snuffled at it, and Gwyn and Drax went a few paces upstream of them to fill their waterskins.

"So, what do you propose we do now, Gwyn the Savage?" Drax asked.

"Pick a direction and start walking," Gwyn answered. "When you think they're probably close enough, pop over the ledge and shoot them with magic or lightning or whatever it is you do. And try to do it quick enough that they can't spot you and shoot you in the face with a crossbow bolt."

"I especially like that last part. So, which direction?"

"Best to head west for now, up into the foothills. We'll be harder to spot than on the plain, and we might need shelter from weather."

Drax shrugged. "Sounds reasonable. Shall we eat something while we rest?"

Gwyn opened her saddlebags and shared out some trail rations. "I'd planned to resupply at Tira's ranch. We're going to start running short on provender soon, and there's no time to forage when we're getting chased across the landscape."

"Flamewind's carrying a day's worth. Two if we stretch it," Drax offered.

Gwyn passed close to Drax on her way to the horses, leaning in close to his ear. "Karon gets full rations. Even if we have to do without. Understood?"

"And agreed," the elf responded, his voice affronted and not, Gwyn thought, at the notion of an empty belly. She found she still didn't quite have the measure of him.

CHAPTER III

Half an hour passed before the trio felt rested enough to start heading west. Karon sat Thunderhead alone as Gwyn and Drax led their mounts. Drax accompanied them only a little way before stopping to wait in ambush for their pursuers. Twenty minutes after that, Gwyn heard a thunderclap smite the clear sky and looked back to see Drax hustling toward her at the top of the ridge. He was clearly unhurt and in possession of the two enemy horses, so she settled in to wait for him.

At last he came near enough to shout. "No more following. And our transportation and armament situations have both improved." Drax led the two enemy horses down a cutting into the main stream course, and both had crossbows and smaller hand weapons hanging from their saddles. "There's a little food, too, and extra waterskins. I thought we'd hang on to the mounts for as long as the forage holds out, then turn them loose to find greener pastures if we have to."

"Anything saying where the riders came form or who sent them?" Gwyn asked.

"No such luck," Drax answered as he drew up next to her.

"I thought as much. I'd be surprised if they could read in the first place."

"Well, they certainly can't *now*, nor report back where we're going. I think we're in the clear, at least momentarily." Drax shook his right hand as though trying to cast off the pins-and-needles feeling of a sleeping limb. He flexed his fingers, then twisted one of his rings, an amber stone set in a band of gold. "That'll need new enchantment soon, and I don't expect to come by the requisite time or materials in the near future." Drax caught Gwyn's eye as though hopeful she would ask after details of his magical processes.

"Spare me your wizard lessons," she scoffed as she began walking west, unable to think of anything offhand that interested her less. After a moment the elf fell into step behind her.

Gwyn pushed the group's speed less aggressively, and with four horses now they had ample opportunity to ride instead of walk when feet got sore. As they went, they passed small forks joining the gully on either side, angling upward from the east, and they realized a sizable stream coming down from the mountains had split many times as the land flattened to produce the trickle in the gully. By the fifth fork, the water covered the full width up to their ankles, so they found a place where the wall was less steep and left the protection of the defile. Gwyn and Drax kept wary lookouts, but they saw neither man nor beast throughout the day save a few antelope growing shaggy for the winter.

As dusk approached, they climbed a gentle escarpment into a land of craggy hills and scrub. Drax purported to have passed that way before, years ago, and located a shallow cave cut into a hillside where they sheltered for the night. It was not large enough to conceal the horses, and with recent developments they wouldn't risk the smoke of even Drax's dark fire, but otherwise they passed the night restfully enough, except for Karon. He tossed and whimpered throughout Gwyn's watch despite her unpracticed efforts to calm him. He had barely spoken or eaten throughout the day; he was bearing his circumstances better than Gwyn would have imagined, but even so, they were slowly chipping away at him. She feared if something didn't change, soon there would be nothing left.

Morning did bring change, though of a wholly unpleasant sort. The new day dawned an angry slate gray, forcing the group to delay setting out until the weather made up its mind. The storm broke before midmorning, thunder booming over the land as wind whipped the rain. Karon sat wide-eyed, wincing at each crash, but he said nothing, staring vacantly out into the storm. Gwyn thought to take his mind off things somehow, but speech was slow and difficult over the roar of wind and rain, so she just held him on her lap as they waited.

The hillside and its little cutting served them well for another hour, but the wind shifted after that and lashed them with cold, stinging rain. The lightning had subsided by then, so they struck camp, rather miserably, and went in search of other shelter, or at least hoping to cover some ground since they were getting soaked anyway. The land was too broken to continue west, especially in such poor weather, so they turned back to the north. Shortly after they left the cave the rain slackened off, but a misty drizzle persisted for the rest of the day, enough to keep the travelers, and any potential tinder, persistently soaked. Gwyn didn't understand how Drax's fire-making rings worked, as he seemed to have two, but she trusted his desire for comfort as much as his competence that if they'd been enough to overcome the soaked conditions, he would have said so. The wind calmed, mercifully, but the persistent chill in the air combined with the damp conditions to keep the travelers in a state of unrelenting distress.

As they rode, Gwyn peered back through the drizzle to the higher elevations in the west and was sure she could see snow blowing around the stony heads of the highlands, stern harbinger of winter's steady advance even in these southern latitudes. They ate in the saddle, chewing hard biscuit they let soften in the drizzle; the method forced them to eat slow, which was probably for the best. By midday Gwyn felt too worn and anxious over the quantity of their rations to eat, but she called a halt anyway to take a meager rest. As Karon tore at a strip of dried meat, she noticed the boy stared fixedly into the east, down onto the broad plain.

"We should go that way," he declared suddenly. These were the first words Karon had uttered all day or the one before, and now he spoke decisively, his arm pointed to the east. The grownups looked down at him in bewilderment.

"Why do you–?" Drax began.

"No," Gwyn interrupted, "he's right. I can't… Don't ask me how or why, but… There's *something* that way."

"A pack of ravenous wolves is 'something,'" Drax countered, "but that doesn't mean I want to go closer."

"My horse is going east," Gwyn snapped. "I don't care whether you're on it or not."

"I wasn't trying to argue–"

"Well you're doing a damn fine job of it."

"–I just like some idea what I'm facing. You must admit it's a bit strange. Even for an Atlunder."

Gwyn nodded, ignoring the elf's thin attempt at jest. "I do admit it's strange. It's just a feeling, and I trust it."

Drax shook his head and muttered something in his own tongue, and Gwyn felt some satisfaction at making him feel as bewildered at her as she so frequently did at him.

Nevertheless, after they had rested the elf took forward lookout without complaint as they rode down the slope to the eastern flatland.

Hours passed. The sun remained invisible behind the clouds, but by a general deepening of the gloom and her increasing exhaustion, Gwyn knew evening was hastening by when she spotted the silhouette of a solitary tree standing a couple of miles to the north. The land sloped down toward it as the line of the hills made a shallow curve farther to the west. The tree was the closest thing to shelter she'd seen all afternoon, so she made toward it. Soon they were close enough to make out its kind, and she realized it was a hadun tree, the traditional guardian of all Atlund towns, though rare this far south. "This is a good omen," she called, her spirits lifting slightly. She quickened her pace.

"*That* isn't," Drax added, pointing toward the west where distant lightning flashed over the hills.

"Dammit!" Gwyn shouted. "This day is accursed, I would swear." They finished their jog to the tree, its shelter welcome if meager. On its north side the land continued to fall away in a broad, easy slope to a small stream at its bottom. Just past the water sat a solitary cottage, small and alone on the vast plain. The grounds and exterior were in obvious disrepair, but a warm light glowed from within.

After the miserable course of the day, the mysterious dwelling filled Gwyn with a sense of terrible unease, but they needed shelter in the worst way. They were all shivering, to say nothing of the approaching lighting. "Drax," Gwyn ordered, "stay here with Karon and the horses. I'm going down the slope to see who's at home." She pulled her sword from Thunderhead's tack and carried it against her shoulder in what she hoped was not an overtly threatening posture. A minute later, Gwyn came toward the cottage's front door. She was tempted to peek through the windows at whoever was within, but anybody living in so desolate a place would no doubt be armed and wary, so she thought it best not to approach as a thief in the night. Her nerves and senses were taut as she rapped on the weathered planks.

"Who's there?" came a woman's voice, calmer than Gwyn would have expected, and somehow familiar, though in a way that brought no comfort.

"I am a traveler with two companions seeking shelter," she answered through the door. "We can pay a little. My name is Gwyn."

"You may enter," the voice replied.

Gwyn turned the worn latch and eased the door open, her sword before her. As the door swung wide, she saw a woman sitting behind a simple table, backlit by a fire crackling in the hearth. Her features were hard to discern, but Gwyn guessed the stranger was shorter than average and passing out of her middle years. She listened for breathing or movement behind the open door before stepping across the threshold and lowering her sword. A rainy gust blew in behind her, and she reached back and closed the door. "Are you alone?" Gwyn asked.

"That's an ominous question, especially from someone armed."

"There are dangerous men about; I only wondered if you were protected."

"I am more capable than I appear," the woman stated, "and I shan't be here long. We have much to discuss, but I risk greatly for us both the longer I remain."

Gwyn shifted her weight, preparing to fight or flee. "What are you talking about?"

"I have been waiting here for you, *Gwyn et Sheevasa*. Have you not felt me drawing you? Out of the hills, and to the tree above?"

Gwyn nodded warily, noting the woman's use of her

proper Atlund name, not the "Gwyn the Savage" sobriquet she had acquired here in the South. Her homeland was full of stories that began in much this way. All ended badly. "How do you know me?" she asked, her voice heavy with superstitious dread.

"I have always known you, Little Gwyn," the woman replied. "Do you not remember?"

As Gwyn's eyes adjusted to the firelight, she took a more careful look at the features of the strange, serene person sitting before her, trying to recall her soft, brown hair with its sheen of silvery strands, her rounded features that held a beauty defying the advance of time. "Yes," Gwyn finally remembered. "Early last year, at the southern fringe of the Elven Forest. You were as strange to me then as you are now."

"That was not our first meeting. I have watched at other times when you didn't see or don't remember."

"Why?" Gwyn tightened her grip on her sword. She didn't mean to use it, nor suspected it would do any good, but the solidity of it in her hand gave her some comfort.

"My eye is drawn to that which is unusual and consequential. The boy, for instance, is special. You know this as well. He needs protection, fosterage, but it is dangerous for you to remain together."

"How?" Gwyn challenged.

"You are alike, as you and his father were alike. Already the time you spent with Shon, his dying deeds and your vengeful curse, have drawn the attention of dangerous enemies, putting them on the trail of things that had better been kept hidden."

"How do you know all this?"

"As I said, I watch, perhaps more intently than my foes." The woman pulled a necklace from under her robe and lifted the gold chain over her head, allowing a pendant of black crystal to dangle from her hand. Suddenly she began to swing the necklace in a vertical circle, faster and faster until it appeared as a ghostly yellow disk bound in a ring of blackness. Before Gwyn could question this strange behavior the disk shimmered, transforming into an image of the outside of the cottage where she now stood. The firelight dimmed, making the image appear sharper and more solid, then quickly the viewpoint seemed to travel north, following the stream outside. Gwyn's bewildered eyes were shown the stream course entering a broad valley that soon narrowed into a canyon. Finally the vision rested on a great fortress, its white granite walls dwarfing even the Southern Capital's, the red roof tiles on its many buildings looking perfect and new.

"This is the path to the Abbey of the Shield," the woman said. "It is the most guarded place in all the world, and you must bring Karon there for now. He will be safe and well cared-for throughout the dangers that lie ahead of you. I will await you there."

Suddenly the fire flared back to life, and the woman was gone. A faint, tinkling sound drew Gwyn's attention to the table where the woman's crystal necklace was just coming to rest after her disappearing hand had dropped it, the only proof she had really been there at all. The cottage was warm, but a chill ran down Gwyn's back, and she could feel the hairs on her neck bristling like an angry cat.

She heard footsteps from outside and brought her blade into guard, standing at the ready beside the door. The latch turned; the door inched open. Gwyn swung her mighty sword.

"Hello?" Drax's voice sounded nervously.

Gwyn growled and averted her strike, the blade burying itself a solid inch into the doorframe. Drax's eyes went wide with shock as lightning flashed behind him. Gwyn heaved a sigh of mixed relief and frustration as she levered her edge free. "You thrice-damned fool. Don't you know to announce yourself in a situation like this? I nearly took your head off."

Drax ducked under the blade and stepped inside. "I didn't know *what* the situation was. You say you're going to check out the house, you walk inside, and the next thing I know the place is blazing with all kind of magic, strongest I've ever felt. I started down the slope to help, but by the time I got here, it had stopped. You could have been dead for all I knew, and I didn't feel like 'announcing' myself to whoever was left."

"And where is Karon?"

"Back by the tree. The horses are watching over him. You know, Thunderhead is exceptionally intelligent, and I asked–"

"You were talking to my horse?"

"…Yes."

"No more. I don't want you striking up conversation with my animals."

"And if *he* speaks to *me*, I'm just supposed to be rude?"

Gwyn sighed as she laid down her sword and began moving a nearby chair into one corner. "They don't really talk, Drax."

"Thunderhead did. Well, not 'talk' as we do, but communicate. I can only suppose he has unbroken lineage back to the noble breeds that could understand the speech of men."

"You mean…that's not just a legend?"

"Who told you it was?"

"Never mind. We need to get out of the storm. Go get Karon while I shove this furniture away to make space for the horses."

"Inside?"

"Just go!"

"Alright, alright."

In a few minutes Drax was back, and by then Gwyn had

moved the table and benches into a corner and stoked the fire with wood from a stack near the hearth. After that, they shared a quick supper, then put Karon to sleep on a bedroll from one of the bandits' horses. Finally, Gwyn related to Drax all she'd seen in the cottage.

"You'll take the boy to this abbey, then?" the elf inquired.

"It's not out of our way, to the extent we even have a 'way' anymore. If nothing else, I want to get a look at the place. In person, I mean."

"What if it's some kind of trap?"

"To what end? You said her power was vast. If she wanted to harm us or take Karon, why not just do it?"

Drax shrugged. "That's fair logic, but with that much magic involved, logic may not hold sway."

Gwyn nodded in acceptance, though not understanding. "Still, do you have a better idea?"

"I suppose not. If someone's after the boy, someone with money or power or both, I don't know that he'd be safe anywhere else."

"We're decided on the course, then." She hesitated. "Do you have any knowledge of the other things she said? About me and Karon being 'alike,' about what may be special about either of us?"

Drax narrowed his eyes in thought. "There's something. Not magic as I know it, just…a sort of force that I sense in you. It's subtle enough I didn't make anything of it until now. It isn't in the open, it's…like being on a still pond at night, with the big moon full, and you know there are fish teeming under the surface, but all you can see are ripples and silver flashes. That's the best I can explain it."

Gwyn was raised in a place where magic was thought to weave itself throughout the very land, but few had any truck with it, at least not that showed overtly in their lives. She hadn't been inclined to give such legends much thought for most of her life, but since her strange connection to Shon, and especially since his death, inexplicable happenings and sensations became increaseingly regular in her days. "That's not much," she finally responded to Drax's description. "What do you think it is?" she asked, desperate enough for insight to ask even him. "Where does it come from?"

"I don't know," the elf replied. "I've never felt its like. At first I thought there must be something to those rumors that surround you, the whole 'Windborne' superstition, but I sense something similar in Karon. Different, but the same."

"And he's never been within four hundred leagues of Atlund or the Wind."

"Exactly."

"Just one more reason to go to this place. The woman knew more than she told. Get some sleep. I'll take the first watch; I want to think."

Drax nodded off immediately. He seemed to have an uncanny knack for catching sleep whenever he could, a trait of soldiers Gwyn had never learned herself. He appeared to take full advantage of the protection of solid walls around them as well; Gwyn thought his sleep was deeper than it had been on prior nights, leaving her to tend the fire and strain her ears for intruders as rain and wind slashed at the ramshackle cottage. As the night drew on, Gwyn grew more and more uneasy, her skin crawling as though someone watched her with malice and desire. She paced to where her cloak was drying by the fire and put it on, wrapping it tight around her, though she wasn't cold. Finally she rose Drax and lay down, her mind heavy with a sudden press of weariness.

She had no idea how much time had passed when she awoke to the noises of three heavy knocks on the door. The fire still burned, but Drax was nowhere in the cottage. "Dammit, Drax," Gwyn shouted, rising, "I told you to announce yourself." She crossed to the door and reached for the latch. The second she touched it, the door exploded inward, battering her to the floor. She shoved the broken planks away and looked through the doorway, but outside was only blackness.

Only blackness. No stream, no rain, no lightning flashes, just darkness beyond description, swallowing up the light of her little fire. A fear gripped her as she rose and started to run for her sword, but her legs would not obey. The black came into the house, seeping and oozing like oily smoke, and then it was around her, touching her, lifting her up, enveloping her. It made no difference that she'd slept in her clothes; it reached inside them, leaving her naked to its menacing embrace. It covered her to the neck, then oozed up over her face, smothering her, seeping into her eyes, pooling into her memories, stripping her from herself, carting off her every thought and leaving only the dark…

"Gwyn!"

Gwyn gasped and bolted upright at the sound of Drax's voice and the feel of his hand shaking her shoulder. So desperate she was to feel anything warm and real after her nightmare that she reached up and held Drax's hand to her arm instead of shrugging it away. Drax noticed her unusual manner.

"Gwyn, are you alright? Karon was tossing and whimpering, and then you started *screaming*, fit to wake the dead."

Gwyn looked over to Karon and saw that he had awoken as well; he sat with his back against the wall and his legs drawn up tight against himself, his eyes wide and darting.

"We have to get out of here," Gwyn ordered, throwing her blanket off her legs.

"It's not light yet."

"Now! Something's coming."

Gwyn had never saddled a horse so fast in her life, and the sky was only just graying as they set out from the cottage at a quick trot. Soon wisps of cold fog were curling up from the stream and damp grass, smothering the plain. Gwyn never allowed the group to flag. Drax kept looking behind them, but whatever dogged Gwyn's thoughts, he never saw it.

They ate in the saddle after the sun was fully up, but the sun reached its southerly, winter zenith before Gwyn would call a halt. The stream was just turning into the broad valley she'd seen by the strange woman's magic.

"Half an hour for food and rest, then we walk to save the horses," Gwyn ordered. As she doled out the food, she made a sign to Drax that this was the last either of them would get, and he nodded understanding. Gwyn doubted it would matter; if they couldn't make the abbey soon, whatever she knew was after her would give them greater worries than their bellies. The trio ate in silence, Karon staring at the shadow of every passing bird. Even Gwyn remained tense and restless.

Finally Drax spoke, quietly enough that Karon couldn't hear. "We haven't traveled together long, but I've heard every rumor and minstrel's song of you, and in no wise have I ever known you to flee like this."

"I've never met an enemy I couldn't fell before this."

"Are you sure it wasn't just a dream? I didn't feel anything."

"It wasn't after *you*."

Drax sniffed, trying to lighten the mood. "I can't see why not. I'm much more interesting than you."

Gwyn glared at him, and the remainder of the brief rest was taken without further attempts at levity. In a few minutes they moved out on foot, except Karon who rode Thunderhead, leaning against the saddle horn to keep from sliding off the big horse's back. After the best part of two hours, the valley narrowed into a steep-sided canyon, perhaps a hundred feet wide, the stream babbling away down the middle fifth of it. They'd been in the canyon for a mile when Drax whispered, "Gwyn?"

"What?"

"Something's not right. Whatever you thought was chasing us, I think it's getting close."

Gwyn had felt a growing unease over the last few minutes but put it down to the memory of her terror. With Drax's confirmation, she no longer hesitated. "Best get mounted up," she declared, taking no time to wait for Drax to ask Flamewind for help; she grabbed the shorter elf about the middle and heaved him onto the saddle, then jumped onto Thunderhead as Karon made himself small against the horse's neck.

With that they were off like a bowshot, the two bandit horses in tow, but no sooner had they started running than Drax reeled suddenly, Flamewind's head lolling to either side crazily. Gwyn felt an icy claw grip her heart. She looked back, and something was there.

At first she thought it was a zil'bast on one of their cantankerous, rangy horses until she realized this horse, such as it was, had no skin. It just stood there, maybe fifty yards away, tossing its head so that a mane of sinews slapped back and forth over its neck in grotesque mockery of horsehair. Its teeth were needle-sharp fangs, its whinny like the scream of a wounded beast. Its rider was formless beneath a heavy, black cloak, but its hands protruded, hands that ended in long, claw-like nails. In its right was a rod of black iron topped with a standard like outstretched bat wings; he held it light as a feather though it must have weighed double Gwyn's great sword.

The creature started forward, and Gwyn's breath froze in her lungs. She could swear the water in the stream parted to flow around the sickening mount's feet, and even the canyon seemed to widen as it advanced, as though the stone itself shrank back.

All this Gwyn saw over her shoulder as Thunderhead continued his mad dash forward, his breath coming in heavy, panicked snorts, but though the beast behind them appeared to move only at a stately walk, impossibly he gained. The sun dimmed, and the air grew colder.

"Drax!" Gwyn shouted to the elf, his body still reeling. "Drax, come back!" Drax shook himself as though casting off a bitter thought, then slowed his horse. As he turned back to Gwyn, she saw sweat standing out on his forehead. "Take Karon," she shouted over the thunder of hooves and terror, grabbing the boy with both hands. "Take him and run!"

There was fear in Drax's eyes but no cowardice. He didn't argue, dropping the riderless horses' reins and catching the boy as Gwyn shoved him through the intervening space. As the bandit horses bolted with their share of the party's gear, Drax whispered a few words to Flamewind that redoubled his already considerable speed. At the same moment, Gwyn reined in Thunderhead, who reared up hard onto his hind legs and spun so quickly Gwyn was hard pressed to remain in the saddle.

The hideous beast continued to advance at the same implacable pace, like the glaciers on Atlund's northern frontier, and Gwyn struggled to free her sword from its lashings on the saddle, heeding an instinct that only the blade of her ancestors could serve in this battle. The rider pointed its black staff, and something inside her screamed.

Her body thrummed with the same prickly thrill she had felt around Shon, but now the underlying emotion was not enticing and persuasive but vast and indomitable, an assault demanding utter submission. Gwyn had slain sorcerers, lifted sieges, led dozens cheering her name into the teeth of death, yet all her confidence was as a windblown mote before this advancing power, raw and insatiable, and she coveted it. Then something flashed hot insider her, and the battle light sparked in her eyes as she gripped her sword in both hands, making ready to spur Thunderhead into a charge. The reins hung slack between the bit and her sword grip, but she knew by the shift of his weight and the point of his head the steed needed no guidance.

Suddenly another sense shot through her, as pure and familiar as the pale sunlight of her homeland. The voice of the woman from the cottage filled her mind. "Not now," it said. "You can't win; he'll take you. You have to run." And the truth of the words was in her, known to her as she knew her name or the feel of the sword in her hand. With a jerk of her arms she flicked the reins to one side. Thunderhead turned and bolted.

All had passed in only a few seconds, but already Drax was two hundred feet away, the bandit mounts fleeing in panic but flagging quickly behind. Thunderhead's power-ful hooves smote the earth as Gwyn struggled to make up ground against Flamewind's incredible speed.

The dark rider swept his staff.

A wall of iron shot up from the earth in front of Drax and Karon, forcing Flamewind into a sudden, rearing stop. Gwyn continued forward as Drax searched for a way over, his head sweeping side to side as he clutched Karon to his chest.

Before Gwyn was forced to slow, a sudden concussion ripped the air, showering horses and riders alike with sparks and hot slivers. The spots cleared from their eyes, and a tunnel was now visible through the wall. Gwyn shot into that opening with Drax abreast and regaining his speed, horseshoes splashing through the shallow, disrupted water and clanging against the unnatural iron of the tunnel floor. Then the metal shook with something more than the rush of their passing, and a spar of twisted steel shot up from the ground right in front of Flamewind. The horse leapt, missing the point by inches as another cruel spike burst from the earth at Thunderhead's right flank, thrusting into the space he'd occupied only an instant before. Suddenly the ground was alive with twisting barbs, but Thunderhead and Flamewind danced through them, leaping and sidestepping with inexplicable grace. Further behind, Gwyn heard horrible screams echoing up the tunnel and knew the bandit horses had not been so skilled or lucky.

At last they were clear. Gwyn looked over her shoulder to see the creature start into the tunnel, weaving through the space between the spikes. Then a curtain of light fell from the sky, blinding them for a moment, and when it passed they saw vines erupting from the earth everywhere the light had touched, all along the base of the wall, spreading over its face and rapidly filling the tunnel, completing decades of growth before Gwyn's astonished eyes. In moments the vines grew thick as Gwyn's arm, crumpling the forest of spikes like so much beaten tin. At a stroke from the dark rider's staff the wall started to crumble, but even then it was too late, the countless spreading roots pitting the iron's surface, holding it in place, anchoring it to the ground and sides of the canyon.

An enraged shriek sounded from the other side of the wall. The sun blackened for a moment, hiding, and Gwyn knew their pursuer was gone. Finally she dismounted and stowed her sword, leading Thunderhead away from that frightful place.

The canyon widened as they went until it stretched more than a furlong across, and afternoon lay golden and expectant on the land when the trio reached the abbey. Its alabaster walls stood out in contrast to the dusty sandstone of the canyon sides against which they were built, using as their fourth wall the western cliff face itself which even inexorable time had not conquered. The southern wall stretched to a round corner tower on the other side of the stream, which flowed through a barred grating in the base of the granite. The eastern wall stretched north, paralleling the far cliff as it made a wide, eastward bend out of Gwyn's sight. A pair of huge, wooden doors broke the southern end of the fortification, and they stood open, the silhouette of the woman from the cottage framed on the threshold. As they neared, she spread her arms wide and called to them. "*Gwyn et Sheevasa*, Drax of the Western Vale, Karon son of Shon, noble Thunderhead, and loyal Flamewind. I invite you as friends into the Abbey of the Shield. I welcome you!"

Gwyn was too exhausted and confused to offer thanks or pleasantries; she merely lifted Karon down from his perch on Thunderhead's saddle and asked, "Stables?"

"This way," the woman replied, betraying no offense at Gwyn's manner as she extended a guiding hand toward the near side of the green. Standing beside her for the first time, Gwyn realized the mysterious woman stood only as tall as her shoulder. Drax followed Gwyn as she led her horse in that direction, following her ears and nose to the lodging she sought. Their mounts had been drinking their fill at intervals from the stream, but their relief was palpable as Gwyn finally removed their tack and baggage, and she brooked no interruption as she rubbed them both down, letting her mind wander as she did.

Finally she left the stables, only then taking in the sights all around her. The abbey grounds were at least a hundred yards wide and stretched away along the canyon wall as far as she could see. Further back, past a half dozen white buildings with roofs of red tile, she saw fields tended by people in green tunics, and past that an orchard, the scent of its fruit even now wafting to her on the unseasonably warm breeze. Closer at hand, warriors in blue and red uniforms drilled on the green as armored guardsmen patrolled the tops of the walls, walls so thick half a dozen men could stand abreast upon the alures. All this lay in the heavy shadow of twilight, and in another moment a horn sounded out over the land. As the guards continued their ceaseless patrol, everyone else set aside their labors and disappeared into the various dwellings, kindling lanterns hanging to the right of each door as they went. Just a few feet away, facing Gwyn, stood the woman from the cottage, looking dignified in a simple, purple dress, her silvering auburn hair unbound.

"I have many questions," Gwyn said.

"I have many answers," the woman replied. "Trust that I will offer as many as I dare, but I must keep my own counsel on which those be. Ask."

"Where are Drax and Karon?"

"Abed. They were bone weary, even as you are, and they have not the endurance of your breeding."

"Who are you?" Gwyn asked.

"You may call me Daruneh."

"Thank you for the name, but it isn't what I asked for. Who *are* you?"

"I am…a guardian. I am your ally in a struggle you do not yet realize you fight. I am a worthy protector for the boy. I am the custodian of this abbey. More than that you will not learn from me today."

"What attacked us out there?"

"A being of power and malice, neither man nor orc nor elf," the older woman replied.

"Some new race?"

Daruneh stared hard at her but did not answer.

Gwyn sensed waiting would gain her nothing. "Then what does it want?"

"It wants the North as its seat and the South as its footstool. It wants the East for its plate and the West for its cup. It wants the Sky for its raiment and the Stars for its crown. Its bread is pain and its water is hate. There is nothing it does not covet, but few things it truly desires. You and Karon are among them."

"Why?"

"I may guess, but I do not know. In this I choose silence over the possibility of error."

"And you fought him off?"

"I did not challenge him directly; I only thwarted his attempt to take you. It had been better that he not know you came here, but I had to take care not to call to you too loudly. I chose stealth over speed, and my choice may have been poor. But you are safe here, for the present."

"I cannot stay here forever," Gwyn stated. "Does he wait for me even now, beyond your protection?"

"Somewhere, certainly, but he cannot simply hang about my threshold. Not while I live."

"What must I do?"

"For now, you must sleep. We will speak again tomorrow."

CHAPTER IV

Gwyn did not remember going to bed after that. The next morning, or it might have been the next year, so rested she felt when she awoke, she had only vague memories of Daruneh helping her to a bedchamber. Sunlight and birdsong filtered through her window and echoed from the stone walls, and when she rose, she found a bath had been drawn for her in a square tub of grey-veined, white marble. A side table stood covered in brushes, combs, bottles of oil and perfume, and a pair of silver looking-glasses. The Atlunder approached the bath with a dubious posture, her eyes darting to see if anyone was nearby. Satisfied, she picked up a bottle of purple liquid, removed the glass stopper, and sniffed it, her head snapping back immediately as she coughed and sputtered. The scent was floral and not unpleasant in itself, but it was strong beyond description. Gwyn resisted the urge to throw the bottle to the floor, set it back on the table none too gently, and started to walk away. Half turned, she stopped and picked up one of the looking glasses, angling it up and down to give herself a quick view. The muslin shift she wore as an undergarment, acquired in Sutherset to replace the woolen ones she'd traveled south with, was worn and sweat-stained. Her face was grimy, and she suddenly shuddered to consider her odor, realizing the notes of horseflesh were probably the best of it. She was fit for a bloody campaign or even an Atlund feast hall after a day of training or games, but not to go amongst properly civilized folk.

With a stuttering reach she picked up a second bottle and held it away from her face as she opened it, taking only the barest sniff before thrusting it back to arm's reach. After a moment of hesitation though, she brought it closer and breathed more deeply. This green elixir had a more subtle aroma, hints of wildflower over a strong base of pine. It reminded her of the evergreen forests of her home, and she smiled. Finally she poured it liberally into the steaming water of the bath, pulled her dirty smock over her head, and climbed in. At once the heat soaked into her, relaxing muscles she hadn't realized were tight. The scent she had poured into the water was sharp, opening her exhaustion-dulled senses, but a sensation of peace overwhelmed her, too; she found herself not alert but simply aware, savoring the heat of the bath, the sounds of birdsong and laughter that gamboled through the round windows, the contrast of the cool air wherever her wet skin rose briefly from the water. Her life had not been an easy one, and Gwyn had never been given to sitting idle, yet she couldn't fight the calm and didn't want to. The dangers and questions hadn't disappeared, and though she didn't feel exactly content, she experienced the liberty to simply be at rest, and she remained so, soaking for what felt like hours, though when at last she opened her eyes the sun had barely moved and the water still steamed hot. Not only hot but clear, though days of road dust and sweat had dissolved from her skin. She trembled for a moment, realizing she was in a place of subtle magics, but she put aside her apprehension. Drax's spells, after all, had proven useful and consistent, and though she could barely fathom Daruneh, Gwyn found herself trusting her, and if nothing else the mature woman was undeniably more clearheaded than the flippant elf.

Finally Gwyn reached to the table and picked up a bar of soap that smelled of lavender, followed by a pumice stone. Using them in turns she set to, scouring every inch of herself, scrubbing away the dirt and grime and lingering fear of yesterday. After that she emerged, her northern ruggedness happy to let the cool air dry her as she found the stoutest comb on the table and took the weeks of tangles from her wild hair. Once done it stood out from her head like a mane, untamable, and Gwyn shunned the decorative pins and combs and reached instead for a simple strip of brown fabric to tie it back out of her eyes. Only then did she go in search of her clothes, and only then, with a pang of guilt, did she realize she hadn't even accounted for her sword before going to her bath.

To her relief she found the blade nearby, hanging from pegs near the headboard as though she'd lived in the room all her life. Fresh clothes were laid out for her as well, though she was certain none had been at hand when she awoke, in cut and style much like her own, and they fit perfectly. Her cloak and mail hung nearby, both cleaned and the armor oiled like new. She forwent the armor but couldn't help picking up her sword as her stomach growled its impatience. Only one door stood in the walls of the room, so she opened it, stepping out into a sunlit hallway. A pleasant-looking young man in red and blue stood at easy attention outside her door.

"Lady Gwyn," he said with a graceful bow, "may I do you the honor of escorting you to your breakfast?"

Gwyn cleared her throat. "I'm no lady," she answered, though she felt more like one than she had in, perhaps, ever, "and I don't know what 'escort' means in these parts, but if you're leading me to the food, then lead on."

The man laughed, a clear, unfettered sound, and turned to the left, leading Gwyn down a spiral staircase and out onto a broad, green lawn between a quartet of buildings. He did not presume to take her arm, but he kept the pace so she was at his elbow all the way to the long table laid out on the grass, surrounded by abbey dwellers sitting in simple chairs of wood and canvas. Drax and Karon sat with Daruneh at the far end of the table, but Gwyn didn't see them; her eyes were only for the food. Great mounds of it piled on platters all down the length of the table: venison, bacon, and sausage; breads, muffins, and pastries; fresh fruit, some of varieties Gwyn had no name for; pies both sweet and savory. Off to one side a pair of chefs in green tunics prepared fresh eggs to order, and opposite that stood a sideboard of milk, water, teas, and juices. In her life Gwyn had met two kings and a handful of nobles, and not a one of them ate like this. Here, worker and warrior and stranger and leader all sat to such a feast side by side.

"Lady," her escort said softly after allowing her a moment to take it all in, "your companions and Miss Daruneh await the pleasure of your company."

She nodded absently, and the young man led her down the table to an empty seat next to Daruneh.

"Gwyn," the woman said, "I trust you've rested. You look lovely and fierce at once, with your sword in hand. Please, sit."

Gwyn obliged, laying her sword in the grass under the table, and Drax passed her a plate mounded with what looked like some of everything. "These folks know how to lay out a spread," he commented through a half-full mouth. "Tell me how you take your eggs and I'll bring you a plate."

"Any way you bring them, I'll take them."

Drax stood, allowing Gwyn to see Karon sitting on the

elf's other side. He held his arms across his stomach, and his face was the picture of concern. "What's wrong?" Gwyn asked.

Karon turned to her and mumbled miserably, "I ate too much."

"No such thing!" Drax shot, clapping the boy on the back. Karon winced and belched as graciously as he was able, and Drax laughed as he sauntered off toward the egg table.

Daruneh smiled a benign smile. "We warned Karon to slow down, didn't we?" Karon nodded. "But the poor boy was half starved, and he's got a lot of growing to do yet."

Gwyn needed no invitation and began blunting her own hunger pangs with abandon, slowing down sometime during her second plate and finally cleaning a third. People around her traded stories and asked questions, but she only nodded or shook her head when they did, her mouth occupied with chewing. Drax was more garrulous, though Gwyn noted he most often made light with his answers or turned the discussion back to the abbey and its people, rarely revealing anything of himself. Only after eating her fill did Gwyn finally speak again. Looking to Daruneh, she asked, "Who are all these people?"

"The lost and the found," Daruneh answered, "the wreck and refuse of a world that is rich in cruelty and poor in compassion. I call out to them, and some answer. Some, once mended and restored, return to the world with only scant memory of this place; others choose to stay. Those live and love and bear children as in other places, adding to our community of peace."

"Peace?" Gwyn asked. "Do I not see guards even now patrolling the walls? Did I not see men training to battle last night?"

Daruneh's eyes narrowed just slightly. "Yours are a warlike people, and I respect their bravery and skill...but don't assume being peaceful is the same as being harmless."

"I don't," Gwyn answered, "at least, not anymore. One of many lessons I learned from Karon's father and men like him."

"That reminds me," Daruneh said. She motioned to a younger woman down the table who came to stand behind them. "Karon?" Daruneh addressed him.

The boy, apparently over his stomach pains, looked up from a pastry.

"Karon, this is Miss Elnor. She'd like to introduce you to a few of the other children here. Would that be alright?"

Karon looked up at Gwyn, and she thought he was nervous.

"It's just right over there," Elnor reassured in a voice like song, pointing to a corner of the lawn where a handful of children sat under a spreading tree with slates while another woman recited letters. "Gwyn and Drax will only be a call away if you need them."

Gwyn nodded. "It's alright. Go along with Miss Elnor."

Karon got up from the table and followed the willowy woman over to the other children at their lessons. Gwyn watched them go, feeling an inexplicable apprehension at letting the boy walk away, and when she turned back she saw Daruneh still looking at Karon across the green. Her face was calm, but there was a great distance in her eyes, and if Gwyn had ever seen a look more perfectly sad, she couldn't remember when.

"The pages were written so long ago," Daruneh muttered, as if to herself. "So cruel the hand that would pen so innocent a child into such a dark and twisted tale, and so near its ending, when so many will pay so much for the sins of their forebears."

Gwyn felt a chill at the words, though she could not reckon their full meaning. "Do you see the future then as well, woman?"

Daruneh returned Gwyn's look and smiled. "Not in the way you mean it. There are some gifts and curses that are denied even to the deepest magics, as your Master Drax knows well. But I can see the flight of the arrow and suss where it will strike. Many things have lain long dormant, but now that they move, their trajectories are plain to me. They fly to a resolution that, though never predestined, has long been inevitable."

"Will you not speak plainly to me?" Gwyn demanded.

"I dare not. In the past I have spoken too rashly to others, and it came to a bad end. When the time has come to loose the final arrow, then I shall, but nary a moment before."

"Then why did you bring me here?"

"*That* I have admitted plainly from the start," Daruneh answered. "I brought you here to bring the boy here. He will be safest in the abbey. You would be, as well, but I know you will not remain, and that safety is not something you seek."

"But why is Karon so important?"

"The boy has a proud heritage."

"I already know that," Gwyn interjected, her tone curt.

"You mean his father. But his father's heritage was the same, as is yours in kind. There is power in your blood, Gwyn, handed down from your father and his mother and her mother and her father, through the firstborns stretching back to a time when your people still lived in rude huts and hid from the moons. Even dormant within you it calls for a response from everyone you meet, granting you the influence to inspire mighty deeds and apocalyptic changes. Fully awakened, none now can say what it might mean, for good or ill, but our enemy both fears and lusts after that power. Once it was held by many, but now you and Karon are the last. To ensure it is not snuffed out before it's time is worth any price."

"But how can you keep Karon safe here from so

powerful a foe?" Gwyn challenged. "What is this place? You don't even hold the high ground," she added, casting her eyes to the clifftop looming behind her.

"Not high ground, but sacred. And not sacred in the sense that human or elf seek to consecrate places, but special in its own right. I do not know how it became so. No force of arms, however mighty, can assail this place, nor even find it unless I will it, and with my help its natural wards are proof against even the most powerful magics. The abbey is impregnable as long as I remain in it."

"Well, I have done as you bid. Karon is here. I can sense you seek only to help, as surely as I sensed the thing in the canyon sought ill, and it's clear enough the boy will be well cared-for here." Gwyn looked over her shoulder at the boy for a longing moment. "Better off than he could be where I'm going. So I ask again what I asked last night. If you will tell me no more, then what must I do?"

"You are welcome to remain here for as long as you like, though I know time is precious to you and to your homeland. Go, when you must, with my blessing. That which seeks you may predict you will leave, but my power will conceal you; he will not know when or where you go, unless your ways are reported to him by mortal means. In the fullness of time, we will speak again."

Gwyn looked at Drax, who continued to eat like a starving man. "Well, elf," she asked, "how urgent is your need to be home?"

"Less than yours, by the sound of it," Drax managed around a mouthful of bacon. He swallowed. "What did she mean about time being 'precious'?"

"It made about as much sense to me as the rest of it," Gwyn dissembled, glad the elf had never pried into the reason for her insistence on travel during such a harsh season. Gwyn toyed briefly with the idea of remaining in the abbey until the first breath of spring. After all, traveling north as the year waned, proper winter would descend on them quickly if they departed now. The cold didn't trouble her, and heavy snow was rare in the lee of the mountains, at least until much later. Forage would grow scarce, though, especially for the horses. Then she considered the note from home now stowed with her gear and the urgency of its wording. She dared not delay. "Alright," she announced. "Be ready to leave at dawn tomorrow. Daruneh, we could desperately use some supplies. I can pay for them."

"I will see to it, and don't concern yourself with money. On the contrary, I can offer you a little. We have no need of it here, but travelers we've allowed to find this place sometimes hide it in out-of-the-way corners, in gratitude, when we aren't looking."

"Thank you. I am in your debt."

"Not at all. It is I who carry that burden, one my modest support will never repay." The woman remained composed, but her eyes sparkled with heavy emotion. "Please excuse me. I have many duties. Make yourselves at home. The abbey and its people are fully at your service." She stood and gave a slight bow, then left.

"Drax," Gwyn rumbled when she was gone, "it's said most wizards are students of lore as well as sorcery. Is that true of you?"

"Probably less than most. Why?"

"Daruneh speaks of many things that were set in motion long ago. I know the history of my own people, and some of the Southern Kingdoms, but neither are enough to solve this riddle."

"Yours is the oldest civilization that still survives," the elf answered. "I don't know what the knowledge of my people could add."

Gwyn nodded. "Wars, famines, the march of centuries. We've lost much and forgotten more. My people sing of days before history, the Once Times when dragons roamed the lands and the mothers of man sheltered beneath their wings, when the elder peoples grew gluttonous in their pride and made war against Terillah Himself beyond the veil of the Physical Realm."

"And?"

"I never heeded those stories much, but if Daruneh's belief is true, this place was built during such times. Perhaps some doom of my own written then as well. But my people have only the old myths of them. Nothing I'd stake my life on."

Drax smiled. "Myths like…talking horses? Maybe the lack isn't in what your people know, but in what you've bothered remembering." Gwyn scoffed but knew he may be right. "Perhaps when you return home you'll find the scholars know more than you think," the elf concluded.

"Perhaps." Gwyn's tone was unconvinced. "I'd like to walk awhile. Can you keep an eye on Karon?"

"Of course. We'll be here when you get back."

Gwyn sauntered off to sift her thoughts.

Her day in the Abbey of the Shield was a memory of comfort Gwyn would treasure all her days. The sun was warm, the air was sweet, and the people were kind. Many trained at arms, and Gwyn accepted their invitation to join them for an hour of sparring. None bested her, but their skills were sure enough. Yet all was tinged with a strain of melancholy, for Gwyn knew in her bones that a place of such peace and ease was one in which she could never belong.

She and Drax took it in turns to stay within sight and earshot of Karon, and by lunchtime they could see the boy was acclimating rapidly to the routines of the abbey. He accompanied the other children in lessons, chores, and play, and by suppertime he even appeared to have become something of a ringleader, using his tales of the wide and wild world to impress his peers, many of whom Gwyn supposed had never so much as left the abbey grounds. She noticed his particular zeal for helping in the gardens and wondered if he took after his mother in that way. His recovery from the shocks and pains of his life, so recently in doubt, now seemed to be progressing with alacrity. Gwyn felt certain that powers of healing suffused the very air and land of the place, powers nurturing not only the body but the soul.

Gwyn walked the fields and orchards, seeing some portion in every stage of planting, tending, and harvesting, as though the seasons held no sway inside the abbey's borders. She followed the stream where it flowed through a grating in the north wall to water the crops and pasturelands, meads that housed sheep (a surprising fraction of which were black), horses, and dairy cattle. A little apart from the rest they raised pigs in a large sty, and even this was cleaner and less fetid than those in normal lands. As she turned to follow her ears to the chicken coops, she saw Thunderhead and Flamewind racing and playing like colts with other beasts from the abbey's herds. The fatigue of their urgent journey seemed washed away, and she felt the same refreshment in her own being. A part of her wished she could leave them here to their happiness, but her need for them was too great. At last the shadow of the western cliff fell over the grounds, and shortly thereafter the horn sounded, sending the residents of the Abbey of the Shield to their various dwellings. Gwyn and Drax returned to the common house where they'd spent their first night and ate another meal finer than any king's, checked on Karon, and returned to their beds.

Dawn came too quickly, and when it did Gwyn found Daruneh was as good as her word: In her chambers were layers of warm clothes, mostly in black wool, ending in a heavy cloak of dark brown fur. Once she reached the stable,

Gwyn saw Flamewind's saddle had been so refurbished as to rival Thunderhead's that was nearly new, and both had been cleaned and polished. Both mounts had been loaded lightly with provisions and a bit of coin, but most of the supplies and supplemental fodder for the horses were stowed densely on a sturdy mule with a well-crafted pack harness, all gifts from the people of the abbey. Daruneh was there to see them off.

"The mule is called Bully," she explained, "for reasons that would have been obvious had not Thunderhead already put him in his place. I'm sure you're concerned over supplies in the wilds, Gwyn. Rest assured, our produce keeps well and sustains the body even better. Ration carefully, supplement with whatever little forage you can, and these stores will see you and your beasts to the fringes of the Elven Forest. I daresay you'll have no trouble with provender in that place."

"That we most surely won't, Lady," Drax proclaimed as he climbed astride Flamewind.

"I must ask one more boon," Gwyn spoke up.

"Name it."

"Can you send word to Lord Major Baraxis in the realm of Sutherset that Karon is safe? I directed news of the boy's abduction to him, and if it got there, I don't doubt he has men, and maybe himself, out risking their lives to find him."

"I will find a way," Daruneh replied. "Be well, warrior. We shall meet again."

Gwyn nodded her thanks and turned Thunderhead toward the main gate. "You aren't saying goodbye to Karon?" Drax asked.

"It's early," Gwyn answered. "I didn't want to wake him. And you saw how content he was with the other children. Best not to confuse him. Let him be happy here and forget about us and all the pains of before."

When Gwyn came to the main gate, though, Karon was

there, standing in the open and waiting for her, looking healthy and confident in his new, green tunic.

"Karon," Gwyn said, "I thought you were still asleep."

He walked up to Thunderhead's right side, and Gwyn offered her hand, swinging the light child up into the saddle when he took it. Karon said nothing but threw his arms around her neck. Then he pressed something into her hand and kissed her cheek, his touch reawakening the feeling of fierce protectiveness that tempted Gwyn to gallop straight out the gate with the child safely on her saddlebow. It took surprising effort to let him go as he slid down her leg to the ground, and she realized her eyes stung as she watched him run back to a group of other boys hiding behind an outbuilding. "You kissed her," she heard one of them hiss, followed by Karon's shout of, "Did not!"

At last she looked down at her hand to see what Karon had placed there. Nestled in her palm was a tiny purple blossom, a mountain crocus, a flower only to be found in the northern highlands. Even in her walks about the magical abbey she had seen none growing. "How?" she started to ask, but Karon and the pack of boys had disappeared. Gwyn clutched the flower gently to her breast and clicked her tongue at Thunderhead, who trotted forward out the gates. Drax cast one last look about the abbey grounds before whispering to Flamewind and riding off after Gwyn, Bully the pack mule in tow.

The pair turned north out of the gates and followed the cut stone wall of the abbey through the canyon. Gwyn reckoned they had been traveling for three quarters of a mile when the dressed stones finally curved away into the side of the cliff, demarking the end of the Abbey of the Shield. After another three miles, Gwyn felt a sudden, inexplicable hollowness. Looking over her shoulder, she caught a look on Drax's face and believed he was feeling the same sensation. "What was that?" she asked.

"I believe we've just left Lady Daruneh's protection," Drax answered, "or the natural ends of whatever enchantment lays upon the abbey. Probably both."

Gwyn felt suddenly naked before the cold world at the thought of journeying forth without the mystical woman's aid, small and vulnerable under a menacing sky. She believed Daruneh when she said her enemy couldn't simply linger about the border, but when Gwyn remembered the blackness that invaded her dreams and the crushing despair that had gripped her heart in the canyon, her surety was deeply shaken. That terrible sorcerer may not know when she would leave, but it must suspect she would go north when she did. How far could she go before it found her again?

To distract herself from the dread as they rode on, Gwyn turned her mind to the magics of the abbey and her brief discussion with the woman who fortified them. "Drax," she asked, "what did Daruneh mean about some things, some 'blessings and curses,' being denied even to magic?"

"To call them 'laws' would miss the mark," the elf replied after a moment, "but there are certain realities that can't be outwitted. The past is a stone carving, not a chalk drawing. No power can change it. The future, on the other hand, is not *even* a chalk drawing, but an ever-shifting sand painting. There is no glimpse of it that does not change the moment it is seen, fracturing into an infinity of possibilities. At least I've heard it so, for I've never attempted even a peek. Some say if it was possible to catch a fixed image then even the seeing itself would change the outcome, though that's as much an argument for philosophers as sorcerers. Better wizards than me have tried and failed; tales tell of some who wouldn't relent and were driven mad. I suspect those are more cautionary fable than truth.

"Anyway," Drax continued, "that's what she meant about not seeing the future. Magic, by and large, is a product of the 'now.' It has no mastery over time; it cannot alter or circumvent it. Mostly."

"What do you mean, 'mostly'?"

"Well, you could speed something up or slow it down, say, at least for a few moments. That's about as far as it goes. A wizard can't take something out of time altogether, or even move anything from one place to another without, somehow, passing through the space in between. Everything has limits."

"Daruneh seemed to disappear into thin air in the cottage."

"*Seemed* to," Drax reinforced. "Magic can move things in a lot of different ways and fool the senses in just as many, but it can't make something vanish from one place and reappear in another. Especially not a *living* thing."

Gwyn was silent for a moment. "And the dead?"

"Stay dead." Drax shuddered. "Magic is a thing not only of the 'now,' but also of the Physical Realm. Once a spirit passes into whatever lies beyond, it's out of magic's reach. No force can claw it back."

"My people have stories of spirits or images of the dead returning. Usually to give warning of peril."

"If those tales are true they're bound by laws of the next world, not this one. Perhaps a will from that side could return of its own volition, but it can't be compelled, and it couldn't retake flesh…I don't think. A body can be made to move again, after a fashion, but it isn't the person it was before. It's, just, a *thing*, an abomination, and the arts to do it are corrupting and perverse. Even the zil'basts never raised up their dead."

"How did you come to learn all this?"

"Magic for elves comes as natural as walking."

"But not all this kind of magic," Gwyn pressed. "Surely you aren't a nation of people who can shoot lightning and detonate zil'basts with a thought."

"Surely not."

"So then, since you said you study less than most, how did *you* come to learn all this?"

Drax didn't answer immediately. "That's a story for another day. Will you take the mule for a while? I'm still supposed to be the guide. I'm going to scout ahead a bit."

Drax handed off the mule's reins and rode on, and Gwyn let him be.

In time the canyon widened once more into a proper valley, and by the end of the day they could see the vast plain stretching out before them in the twilight, the westward wall shrunk to less than the height of a tall house and the eastward one disappeared altogether into the earth. As the west cliff face stuttered likewise into nothingness, Gwyn led the way up a cleft between two outcroppings to find shelter from the wind, then set their cold camp.

She dreamed again that night. Just as she had during her search for Shon's killers, she saw the forms and faces of the marauders she'd slain, each annihilated and banished before her. As the vision began, her dreaming heart filled with panic at the notion of the dark-robed figure searching her out once more, the memory of their encounter lending a cold edge to the unnamable dread the being had always inspired. This time, however, the menacing shade was nowhere to be seen. Neither did Daruneh speak, though Gwyn sensed she was nearby, just out of sight. Freed from such unfathomable entanglements, Gwyn focused on the three faceless visages that remained, but after a few moments the murky figures wandered away. In the unnatural darkness she knew not where they might be going, and the notion of their escape sickened her heart.

Their passage revealed a tangle of charred timbers behind where they had stood, and a young man, perhaps a few years older than Gwyn, sat upon a piece of it, looking at the ground. His profile was somehow familiar, but she couldn't remember why.

"I'm not the monster I'm made out to be," he said.

"You tried to kill me," Gwyn answered flatly, feeling strangely detached from the encounter.

"I didn't!" the man insisted, still not meeting her gaze. "I only meant to keep you from *her*. And her lies."

"Your shadow has plagued me enough, and now I've seen your real form. It is no better."

"So she sees me, and so she's made me to appear. Now you see me thus, as I am."

"I dream. This is not real."

"The Physical Realm is not the only one. Your vengeance is intangible, but nonetheless real. Nor the less righteous."

An offer rested unspoken beneath the young man's words, and it's potential, against the mocking laughter she now heard of the three disappeared shades, chipped away at her apathy. Her curiosity, however, quickly gave way to frustration. "Spare me your riddles," she spat. "I have no time for them, nor any patience."

"On that, *Sheevasa*, we agree," the man said as his form melted into the darkness.

The next morning, Gwyn recalled most of her vision only vaguely, but the mockery of Tira's surviving murderers rang in her ears and clawed at her mind. After they had struck camp and repacked the mule, Gwyn announced, "I'm going to start heading east."

Drax's eyes narrowed in confusion or suspicion. "What for?"

"If my dead reckoning is right, we can't be too far west of that northward road the first bandit mentioned."

"Right," Drax replied without agreement, "the *bandit* mentioned it. Because it's full of *bandits*."

"I have reason," Gwyn countered. She waited a few heartbeats before adding, "After I killed that one, you said you were with me at least until we found Karon. Well, that's seen to, now. If you don't want to be part of the work I have yet to do, I understand."

Drax looked long into Gwyn's eyes. His searching stare felt intimate somehow, and though she resisted the urge to protest, it filled her with discomfort. Finally the elf said, "I won't kill anyone in cold blood, nor in hot if they've turned to run. Don't ask me to."

Gwyn clenched her jaw and nodded.

"If Flamewind's going east, then," Drax relented, "I'll be on him."

By midday they struck the road under a clear sky, forcing Drax to remove his shading lenses to make a better survey of the tracks. Even Gwyn, whose tracking experience focused on forest loam and undergrowth, could easily see the heavy and repeated passage of horse hooves, both shod and otherwise, almost exclusively heading north, but she had no sense of the critical details.

Drax spent no time on enchantments and reported, "These tracks were laid down before the storms that hit us a few days ago. I can say that much."

"How much before?" Gwyn demanded.

The elf shook his head.

Gwyn pondered only for a moment. "I'll have to go south, then, to the ruined town the bandit spoke of. With any luck, the men I'm after are still there." She turned Thunderhead to the south and started walking, the pack mule following behind.

Drax took a last look before trotting up to come abreast of Gwyn. "How will you know them when you get there?" he asked as he fell into step.

Gwyn declined to share her dreams, but since they

showed her no faces this time, she had no need to lie. "I won't," she confessed. "If there are any horses with Shon's brand still there, I'll know the killers are likely nearby. I doubt they'd go far without orders, and we killed their boss on the road."

"*I* did," Drax clarified.

Gwyn said nothing, keeping her eyes on the horizon in case trouble presented itself. She would have preferred to leave the thoroughfare and travel parallel, but with no cover on the flat plain to hide her silhouette, it seemed of little use. The wind whipped at their backs as the sun hastened on toward evening, bringing a chill that showed first the horses' breath steaming, then their own. Gwyn had spent only one winter in the south, preoccupied with Baraxis' training and rarely outdoors after dark. Now, in the open, she had to fight her Atlund instincts not to flee the night wind in winter, and though her mind knew it was safe enough, her heart tensed with apprehension. The big moon, now, was waning, but thanks to Drax's nocturnal vision they pressed on for two more hours before a dilapidated waystation rose up before them in the gloom, offering shelter from the wind. It was a squat building of mud brick with door, shutters, and roof of wooden planks.

Drax approached first, peering through cracks in the shutters, then signaled to Gwyn that he saw nothing. She dismounted and readied her sword, preparing to enter through the half-rotted door. Before she could cross the threshold, Drax stopped her with an urgent wave of his right hand, then twisted one of the rings on his left, a simple band carved from some green mineral. To Gwyn's surprise, it began to glow with a soft, golden radiance, just enough to banish the shadows and clearly show shapes to her dark-adjusted sight. Drax removed the ring and handed it to Gwyn. She found she could only slip it over the first knuckle of her index finger, the elf's digits being so slight, but with it thusly in place she gripped her sword and whipped open the door, quickly scanning the room.

Before Gwyn could observe a quarter of it, a shadow burst from the far corner and rushed her. Giving back with a startled cry, she made a quick slash with her sword, then something struck her face as she whirled and tried to duck out of the way. Bully the mule brayed and kicked. She heard Drax shout in alarm and turned toward the elf, washing him in golden light as she brought her blade back into guard, but by the time she could take a step toward him she realized the enchanter was laughing, one hand over his mouth as he readjusted his skull cap with the other.

"What in all the hells was that?" Gwyn gasped. "What are you laughing at?

"Barn owl," Drax chuckled. "I didn't see it in there, I swear."

"Go on, laugh yourself to death, elf," Gwyn chided. "It's a miracle the mule didn't bolt. Next time *you* can go in first."

"Gladly," Drax answered with a slight bow, recovering from his mirth. Satisfied any other occupants would have already frightened off the owl, he took his glowing ring back from Gwyn, entered incautiously, and looked about once more, finally declaring the place empty and safe enough.

Making a quick survey of the exterior, Gwyn found the place once had a stable on the back side, but it had collapsed into a weathered heap. A few boards had broken or rotted off at convenient lengths for a fire in the collapsed hearth, and soon she had the animals settled on one side of the cramped shelter.

"I could do without another night sleeping with the reek of horse excrement," Drax complained as he warmed water in a small kettle from his pack, nestling it down in the outer coals.

"There's plenty of fresh air outside," Gwyn countered around a mouthful of jerky.

"Fresh enough for the animals, too," Drax insisted. "It isn't even raining this time."

"We're in a region crawling with horse thieves, as you were quick to point out just this morning, and now you want me to leave two exceptional horses and a perfectly serviceable mule outside in the dark?"

"*I* wanted you to go the other way altogether," Drax pointed out.

Gwyn sighed. "How can you not understand this at all? Has nothing bad ever happened to your kin or people, then? Nothing that had to be answered? What is it in the Elven Forest, all dancing about catching glowworms and picking daffodils?"

"Yes. That's exactly it; how did you know?" Drax ripped the lid off his kettle and tossed in a handful of herbs with uncharacteristic aggression, and Gwyn decided to say no more.

CHAPTER V

They continued south throughout the next day, speaking little. The wind slackened off by noon, which was fortunate, since no shelter presented itself that night, forcing the small band to huddle in a gully around one of Drax's dark fires. One end of the depression had filled with stubborn scrub and blowing tumbleweeds, but this they had to feed into their invisible, little blaze constantly as the fuel burned hot but too quickly. By midnight they gave up, the temporary warmth the fire provided no longer worth what they gave up in emerging from their nests of blankets to gather it. Gwyn tossed on the cold ground, gnawing her lip in concern and frustration. Despite her protests to Drax, she knew her course was now opposite from her ultimate destination, and every day was precious in this harsh season, to say nothing of whatever may be transpiring in her homeland.

The sun was well past its zenith the following day when Drax called a sudden halt. Gwyn had barely noticed the low bumps on the horizon, which at this distance might be anything, but the elf, eyes invisible behind his blue lenses, insisted they were a collection of buildings. Gwyn nodded. "That must be the place, then."

"How do you want to do this?" Drax questioned.

"We need to get close enough to see how many men are about." She paused. "Could you make me invisible again, like you did against the orcs at the Capital?"

"I didn't really make you invisible," Drax clarified, "just tricked orcish eyes into not seeing you. If I work that spell on a human to fool human sight, things go a little, ah, well, you wind up practically blind for the duration."

"You have the damnedest exceptions, you know that?"

"I was working on it a while back, but I needed a better understanding of how eyes function, and…" He noticed Gwyn's scowl. "Right. No 'wizard lessons.' You were curious enough the other day. I'd have thought by now you'd have developed more respect for the finer points of my craft."

"I respect blacksmiths, too," Gwyn rebutted, "but I don't need to know what color the iron glows before they smack it. Since it's a safe bet there are only human eyes in the camp, could you use this magic on yourself?"

"Naturally."

"Alright. We'll leave the road and find whatever meager cover we can. With luck they won't have lookouts, or at least not good ones. Once we're as close as we dare, you'll go in the rest of the way and have a look about."

Davax had never caught a good break in his life. No one had ever done him a good turn just for the kindness of it. His father had died in the war when he was too little to remember, and maybe if his mother had died then, too, he could have been adopted by a family with money or means. People always said he'd been an angelic little child, after all. But no, the sour, miserable woman had held on until he made his fourteenth year, and where was a young orphan to go at that age but into the army? Well, that life had been all well and good for his father, and look where it had got him.

He ran northward, looking to earn his keep with a trade caravan or some such. He knew his way around horses. What a miserable lot that had been; sunup to sundown, sometimes longer, feeding, currying, walking, fetching water, feeding and currying some more. For what? A pittance. The traders bought and sold weapons and beasts and every other thing for more than he could make in a lifetime. Once Davax realized he was surrounded by such wealth and, in rougher parts, surrounded by people that wanted to take it, the problem seemed to solve itself. Tipping off the thieving bands to their whereabouts, "losing" a horse or two in their territory, maybe weakening a few bowstrings when nobody was looking, all a lot easier than the work he was paid for, and the robbers tossed him a fair cut of their take, not the scraps he got from his "gainful" employment.

One thing led to another, though, and if the life of a horse thief was easier than of a groom, it was often just as boring and occasionally far more dangerous. So here Davax stood, leaning against a near-empty corral in an abandoned town, doing what? Fetching damn water for damn horses. Never caught a break in his life.

He gasped a freezing breath when he saw a man approaching down the westward lane, stepping from behind one of the farther buildings. After a moment of initial surprise, he first thought it must be one of his four compatriots, for who else could it be in this desolate place? Then Davax realized none of his fellows had a fur cloak that finely made; if they had he'd have heard no end of bragging about it. A moment later he saw three animals stepping into view, led by this unknown man, two fine horses and a mule. The stranger led them toward the corral with a purpose.

Clearing his throat, Davax called out, "Who goes there?"

"Nobody you know," the answer came back. The voice was strange, sort of high and raspy, but this time of year a strained throat was as common as a cold day.

"What do you want?" he yelled.

"Money. Looking to sell these beasts."

"Come on, then." Davax laughed to himself. He couldn't recall the last time he or any of his gang had *paid* for a horse, or much of anything else. Two of his friends, hearing the exchange, had sauntered out of the nearest building. The other two were probably sleeping, but let them. Three-to-one odds were fine, and by now the man was close enough to see he carried no crossbow or anything else that could harm them before he got within reach to be harmed himself. Siris, the one left in charge of the camp, took a step forward. He would probably let the exchange go forward, the easier to get the animals into the corral without any trouble, then just kill the seller before he could leave with the money. Davax had seen him play it that way once before.

The man approached slowly, his face still in the shadow of his hood, until he stood about a couple long paces from Siris. "Well, out with it," Siris growled. "How much do you want for them?"

With his right hand the man reached forward and to his left in a strange gesture. With his other hand he pulled back his hood, revealing that it was no man at all but a young woman, her features grim and hair a fiery mane. A sense of dread flooded over Davax, though his brain couldn't work out why. The woman drew her right hand sideways and suddenly it was full of a massive, shining sword, and before Siris could land a strike with his own weapon she had cut him down like it was nothing. Suddenly Davax's brain caught up. He didn't know the face, but he knew the height, the gender, the hair, the *sword*. "Gwyn the Savage!" he screamed. "It's Gwyn the–" before he could repeat the cry, Davax caught the pommel of the great sword full in the face, breaking three of his teeth and instantly filling his mouth with blood. He fell backward, whacking his head against the rails of the corral, and closed his eyes, no stomach for watching the death stroke find him. No, no one ever did him a good turn.

The fight was over in seconds. Gwyn peered about at the wreckage. The leader, apparently, would be dead in a few more spurting heartbeats. The sentry, or what passed for one, cowered and sobbed against the corral fence. The third man had rushed Gwyn with a club as she pommel-smashed the sentry. In the split second before the club wielder died she saw the regret in his eyes as he processed who she was and how foolish his charge had been, but by then it was too late. Gwyn had quickly put her point back on line after the pommel strike, and the brigand had stumbled right onto it. As she put her boot against his chest to shove the body off her blade, she growled in frustration without sentimentality; until she could determine who knew what, she needed to keep most of these curs alive.

Meanwhile, Drax had reappeared at the doorway to a nearby building just as two more enemies tried to emerge in response to the screams and commotion. Both were now rendered noncombatant, one cradling his withered right arm against his chest and screaming, more in fear than pain if Gwyn heard it right, and the other leaning against the doorpost and wheezing through a neck that now looked as scrawny and wrinkled as a vulture's.

Gwyn cleaned her blade quickly, then stowed it back in the sling on Thunderhead's tack. Following that, she looped the horse's reins over the corral fence; that would be sufficient to keep Flamewind and Thunderhead from wandering, and she dared Bully, who was tied to Thunderhead, to move the powerful charger anywhere he didn't want to go. Finally she heaved the sobbing bandit to his feet by the back of his shirt and frog-marched him to the doorway. The wheezing man scrambled to get out of the way, and Gwyn shoved her charge through the cleared opening. The screams of the brigand with the withered arm, especially now that she was closer, grated on her nerves in the relative silence of the plain. "Shut up!" she ordered him.

He didn't seem to hear. As Drax looked on, she spun the man around to face her and slapped him, hard, which finally quieted his horror. "You're sure there's nobody else about? No more 'barn owls' you missed?" she asked Drax.

"For the third time, yes," Drax answered. Gwyn did suspect he was right; smoke only curled from one chimney, and she doubted anyone else in the abandoned town would elect to sit shivering in the cold, especially given Southerners' disdain for it. Still, she'd felt conflicted at Drax's earlier scouting report of only five men, the words seeming to issue from the very air as he sustained his invisibility rather than remove the bracelet he'd enchanted, which he claimed would tax its power. On the one hand, she'd had no good plan for taking the outpost if it was guarded by more enemies than they could handle; on the other, the fewer the inhabitants, the worse the chances the men she was after were still there. "You found no defects in your sword, then?" Drax asked, his tone facetious.

"I did not," Gwyn admitted.

"I told you just holding it wasn't the same as putting magic on it again. As I endeavored to explain, the magic wasn't even on *me*, just emanating onto the people trying to see. If you'd be more patient you might learn to understand these things." Gwyn glared at him. "In any case," the elf finished as he herded the last bandit through the door, "magic or no, I'm still surprised you deigned to let me carry it."

Gwyn was secretly surprised at that as well. Walking in with sword in hand would have ruined the element of surprise, and even if no one noticed the weapon on Thunderhead's harness, she couldn't free it from there as quickly as she wanted in such close quarters. Drax had suggested carrying it for her and placing it in her hand when she reached for it, and apart from initial concern at having the ancestral weapon exposed to any kind of Drax's magic again, the mere thought of letting the elf carry it hadn't troubled her at all. Indeed, she didn't even consider the act to be any kind of affront until Drax voiced his assumption that she would. The realization shamed her for a moment, the thought she may not be properly safe-guarding the dignity of her family's blade. She looked at the short wizard's back as he entered the building in front of her, puzzling. She had traveled and fought both alone and in a company, but this practice of investing so much trust in a single companion was strange to her. Nevertheless, Drax had proven himself to be brave and competent, and even tolerable company, if a bit waggish and squeamish at times. Why shouldn't he carry the sword, given a strategic need? As long as he didn't actually try to fight with it. Never that, and may Terillah forbid it.

Gwyn stepped into the dim dwelling behind Drax. She left the door open behind her for better light and knowing the cold seeping in would trouble her enemies more than it would her or even the elf. Looking about, she saw cots set out on either side of the hearth, leaving only a small space between them to access the fire. A few tables and a motley array of chairs and benches filled the rest of the space, save a corner where foodstuffs were piled on shelves. Nearest that the tables were covered in cups, boards and utensils. A table nearer the door boasted some dice and game tiles in disarray, a Southern pastime for which Gwyn had little opportunity and less interest during her months of battle. Across from this, Drax prodded and ordered the three men into line on a bench, and the two he'd enchanted shrank from him as fearfully as anyone ever had from Gwyn, though it seemed the effects of his magic were fading. Once the survivors were arranged in an orderly row, Drax stepped out of the way and looked to Gwyn.

Gwyn looked back, then to the sullen men before her, two massaging and flexing their recovering body parts, the last spitting a mouthful of bloody saliva and one more tooth onto the floor before wiping his mouth with his sleeve. "Go ahead," she said to Drax.

"Pardon?"

"I've noticed you don't like the way I question prisoners. Have at it, then. You know what I'm after." She leaned against the wall to highlight her passive intent.

Drax's eyes widened a bit, then he stood up a little straighter. Gwyn looked on as he whispered some strange syllables under his breath and slid his left index finger over the silver ear cuff he wore, and when he took his hand away she could see the spidery lines glowing on it as she had before. Drax pointed at the man with the withered arm, the one most able to talk given the group's injuries. "You," he began, "when was the last time you left this place?"

The man looked back and forth between Drax and Gwyn as if deciding which one he was less afraid to talk to. He returned his gaze to the floorboards and shrugged. "Last month sometime."

"Ten days ago, or so," Drax continued, "some of your partners in villainy were doing a job far from here, twenty leagues east. Were any of you a part of that?"

All three men shook their heads, and the speaker added, "Those weren't with our lot, exactly. There's four gangs who gather up horses here to drive north, and split the take."

"Why, you're just a regular trade guild, aren't you?" Gwyn snarked. The thief seemed to take the question as rhetorical and remained silent.

"So none of you were doing jobs that far east in the last couple of weeks? Look at me," Drax ordered, making eye contact with each man in turn as they shook their heads. "But three men *did* come through here a week ago, from back east, did they not?"

The three men looked at each other, none speaking. Gwyn wasn't surprised to realize they offered up denials more readily than useful knowledge. She pushed off from the wall and took half a step forward. The wheezing man held his hands up to stay her and nodded. He coughed and cleared his throat. "Yeah, they did," he rasped. He rubbed his throat for a moment before continuing, his voice becoming a bit less hoarse with each word. "We'd had a sizable herd stored up, and they had orders from the bosses to start the drive as soon as they got back."

"Dammit!" Gwyn cursed, kicking the table in front of her so half the dice and tiles scattered onto the floor. The brigands shrank back from her outburst, not knowing how relatively mild it had been. As she spun a chair around and sat on it backwards, a habit she'd developed from so often wearing her great sword in a back sling, she realized she'd already known this truth. She couldn't explain it. When tracking down the orcs that had killed Shon, she'd attributed her knowledge of them to the fact that she'd seen their faces, though from very far away. Even when she dreamed their deaths after the fact, those slain in battle by others' hands, she wondered if she'd somehow seen them first, in the distance or from the corner of her eye, in ways she couldn't have noted in the moment due to the heat of combat. Even though a part of her knew that wasn't possible, it was a shred of rationality she could cling to.

Now, layered atop Daruneh's vague statements about

her and the dream she'd had of Tira's ranch, she had no way to explain away her certain knowledge, even before Drax's questioning, that neither the two men she'd killed nor any of these three that remained were under the condemnation of her vengeance. The legends of her homeland certainly allowed for such things. Still, believing in legends and seeing their realities play out in her own life were wholly apart, an irreconcilable gulf between them. Then Gwyn felt the weight of the immediate need hit her shoulders, far greater than her existential confusion. "Two days here and two days back," she muttered, shaking her head. She looked at Drax and spoke clearly, her voice thick with self-recrimination. "I wasted *four* days."

Drax grimaced. "It was always a risk. You can only reckon with what you know at the time."

"Why are you trying to salve my conscience? You didn't even want to come here."

He shrugged. "Have any of you ever been to this place up north?" he asked, returning to the outlaws. "Do you know anything about it?"

They all shook their heads at first. "Only been one drive where the men came back straight away," the man with the busted mouth finally spoke, lisping a bit as he struggled to adapt to his new dental architecture. "Took, mebbe, what? Four weeks?"

"More'n a month," the first speaker corrected. "Said it was a newish place, a stockade fort. Lots of blacksmiths, not much booze or women to be had, unless you're one of the guards of the place." He shrugged. "That's all I remember 'em saying."

"Is it on the north road?" Gwyn demanded. "No forks or turnings to take?"

"Road goes within clear sight of it, far as I know," the first man replied, now rubbing his shoulder.

Drax walked back toward Gwyn and bent to her ear.

"What are we going to do with them?" he asked, his voice tight. "I know they're bad men, but none of them even tried to lie."

"They'd have killed me for the worth of two horses and a mule," Gwyn answered, not bothering to lower her voice and with her eyes on the prisoners. Despite her words, she was surprised to find she had no special desire to kill any of these men. Her mind flashed quickly through her years of battle to consider the two beings, one orc and one man, she'd killed in truly cold blood, and in both cases she knew their crimes against those she cared for. These three, yes, she could slit their throats and sleep well afterward, but she felt no passion for it. She wasn't motivated to investigate the meaning of either fact.

Hope of discretion now lost, Drax straightened and spoke in normal tones. "You know I'd rather they weren't killed."

"I'm indifferent," Gwyn replied. She thought she noted something like surprise in Drax's expression, but before she could remark on it, the bleeding man, sitting closest to the wall, bolted toward the door. Gwyn stood and whipped her chair at him; it struck his legs and tripped him, and the fleeing criminal hurtled into the doorjamb, striking his head and collapsing in a tangle of limbs and broken chair parts. Gwyn glared at the other two, and they sat still, too afraid to move. She couldn't leave any of them here to report on her movements, nor would she risk dragging them along with her. "Can't trust them," she growled. She reached for her dirk as the men on the bench began to babble unintelligibly.

"What if I could make them forget?" Drax interjected.

Gwyn narrowed her eyes at him as the two conscious brigands went silent once more. "Can you do that?"

"It's been done," he replied. "Not by me, I admit. I can work it out."

"How long?" Gwyn asked, still suspicious.

"The rest of the day. At least."

Gwyn sighed. "Fine. We'll rest the horses and take advantage of the extra feed here. You have until morning." The man on the floor began to stir, so Gwyn hauled him back onto the bench. She turned to address the three of them. "This enchanter has work to do. It's the only hope you have of leaving this building alive, so I wouldn't interrupt him if I were you. I'm going to bind you all so I can go see to the animals. If you give me any trouble, I'll gut you just as happily. Understood?"

They nodded, and Gwyn found cordage around bundles in the foodstuffs that she used to tie the bandits hand and foot. Before she left the structure, she stopped at the table where Drax had taken a seat and begun leafing through a small journal he produced from within the folds of his robe. "Will you be in a trance, like when you did your enchanting at the crossroads?"

He shook his head. "Not for a while. I have to study my notes and test a few minor invocations before I get to that stage."

"Keep an eye on those three, then. I don't trust my knots much more than I do them."

The elf nodded, and Gwyn paced outside.

When Gwyn returned, her mail removed and bundled with the mule's pack, the sun was sinking behind the peaks of the Tunari Mountains. *Bia Creg* cut the sky like an errant star, but *Aridan*, waning through his last quarter, would not rise for hours. The three prisoners leaned against one another on the bench, nodding and waking in restless turns.

Drax looked up from his work, now lit by a dripping candle. "Did you turn the stolen horses loose?" he asked.

Gwyn shook her head. "Even if they found their way home, they might find 'home' abandoned. Your supposed conversations with my animals aside, I can't imagine most horses know whether they've been stolen, much less care. I don't see any evidence the ones outside have been mishandled."

"Well, I was just about to come find you. I'm ready to begin my spell. I'll be oblivious awhile. Can you stand watch?"

Gwyn nodded and crossed the room to add wood to the fire. Despite the relative gloom, Drax covered his eyes with his spectacles before slumping a bit in his chair, his mouth twitching with barely audible incantations as his hands worked patterns in the air before his breast. Gwyn found clean water and ingredients enough for a decent soup amidst the foodstuffs. She threw everything into a pot hanging from an iron bar before the fire and swung the vessel over the flames. She'd rarely had to cook for herself, making do with hard biscuit and dried meat when journeying alone, and didn't much relish the prospect of the flavorless concoction she knew would result, but it would satisfy her empty belly.

While the water heated, Gwyn crossed to one of the front windows and pulled a chair before it, cracking open the wooden shutter to peer into the twilight, trying to reckon the hours until moonrise. Nothing stirred. She closed the window and waited, leaning against the wall and resting her eyes a few seconds at a time while listening for any sounds other than Drax's sibilant whispers and the bubbling of the pot. Finally she decided the soup was done, or close enough to be edible, and rose to swing the vessel away from the fire. She ladled some into a wooden bowl and found a farl of dry bread to dunk in it. By the time the soup cooled, the darkness outside was complete, but after sitting back on her stool with her steaming bowl, she opened the shutter again to see if anything showed under the starlight.

"Shut the window," one of the prisoners muttered, shifting on the bench. "It's cold."

"Yeah," mumbled another in half-waking response, "there won't be anything to see out there 'til morning."

The first speaker hissed and elbowed the second. Gwyn's face went slack in realization, then tight in self-reproach. In her zeal to learn of the northbound murderers she sought, she'd forgotten to inquire about the rest of the raiding bands and where they might be. Drax had done likewise. She suddenly imagined a gang of marauders approaching in the dark. Surely the time of their planned return, as accidentally revealed by their compatriot, could be no better than a rough estimate. They might be nearby even now, and on familiar roads, even after sunset a single lantern to show hazards to the lead rider would be enough to continue progress despite the late moon. Whatever she might disregard as pure speculation, one fact couldn't be denied: If there was even a chance more enemies could be there by morning, they were closer than she wanted them. Cursing, she stood and called out to Drax, setting down her uneaten supper. The elf didn't stir. "Alright," she ordered the bandits, "get outside."

"What?" one of the outlaws scoffed. "Why?"

"I've got work to do, and I want you where I can see you."

"You going to loose our feet?" a second asked, stirring.

"No."

"Then how—?"

"Hop, roll, inch on your bellies, what do I care?" Gwyn shot back. "Just go before I lose my temper."

The one closest to the door, his jaw swollen from Gwyn's pommel and his eye blackened by the doorjamb, lunged through it, falling and rolling out of the way. The other two rose and hopped, fell, crawled, and shimmied until they had cleared the building. Lighting a lantern,

Gwyn followed them outside and set to work saddling the horses and repacking Bully's harness. She moved as quickly as she could in the dim light, but every task seemed to drag on for an eternity. Her lantern hanging from the nearest corral post cast eerie shadows with every movement. She'd loaded a quarter of the fodder from the abbey when she looked to the patch of firelight outside the door and realized her captives were gone.

Gwyn looked in immediate alarm through the open window, but Drax still sat where she'd left him, immobile. She rushed to Thunderhead's side and reached for her sword when a lance of pain shot through her left triceps. Too late her mind registered the springy *thunk* of crossbow limbs that had preceded the agony. She heard a curse from beyond the lanternlight, on her left flank, and the sound of movement. Pulling her dirk, she slashed the leather thongs holding her shield to Thunderhead's harness and gripped it as best she could, no time to strap it properly. She charged the frantic sounds and heard crossbow quarrels clatter to the ground, another curse. A shadow appeared before her, outlined against the lowest stars, and she thrust forward with her dirk, keeping her hand within her own silhouette to hide the movement. She felt the point rip fabric and flesh, and the enemy cried out in pain and alarm. Now nearly on top of the man, Gwyn pulled her blade free and slashed with it, feeling a spray of blood as the shadow melted to the ground.

She sidestepped away from the lantern's glow, wary of another attack, but before she'd gone three paces she heard dull footfalls on packed earth, hurtling pell-mell southward. Two sets of footfalls, she was certain. Sighing, Gwyn wiped her dirk on her pant leg and sheathed it as she walked back through the doorway and closed it behind her. Finally she dropped her shield and felt the back of her burning, aching arm. The bolt still hung there, buried deep, but as she probed at it, wincing at the fresh pain, she didn't believe it had struck bone. Every move of her arm and twitch of the muscle shot her through with a painful shock; she wanted to yank the quarrel out but knew she shouldn't, especially since she couldn't tell if the head was barbed.

"Drax," she yelled, hurrying across to where he sat. "Drax!" Still the elf didn't react. Gwyn stooped, putting her face just an inch from his and preparing to yell again and slap him if that didn't work. So close, she suddenly saw, even through the shaded glass, the elf's eyes glowing and sparking in erratic pulses of yellow and purple. "Hells!" she gasped, stumbling backward. She had no idea what catastrophe might result if she managed to force him awake in that moment. Sighing again and marshaling her resolve, Gwyn wrapped her right arm around Drax's narrow waist and heaved him up onto her shoulder, hustling out the door and sliding him awkwardly onto Flamewind's back. "This is what I get for letting people live," she grunted as she shoved one of Drax's legs over the saddle and worked his foot into the stirrup. The rope harness she'd made at the crossroads was still in one of the saddlebags, and she slipped it over Flamewind's neck and forced Drax's arms through it, finally looping the reins around his arms, the harness, and the saddle horn before cinching everything as tight as she dared, still leaving the free ends long enough to lead Flamewind by them.

She returned to the building to retrieve her shield and quickly loosened the strap so she could sling it on her back, growling in frustration when it glanced the embedded crossbow bolt and highlighted the pain. Still working in the light of the single lantern and what little firelight flickered through the door from the hearth inside, Gwyn loaded another bundle of the abbey's fodder onto the mule, but before she could grab a third she heard the sound of hoofbeats thudding up from the south. Without hesitation she mounted Thunderhead, grabbed Flamewind's reins, and galloped into the darkness of the north.

She ran only a mile, the bolt in her arm searing with every step, before leaving the road and slowing to a speed she hoped wouldn't be audible as she paralleled the path thirty or forty yards away. The passage of so many horses had flattened the plain a substantial distance from the road proper, so at a walk she had little concern that any of the beasts would make a false step, even in the dark. She dismounted to reduce Thunderhead's burden and shorten their silhouette against the stars. If any pursuers used lanterns in the pursuit, she would see them coming miles away on the flat prairie. If they didn't, she hoped they'd ride straight past her on the road, at least until the moon rose. She didn't think she'd bled much, but between the wound, missing meals, and lack of sleep, she felt exhausted and weak. She doubted she could wield her sword until her arm was seen to.

"What… What…in every…single one of the hells is going on?" Drax gasped after an hour, slowly coming back to awareness.

Gwyn halted and turned, fumbling in the starlight to loosen the ties holding Drax to his horse. "We forgot to ask when the rest of the gang was coming back."

"Oh."

"The prisoners got loose while I was loading the horses. One's dead. Two got away. I got shot."

"Shot?" Finally freeing himself from the harness, Drax sat up. "How bad? Do you need help?"

"Left arm. It's been better." Gwyn could still move her fingers, but her elbow felt sluggish and swollen. "Can you heal it?"

"Not… I'll do what I can. Is anyone after us?"

"Can't tell."

Drax stepped down from Flamewind and removed his lenses. A moment later Gwyn's wide pupils were assaulted by the light from Drax's ring.

"Put that out," she ordered. "Don't be stupid; anybody looking could see that for miles." Gwyn couldn't be sure how well even the elf could see by starlight alone, but making any light was a risk they couldn't take.

With a sigh he brought his eyes close to Gwyn's wound and probed it with his fingers. Gwyn was alarmed to find the ache of his prodding felt dull and somehow distant until he poked harder, forcing her to hiss as a renewed, sharp pain shot deeper through her arm. "Do you have to keep doing that?"

"Sorry. I think there are small barbs on it. I'll have to cut it out. If we can't afford a light, it'll go better after the moon rises."

Gwyn nodded. "I can stand it a couple more hours."

"You rest here with the horses," Drax insisted. "I'll look about for whatever brush I can find for a dark fire."

"I can help."

"Now *you* don't be stupid," Drax interrupted, continuing over Gwyn's impolite rebuttal, "you can barely see, and you had more vigor after going hand to hand with a few dozen orc sorcerers than you do now. You carried me out of there, and thank you, by the way, now let me handle things awhile. Just rest and try to stay warm."

"Alright," Gwyn relented, slumping to the ground. "Don't go too far. And if you feel like passing out, give a cry first so I can try to find you."

"I'll be fine," the elf assured her as he padded away. "The preparation doesn't take so much out of me, and the actual spell never happened. Real waste, though. Wonder if it would have worked." Drax continued to mutter as he looked for brush or other fuel, occasionally returning with armloads. Gwyn lay on the hard ground, wrapped in her cloak and blanket, and dozed a few minutes at a time.

The moon was well up when she awoke to Drax shaking her. There was no need for words. With only a nod she doffed her outer coverings and turned to lay on her chest to give the elf better access to her wound. He pressed a short length of thick rope into her hand, and with an emotion as close to fear as she would ever admit, she gripped it between her teeth. She heard as much as felt Drax cutting the left sleeve of her gambeson away from the quarrel, though with the many strokes required to slice through the tough, layered linen, the elf's knife often struck the bolt and forced her to wince. Once the fabric was clear, she waited, tensing, through a long pause.

"Try to hold still," Drax cautioned, positioning Gwyn's arm a bit away from her body and laying his shin across her forearm and his knee on her shoulder blade. Then he cut flesh.

Gwyn grunted in agony and heaved off the ground, her brain heedless of her body's reactions. The lighter elf was cast away on the dry, crackling grass, cursing under his breath.

"This may not work," Drax hazarded as he collected himself. "Maybe we should–"

"Go again," Gwyn ordered, taking the gag from her mouth for a moment. "I'll keep still. I'll make myself." Drax took position again, and this time Gwyn clenched every muscle in her body, willing herself into a rigid statue of muscle and bone on the frozen turf. Drax cut, and she felt the pain, felt it rush up into her skull and spin her world about weird axes. She expected Drax to wrench the bolt free at any moment, but he didn't, instead making cut after cut. Gwyn was sure he must be flaying her arm wide open under the moonlight, peeling muscle from bone, and that image, as much as the pain itself, forced her over the precipice into blackness.

She awoke once more to a scorching anguish in her arm, her involuntary scream splitting the silence of the winter plain. The burning Gwyn felt dissipated slowly to a tight, violent ache as she looked about, sweating in the cold. "What was that?" she mumbled.

"Bolt's out," Drax answered from behind her. "I bled it clean. It's cauterized now."

Gwyn tried to flex her arm but found it immobile. "You lashed it down?" she asked, not panicking as she had when she'd woken to the same treatment on her other arm, two and a half years earlier.

"Yes," the elf answered. "Keep it totally still tonight, and tomorrow I'll rig you up a sling."

"I was hoping you'd have some fancy elven magic for this," Gwyn pressed.

"It's…a bit more complicated than that," Drax replied. "I've done all I can. Sleep now."

Gwyn needed no additional urging.

Chapter VI

In the morning Gwyn found the pain in her arm to be harsh but manageable. Drax provided the sling he had promised and did most of the work in striking what had passed for their camp. With the midmorning sun revealing no travelers in either direction, the pair pointed their horses to the north and began the long trek toward their goal.

A week passed with no sign of other travelers, neither friend nor foe. With no fighting to be done and Drax eager to take a greater share of the work of camp life, Gwyn fought her instincts and forced herself to rest her left arm. Drax's efforts seemed to have staved off infection, and the wound gave her less pain with each passing day.

Though the air grew colder the weather remained dry, so it was bearable. Bundled carefully they could travel in relative comfort as long as they found nightly shelter out of the wind. This urged them to the west, where the rising foothills of the Tunaris provided more variable terrain for windbreak, but the more rugged ground also slowed their northward progress, and the daylight hours were short. The lower pockets did catch adequate water to stave off thirst and provide enough windswept, stunted trees for firewood, and in the empty land Gwyn felt safe enough to light campfires each evening, only occasionally feeling a sense of unease that prompted her to request Drax's dark fire (a resource he assured was abundant but not limitless).

On more than one of these windswept nights Gwyn dreamed the vengeance dream again. The young man appeared each time after the three surviving condemned murderers had faded into the blackness, and Gwyn woke the moment she saw him. On his last appearance, the dream continued, and the man spoke. "They won't elude you forever. Have courage."

"I need no words from you," Gwyn spat. "I know you sent them after the boy. After I'm done with them, you should worry for yourself."

For the first time the man turned his face toward her. It was a pleasant face, strong of feature and with cool, blue eyes beneath light brown hair left shaggy. "Why do you think I sent those murderers?"

"You tried to take the boy, and now you're here, showing your face among the damned."

"Is that right?" the man challenged. "Did you dream the face of the orc general who ordered the sentries out that killed your friend? Did you dream the warlords who drove the invasion?"

Gwyn didn't answer.

"So why am I here?" the man asked her unvoiced question for her. "Where do you think these dreams come from?" His smile was thin.

"They come from me," Gwyn insisted, thumping her chest, "from the power you want for yourself."

"Those are *her* words again. Men tried to take the boy, they failed, and now only one of us has him. I will tell you no lies, nor truths you will reject. It isn't my way to force your path. I will only ask the question. Are you sure you rescued him from me? Or did you deliver him finally to his abductor?"

Gwyn woke with a start. She didn't believe this voice in her dreams. The sense of calm and peace she'd felt in Daruneh's abbey was too pure to be ignored. Yet were not Atlund's legends filled with tales of warriors who had been lured to catastrophe by the spurious promise of comfort and ease? She cast the thought aside, trusting to her instincts that had carried her this far, but she tossed in her bedroll, sleeping no more until dawn.

As Drax lit their fire on the seventh night out from the outlaw village, he risked a question to Gwyn. "You have something else gnawing at your mind, aside from the vast panoply of problems before us, don't you?"

She hesitated. "Do you trust Daruneh?" she finally asked.

Drax started for a moment, clearly astounded by the question. "You ask this *now*?"

"I didn't see the need before," Gwyn replied. "It seemed clear enough at the time, but I've been having doubts."

"I didn't sense anything false in her," the elf assured.

"But, she isn't...human. Is she?"

"I doubt it," Drax answered.

"Then what is she?"

"Lore beyond my ken, I'm afraid."

Gwyn knew the elf meant nothing in using the word 'afraid' in reference to the enigmatic lady, but she winced at it nonetheless. For several minutes more Gwyn stared at the fire, glancing occasionally at Drax with an unsettled expression.

"What is it now?" the elf asked.

Gwyn scowled. "Nothing important."

"Well, perhaps an Atlund mind is content just staring at

the horizon day after day, but I require a bit more diversion. No matter if it isn't important; with everything else happening I'd relish something trivial."

Gwyn kept her eyes on the fire as she finally mumbled, "I want you to ask Thunderhead something for me."

Drax smiled. "With your permission, I'd be happy to. What do you want to know?"

Gwyn still wouldn't meet the elf's eyes, her embarrassment overwhelming her confidence. "Well, I've been wondering since Daruneh greeted us all by name at the abbey, if that means... Does he consider Thunderhead his real name?"

Drax stood and walked the few steps to Thunderhead and closed his eyes, petting the great beast's mane. After a few moments the horse dipped its dark head, and the elf whispered in his ear. What followed looked to Gwyn like the animal was having a minor fit, nearly a minute of mane tossing, head bobbing, and foot stamping, interspersed with snorts and quiet nickers. At last Drax turned back to Gwyn.

"This is what I was trying to tell you about before. He spoke almost like a person!"

Gwyn arched one eyebrow.

Drax rolled his eyes in turn. "Alright, not like a person, but what I mean is, when I talk to other animals, even Flamewind, it's all feelings and urges, maybe a simple idea like food. I was just hoping to get a 'yes' or 'no,' but what Thunderhead just did was more like actual language. Primitive, but still language."

"Fine, then what did he *say*?"

"Well, if I understand him correctly, he says his ancestors have been serving Baraxis' family for many generations. They're considered humans of great honor by the herds there. In respect, they've been letting the Sutherset family name them for a long time. So, yes, he considers Thunderhead his true name." Drax looked at

Gwyn as he paused, then asked, "Why does it matter so much?"

Gwyn explained the Atlund legends that men and horses once knew each other's speech, and that horses would tell their true names only to their most trusted riders. This led to a tradition that giving a name to a horse, without earning its real one, was an act of disrespect and arrogance. Thunderhead stamped and snorted, then Drax whispered to him some more, followed by more motion and sound from the horse. Drax smiled. "See how smart he is? He knew we were still talking about him. I translated for you. He seems to think your ideas are old-fashioned, but he says when we get to Atlund you can tell all your people he told you his name if you want to. He's proud to be your horse."

Gwyn stood and walked over to Thunderhead, running her fingers through his mane as she offered a slice of candied apple from Daruneh's provisions. Thunderhead took it gladly, bobbing his head in seeming appreciation.

"Well, that's something I've never seen before," Drax mused.

"What, me spoiling a horse?"

"No. You smiling."

"Shut up," Gwyn shot, offering a piece of apple to Flamewind in turn so he wouldn't feel left out.

Drax sat back down, leaving Gwyn to continue petting Thunderhead, then the elf said, "While we're on the subject of names, I have a question of my own."

"You can ask it," Gwyn offered. "I might not answer."

"What's your sword's name?"

Gwyn stopped her attention to the horses and looked at Drax. "What?"

"You heard."

She hesitated. "How do you know it has one?"

"Just a hunch, but the way you're stalling proves I'm right."

Gwyn returned to the fire, wrapping her cloak and staring into the flames. Several minutes later, after Drax had returned to his supper, she finally said, "I ran away from home after I turned sixteen. It was in the winter, and I was gone for three nights. The third night, all I could find for shelter was a hollow tree trunk, still standing up with a gap at the bottom. I didn't know if it would be enough. I didn't really expect to wake up. Do you know about the magic of the winter Wind in Atlund?"

Drax nodded in silence as he stared at Gwyn. She continued, trancelike. "The space was so small, I could only barely squeeze myself in and block the opening behind me with dead leaves and loam. I had to leave the sword out in the Wind. The next morning, when I did wake up, first thing out of my shelter I checked for it, half in a panic. It was right where I left it, but when I gripped the hilt, I could swear it was colder than it should have been…like the Wind had gone into it somehow. So that day I named it after the word for the Wind in the ancient Atlund tongue: *Tyralist*. It's felt cold like that every time I've touched it since, a little less since Baraxis had it reforged and you put your runes on it, but still there. I don't mind. The ferocity of the Wind is in it. Just like me." Gwyn cleared her throat and looked up at Drax. "Nobody else knows that. You speak it to another at the cost of your life."

"I wouldn't have pried if I'd had any idea it was so personal. You didn't have to tell me."

"Someday I'll ask you something," Gwyn replied. "Remember I trusted you first."

For another week they traveled in the same way, replenishing their water skins at every stream and trickle and rationing Daruneh's supplies with discipline. Bully seemed well enough foraging in the scrub, but Gwyn insisted they walk as much as possible to save Thunderhead and Flamewind's energy after losing half the abbey's nourishing fodder at the bandit town. Drax boasted he had long ago enchanted his boots to endure for years, but Gwyn grew ever more footsore, and every northward mile and every passing day grew colder.

Occasionally a road from the mountains would wind its way down and hurry off toward the northward thorough-fare they paralleled. These often led to a waystation at the crossroads, but all were abandoned, save two. These had been commandeered by outlaws who attacked as soon as the traveling pair, seeming by every outward appearance to be wooly for the fleecing, drew close. Against Gwyn's hammer and Drax's spellcraft the highwaymen were little threat, and as Gwyn's dreams almost nightly confirmed, none proved to be the three men she sought. No, the most dangerous enemy on the long journey across the plains was neither winter nor men, but boredom.

"Did you hear the one about the Southern merchant and the Priest of Terillah?" Drax asked one day. It was sometime during the second week, but beyond that the days all ran together.

"I'd heard it before I ever met you," Gwyn growled back, "and I've heard it three times since we left the abbey."

"Why didn't you say so?"

"At the time I thought it was better than the sound of the endless wind or the soul-numbing silence, but I've changed my mind."

"Then how about–"

"If you try the one about the Atlund clan chief and the fishmonger's wife again I swear I'll kill you. I'm not kidding."

Drax bit back the joke but after a moment couldn't help remarking, "Have you ever noticed how you threaten to kill me a lot?"

"A girl can dream," Gwyn growled.

Such was the strained state of affairs near the end of the third week when, in the hour before noon, they espied the telltale, jagged-top silhouette of a log palisade on the horizon, jutting from a low rise to the north and a point west. "I know we haven't been followed, much less overtaken," Gwyn reasoned, "so they can't be on the lookout for us. What else can you see, Drax? Can you tell what sort of place it is?"

The elf peered ahead. "It looks to have been built recently; the logs aren't weathered much. The gates are open. I see some oxen milling around. I smell horses on the north wind, no surprise, but I can't see them. Maybe they're corralled inside? If my judge of the distance is right, it's big, a few acres inside. This has to be the place, but it doesn't have the seeming of a rude, outlaw fort to me." Drax then gazed at the mountains, flaring his nostrils. "I can't be certain, but there may be a storm coming down. Might be nothing, but could be snow, if I'm right."

"We'll risk walking in, then," Gwyn decided. "We need rest and supplies, and if we get snowed in we could be here awhile. All hard to achieve if we're sneaking about the place, even if we could." She dismounted and retrieved her sword from its lashings, moving it to its back sling, just in case. She flexed her left arm and felt confident she could fight with it again, and she felt safer with the sword than other armaments. She'd watched the road carefully during their journey; as certain she was they weren't followed, she was equally sure none had gone past them headed south. Her heartbeat quickened at the probability that the last of Tira's killers took their ease somewhere inside, unaware their death drew near the gate. Remounting, she clucked her tongue at Thunderhead and trotted toward the road, her pace eager.

~ * ~

The sun had passed its zenith by the time they came within a stone's throw of the walls, granting Gwyn a closer view of the outpost. Outside the palisade sat a handful of wagons, their oxen unyoked and left to graze and drink water from a ditch apparently dug for the purpose, its sides hidden by a layer of ice. Gwyn supposed these wains belonged to merchants, the most eager or desperate, who had come to the place as soon as word of the peace reached them, looking for caravan guards or resolving to wait until more of their kind gathered for mutual defense on the southward journey. She looked and listened for other Atlunders, suddenly anxious for news of home, but the people camping outside seemed all to be of the northmost-dwelling Southern stock, rugged and self-reliant like her countrymen but without any connection to that land beyond the wilds and the Elven Forest.

The wall of the outpost itself was composed of upright timbers, uneven but around twelve feet high and sharpened at the top. At this distance she could see the heads and shoulders of men standing guard, wearing an assortment of helmets or none at all, and occasionally the unmistakable outline of crossbow limbs cut the backdrop of the cloudy sky. Confirming Drax's observations, the walls were new and roughhewn, giving the impression the fortification had been erected quickly, and they enclosed a rectangle perhaps half a furlong on the short sides and only a bit more on the long. Against the north wall a rail fence enclosed another narrow acre where men exercised the horses Drax had smelled. A few merchants looked on, and the men who seemed currently responsible for the beasts were unkempt and armed. They gave Gwyn baleful looks from a distance, and with a frustrated grunt she elected to turn back toward the gate, losing an opportunity to see if any of the animals had Shon's brand.

As she and Drax approached the open gates, situated in

the eastern wall, the guards stared down at them but made no challenge. Passing within, Gwyn looked up at a scaffold running along the inside of the stockade that could accommodate many defenders. It seemed clear the installation had been erected as a military fort, but presently its purpose wasn't so obvious, nor who controlled the garrison. In addition to the open gates and civilians milling about, the guards wore no regular uniforms or arms, though each did display a sash or armband of purple and gray.

Buildings on either side of the main gate funneled entrants through a space barely wide enough for a large dray, and while still in this narrow alley Gwyn and Drax suddenly heard the wet snap of a lash and peals of mocking laughter. Glancing at one another, they slowed their approach, their movements still tracked by two of the crossbowmen Gwyn had seen the moment before.

Once through, they found themselves standing at the back of a large crowd gathered around an open square. A voice called out, "Twelve!" The lash cracked and the mob laughed again. By virtue of their mounted height, Gwyn and Drax could see over the heads of the throng to the focus of their derision: a small man, practically naked, with his head and hands through a pillory. A burly figure stood behind him with a many-thonged whip, dealing strokes to the captive's legs and back as a large man off to the left, well dressed in yellow and red, continued to call out the count.

"What do you suppose he did?" Drax asked out the side of his mouth.

"How should I know?"

"I don't know that you should, but if you have even a guess I'd like to hear it. Whatever *he* did, *I'd* like not to."

Gwyn remained silent, no stomach for spectating such an event. Though she couldn't guess the man's crime, she doubted such a small and underfed wretch could be dangerous enough to warrant such a whipping. Legal punishments in Atlund ran the gamut from simple restitution to hard labor to swift execution, but to beat a helpless man was dishonor and cowardice, and no Atlunder could be found to carry out such a sentence. She knew corporal displays were legal in the South, but given the dire circumstances during her tenure in the cities, mis- demeanors had either gone unsolved or been corrected immediately at the back of a soldier's fist. For all her bloodlust, it galled her to see a man bound and beaten this way, but it wasn't her place nor in her interest to interfere.

Instead, she was just about to turn away and find a path around the crowd when the well-dressed man yelled, "Fifteen!" The lash fell one more time, the pilloried man screamed, and the crowd broke apart, still chuckling at his misfortune. As the mob dispersed, one of the crossbowmen pointed at Gwyn and Drax, at which a rough-looking guard in a few mismatched armor plates stepped forward with a halberd, barring their way.

"State your business," he demanded.

"We're travelers, bound north," Drax answered amiably. "Just passing through to rest and refresh our supplies."

"Do you have money?" the guard asked.

"We have enough," Drax replied, jingling the coin pouch he'd received from Daruneh.

"Why didn't you say so?" cried the well-dressed man from a few paces away, turning from his hurried walk out of the square. Gwyn regarded him carefully as he sauntered back toward them, his six feet of height heavy with fat. Still, by his gait, the breadth of his shoulders, and his meaty hands, Gwyn guessed at powerful muscles beneath the more recent padding of indolence. His round face cracked into a sickle of a grin, a white flash in a red smudge. "Welcome to Finn's Station!" the man continued. "Forgive the initial unpleasantness, I beg you. The methods required to keep the king's peace here are distasteful but effective. I'm Lord Finn, and this is my waystation. Glad to have you visiting! What's mine is yours, for a reasonably negotiated price, of course. Do you need weapons? Armor repair? Horse grooming? My team of master craftsmen stand by, awaiting your every need."

Finn kept talking as Gwyn surveyed his stable of "master" craftsmen exiting the square; most looked honest enough but were thin and dirty, their backs bent by hard toil. Even Drax was shifting impatiently when the lord finally paused.

"Hells, would you even sell us the blades of grass here on the green?" Gwyn wondered, the need to stay out of trouble no match for her irritation at the lord's patter.

"Heavens no, beasts as fine as your horses there need proper fodder, and with a purchase of food or boarding any one of the stable masters can provide a voucher that will exempt you from grazing fees during your stay, which I assure you are nominal in any case."

Drax started to chuckle before realizing Lord Finn was serious. Gwyn's face went slack as a new wave of weariness and frustration washed over her. "Is there a tavern?"

"Indeed, young lady, indeed," Finn responded, scarcely breaking rhythm. "Take the north road out of the central market, third building on the left. Tell them Lord Finn sent you!"

Gwyn and Drax took their leave before Finn could enumerate the many goods and services available at the establishment. As they moved into the station, its origins as a military post became all the more clear. The market of stalls they passed through could be discerned as a former drilling green. Beyond that, a lane ran from the gates straight to a building against the back wall, a command post and officers' residence by the look of it. A single track crossed the lane, running from left to right, and both "streets" were fronted by shops and other establishments, all bearing the scars of their previous uses – a mess hall there, an armory across the street – save a few that scorned their martial history with coats of garish paint and breezy curtains. At the north end of that crossing track Gwyn saw large stables and the smaller gates, probably widened sally ports, that accessed the corral she'd seen outside. Smoke and the ringing of forge hammers permeated everything, suggesting more smithing stalls than Gwyn would expect in a place of this size.

The pair soon arrived at a newer building of rough beams and cheap clapboard with a square sign above the door that proclaimed, "Edgewild Tavern, Northmost Booze in the South." Gwyn cast a suspicious eye over the façade before dismounting and turning to Drax. "I'll go inside and check things out. Best stay out here with the animals."

"I heartily concur," Drax replied, his head turning to follow the motion of a large man on the other side of the lane whose stare lingered on Flamewind and Thunderhead as he passed.

Gwyn opened the tavern door; a bell inside swung inward, but its sound was dull and clunky. The interior swam with shadows as her eyes adjusted from the midday sun outside. A fire burned in a huge hearth to her left, but it cast deep shadows and only barely took the edge off the cold.

A voice rang out from the back of the room. "Never figured to see your face again, leastways not alive."

Gwyn strained to see the speaker through the shadows, finally resolving a deeper smudge against the dark into the shape of a small man behind a long, bottle-covered table. As her vision further acclimated, she was able to discern a gray, shaggy head with a hardscrabble beard and a cloth tied over one eye. Meanwhile she moved away from the door in a sidestep that kept her back to the window where Drax stood, trying to stay in view of her only ally. "I'm sorry, man," she replied, "I don't know you." She took a few cautious steps in the speaker's direction.

"Don't blame you, Captain," he spoke again. "I've lost some weight and some hair, not to mention the eye."

Hearing more of his voice, and closer now, Gwyn studied the man more carefully, then quickened her gait. "Adezavax?"

"One and the same," the old soldier answered. He did, indeed, look leaner and older than when he'd been Gwyn's guard captain on her southward caravan journey, older than the year and a half would allow. Seeming to catch something in her gaze, Adezavax said simply, "It takes a toll, don't it? It was mead, if I remember right?"

Gwyn nodded to both questions, reaching into her coin pouch as the small man found a bottle and began to pour. "Why do you call me 'captain'?" she asked.

"Everybody in the South knows your story, at least as the harpers sing it." He placed a full, pewter tankard before Gwyn. She dropped her coin down in turn, but he waved it back to her. "Once a captain in the orc wars, always a captain, if you ask me."

Gwyn lifted her cup toward Adezavax and said, "Fair enough, Captain," as the man found his own tumbler and drank a wordless toast with her.

"No," he clarified, "captain in a caravan don't count. In the war I made sergeant, so that rank I'll answer to."

"You went back to the fight," Gwyn surmised.

"After the bridge fell," Adezavax confirmed after another drink. "Trade pretty well dried up with the Capital surrounded, and I figured I had to do my bit. Had some action in the western fiefs, plenty of bloody work trying to kill or corral all the orcs that scattered after you lot broke the siege. That's where I lost the eye. Job wasn't done yet, but I wasn't much use with all the orcs on my left side as good as invisible, so I headed back north waiting for trade to start up again," he paused to gesture about himself, "and here I am."

Gwyn started to speak, but the sergeant continued, "You can tell your friend to come inside. Nobody'll steal your horses."

Gwyn started toward the window as she replied, "Hard to believe, since I know full well there's horse thieves about."

"Sure enough, the place is lousy with 'em. They just won't steal *your* horses, not so long as they're outside my tavern."

Gwyn tapped on the windowpane to get Drax's attention, then motioned him inside. As he entered she moved back toward the bar. "You think you have that much influence around here?"

Adezavax smiled. "For now, let's just say I have an understanding with some of the players about the station. That satisfy you?"

"For now."

"We have a new friend?" Drax asked, approaching the pair.

"I'm Adezavax," the older man answered. "Folks call me Dez, when they've call to call me anything, and you might as well do the same. That goes for you both."

"We rode south together," Gwyn clarified, offering no more to the elf. She pondered her course as Sergeant Dez took the elf's order for a glass of port and poured it. "Who knows about the horses coming in here, where they come from and who brings which ones?" she finally asked.

"I keep track of what I can," Dez replied, "but the man

in charge of all that is Roxen, Finn's right hand steward. You won't get anything from him, though. Why do you want to know?"

Gwyn paused, unsure how far to trust Dez. He'd seemed decent enough when they rode together, but she'd been a different person then, less observant of character and not looking for anyone to trust, much less who was worthy of it. "Horse thieves killed a friend of mine down south," she decided to answer. "I have good reason to believe they're here in the fort, somewhere."

Dez narrowed his eyes. "And there's no chance you'd just let that go."

Gwyn slammed her mug down. "No chance in all the hells, and if you ask me to, I would know why!"

Drax reached for Gwyn's arm as if to stay her temper, but she batted him away. Meanwhile, Dez said in a low voice, "Easy, Captain. I'm not asking, and if I was it would only be for your own sake. This is a dangerous place you've come to." He glanced over their shoulders at the front windows, then added, his voice low, "In fact I'd like to hire you. We've–"

A pair of men passed by the left window and paused in front of the door, and by the cadence of their conversation it seemed at least one of them was coming in. Dez began speaking and moving quickly as he pulled a warded lock key from his pocket. "Here, this is to my place, in the very northeast corner of the fort. Put up your hoods; try to stick to the shadows as you leave, and give this man a wide berth. Go now!"

Gwyn felt anxious at Dez's manner, and she wasn't inclined to take orders from him, but under the circumstances she decided she couldn't afford not to. Moving as instructed, she saw that, indeed, both men entered the tavern and went straight to the bar, hailing Dez as they did. She and Drax kept to the shadowy side of the room across from the hearth, then cut quickly to the door and reclaimed their mounts.

As Finn's Station had only the two main, crossing thoroughfares, reaching the far northeast corner required picking through narrow lanes and alleys where it was easier to lead the horses than ride them. The pair tried to stay discreet, with Gwyn stopping as soon as they were out of sight of any passersby to return her sword to Thunderhead's tack where it was somewhat less conspicuous. At length they reached the corner that was reportedly Dez's house, a low cottage with a sizeable stable attached. After seeing to their animals, they entered the house through a back door and settled down to wait, taking their ease on roughhewn benches at either side of a long table. After a time, Drax spoke.

"What do you think is going on around here?"

"What's to think about?" Gwyn retorted. "Seems a noble, Finn or some other, had the fort built to promote trade coming through his lands, and as the armies all got pulled south to the front, the locals came in for protection from the outlaw gangs. Then the horse thieves started bringing stock here; the first man we questioned said this was the place to get the best price."

"You mean before you cut his throat out?" Drax shot.

"He sure as hell didn't say it *after* I cut his throat out," Gwyn answered, unperturbed.

"But why gather any horses *here*, stolen or otherwise?" Drax went on. "This is the northernmost edge of the Southern Kingdoms, there's nobody here to buy them. Off to the east are pasturelands where they raise horses for sale *to* the south; no reason it should be running the opposite way here."

"I assume you heard the forge hammers and smelled all the smoke as we came in, too," Gwyn pushed.

"I did."

"So…gathering up horses, lots of smithing. All adds up to what?"

Drax shook his head.

"Somebody's raising an army," Gwyn asserted.

"Why?"

"I have no idea."

"I don't like it," Drax muttered.

"Usually I'm in favor of armies, but I like to know where they're going. And why." Gwyn considered the very few possibilities. Unless the elves were rallying to war, an idea so unlikely as to be laughable, it seemed matters in Atlund were already worse than she'd feared.

"You think your friend, Dez–"

"He's not necessarily my friend," Gwyn corrected.

"Whatever. Do you think he has something to do with it? Maybe that's what he wanted to hire you for?"

Gwyn shrugged. "Assuming we're not already in some kind of trap, we'll find out when he gets here."

The pair was quiet for most of the afternoon. Whatever peace Drax had made with Gwyn's vengeful intentions on the road seemed strained by their sudden imminence. Gwyn lit the fireplace, then they dozed in turns, the first rest they'd had in warm shelter since the abbey and with no guarantee of when they'd be so comfortable again. Gwyn was sure the elf slept better than she did.

An hour after sundown there came a knock at the door, followed by Dez's voice hissing, "Open up, I only have the one key."

Gwyn cracked the door, and Dez slipped inside, moving immediately to the fire to warm himself.

"You'd best start explaining things, Sergeant," Gwyn rumbled.

Dez was silent for a moment, but Gwyn could see by his distant stare he was composing his thoughts, so she sat back on the bench and tapped her fingers on the table. Dez removed his coat and hung it by the door, then moved to the back of the cottage, drew the curtain on his pantry, and retrieved a small sack and a pair of soup bones. Tossing the bones into a small cauldron of water hanging near the fire, he swung it over the flames on an arm of iron before dumping most of the sack's contents in front of Drax and Gwyn. He then took the remainder with him to a three-legged stool near the fire. Finally he pulled a knife from his belt and pointed its tip toward the piles of potatoes and assorted root vegetables before each of his guests, then started cutting his own portion and tossing them into the pot.

"The local lord put this stockade up a couple years back," Dez finally began explaining, "when the orcs pressing harder started pulling levies from farther and farther north. With a shortage of defenders and the raider bands growing, it was easier to protect one fort than miles and miles of countryside. Not too long after that the noble got called south, too, and word is he won't be coming back. Nobody knows quite where 'Lord' Finn came from, but he had a writ that looked legitimate and a dozen or more fighters to back it up. At least that's the story. I've been here three months or so, and Finn had been in charge twice that long when I got here, give or take.

"Anyway times had gotten real lean in these parts before he showed up, as you could imagine, and Finn promised to make necessities start flowing again. Somehow he did. Between that king-sealed writ and being the only man around with extra goods, it wasn't long before he started setting his own terms and taking what he wanted. Food, clothing, money. Eventually even sons for his levy and daughters for his bed, or his men's. Lots of folk are bound to the land; those free would have left, but before the war there was nowhere to go, and now it's over, Finn and his guard keep close tabs on everybody. More than a few have been dragged back here and whipped for trying to leave without settling their debt, which everyone's in thanks to his strangling prices."

"That's despicable," Drax spat. "They're funding their own jailers."

"Agreed," Dez replied.

Ignoring the ethical concerns, for the moment, Gwyn pressed on. "What of the horses and weapons?"

"Soon as he got here, Finn sent couriers all through the north inviting every smith and offering to buy any horse he could lay hands on. In the beginning he said he was stockpiling for a caravan south, to the front, but there were always delays, then word came the war was over. Still, Finn kept everyone working, and so far one full train has left with a sizeable herd, but they didn't go south. They went north."

"How *far* north?" Gwyn asked as she put down her knife and stared at Dez, the suspicion clear in her voice.

Dez nodded. "Atlund. At least that was the rumor."

Drax had started on the toughest, longest-cooking tubers first, so he stood and carried a double handful of pieces to the soup pot, asking, "What would Atlund need with all that? I know the nomad tribes across their eastern border give them a fair bit of trouble, and sometimes there are beasts to slay on the north and west frontiers, but their own armorers more than keep up with that. They've been helping arm the South against the orcs for decades."

Gwyn sighed, which brought looks from both men. She returned their gazes, then began, "Seven odd months ago my mother and, well, the man that raised me, they wrote me a letter. It finally found me before I left Sutherset. Our king was dying, some believed it was poison, and the clans were rallying to war. I guess some of them regretted not laying aside more weapons for themselves all these years."

Drax shook his head at Gwyn. "All those weeks on the road and you never bothered mentioning your homeland on the verge of civil war?"

"Why would I? Were you planning on going all the way to Atlund?"

"Well, no, but–"

Gwyn looked away from him and back to Dez. "When did this caravan leave?"

"Ten weeks ago, thereabouts. Not long after I got here. Finn wanted to get another shipment out soon, but nobody will set out now. Too cold, too much chance of snow."

"Why were you so anxious to get us out of the tavern today?"

Dez grimaced. "Just trying to delay the inevitable, I guess."

"What does that mean?"

Dez cleared his throat and shifted on his stool. "There's a price on your head."

"What?" Gwyn and Drax both exclaimed.

"Well, not a bounty exactly, but somebody's offering a heavy weight of silver for knowledge of your whereabouts."

"Who?" Gwyn demanded. There could be no doubt Daruneh's great enemy was ultimately behind it, but if Gwyn managed to put a human name to the plot it could only help her unravel it.

"That's the odd thing," Dez answered, "nobody seems to know. It's always that somebody heard about the job from a 'friend of a friend' and that fellah knows where word is to be sent, but try to trace it up any higher and folks start getting quiet. I'll admit I lost some contacts when I left the merchants and went back to the war, but it's still strange I can't learn more. Confounding. Anyhow, you're a unique character; anybody'd know you from description alone. It's only a matter of time before Finn knows you're here, and he surely knows of the bounty. It isn't big enough to excite him, but he'll use you to get close to anyone with that kind of coin."

"He's known for hours," Drax declared. "We spoke to him on our way in, and if Gwyn's reputation has spread this far, it's a sure bet he knew her, even though he didn't let on."

"Well," Dez replied. "That's a bit of a dip in the trail, ain't it?"

"What will Finn do?" Gwyn asked.

"It's hard to say. He's smarter than he looks, too smart to make a clear guess how he'll jump. One thing's sure enough: he'll know you're staying here. We'd best sleep in shifts tonight, just in case. Then, tomorrow, well, maybe we just solve the problem once and for all."

"How's that?" Gwyn asked.

"Well, like I said, I wanted to hire you."

"What for?"

"To kill Lord Finn."

CHAPTER VII

Gwyn narrowed her eyes at the implication. Clearly she had no compunctions about killing, even in cold blood if the reason seemed right to her, but she'd never thought herself an assassin. "I sell my sword arm," she finally said, "not a dagger in someone's back."

Drax snorted. "*This* is where you draw the ethical line?" he snapped. "You'll murder someone for a dead woman but not to help hundreds of people who are still alive?"

Gwyn turned to Drax at her right, swinging her leg over the bench so she faced him square on. Unclenching her jaw, she murmured, "I once strangled you and slammed your head against a wall for something you didn't deserve, so I'll stay my hand this once. If you ever refer to Tira as the 'dead woman' again, your next words had best be a prayer to Terillah that your spells are faster than my fists. Am I clear?"

Drax stood and faced Gwyn. "I'm not afraid of you, Atlunder."

For several long moments their eyes burned into one

another, and Dez shrank back from the point of tension hanging in the air between them.

"I meant no disrespect to your friend," Drax finally added, breaking the stalemate. "She is gone from the struggles of the Physical Realm, though, that you cannot deny. Unlike the people here who need someone like you."

"The people I fought for in Sutherset I also fought *with*," Gwyn replied, "side by side. Why should I risk my blood for these people who won't risk their own?"

"You sound like the cocksure maid who sauntered into my camp a lifetime ago," Dez remarked, rejoining the argument. "I wouldn't have wasted my breath on you then, but I know a share of what you've seen and done since. You know it ain't so simple as these folk not *wanting* to fight for themselves. You've had arms and training all your life; they haven't."

Gwyn sighed. "Fine," she relented after a minute of thought. "Still, we may both have changed, but I never knew you to give an order you wouldn't follow yourself, and I don't sense you've changed in that."

"No," Dez agreed, though his tone revealed he wasn't sure where Gwyn's reasoning was leading him.

"So if killing Finn was as simple as someone jamming a knife between his ribs, you'd have done it a long time ago."

Dez dropped the last of his vegetables into the soup pot. "Finn's cagey, doesn't trust anybody too far. Always got two or three guards around him, at least, rotating through his toughest fighters, and I've seen he's no slouch with a blade himself." Dez stood and retrieved the rest of Gwyn's vegetables as her attempts at peeling had ranged from painfully slow to outright butchery. "I do have a dozen men of an age and willing to fight," the sergeant continued. "Half of them know how. One is on the inside, in the house guard, though never on Finn's actual person."

"Then why does the man still breathe?" Gwyn growled, exasperated.

"We figured, at best, anybody who could get in a killing strike would be cut down before the bodyguard even realized their boss wouldn't be around to pay them for the job. Risking life is one thing," he quickly added, cutting off an objection from Gwyn, "sure suicide is something else. Anyway, it's more likely the attempt would fail, and the men trying it would have died for nothing, and maybe the rest of us, too. We can't be sure how much Finn or Roxen knows about our little association."

Gwyn felt the temptation to involve herself in Dez's coup as a tingling tension in her sword arm. She could scarcely remember the last time she'd had a decent fight. On the other hand, she loathed the distraction from her immediate oath to avenge Tira, as well as her urgent need to be home to Atlund, now grown all the more pressing by the knowledge she'd gained in the station. The latter couldn't much be helped, but perhaps she could force a way to advance the former in conjunction with Dez's need. "So you think signing me on with your gang of usurpers will make the difference?" Gwyn asked, softening to the notion.

Sensing the shift in mood, Drax added, "Me, too. Gwyn didn't properly introduce me, but I'm called Drax of the Western Vale. Perhaps you've heard of me? My enchantments earned no small renown in–"

"He's good," Gwyn interrupted. "Now answer my question."

Dez stirred the soup and put a lid on the pot. "You're worth any five of Finn's men, and you're a captain, a proper leader. Give me a caravan to defend on open ground, and I can give a good enough account to convince ruffians my goods aren't worth the trouble, but apart from that, I'm no strategist."

"Can't say I have any experience breaching guarded

manor houses, either, but between us, and Drax's spellcraft, I'd be ashamed if we couldn't come up with something," Gwyn replied. "No illusions, though. Even if we carry the day, some of your dozen men are sure to fall."

"They have the courage," Dez assured, "if you can give them a real hope of victory." The trio was silent for a time as gusts of wind whistled past the shutters. "I'm afraid to ask this," Dez finally hazarded, "but what's your price? Both of you."

Drax spoke before Gwyn could. "I don't want anything. Fate has brought me here, and I'm able to help. That's enough."

Gwyn looked sideways at the elf. "You were never shy about extorting lords for your magic during the war."

"Living in the South has expenses, and I had my reasons then, just as I have my reasons now." Drax's tone had a note of finality, so Gwyn let his answer rest, thin as she found it.

Her thoughts focused, instead, at the opportunity she sensed at last as Dez looked to her, waiting for her to state her terms. "I don't want money, either," she said, eliciting a look of surprise from both men. Drax even seemed pleased, if she read him right. "I want something else," she continued, picking up a largish chunk of sweet potato peel and scraping a symbol into it with her belt knife, a circle topped by a diamond. "Find out where the three men are who brought in horses with that brand, maybe a week or ten days ago. And let me kill them." Drax muttered a string of words in elven, and Gwyn didn't need to know the tongue to guess their meaning.

Dez took the peel to look at the symbol, then tossed it into the fire. "I'll see what I can do."

"If you want to start your maneuver tomorrow, I'll need the information tonight," Gwyn pressed.

Drax cursed again, and Dez looked to the shutters where the wind keened ever more sharply. Standing with a sigh, he crossed to the door and lifted his coat from the peg. "Stir the soup," he ordered. "I'll be back."

Once the sergeant had gone, Drax turned back to Gwyn with a scowl. "Would it kill you to just do something right for these people?" he challenged.

"It might," Gwyn answered. "I'm good. Maybe I even doubt there's anybody better in this place, but it only takes a moment of bad luck to die." She pulled her left arm across her chest, stretching the wound, which still felt stiff much of the time, to prove her point.

"You know what I mean," Drax replied, unconvinced. "Your name may mean 'Hand of Vengeance,' but that never meant anything to the people in the South. They don't even call you that; they all say 'Gwyn the Savage.' You became a hero to them because you fought like a savage to *save* them, not to avenge them."

"I never asked to be their hero, and I don't care why they thought I was one," Gwyn snapped back. "I can't see how *me* being reluctant is any stranger than *you* being so eager."

Drax looked suddenly away, and Gwyn could see her suggestion had hit something dear to Drax, some memory or conviction she couldn't guess at. She felt an unusual curiosity toward this strangely ardent enchanter who had somehow come to populate her vanishingly small circle of comrades, but not enough to press the issue. After a moment Drax looked back. "Someone helped me once," he answered. "I had nothing to offer in return, so I do what I can, when I can. Satisfied?"

She felt this reply brought more questions than answers, but again she let the elf be, albeit with a growing realization of how little she really knew about the impudent, if competent, elf. Drax stood as the wind lashed at the cottage, a sudden gust shooting down the chimney to set a new rhythm to the flames' dancing. He stirred the soup for a moment before cracking the shutter and peering outside, his nostrils momentarily flaring. "I hope Dez doesn't take too long," he mused.

Gwyn looked at him, her expression questioning.

"Snow," Drax replied.

At least an hour passed before Dez returned, and when he opened the door the cottage's light showed flakes falling and whipping about in the gusting wind. He hung up his coat again and stood by the fire, rubbing his arms to speed its warmth.

"What did you learn?" Gwyn asked, leaning forward.

Dez walked to his pantry and cut down the lowest bundle of dried herbs from a hanging cord, then crumbled them into the bubbling soup. "I spoke to as many of my men as I could. Those that get the message will gather in the tavern as soon as they're able. If this snow keeps up, we can hope it will slow the guards rallying to the big house when the alarm is raised."

"But did you get what I need?" Gwyn demanded.

Dez looked to Drax, then back to Gwyn, hesitating. "I need your word you won't back out once I've told you."

"You should know better than to ask," Gwyn replied. "As bad as I am at following orders, you've seen I'm even worse at staying out of a fight."

Dez relented. "A couple of my comrades had noticed the brand you showed me. It stands out, not being one of the nobles' symbols we usually see, and a lot of the animals aren't marked at all. They took note of the men that brought them in, three, just as you said. One was short and gap-toothed, another tall with long, dark hair and a hacking cough. Both of them are staying in the inn and retire to a private room upstairs when it's time to sleep, though neither of my men knew which one. They said the third highwayman was a bit better dressed and kept a nicely trimmed beard. He spoke for the group. He's been making plans with Finn and a couple of other merchants, got himself a room in the big house. I'll see to it none of them gives the slip while we're about our business tomorrow."

"By morning," Drax added with a nod toward the shutters and the falling snow behind them, *"nobody's* leaving Finn's Station."

At last the blizzard fell hard, lashing the fort with gales out of the northwest driving heavy, wet snow before them. For the first hour Gwyn looked out occasionally, seeing men with lanterns or guttering torches hurrying about, some only trying to make it home and others rushing to the corral to bring the horses into whatever shelter could be had. Thanks to Gwyn and Drax's beasts, Dez's stable was too full to be pressed into service, and he was only challenged on the point by one man who came to his door. Dez seemed to trust him and asked him to spread the word his place was off limits. Gwyn catalogued this indication of his influence before going back to the window.

"Isn't it usually dry this time of year, in the lee of the mountains?" she asked either of the men in the cottage.

"Usually," Drax agreed.

"The years we get a blizzard like this, it's usually a few weeks later. Sometimes they're early," Dez added.

"Sometimes," Gwyn allowed. "Not oftentimes." Sussing out the forces arrayed against her was beyond her ken, and she knew it, but remembering walls and spikes of iron shooting up from nowhere, the sun going black in the canyon, she couldn't help but shudder to think this uncommon snowfall was somehow being sent to trap her here. Could Daruneh's great enemy have eyes and ears in Finn's Station even now? Had the bandits she failed to kill in the south, should have killed, in hindsight, sold the knowledge of her whereabouts to some intermediary in the intervening weeks? Dez's walls protecting her from the blizzard felt more and more a cage the longer she sat, a gale of anxiety slicing through her anticipation of imminent blood and battle.

After that first hour the lanterns and torches stopped moving, leaving the outdoors in darkness too deep to penetrate from inside, but by that point several inches of wet flakes had already fallen.

Finally Dez served the soup, and with some sippets for dipping the simple meal was pleasing enough, certainly more flavorful than the rations Gwyn had grown accustomed to over the weeks of her recent travels or, for that matter, the months at war. The old soldier didn't keep much variety in his libations, but his ale was good enough.

They talked little, the natural inclination to trade stories and fill gaps since their last meeting buried under the howling wind and the knowledge of battle that lay ahead.

"There's just the one inn, then? At the crossing of the two main roads?" Gwyn asked while filling her soup bowl a second time.

Dez nodded.

"Gwyn," Drax cautioned, "you aren't going to do anything rash are you?"

"I'm not planning to go freeze to death in this blizzard, if that's what's worrying you," she answered.

Drax scowled but nodded before going back to his soup.

"So," Gwyn continued to Dez as she sat, "you've set up a nice little kingdom for yourself here."

"Just a few likeminded scofflaws," he deflected.

"Don't be modest, Sergeant. It's impressive work having only been here a few months."

After another swig of ale, Dez expanded. "Not all of Finn's men were real cutthroats. A few were guards I'd employed at one time or another. Nobody you'd want at your side going to meet the king, mind, but decent men.

They'd been doing what they could for the better folk here, the ones that called it home before Finn started importing scum. As more fighters came in with less compunction about the lord's way of doing things, the honest few were elbowed out to make room. They were in need of a leader, and they looked to me when I showed up, got me work at the tavern so I could keep track of the comings and goings. This cottage was empty, and I'd made a fair bit before I quit the caravans, so I picked it up. Like I said before, we haven't had a real chance at taking Finn down directly, but we do what we can in secret: gather up extra necessities for families Finn taxes too hard, make sure the young lads and lasses, those that are willing, have what they need to get married before Finn's guards take too keen an eye, or get the boys in binding apprenticeships so he can't conscript them and pound out their decency. So far he hasn't crossed those lines. So far. We do what we can. It isn't enough."

"Well, tomorrow will answer for all," Gwyn vowed. "One way or another."

With that she withdrew the little space available to her, staking her claim on a rocking chair near the front door. Dez and Drax chatted a bit, both being more affable than she was, but in less than an hour the hearth burned low and the time came to sleep. Gwyn rose to help move the table and benches to one side, and Dez deployed a pair of canvas cots with extra blankets before going to his own bed in a screened corner. Gwyn returned to her chair without speaking as Drax lay down.

She pondered the coming fight and the worth of it. Were these people merely lacking in the ability to rise up, as Dez had suggested, or were they cowed beyond even the desire? Did this group of Southerners, who couldn't be lacking in hardihood to have lived in such a far-flung place for so many generations, also represent simple, peaceful people of untold grit and courage, like Ardos and his ever-sacrificing family, or merely those glad to live far away from the brutal wartime demands on their countrymen? Did they deserve her help, the risk of her body and blade? She considered the time, not so long ago, when she gave no thought to the people living in the lands where she fought, even in her own home. The fight itself was all that mattered, at least once her destiny to avenge her father had been snatched away. Who now was this woman sitting in her skin, wondering if the fight was worth having? Again she stretched her wounded arm. Perhaps it was not the months that had changed her, but the scars.

Late evening wore into deep night as she fled from weariness, thinking her thoughts and occasionally casting a glance on Drax in the umber light of the dim coals. The elf was a light sleeper at need, but here in the warm house she could count on him to slumber deeply. Dez, meanwhile, was snoring behind his screen. It was time to move.

Gwyn rose and took a cloth from the table, using it to cover and tie down her hair. She left the heavy fur cloak she'd received from Daruneh on the chair where she'd been covering with it, taking back the black wool overcoat she'd left drying by the fire and fastening it closed with its horn toggles down to the waist. The fur would have been warmer but also heavier and more conspicuous. Likewise, she gazed for a moment at her sword on the table, reflecting the ember-light, but left it behind. It drew too much attention, and, anyway, it was knifework where she was going. Neither Dez's assurance her enemies would be watched, nor Drax's observation about the besieging blizzard, gave her any confidence. They did nothing to quell the violence in her heart.

A moment later she stood outside in the wind and snow. She'd told Drax the truth before, in a way. She had no intention of freezing to death. Indeed, what these Southerners called a blizzard held no fear for her. She'd known, as a matter of pure fact, she was coming closer to home with each passing day, but now, standing in the punishing wind, she *felt* it. This cold *was* her home, the snow her element. For minutes she stood there, absorbing the frigid night and letting her skin numb to the pelting snow. Meanwhile, her vision acclimated to the dim light leaking out of numerous windows and shutters to reflect off the white drifts. Even straining, Gwyn could make out only shadows, but it was enough.

Taking advantage of her long legs, Gwyn forced her way through the knee-deep banks, moving from lee to lee of buildings to conserve her strength. The wind drowned all noise, she avoided the halos around windows, and no guards would brave the wall this night. She was a ghost in the darkness. Movement slowed in the north-south street where nothing blocked the snowfall, but the gale was mostly at her back, giving her face a rest from the slashing wind. The distance wasn't great; even fighting the weather she reached the inn after only several minutes, not even long enough for the cold to reach the bones of a hardened Atlunder. Through a gap in the shutters she could see the occupants moving tables to make room for sleep in the common room, half a dozen men, a couple of whom showed drunkenness in their movements. By Dez's description, none were her targets. She trudged toward the back of the building, leaving the reflected firelight and feeling her way to a chest-high fence that blocked the inn's rear yard. Using her boots to clear a foot-wide patch of snow so it wouldn't drag at her legs, she vaulted the barrier and crunched down through the drift on the other side. In a moment she'd reached the back door and tried it. It yielded, as yet unlocked and unbarred. She slipped in as quickly as she could, checking that the snow she tracked in was inconspicuous atop the preexisting pile and praying the sounds of scraping bench and table legs would cover the noise of her entry. Glancing about, she saw by the lantern glow slipping through cracks of an inner door that she was in an attached kitchen with a set of narrow stairs to her right. Taking these for the way up to the innkeeper's rooms, she moved to the far corner and crouched in the inky shadows.

At length a short, round man, the proprietor it seemed, came into the kitchen holding a single candle and moving toward the stairs. His head never turned in Gwyn's direction, and in a moment he had ascended out of sight. The only light beyond the inner door now was a deep red glow, and Gwyn knew the lights in the great room had been extinguished, the fire down to banked coals. She settled in to wait until the men in the common room had found sleep.

It seemed the best part of an hour before the last of the chat and jibes died out, followed by the rise of snores from some. Shortly thereafter the tossing and turning became infrequent, and Gwyn took her chance. She opened the inner door, which squeaked only softly, and moved quickly into the common room. It was now thick with shadow, and she hoped if any sleepers had come half awake at the sound of the door they would mistake her for the innkeeper checking some late detail. With cautious steps she threaded her way to the base of the main stairs in the far right corner of the room, near the front door, and began her climb. She knew the treads would squeak but moved with careful confidence as any legitimate resident of the inn might do. The wind still howled outside as well, obscuring some of the noise, or at least she hoped so.

Once at the top of the stairs, Gwyn found herself at the end of a hallway stretching the length of the house. Three doors stood on either side. To her surprise, yellow lanternlight still leaked from under one, so she moved silently to it and listened. A man's voice murmured from within. After several such comments without reply, Gwyn decided the occupant must be speaking to himself. She could only make out a few of the words, but he seemed to be a trader pondering where to invest his coins. Not one of the men she sought. Two other doors stood open, so these Gwyn looked in, finding them empty. In one she procured a small oil lamp and risked lighting its wick with flint and steel from her pouch. Now with the clay vessel in her left hand, she returned to the hallway, pulling the dirk from her boot with her right. Her heart beat against her ribs; she could sense her quarry was close.

She tried the first closed door, lifting the latch with agonizing slowness before pushing it forward, only to find it barred from the other side. The second was likewise warded. The third swung gently open; it's occupant lay sprawled on the bed, uncovered and shivering in the drafty room, seemingly too drunk to bar his door or even crawl under his blankets when he retired. Gwyn lifted her lamp and saw the man to be of average height and thinning hair, matching neither of Dez's descriptions. Having exhausted all other possibilities, she returned to the barred doors. She pressed her ear against one, straining to catch any betraying sounds over the constant rush and whistle of the wind. At first she heard only silence, then her gaze snapped to the other door, nearest the stairs, as a wet cough sounded through the planks. She moved to it and listened, perceived the confirming sounds of fitful sleep and tossing that seemed to come from both sides of the doorway, and finally the racking cough once more.

Someone must be in the silent room to have barred it; there was no shortage of coughing men this time of year, and even one known to cough might be silent for long stretches. Weighing her odds, she chose the door most certain to conceal two men. Gwyn held her breath and moved the lantern light across the door, searching every inch of it for any weakness. A tiny gap presented itself between two of the vertical planks at about the right height for the bar, but it was too narrow for Gwyn's dirk. Setting down the lantern, she drew her belt knife and pressed its thinner blade against the crack, felt it barely slip through. She could dig the point into the inside of the wood bar, but there wasn't enough space to force it left or right. She found its bottom edge and worked the blade underneath; she knew she could lift the bar on the left side but had no idea how far. She had to try.

Raising her knife handle by fractions, she felt the blade take the weight of the bar. Wood raked against wood, a sense of vibration at her palm stronger than the grating sound that barely registered to her ears above the wind. An inch. Two. Three, and she felt the weight shift on the blade. Had she cleared the left bracket? She lifted the latch with her left hand and leaned gradually into the door. The left side shifted. She felt resistance as the right end of the bar began to bind between the bracket and the frame. She pushed farther. The door inched open under protest. She could almost slip through the gap.

Suddenly a crackling snap sounded from the right edge of the frame, and it gave under her weight. With the reflex of striking a gap in an enemy's guard she shoved through the opening and closed the door behind, holding her breath as she listened for the sounds of anything stirring throughout the inn. Before she could assess more distant noises, she felt a shadow move to her left.

Gwyn pounced. Her left hand fell across the shadow's head and slid to its mouth, muffling a cry. Half a heartbeat and her knife blade had come to rest against its throat, her knee on its sternum. She could sense the bends and joints of the body beneath her, knew it was short. Against the hand over its mouth she could even feel the gaps of missing teeth through its lips. She sought a confirmation she didn't truly need; the moment her hand touched flesh she knew this man to be a breathing corpse, a being she'd marked for death a month and over a hundred leagues ago without ever seeing his face. The certainty startled her, her desire to trust it matched only by her fear. Gwyn's lips were against the man's ear as she whispered, "Any sound above a whisper, and you die. Nod if you understand."

The man nodded.

Gwyn shifted her weight so her shin now rested across the man's chest and left arm, still trapped beneath the covers. She moved her left hand from his mouth to hold his right wrist against the wall. "Who's the other man in this room?" This other man had begun to stir but, by illness or intoxication, seemed slow to awaken.

"M-my partner," the trapped man replied, his voice aquiver. Gwyn couldn't know how the battle light flashed across her eyes, complementing the man's helpless position with diabolic terror.

"You rode all the way north with him?"

He nodded slightly, his throat bulging against the knife blade as he tried to swallow down his fear.

Gwyn slit his throat, deep, his blood spraying her face for a moment before gushing over his chest and soaking his blankets. He gurgled and retched as she climbed off him and turned to the remaining bed. The other shadow sat suddenly upright, making confused mutterings at the horrible sounds, but Gwyn struck before he could remove himself from his blankets, covering his mouth and plunging her knife twice into his chest. On the third strike it lodged in his ribs, so she drew her dirk and slit his throat in turn before he could scream. As he writhed she tried again to wrench her knife free; something gave and it came loose in her hand. She tried the room's window but found it didn't open, returned instead to the door and stepped back into the hallway.

A man stood there, outside the lighted room's door, wearing a long, linen nightshirt and holding a clay lamp like the one Gwyn had used. Hers still sat on the floor, but the merchant's illuminated her clearly, her bloody clothes and blades. "Who–? Help!" he began to shout. "Help! Murder! Help!"

Gwyn's first instinct was to threaten him to silence, but she knew it was too late. After that moment's hesitation, she turned and dashed to the head of the stairs, passing the shouting man who backed away in fear but didn't stop raising the alarm, as though the working of his voice had become reflexive through his panic. At the bottom of the stairs Gwyn saw, by the faint hearth embers, the denizens of the common room jumping from their pallets and reaching for weapons or clothing, but before they could move toward her she had pulled open the door, allowing the frigid wind and a tumble of deep snow to breach the threshold. She leaped into the night, plunging into snow that was now thigh-deep but sinking only to her shins before it packed enough to bear her weight. No longer caring for stealth she ran through the crossroads with all speed, cutting between two buildings on the far side to be out of sight from anyone in the inn who might peer after her into the dark. She heard more shouts but only faintly, the cries carried away southward on the howling wind. Passing behind two small buildings, she cut back to the main road to observe the inn's front door, her eyes squinted against the blizzard. It was now closed, but someone had popped open the nearer set of shutters before retreating inside. Lanterns had been lit, their glow obvious on the fallen snow. Silhouettes of faces could be seen trading places at the window, but darkness already obscured Gwyn's escape, and even now the drifting snow began filling her footprints just outside the inn's door. Taking a more careful path, she moved through drifts and piles, cold minutes passing as she picked her way back to Dez's cottage.

When she arrived, she could see by the glow through the shutters the fire was once again high. She pounded on the door twice and waited.

"Who's there?" came Dez's question from within.

"Open up; it's me."

The lock rattled, and the door opened a crack. Gwyn slipped inside the warm home and immediately began to remove her wet overcoat, only then realizing her knives were still in her hands. The blade of her belt knife was broken off three inches above the grip. She took a step and tossed both on the table, then returned to the coat's toggles.

"By Terillah, Gwyn," Drax gasped. "What did you do?"

She looked sidelong at him, her jaw set, as she hung her bloody coat back on the peg. "You know damn well what I did."

Dez, still in bedclothes but with a short sword now belted to his hip and a round shield leaning against the rocking chair, narrowed his eyes. "Is this what I think it is?"

"She's murdered the horse thieves," Drax confirmed.

"I killed them," she corrected. "Whether it's murder will take better men than you to judge."

Drax dropped onto the nearer bench, his eyes on Gwyn's bloody weapons. He shook his head. "Do you even know they were guilty? *Really* know?"

"I'm sure."

"But how? What if the ones you wanted met some other gang on the road and traded–"

"I *know*," Gwyn insisted. Her tone was not fully anchored to reality.

Drax went silent, but Dez spoke. "Drax filled me in on the particulars after we found you gone, and we can debate the moralities of this over drinks sometime. I'm sure it'll be the scholarly moot of the ages, but for now we have bigger worries. Finn won't let a murder stand within his walls; he can't, if he's to keep control. The blizzard gave us a chance, but someone from the inn is bound to make their way to his manor sooner than later, now. Did you at least get away clean?"

Gwyn didn't answer, walking back to the table and sitting on it, taking up her dirk to wipe with a cloth from her pouch.

"Gwyn?" Dez insisted.

"A man saw me, a merchant, I think. It doesn't matter; he won't have known me."

Dez growled a wordless, frustrated sound. "You stand out more than you know, Captain, and Finn will be looking for an excuse to get at you, to find out all he can about this bounty on you. You've given him more than he needs on that score."

"What can we do?" Drax asked.

"Why are you both so worried?" Gwyn challenged. "The plan was to kill Finn tomorrow, anyway, and nobody's going to come after us tonight. You Southerners are too squeamish about the cold."

"Forgive me if I don't have the confidence of your contempt, Gwyn," Drax spat.

"He's right," Dez agreed. "If anybody is on his way from the inn to the big house now, or will start digging out sooner than first light, we need to know it."

"What about your man on the inside?" Gwyn asked.

"I couldn't risk talking to him when I went out; he was on duty at the house, and I didn't have any excuse to show my face there at such an hour. Even if he hears anything, he won't know it has anything to do with me."

"Drax can get in if you're anxious," Gwyn offered.

"Excuse you?" Drax objected.

"You said you wanted to help," Gwyn replied. "Taking this part, you probably won't even have to kill anybody."

Drax sighed, but Gwyn could see the appeal of her point playing across his features. "Fine," he relented.

"How's he supposed to do this?" Dez questioned.

Dez proved to be a more fascinated audience for Drax's explanation of his craft than Gwyn ever had, and, once satisfied, he gave Drax a description of Vawz, the inside man, and where he could be found. Between the two of them, they were to provide as much warning as possible if anyone brought news of Gwyn's crime to Finn or if the lord showed the barest sign of sending anyone out of the house. If no emergent threat appeared by midmorning, one or the other of the infiltrators was to report to the tavern with all the information they could gather on the disposition of Finn's defenses. Finally the enchanter bundled himself against the cold and, with an elven grumble, slipped out the door into the darkness.

CHAPTER VIII

The blizzard continued to bury the fort through the night. Dawn fell through ashen skies on an alabaster world, the winds becalmed as flurries continued to drift down over the station. The sun was well up, though barely visible, when the community began to stir, residents digging their way first to their animals, then some to their shops and others to help their neighbors, especially those with north-facing doors. Dez's cottage, sheltered in the lee of the northern wall, fared better than most, so he set out as soon as there was light enough to see. On his errand the night before, he'd started his people spreading the word to meet up in the tavern as soon as they were able, so Dez trudged there to await them. He had only the threads of a plan, but if he could pull those together into some kind of framework, they might move as soon as Drax or Vawz emerged from Finn's house with a report.

Gwyn, of course, after her brutal adventure of the previous night, would need to lay low until the others could assess the extent her crime was known and how eagerly anyone may be seeking her. After seeing to the needs of the horses and mule, Gwyn sat at the fire, listening as the sounds of shovels and shouts dispelled the eerie silence of a post-blizzard morn. She watched the flames dance and the sparks shoot up the whistling chimney, taking the opportunity for a rare bout of introspection. She'd scrubbed most of the blood out of her overcoat in Dez's wash basin before going to sleep, and now it hung drying by the fire. The metallic scent of it still piqued her nose at sporadic moments, an odor that never seemed far from her. Her memory of the horror in Drax's eyes stood opposed to the excitement she felt for the coming battle. The evidence suggesting there might be something frighteningly wrong with her conscience warred against the conviction that Tira's last murderer mustn't continue drawing breath.

She'd resolved no dilemma and started to grow restless in waiting when she heard the lock on the back door rasp open. Grabbing her blade from the table, she leaped into the pantry and pulled the curtain to conceal herself, breathing silently as she peered through a gap between the canvas and wall. The curtain had barely stopped moving from her passage when a man entered her view, taller than Gwyn and seeming as broad in the shoulders as two of her. His movements as he paced the cottage, observing the displaced table and cots still laid out before the fire, seemed familiar, and as he turned toward the pantry, revealing his bushy black beard and soot-stippled features, Gwyn immediately recognized the giant as the man she'd seen delivering a whipping to the pilloried wretch the day prior. He was unarmed, and Gwyn was confident she could kill him, but she had no idea what additional trouble that might bring. She also very much doubted she could subdue so large an enemy for questioning without doing permanent harm. Frustrated by the need for inaction, Gwyn withdrew as deep as she could into the pantry, her back pressing against the rough shelves, and waited behind her sword, her grip high on the hilt and hands held lower than her belt just to keep the point clear of the ceiling.

"Hello?" the man called, and Gwyn saw his fingertips grasp the edge of the curtain.

She brought her right knee to her chest and kicked forward, slamming the intruder's sternum through the canvas. She heard the air whoof out of him as she batted the curtain aside with her blade and moved forward and left, pivoting back to her right immediately to square up on her attacker and seeing he was doubled over from her kick, one that would have sent a smaller man reeling. Taking advantage of his vulnerable position, she let go of her sword hilt with her right hand to bring her fist down on the base of his skull. Still the massive brute didn't go down, though he staggered sideways against the hearth and held up one hand as the other went to the back of his head.

"Don't kill me," he pleaded, "I'm a friend."

"What are you doing here?" Gwyn demanded, whipping her sword in a short slash that made clear the stranger shouldn't try to rise while also bringing her point on line with him. "How did you get Dez's key?"

"I made a copy weeks ago. At his request," the man replied and quickly clarified. "Please, lady, put down your sword. I swear I won't come closer without your leave. If you'll stay your blade I'll even sit here calm-like, and we both know you could carve me up before I could stand if you had a mind."

Gwyn moved to the side of the room so the door to the stables was in her peripheral view, then occupied a space that kept the stranger at the outer edge of her lunging range. Thus positioned, she rested her blade against her shoulder, a less threatening stance but one easily transitioned back into guard. She nodded to the man.

In response, the stranger eased his bulk down until his

rump found the floor, then stretched his legs out before him, angling them in front of the fire. Before Gwyn could begin interrogating him, he offered, "I know who you are, so let me make it even. I'm called Brae. I'm one of the farriers hereabout."

"I've seen you as a torturer, not a horseshoer."

Brae broke eye contact with Gwyn and mumbled, "It isn't what you think." His voice was a sonorous baritone, but even that pitch was higher than suggested by his barrel chest.

"It doesn't matter what *I* think," Gwyn answered. "Your crimes are against your neighbors, not against me or mine. Why are you here?"

"I'm a friend of Dez. He told me to come here and fetch you."

Gwyn began to scoff.

"Those were his words, mind," Brae added.

"Why didn't you announce yourself?"

"I meant to, Dez told me to, but…" Brae blushed. "I got distracted admiring your horse and forgot. I'm no warrior, lady, these sentry calls and such don't come natural."

"I'm no lady," Gwyn corrected. "You call me Gwyn. Doesn't mean I trust you."

Brae nodded.

"Where am I to be 'fetched' to, then?" Gwyn asked.

"Tavern. Dez is still there. He's put the word to enough of our men to get them in positions, and the time's getting near enough we need you close to hand."

Gwyn found this reasonable, though Dez's insistence that she not cross paths with at least one of the tavern's patrons just the day before cast some doubt on the story. "Why wouldn't he send my traveling companion? He had to know I wouldn't want to come with you."

"That elf fellah?" Brae clarified. "Still not back yet, and, well, Dez is starting to worry. Said the elf told him he couldn't be seen as long as only humans were inside, but Dez's afraid the magic wore off or maybe Finn had a charm to see through it or something."

That at least confirmed Brae had been in good faith discussion with Dez; these specific workings of Drax's magic were too obscure to be guessed at and too subtle to come up under interrogation. "Alright," Gwyn relented, "stay here." She walked out into the stables and retrieved her armor and shield from the pack mule, dropping the bundle back on the inside table before donning first her gambeson, then her mail shirt. Finally she picked her weapons back up from the table and ordered, "Let's go."

Brae stood slowly. As Gwyn moved toward the door to take up her fur cloak, the farrier added, "Dez said you're to leave your big sword and anything else you can't hide. Too conspicuous."

Gwyn barked a laugh. "Not likely."

"But... Well, I..." Brae frowned.

Gwyn looked about and quickly spotted a pile of greenwood poles Dez had in the back of the cottage, matching those used in the woven fence about his property. Gathering them, Gwyn placed her sword among the canes and wrapped a bedsheet around them before tying the bundle in three places with cord. *Apologies, Tyralist*, she thought, *you deserve to travel with greater dignity.* There was no way to hide the shield, so she left it behind, expecting to improvise if she needed one. Clutching the package of sticks to her in a way she hoped belied her strength and skill at arms, she looked to Brae. "Satisfied?"

Brae opened the door for her with a shrug, and the two set out into the cold.

The transformation of Finn's Station since Dez had gone was striking, and Gwyn imagined as she walked in the snow trenches how a vole must feel crawling its open-topped runs. The snow displaced to make the paths had to go somewhere, leading the drifts to be piled higher yet so that in many places the white walls were even with her head. Nothing was dug any deeper than need be, either, so the path from each door was a sort of compacted ramp, leading at last to the streets and alleys that lay still under a foot or more of trample-packed snow.

The pair hurried to the tavern and made their way quietly inside. Indeed a crowd was beginning to gather, though the wide hall wasn't yet filled up with drinkers. Dez stood behind the main table filling jiggers and pints; when he saw Gwyn's entrance he motioned to a man by the fire who promptly took his place. Dez pointed Gwyn and Brae to a table in the back-right corner of the tavern and sat down with three tankards.

"You know how long Drax can keep up this disappearing trick?" Dez asked, his forehead creased.

"Not really," Gwyn answered. "I've seen it done twice, once for only a few minutes and again for something more than an hour. Nowhere near as long as this."

"I expected him back by now, though."

"That was the plan," Gwyn agreed. "He *has* been known to improvise."

Dez did not appear comforted, but before he could say more, a skinny man dropped into the chair next to him. "Evix," he greeted, "you made it. This is a good turn." He clapped the small man between his shoulder blades.

Evix winced. "Dammit, Dez," he grunted.

Dez withdrew his hand quickly, muttering a sheepish apology. At a second look, Gwyn recognized the unfortunate criminal she'd seen in the pillory. He was still reed-thin, but he appeared less pathetic and weak now, being clean and clothed.

"Sorry, Evix," Brae rumbled, his face in his ale.

"Nah, I should thank you," Evix replied. "That's the

lightest fifteen I've ever taken. Whippings barely count since you took over."

"Maybe not the fifteens," the farrier answered. "The eighties still count. Permanent."

Gwyn recalled Dez's descriptions of what his inchoate rebellion had managed to accomplish so far and found rigging the beatings to have been conspicuously absent from the list. Seeing Brae's sour face as he drank, she suspected Dez still felt some shame, or at least regret, at the cost.

Evix and Dez were both quiet for a moment as Brae downed the rest of his tankard, wiped an arm across his bushy beard, and pushed his chair back from the table, stomping to the bar for another. Once he was gone, Evix muttered to Dez, "It was asking too much of the man, Sergeant. Brae may like horses better than people, but he wasn't bred to have men's blood on his hands."

"I know," Dez sighed. "We have a rare opportunity now, Evix," he continued, nodding toward Gwyn. "If everything goes to plan, yours will be Brae's final beating."

Gwyn felt chagrined to have become the focus of these people's hopes and dreams just by her presence, but she knew she could have refused the fight, whatever Drax's opinion of that may have been. Her vow to avenge Tira had led her this far, a job still undone, and the way forward now went through Lord Finn's innards. She would enjoy the fight while she could get it.

"What's our move?" she heard Evix say, bringing her attention back to the table.

"Still working out the particulars," Dez admitted. "Gwyn the Savage here travels with an elf wizard."

"*He* travels with *me*," Gwyn corrected.

"He's gone secretly into Finn's house, on reconnoiter and to apprise Vawz of the impending action. We're gathering everybody we can, and when we have the elf's report, we'll decide how we strike."

"This is happening *today*?" Evix asked, incredulous.

"It's now or never. If you have a clear road home, go get your weapons, and spread the word as you go."

"I hope you know what you're doing." With that, Evix rose from the table and moved toward the door, nodding to Brae as the larger man returned.

"You've told me how many men you have," Gwyn began, "but what do we expect Finn to bring today?"

"Probably ten in the house, motley arms but the most experienced. He has twoscore altogether, but we're still gathering reports on the deployment of the rest. Some half-dozen of those likely won't stand against me and mine when it comes to it. On a clear day a share of the visiting raiders and riffraff would jump for Finn, knowing where their bread's buttered, but the snow will confound anybody mustering, hopefully even the guards. If we move fast, anyone outside the main house won't have much luck coordinating against us."

"I've only seen the house from afar," Gwyn said. "Is there cover—"

Suddenly the tavern door slammed open, shaking the walls of the cheap structure with a heavy bang. A man stood in silhouette against the overcast light, amplified by the snow-bright reflections from ground and roofs. Into the tavern he rushed, charging toward Gwyn's table. Her grip tightened around her sword's hilt, preparing to haul it free from its concealment, when Dez called out, "Renny, what's after you? You're making a scene."

The man, Renny, grabbed an empty chair in his path and dropped it next to Dez, squeezing between him and Brae. "We got trouble, Sergeant. We got big trouble."

"Apart from all the unwanted attention you're drawing?" Dez asked. "What is it?"

"They grabbed the elf. Prob'ly Vawz, too."

Gwyn sat up. "What? What happened?"

"I don't know everything. I couldn't get my wagon out to make my usual delivery up to the big house, but after your warning last night I figured me and the missus should take all the milk and eggs we could hand-carry up there, give an excuse to be close by and maybe get a message from Vawz if he spots us. We didn't get past the front door, but the place was buzzing inside, and I overhears some guard telling another how just before sunup he thinks Vawz is talking to hisself, then he gets attacked by a shadow and calls for help, then other men go tripping over some body they couldn't see. Didn't make a lot of sense, but too strange not to report. I passes Evix on the way here, warns him what I know, and he filled me in on th'invisible elf."

"Damn!" Dez shouted.

"Did the elf go visible?" Gwyn asked. "Do they know who he is?"

"I didn't hear," Renny replied, "but there was plenty o' yellin', and I think I heard yer name. Pleased to meet'cha, by–"

Gwyn ripped her sword from its bundle and stood, turning immediately for the door.

"Gwyn, what are you doing?" Dez demanded.

"I'm getting Drax out of there while he's still alive."

"Finn won't kill him. He'll use him to lure you in."

"You can't know that," Gwyn insisted. "They've seen he can use magic; Finn may decide it isn't worth the risk. I can't leave him in there, he's… He's my *friend*, damn him to all the hells."

"Even still, it's suicide to go now. Wait here, we'll think of something."

"Your man on the inside is likely down, Sergeant, and if Renny here can get there and back, Finn's sure to have messages moving. More guards will be digging out by the minute. Our advantages dwindle with time while Finn's grow. All I need from you is the approach to Finn's house that has the most cover from crossbow bolts."

"Along the west fort wall and through the stables is the best," Renny offered, earning a glare from Dez.

Gwyn nodded her thanks. "Anybody coming along?"

"I'm in," Brae announced, finishing his second tankard and standing.

"Me too," Renny offered.

"No, you're not," Dez rebutted. "You're going to take another pail of milk or crate of eggs and try to get inside the usual way before anybody realizes how strange you just acted. If you can get in, learn what you can and wait for us by the stable door, and if you see an unattended crossbow, sabotage it. I'll go along with Gwyn."

"You hate the plan," Gwyn rebutted. "I don't want you along if you're not committed."

Dez picked up his round shield. "You *are* the plan, Gwyn. I'm committed."

Satisfied, she turned to Brae. "What do you have for weapons?"

"My forge is on the way," the farrier answered.

Renny was already halfway to the door, hurrying off to his mission. Dez had walked to the bar, giving instructions to his confidante there. In another moment Gwyn led Dez and Brae out into the street, climbing up the snow ramp from the tavern door. Gwyn's armor was hidden below her cloak, and Brae was yet unarmed, but her great sword and Dez's shield were plain for all to see. They kept to side paths as much as they could and moved quickly, hoping to outrun the rumor they were moving out in violence.

They stopped only briefly at Brae's forge, long enough for him to retrieve a long-handled hammer and a round shield like Dez's. At the next crossing of alleys, Dez turned toward a voice to their right hissing his name. Gwyn looked as well, spotting Evix moving toward them, now with a long, thin knife buckled at either hip. He fell into step with the trio and held a hushed exchange with Dez, then peeled off down a different row of buildings. Dez turned to Gwyn and reported quietly, "He sent a few more to the tavern; they'll make a charge when we breach."

"Where did *he* go?"

"He's with us. His way."

Gwyn didn't question the reply as they were now coming to the west wall of the fort. So far they'd avoided any clear lines of sight to the officers' quarters Finn had converted to his residence, but there was no hope of that now. They had fifteen clear yards to cross to reach the stables with no cover and only one, narrow path that had been walked through the snow.

Gwyn borrowed Dez's shield and went first, high-stepping to pack down as much powder as she could. Brae came next, widening the track with his bulk. Dez brought up the rear, watching over his shoulder to ensure they weren't shadowed by enemies. The distance was short, but through the snow every step dragged on for eternity. Gwyn heard a shout from the upper story of the house, her glance flicking in that direction. Moving as much by intuition as reaction, she crouched low, turning behind Dez's shield. She felt a thud against the wood, saw the head of a bolt protrude an inch from her arm, but she ignored it. Her blood was up now, and nothing mattered but getting within reach of the enemy. She continued to advance in a sideways shuffle, now plowing rather than overstepping the snow, her long legs driving deep for grip and shoving forward with all her strength. As they neared the lee of the stables the drift grew shallower, and in another moment the group had gained the outer awning. Gwyn heard a growled curse from above and realized they had denied the crossbowman another shot by the time he reloaded.

Gwyn returned Dez's shield, now with the bolt sticking out from just above its central boss. As she reached over to wrench it free, she saw Evix sprint across the last few feet of snow behind them, a crossbow shot missing him by a hair, then wordlessly slip away into the shadows of the stable. Dez now took point, leading the party deeper into the stables toward a side door to the house. They were six or seven paces away when the door swung inward, revealing a guard in oversized mail charging forward with a sword and large shield. Dez tried to slip to his less protected side, which would also block his own blind flank with a stall partition, but the enemy sidestepped with him and slammed his shield into the smaller man, knocking him off balance. As the guard stepped to his right, he revealed two more men charging into the stable, one with a shield and ax, another unshielded but wearing armor plates on his chest and arms and brandishing a spear. Gwyn feinted to her left, at the ax-wielding guard, drawing a swipe from the curved blade, then slashed at the arm that wasn't drawn quickly enough back behind the shield. The quick cut lacked the power to cleave through, but she felt her edge rake against bone just below the elbow. The guard screamed and fell back a step.

Brae stepped behind Dez, swinging his long hammer down against the swordsman's unshielded shoulder. A telltale crunch sounded from beneath the mail, and the guard's arm went slack, the sword slipping from his fingers. The spearman thrust at Gwyn who batted the point aside with her blade. The enemy was skillful, though, and retracted his point before Gwyn could step inside his reach. Before she could move into a guarded counter, Evix sprang up behind the foe and jammed one of his knives into the guard's neck. The wounded axman tried to bludgeon Evix with the edge of his shield, but Gwyn spitted him before his blow could land. Dez, recovered from his stumble, drove his short sword up through the chin of the last guard while Brae looked away.

"Dammit," Dez growled as they reached the door. "Where the hell is Renny?" As soon as he crossed the threshold he shouted in alarm, another crossbow bolt suddenly appearing in his shield. He turned to the left and charged out of sight. Gwyn stepped through into the vacated space, looking left at Dez's back as he clashed with a guard still in the act of drawing his sword, his crossbow on the floor at his feet. That way led to a narrow flight of ascending stairs, but to Gwyn's right the hallway stretched only a few feet before opening into a wide room. She moved in that direction, her blade in a forward guard, and saw a pair of legs stretching out past the left wall that marked the end of the hallway. Sweeping her gaze across the space once more, she turned toward the prostrate form and saw it was Renny, his eye and jaw swollen and blood trickling from his nose. Evix had drawn up behind her, and he cursed at the sight of his friend, kneeling to check for breath while Gwyn stood guard. As she did, she saw the main gathering room of the house taking up the full width of the structure and at least half its depth. Most of the great hall had a low ceiling supported by wooden posts, but to her left a section was open to the raftered roof some thirty feet above her. In that direction she could see one end of a balcony she supposed ran around the room to access the chambers above. A few feet along the wall to her left was a large fireplace facing the main doors, and just beyond that a narrow hallway mirroring the one she'd just left. She looked back down to Evix and Renny when suddenly a small form lunged at her from behind a wood column. Gwyn nearly swung a cleaving strike before realizing her foe was a thin woman, little more than a girl, throwing her full weight behind an iron skillet. Gwyn stayed her blade and turned her left shoulder into the attack which couldn't possibly reach her head; the woman's strike belied her size, but between the fur cloak and padded gambeson, it did Gwyn no harm. Gwyn growled and brandished her sword, and the woman dropped the impromptu weapon, immediately more afraid of Gwyn than she was of Finn or whichever of his henchman had set her to guard the hall. Without raising the alarm, she turned and fled to the far hallway and up a wide staircase Gwyn now noted there.

Gwyn heard stirring behind her and saw that Renny, still alive, appeared to be coming around. "Something hit me from behind a pillar," he mumbled, holding the side of his face with one hand. "Never even saw it."

"Great big fellah with a war club," Evix assured him, looking up at Gwyn as he spoke. "Miracle you survived, but we chased him off."

Frustrated by the untimely levity but wasting no breath criticizing it, Gwyn asked, "Did you find the elf? Where are they holding him?"

"Cellar," Renny answered, "through the kitchens. That way. Finn's there guarding him." He pointed toward the far hallway with his free hand.

By now Brae and Dez had joined the pair, but sounds of shouting and the clash of arms suddenly resounded from outside. Dez sprinted to the front, throwing open the door. "Guards are trying to get to the house," he called back. "Our boys outside are holding them back." Gwyn heard a scream over the general din. "Hells," Dez grunted, "more crossbows upstairs. We've got to get up there." He turned and ran toward the larger staircase.

Gwyn followed as far as the base of the stairs, then pointed down the continuing hallway that led deeper into the house, toward the heat and smell of a kitchen. "I'm looking for stairs down, not up, Dez."

Dez hesitated, then continued up the steps with an aggravated grunt. "I'll go with him," Gwyn heard Evix proclaim before she moved down the hall out of earshot. She knew by the sound of his heavy boots that Brae was still behind her.

"This isn't your fight, Brae," she said without turning. "You can follow Dez or go out the front to help your friends."

"If you're going after Finn, it's my fight," Brae responded.

Shrugging her acceptance, Gwyn paced down the hallway, moving into the kitchen area. Brick ovens occupied the wall to her left, sharing a chimney with the fireplace in the dining hall she'd just departed. A pair of cooks stood against the far wall, keeping their empty hands in plain view. Farther to the right, a small, paneled space protruded outward from the back wall, covering the top of a staircase of hardpacked earth. Gwyn approached it with caution, peering around the edge of the wall. A few feet out and down, the dug staircase stopped at a rough boulder, then turned to the right, out of view. Steady, yellow light illuminated the face of the boulder from below. No sound drifted up from the larder, but Gwyn had no reason to believe Drax or his captors had left in only the short time that could have passed since Renny learned they were there. Most likely, the fighters below stood ready. All this Gwyn observed in only a few heartbeats, and presently the noise of battle issued from the floor above. She couldn't tell from the clamor how Dez and Evix were faring, but they didn't sound to be much outnumbered. Motioning to the descending stairwell, she declared to Brae, "That's death. There's got to be four or five men down there, not counting Finn; they'll either cut us down the minute we turn the stairs or have a hedge of spears at the bottom. Or both. I'd trust myself against the spears, but not after a hail of bolts."

Brae eyed the width of the opening, then turned back to the kitchen and threw over a small table, scattering its cargo of diced garlic and leeks. With his hammer he smashed off three of the table legs, then used the forth as a crude handle to bear the tabletop before his lower body. Sticking his hammer through his belt, he hoisted his round shield high to protect his head and chest and looked to Gwyn. "Ready?"

She gripped her sword and nodded. Brae moved quietly down the first flight of steps, then paused and took a deep breath. Letting out a tremendous bellow, he turned and barreled down the lower flight, Gwyn keeping close to his back. Over the farrier's roar, she could just make out a voice beyond yelling, "Hold, hold! Damn you!"

Brae slowed at the bottom of the stairs, and Gwyn felt the shudder as he struck something. Still his momentum carried him another two or three paces, and Gwyn shoved her shoulder into his back and thrust her legs against the bottom step, driving him a couple more precious feet. This gave her just enough space to step out from behind him and survey the scene. The larder was chill, but even so the smells of musty earth and root vegetables filled the close space. The ceiling was only a few inches above Gwyn's head, forcing her to shorten the grip on her sword, which in turn hampered her reach. The space was twenty-five feet square, not counting the shelving that lined all the walls, but it was difficult to see past a row of freestanding wood shelves a few feet in front of her. Through gaps between the contents, she could just make out two guards with crossbows falling back, and a quarrel had sprouted from Brae's table shield. Taking up the space to her left, three more guards worked to recover from the battering they'd received from Brae, who looked even more giant as his hair brushed the ceiling. Finding their balance, two brought their short halberds to bear against him. One turned toward Gwyn but immediately thought better of it as Brae threw the tabletop into him, knocking the enemy back once more and giving Brae a free hand and moment to draw his hammer. Before the guard could recover, Gwyn hacked at his nearer arm as she passed, and she felt his left elbow give as he screamed and lowered his weapon. Gwyn was loath to leave Brae at even two-to-one odds, but the risk of letting the crossbowmen shoot once again from cover was too high, and she still hadn't put eyes on Drax or Finn.

Moving quickly to the right side of the room, she pivoted around the row of standing shelves to look down a wide aisle running the width of the space. At the far end, she could see Drax and a man in a guard uniform tied up against one wall, watched over by Finn and two other unarmed men she didn't recognize. Finn moved away from the wall as she charged the nearer crossbowman, but he was too slow to intercept her. She swung at the enemy before he could ready a hand weapon, and while she didn't think she took his head off clean, it was near enough as to make no difference. The second fighter had now pulled a mace and reached for a shield at his feet. Gwyn made to spit him before he could get his guard up, but Finn slashed a sword at her from the left, forcing her to step back and throw a hard block.

Finn seemed a cagey fighter, for as soon as he'd taken Gwyn's attention he stepped back out of her limited reach. Now he stood side-to-side with the mace wielding guard, advancing toward her as a united front. "Keep her alive," she heard Finn order. Over his words was the sound of Brae crying out in pain. Holding her sword in a diagonal guard before her, she threw herself suddenly into the central upright of the storage racks now to her left. One of the men standing against the far wall, seemingly noncombatant, shouted "Look out!" but his warning was too late or too vague. Two of the shelf sections toppled; Gwyn had just enough time to see the halberdiers knocked forward as Brae stepped back and brought his hammer down on the back of the rightmost guard's bare head. Gwyn saw blood soaking the front of Brae's left thigh, but before she could make a thrust over the fallen racks at the last halberdier's back, Finn and the guard with the mace had closed to a threatening distance. She turned toward them and stepped back, bringing all the combatants into her field of vision.

The final halberdier's point had been thrown off line in his stumble, and he tried to fend Brae off with the staff. It may have worked against a smaller man, but the huge smith with his long hammer reached the enemy's helmeted head. Gwyn heard the bell-like peal filling the larder even before registering the sight. The guard staggered for a moment, stunned. Gwyn slashed her sword from left to right, forcing the unarmored Finn back. The guard gave ground and moved the edge of his shield across his body to block, but Gwyn let her point fall to deceive the parry, then thrust up and forward. Her enemy was too slow of arm and footwork, and his padded jack was no proof against Gwyn's blade as it slid into his side just above the hip.

Finn stepped around his man and hacked at Gwyn's arms just as she thrust, and with her blade trapped in the dying guard she was forced to release her weapon and leap back just to keep her hands. Brae raised his good leg and dealt the stunned guard a hefty kick to the chest, knocking him onto his rump, then took a step forward into the shelf debris, heedlessly trampling it under his bulk. Finn stepped toward Gwyn with his sword poised as she reached to her boot and pulled her dirk, taking her heavy cloak up with her left arm for more protection and analyzing how best to get inside Finn's reach. Suddenly his head snapped back, his whole body slowly following as blood sprayed from his nose. Brae's hammer had swung so fast even Gwyn had scarcely seen it. She saw the last, floored guard scrambling backward as Brae swung the hammer again, smashing Finn's throat as he fell. His sword falling from panicked fingers, Finn clutched at his neck, gurgling. Gwyn quickly pulled her sword from the guard she'd stabbed, now fallen to his back, and it was clear he would make no attempt to fight on as he bled to death. She spared a glance backward at the first halberdier she'd cut, but he now sat against the wall, cradling his limp left arm and making quick, agonized gasps.

Looking forward again, Gwyn saw Finn's eyes bulge as Brae stood over him. "If I saw a horse or a mangy dog in such a way, I'd put it out of its misery," the smith barked. "No such mercy for you. I whipped men to death for you, put all the strength of my arms and back into making it as quick as I could." He shook his head. "I find I've no more strength for one…more…blow. Lie there…and die…slow." Brae uttered those last words so haltingly not for drama, but from difficulty. He slumped to the ground, and only then did Gwyn see the crossbow bolt buried feathers-deep in his gut.

Chapter IX

Gwyn hoped Brae would live, but as he sat and clutched his wounds and Finn continued to gurgle, she first crossed the space to the two men who hadn't fought, both still standing between her and Drax. Both had their hands forward, palms out, but didn't speak. "Which of you left two partners in the inn last night?" she asked, her voice flat.

One pointed to the other, and that other showed a note of recognition across his bearded face. Before he could concoct a denial, Gwyn spitted him without ceremony. "For the ranch woman you murdered," she growled as he clutched at her blade, his eyes wide with shock. The other man backed into the corner, whimpering.

Gwyn set her sword down and slashed Drax's bonds with her dirk, then pulled the gag from his mouth. His head lolled for a moment, but his eyes didn't open, and his face was a mess of blood and bruises. The bound guard struggled to speak, so Gwyn pulled his gag as well. He looked but little better.

"Finn and a couple of the guards beat him pretty bad,"

the man, who must be Vawz, explained through bruised lips. "Not bad enough to kill him, I don't think, but he'll be out awhile." Gwyn had hoped Drax would be in good enough shape to do something for Brae, and now, before she could do ought else, she heard the sounds of battle echoing down the steps. She cut Vawz's bonds, then sheathed her dirk. "See to Brae, if you can." she told him.

Gwyn stood and hoisted her sword, looming over the guard Brae had booted to the ground. Brandishing the weapon meaningfully, she ordered, "Hold out your hands."

Instead, the guard threw off his helmet and held his hands up but back. "No trouble, no trouble! I won't fight no more, I swear it. I'll go up first. Try to stop the fight 'fore anybody else gets killed."

Grimacing, Gwyn nodded, motioning toward the steps with her sword. "You, too!" she ordered, pointing to the surviving noncombatant whimpering in the corner. "Or die where you stand." He hastened to comply as Gwyn took up position behind them with her sword point in the latter's back. In a few moments they had passed out of the kitchen and down the hall into the great room, where Finn's cowardly guest threw himself to the left to escape Gwyn's sword. The room was the scene of a general melee, a trail of wounded or dead leading back to the open front door and more than ten men still trading blows with an assortment of weapons and armor. "Finn is dead!" she bellowed. "If you were his man, throw down your arms!"

The battle continued, neither side able to pause without risking their lives. True to his word, the guard Gwyn had freed called, "It's true, the lord is dead. Stop fighting!" but his was not a voice made to command. Shoving her way forward, Gwyn pinned her gaze on the nearest man in Finn's colors and stepped into his flank, taking advantage of his embattled situation to slide her blade in front of his throat. "Drop it or die," she ordered, annoyed. His sword clattered to the floor, and she forced him back out of the fight. "Finn is dead!" she roared again. As she spoke, she moved toward the next of Finn's fighters. "Nobody is coming to your rescue. I am Gwyn the Savage of Atlund! Surrender now or I give no quarter!"

The weight of her words filled the room, and the five of Finn's men who remained withdrew a pace, still keeping weapons and shields up for guard but no longer attacking. This allowed Dez's men to ease in turn, and after a few more perfunctory blows, silence settled over the hall.

"You killed Finn?" a voice sounded from the knot of men. Gwyn spotted Dez, small enough she'd previously overlooked him, stepping into the clear space between the opposed forces.

"Brae did," she answered. "He's badly hurt, himself."

Dez pointed to two men and motioned for them to follow before hustling for the back of the house. Gwyn surveyed the room. Finn's men still stood at guard. "Start losing weapons or start losing hands," she offered. At last the fighters disarmed. "Where is Finn's second?" Gwyn asked. "He's called Roxen, I think."

"Dead," Evix answered from where he leaned against one of the wooden pillars, only then coming into sight. The narrow man held his hand over a wound in his ribs, blood oozing between his fingers. "He was hiding upstairs with the crossbowmen."

"I'd hoped to question him," Gwyn stated.

Evix shrugged. "He pulled a dagger on me."

Gwyn once again looked over the room and took stock as Dez's remaining men collected weapons from the surrendered and fallen, then helped the walking wounded to their feet and began checking for life in those that wouldn't rise. On a more careful count, it looked like Dez had lost half a dozen men, assuming Brae survived. Though her fight had been brief, weariness crept into

Gwyn's limbs as the rush of battle subsided, and she'd slept little. She moved to the open door and dragged a dead man from across the threshold, then shut and barred it. Looking out the window to make a final count, she called to anyone who would listen, "Finn's got at least another dozen men out there someplace. Whoever's least likely to get killed on sight, go out the stable door and start spreading the word Finn's dead. Somebody bar the door behind him when he goes." She heard men moving to obey and pulled a stray chair up near the window, resting her sword across her knees as she reached into her pouch and retrieved a rag with which to clean it. After that she removed a whetstone and dressed the edges; spots here and there needed honing, but overall the weapon remained pristine, as ever it had since Drax had cast his runes on it. Her work completed, she rested her chin on her chest and drowsed. If enemies came, she would wake before they could breach the door.

As she drifted off, some conscious part of Gwyn's brain wondered if she would dream one final dream of Tira's murderers, or if the nightmare would vanish now that her vow had been fulfilled, as it had with Shon and the orcs that killed him. She felt chagrin without surprise when the blue-eyed man appeared before her in the dark.

"Once again your enemies are slain, and once again you live to remember the fallen. This is a good day."

"Even if you sometimes speak the truth, that doesn't make you truthful."

The smiling face sounded an easy chuckle. "You are wise for one so young. A life of battle has made you shrewd. Of course, your observation might be applied just as easily to your supposed benefactor."

"'Supposed'? She did aid me. More than I can say for you."

"Indeed, for those in need of protection, the abbey is

always there. You took advantage of its healing, and I begrudge no one that. But where is she now? Does she assist the hunt for your enemies or celebrate your victory? No. And why not? Because she has no use for you, at the moment."

Gwyn could not deny that even if Daruneh's claim of watchfulness over her life was true, the cryptic woman had not revealed the motive for her vigilance except in vague allusions. The only thing she had said plainly, even by her own admission, was her desire to have Karon brought to the abbey. After attaining that goal, she had gone silent.

"Oh, make no mistake," the voice continued as if hearing her thoughts, "she will come to you again, seeking to direct your sword to her own ends. What then? When you've won *her* war for her, she'll no longer celebrate your bloodlust. At best she would shackle you to some croft like her changeless sanctuary, demand you restrict your passions to chastising ruffians or running off dangerous animals. What life is that for a warrior? Your place is leading an army, not a cloister. Why offer up empty prayers when you can devote the spilt blood of your enemies? She has her own vision of the world, and people like you have no place in it."

Gwyn shuddered at how easily this voice matched her own thoughts, recalled her disdain for the guard duty that had sent her running south all those months ago, her certainty that a place like the Abbey of the Shield was one in which she could never belong. She'd occasionally found her thirst for battle slaked, but it always returned, keen as her whetted blade. Her aches and scars, many for one so young, sometimes pressed her to consider a quieter life, but when she thought of battle, the rage of fire and steel, wielding her sword ahead of hundreds shouting her name, all desire for ease washed away, replaced with the deepest passion she knew, intense and intoxicating. The strange man gazed into her eyes, still smiling. She would not pretend he beguiled her; she could sense his interest, but the desires were her own, quickening her blood.

"You see?" the voice challenged, the eyes aglitter. "She doesn't understand. She isn't like us."

Gwyn wanted to protest that they were nothing alike, but the parity of his words kept her silent.

"You begin to question, to evaluate your position by your own will. This is all I ask. By my word, I will press you no further. If she deigns to speak to you again, observe whether she allows you the same freedom. In due time, we will meet again."

Gwyn gasped as her eyes flew open, her hand gripping her sword hilt so tightly it hurt. The speaker's final words unsettled her; her pupils darted around the great room, scanning for threats, but all stood quiet. Indeed the space was empty save for Dez, sitting in a chair near the hearth. After the morning of brief, tense battle, the gentle crackling of the hearth, heard through the lingering unease of her vision and the fog of sudden waking, seemed distant and unreal, as though she still dreamed. The sticky pools of blood scattered sporadically on the floorboards gave proof that her senses now showed reality.

Standing, she crossed toward the fire and set her sword across the arms of a second chair facing Dez. At last she doffed her outer cloak and mail, laying both out on the floorboards. Placing her sword on top of the mail, she sat again before looking at her old guard captain. However dire the threat of her distant enemies may be, nearer matters pressed upon her immediately. "What of Finn's last guards?" she asked. "How did we fare, Sergeant?"

"None offered fight when they learned Finn was dead. Three have crimes to answer for; we locked them in an empty house. They went quietly on the promise we'd spare their lives. We disarmed half the rest. They'll be watched, likely turned out when the snow melts. The others were strict mercenaries, hard men but not corrupt. They've sworn to fight for us as long as we can honor their wages, and I trust them that far.

"It's the best outcome we could hope, but a costly victory. I lost half my fighting men and a few others who had no business in the battle but wouldn't be put off. Brae may live if his belly wound doesn't go septic. Vawz should be alright, less a few teeth. Everybody else's wounds were shallow."

"What about Drax?" Gwyn asked.

"Still unconscious. No reason to think the worst, but no reason not to, yet."

She searched the sergeant's expression while finding her words. "I had to come for him, Dez. I know you must think if we'd waited longer and made a plan, more of your men would have lived, but I couldn't risk Drax's life."

Dez shrugged. "I can't help thinking that's true, but I can't know it. I know if you hadn't been here Finn would still be alive and abusing everyone. Even with the guard slowed by the blizzard, we couldn't have risked a move without you here to tip the scales. We both did what we had to do. We're square."

"Thank you," Gwyn answered. "All my allies are leagues behind me or leagues ahead, if they even live. I wouldn't like to lose one that's nearer to hand." She paused. "Is Brae awake?"

"He was a bit ago, anyway. He's just in the kitchen; it was too cold to leave him in the cellar, but once we got him up the stairs we weren't about to carry him any farther."

Gwyn chuckled as she stood, though it was a mirthless sound, then moved past Dez into the hallway and back to the kitchen. A space had been cleared against the far wall where Brae reclined on a pile of grain sacks. "How are you?" she asked.

"Holding together," the farrier rumbled. "Got the gut and thigh stitched up. Doesn't hurt so bad, long as I hold still."

"You must have borne the pain well. I didn't hear any screaming in the main room."

Brae shrugged. "Came near to breaking my teeth from gritting 'em, but I wasn't about to give the bastard that stuck me the satisfaction. He's still about someplace."

"Whichever gave you the quarrel in the belly isn't, for what that's worth. You fought well, and with a dire wound from the start," Gwyn declared. "I'd stand with you again anytime."

"I'll take the compliment, but even if I survive this hole in my gut, I hope never to take up arms again. My hammer's for iron, not heads."

Gwyn shook her head once as she turned away, thinking Finn would likely disagree with him, but she didn't say it. Brae didn't like killing, and there was no sense reminding him about it, however right it had been. She wished him well as she left, returning briefly to Dez. "Where's the elf, then?"

"Upstairs," the man answered as he rose to go about some other business, "room in the southwest corner. Where we took crossbow shots from on the way to the stables."

Nodding her thanks, Gwyn took her leave and picked up her sword, then headed up the stairs and toward the back corner of the house. The room where she found Drax resting had no decoration but sported a decent mattress. A rough stool sat nearby, so leaning her blade against the wall, she settled in to wait. The sky was finally clearing, and in the light seeping in the south-facing window she could plainly see Drax's face, better than her brief glimpse in the dim lanternlight of the larder. His eyes and nose were all swollen and red, starting to purple. One side of his jaw was twice its normal size as well, and she hoped it wasn't broken so he could eat properly. On the other hand, if it hurt enough to keep him from talking quite so much for a while, that wouldn't be so bad. She could only assume his body was worked over, too, but she couldn't tell; nobody had removed his robes before putting him in bed, and even if it wasn't so cold she wouldn't feel it was her place to do so. He'd become her friend, she had to admit, but there remained a distance between them that she hadn't felt with Shon or Ardos, or even Baraxis, at least not at the end. She missed that camaraderie, somewhat to her surprise. She'd been too focused on getting home alive to think on it much, or on why her association with Drax was growing along such different lines, but as the morning stretched away with nothing of value to do, and facing the prospect of at least part of a winter with no war to fight, Gwyn suddenly could think of little else.

An hour past midday a youth came into the room to give Gwyn a bowl of soup and a farl of bread. "Dez asked to know what to do with your armor, miss," the boy inquired.

"Tell him just don't trip over it," Gwyn said. "I'll take it back with me when I go to check on my horses."

"I'll tell him, then," the boy answered as he left. He seemed a little afraid of her. She guessed that was reasonable.

Gwyn ate most of the bread and stew, then threw the crust into the bowl to soften in case Drax wanted something to eat as soon as he woke up. Even if his jaw worked it didn't look like he'd be able to handle anything as tough as the loaf she'd just endured. As Gwyn pondered her previous line of thought, she first assumed the distance between them must be her own doing. However people responded to her on a battle line, easy friendship with them had never been one of her strengths, after all. The more she considered it, though, the more she realized, while she'd taken some time to get the measure of him at first, she'd been as open with Drax as with anyone once they'd traveled together for a time. It was Drax, rather, that continued a strange formality with her, or at least shallow politeness. He only seemed to show anything of his real thoughts when he judged her. She hadn't minded his remote nature, fearful of how gregarious he might become if he ever felt truly familiar, but now it puzzled her, considering the dangers they'd shared and having been one another's only company for a month. She grunted in frustration and turned to the window. "And people wonder why I'd rather just be in a battle."

The snow-bright day was softening to twilight when at last Gwyn heard Drax stir. She turned to look at him. Only his right eye opened fully, but it scanned the room with sharp awareness, his body tense. His jaw wasn't fully mobile, giving him a mumbling quality, but it didn't seem broken as he spoke. "Gwyn?" the elf asked. "By Terillah, did they get you, too? Where are we?"

"Hells no, they didn't *get* me," Gwyn shot back. "When I heard you'd been taken I stormed the place and came to your rescue."

"Oh," Drax sighed as his shoulders relaxed back onto the mattress. "Thank you. So where–"

"You're still in Finn's house, or it was. A dead man can't hold a deed, I suppose."

"You killed him?"

"No. I meant to, but Brae beat me to it." She laughed in spite of the situation. "It was a thing to see." Once again serious, she continued, "Even if mine wasn't the killing stroke, Finn's life ended the moment he laid hands on you. He just didn't know it."

Drax shifted with a wince to look directly at Gwyn with

his good eye. "And if you'd been too late, if I'd been dead…you'd have avenged me."

"Even at the cost of my life. Listen, we've ridden together, we've fought together, you helped me save Karon and put an end to Tira's killers, even if you don't like how I did it. You're my… That is to say, I count you as one of my people."

"I never asked to be," Drax answered, though his tone was not affronted.

"I never said it was voluntary," Gwyn replied. "And if anybody does harm to one of mine, there's a blood price to pay. That's who I am. I suppose I was born to it, but it's more than that. I've blamed my mother, the Wind, even a friend's last words for a time, but it's none of that. I *choose* it. I believe it's right. Can you understand that?"

Drax was silent for a moment. "Not really," he finally answered, "but I can respect it. I have to admit, there was a comfort in hoping you'd eviscerate my killers if I didn't make it, cold comfort, maybe, but still… I'm not sure it's something I can begrudge for others now that I've felt it myself. I don't like killing, but I've done more than my share of it. We both have our reasons, and I should leave Terillah to judge yours." There was silence in the room for a few minutes. "Did you get the last of them, then?"

Gwyn knew what Drax meant, and she nodded.

"That's good." He paused, then groaned, pain bringing his mind back to his immediate situation. "I feel like I've been trampled."

"Can you speed things up with your magic now that you're awake? Or maybe once you've got a bit better on your own?" Gwyn asked.

Drax shook his head, a tiny motion. "I'm a fast healer, but nothing my magic can help."

Gwyn remembered his rather mundane job getting the crossbow bolt out of her arm, only using one of his rings, she assumed, to cauterize it, and considered how that method contrasted so sharply with the king's wizard in the Southern Capital, though a human, who had made her hand and knee like new in a single night. "People say elves have the best healing magic there is," she pressed.

"I did; I mean, they do," Drax stammered, "for elves in general, but not for me. Not anymore."

Gwyn waited a moment for more explanation, but when none was forthcoming she decided to let it drop, given the elf's current condition. After a few more quiet moments, Gwyn asked, "How'd you get caught, anyway?"

Drax winced, and Gwyn could tell it was from the memory and not from pain. "I waited at the side door until a boy came out to check on animals, then slipped inside while he worked. Between the noise of the wind and everyone hunkering down, finding Vawz was just as easy. On short rest and in a hurry, I didn't want to go visible and put extra strain on my amulet; he was alone, so I tried to get his attention like I was. I spoke his name, not too loud. He looked around, saw the room was empty, and when I spoke again he cried out before I could stop him. It seemed fine at first, but after a minute another guard came in just to make sure everything was alright and heard my voice on the way to the door. All the poor man said as he came in was 'Who's in here with you?' He was just curious, no sign of alarm. Vawz probably could have convinced him he'd been hearing things, but instead he panicked and rushed the man. I tried to cover the guard's mouth so he couldn't call for help, but when I touched him he spun that way by reflex and I got shoved into the doorjamb. I hit my head and fell, right there, and by then other guards were coming to the noise of the fight, all yelling and confused. A couple people tripped over me in the doorway, fell on top of me, and realized something was up before I could scramble out of the way. That's when they grabbed me and started pummeling. I was afraid of what they might do if they couldn't at least see what I was, so I slipped off my amulet and..." He reached into his robes to an inside pocket, his expression showing relief at whatever he found there. Then he looked to his hands. "Where are my rings?" he asked, his tone urgent. "Did I still have them when you found me?"

It was only then Gwyn noticed Drax's fingers were nearly bereft of his magical adornments, his left ear entirely so. The gold one he used for slinging lightning and the iron one that incinerated things were present on two darkly bruised fingers of his right hand. He must have punched something in the struggle and caused those digits to swell. "I guess not," she answered. "You're lucky they didn't cut your fingers off to get those," she concluded, pointing at his remaining rings.

"I'm lucky? I think we understand that word differently," Drax replied, his tone bitter.

"I'll go look for Dez and see if he knows anything. Do you want to eat? I've got a little stew and soft bread here."

"I'll try, anyway. My jaw is throbbing, but I'm famished."

Gwyn handed him her bowl, then said, "Watch my sword. I'll go get the sergeant and more food."

Having not even managed to get into position to try the meal yet, Drax argued, "What if I can't eat it after all?"

"Then *I* will," Gwyn replied over her shoulder.

Gwyn went back through the main room, but Dez wasn't there. She went back to the kitchens next to see what and who she could find. Brae was dozing on his pallet of sacks, so she let him sleep, and nobody else seemed to be about. There was stew left in the pot, but it was starting to congeal. She stirred in a bit of water from a nearby pitcher and swung it back over the fire to warm. The bread seemed to be gone, so she went back down into the larder, which she found had been cleared of bodies, though the shelves she'd knocked down were still in shambles and blood slicked the floor in several places. She helped herself to a strip of dried meat, gnawing it as she located a few hard biscuits that she took upstairs and crumbled into the stew.

When she left the kitchen with Drax's bowl, she ran into Dez and a couple of his men coming down the larger stairs. "Gwyn," Dez greeted, "good, I wanted to talk with you."

"Same here," she answered. "Follow me. Drax is awake; I'm bringing him food."

Dez nodded and fell in behind her, hailing Drax as they entered his room, now swimming with shadows as the sun had fully set.

"Have you seen my rings?" Drax asked, foregoing a greeting. His speech still mumbled around his swollen jaw.

Gwyn proceeded to hand Drax his bowl, then lit a rushlight on the window ledge to give light long enough for Drax to eat and Dez to say whatever he meant to.

"Finn probably doled your ornaments out to his favorites," Dez surmised. "I'll pat down the few we took alive and tell my people to be on the lookout." He scowled. "Much as I hate to say it, as hard as folks have had it here, they might not cough them up if they've already got them hidden away or handed off to the families of the dead."

"I understand," Drax sighed. "I'd appreciate anything you can do. I'd give them all away if I didn't need them, but I suspect I will, and I can't hope to remake them anytime soon."

Gwyn had resumed her place on the small stool as the pair spoke. The room being bereft of other furniture, Dez remained standing. "What did you want to talk about, then?" Gwyn asked.

"Right," the sergeant began. "A few of us met, trying to decide what to do. First there's the matter of your, ah, activities at the inn last night. Since the men you killed were strangers here, and considering what you did for us today, most everyone is willing to let things go, what with your reputation and all. People here aren't too keen on that sorta justice, but I explained the situation and, well, I *may* have implied you had some authority, since you'd gone to the ranch on orders from a proper lord, and that was the only kind of justice his people were ever going to get. That satisfied most everyone."

"That's the second time you've said '*most* everyone,'" Gwyn pressed.

"The innkeeper's irate, Gwyn, and I can't say as I blame him. You killed two people under his roof. You insulted his honor and attacked his hospitality. I did enough trading with Atlunders to know what would have happened if you'd done something like that in your home."

Gwyn sighed. Dez was right; in Atlund a murder over a proper vendetta might be acquitted, but breaking hospitality, under any circumstance, carried a sentence of death. Maybe reduced to exile with the justification she could bring, but it would never have been forgiven. She'd been so fixated on avenging Tira she hadn't even considered the consequences. At last she replied, "I have no defense."

"There has to be some kind of reckoning," Dez confirmed. "It hasn't been decided, but I wanted to warn you."

Gwyn nodded. "I'll try to make apologies first, when I can. Maybe it will help. That whole cadre of you I saw in the hall just now, though, you couldn't have all met just to talk about me."

"No," Dez agreed with a heavy sigh. "You're not the worst criminal here by a long stretch, not anymore. Finn was despicable, but as far as any of us can tell, his writ of investiture was legitimate. So in the king's eyes, we're traitors, to a man."

"You'd wanted to do this a long time," Drax reasoned. "You must have had some idea what you'd do next."

Dez laughed. "You'd think so, wouldn't you? Truth is, until Gwyn showed up, none of us thought we'd get to make a move anytime soon. Once she got here, things just sorta happened."

"What's the difference?" Gwyn asked. "It will be months before anyone from the Capital makes it up here, and when they do they'll only care about taxes. Just have someone pretend to be Finn or tell the king's man he was trampled by a horse or something."

Drax snorted while Dez answered, "You aren't serious, Gwyn. We've got hundreds of people here; you ought to know Finn's killing is a secret too big to keep."

"You should start writing down Finn's crimes," Drax interjected. "His real crimes. As rightful lord he could recruit young men for his guard, but if he forced women to his bed, that's a hanging offense if you can prove it. And find somebody who knows the usury laws. Odds are good Finn broke at least some of them."

As Dez nodded, his forehead still creased, Gwyn added, "Fine, if you can't carry off a ruse I suppose you'll have to tell the truth, and the sooner the better. I'll pen a letter to Baraxis; he knows my signature, and I can make mention of another 'mark' that will prove it's from me. You can send it south as soon as the snow melts. I'll ask him to request clemency from the king or whatever noble Finn held his land from and send a solicitor to you to help prepare your defense. I wish you luck. Drax and I will be long gone by then."

"Too much to hope you'd stay and help keep us from dancing a gallows jig?" Dez hazarded.

"Too much," Gwyn confirmed. "Sorry, Dez. I've got family waiting on me, wondering if I'm even alive, not to mention a war at least threatening, maybe already on."

"I'm bound for home, as well," Drax added. "Not as urgently, but I never made any friends down south who would take my word as holy writ, like Gwyn did. I'm not likely to be much help to you on my own."

Dez sighed. "I understand. You'll be missed, though. Both of you."

"Let this one talk your ear off through the winter and you may change your mind," Gwyn answered. "Now, if someone could offer me the loan of a lantern, I need to go check on my animals."

"You might as well just bring them here," Dez offered. "There's plenty of room now; take your pick of lodgings. The stable's more crowded, but there should be enough empty stalls for you. There's a lantern by either door if nobody's already using it."

Gwyn left the room and went downstairs, walking past her gear and only taking up her cloak at first. After a couple of paces she thought better of leaving the mail and donned it, wary that some of Finn's loyalists may not be as pacified as Dez implied. Her concern proved unfounded, however, as she made her way to Dez's cottage without incident. Thus emboldened to leave her blade in its harness on Thunderhead's tack, she decided to stop at the inn on her return trip. She threw her reins over the hitching rail and walked to the door. Though the winter sun had set behind the mountains, the hour was still early; through the windows she could see some lodgers still ate at the long tables while others took their empty dishes to a cart next to the very kitchen where Gwyn had waited in hiding the night before. She knocked.

Faces looked out from the side window, then disappeared. A moment later a voice called from the other side, "What do you want?"

"I'm *Gwyn et Sheevasa* of Atlund," Gwyn began.

"I know damn well *who* you are," the voice interrupted. "I asked what you want."

Biting back her pride, Gwyn answered, "I want to make apology to the innkeeper."

The door swung open, revealing a man not much taller than Dez but half again as wide. Over his round face sat a floppy, blue tam. "I'm Nedris. This is my place. You can spare your apology; that's no use to me. What I'm after is restitution."

Despite having wronged the man, Gwyn had to fight the urge to strike him. She had come in good faith, voluntarily, but Nedris' response offered no deference to that. Gritting her teeth as her fists balled unbidden, she grated out, "What would you have of me?"

Nedris' eyes flicked away, and his next words were quieter, though just as hard. "Can you restore the belief in my children that their father can protect them from an intruder in the night? Can you convince my boarders that the security of my walls means anything?"

Gwyn was torn. It wasn't her fault the man was incapable of defending his own; on the other hand, she'd traveled enough to see that if only warriors could be innkeepers, the roads would be long and lonely. "No I can't," she finally replied.

"Then you see my grievance, at least," Nedris grunted.

"The men I killed murdered a woman who died under *my* protection, in a way," Gwyn explained. "It had to be done. Likely there were ways to do it that would have spared your honor. I didn't think." Only in the speaking did Gwyn realize the weight of those words. When she'd left her men to kill the orc sentry during the war, avenging Shon, it had only been by great luck and the risk of many volunteers she hadn't died. Obvious as it now seemed, the notion of her peril and injuries being a direct result of that action wasn't something she'd contemplated on, neither then nor in the months since. Her realization was interrupted by the innkeeper's response.

"Knowing what I know now, I've little doubt those men needed killing, and so did Finn and some others. Dez would have me forgive you and let the whole thing rest, but his word don't carry as much weight with me as it does with some." Nedris was silent a moment, scratching the stubble on his heavy chin. "Come back tomorrow at dawn."

Gwyn made a quick bow of her head and turned from the door. She half expected to hear laughter from the great room behind her over taking orders from the humble proprietor, she of such vaunted reputation, but there was only quiet as she collected her animals and made her way back to the big house.

Gwyn confirmed with Dez that the room next to Drax's was now empty and claimed it for her quarters. It was furnished, if so it could be called, much as the elf's was, though with the addition of a large trunk at the foot of the bed. Gwyn emptied it of some clothing and sundry belongings and added them to a pile of orphaned items in the main hall. She supposed she could claim some of them as spoils, but she'd caused enough offense already and had no idea which dead man the things had belonged to or whether he had living friends on either side of the conflict. She did rifle through it in the hopes of finding any of Drax's things left in a corner of pouch or pocket, but she had no luck. On the way back to her new billet she looked in on Drax and found him asleep once more, so she arranged her gear in her room and went to sleep herself. Mercifully, she didn't dream.

The next morning she awakened to the sounds of the stirring house, the sky out the western window still darkling. Dressing quickly, she went to Drax's door and gave it a light rap. "Gwyn?" the elf inquired from within.

"Yes."

"You can come in."

She entered the room only a step. Drax sat at the window, and his small book was open next to the rushlight on a narrow sideboard. The elf had removed his heavy robes and was dressed in lighter, tan garments Gwyn had only seen him wearing when they'd found a warm enough spot to let his usual clothes air out from their journey. His blue skullcap was off as well, and it struck Gwyn, as it had before when he was so attired, how ordinary he looked. Were it not for the elvish features he could have been any Southern youth just preparing for a day on the farm. "I have business to be about early; not sure when I'll be back," she announced. "Do you need anything before I go? Food?"

"I'll be alright," Drax answered. "I can move about well enough. From the waist up I feel I had a boxing match with a battering ram, but my legs work."

"When you're feeling able, then, can you go downstairs and check on Brae? He's in the kitchen with a bad gut wound. I've seen men survive them, but not as often as I've seen them die. I know what you said last night about your magic, but you did alright on my arm, and I'd wager an elf's herbcraft against what anyone else here could do. I don't know that I could have got you out of Finn's hands without Brae."

Drax nodded. "You may be overestimating my knowledge, but I'll do all I can."

"Why, Master Drax, was that humility?" Gwyn jabbed. "I'm going," she continued before he could react to her sarcasm. "I suspect I'll be around the inn if you need to send for me." She turned to leave.

"Gwyn," Drax stopped her. She turned only enough to see him sidelong. "Thanks for checking in."

She nodded to him and went down to the kitchen. Three

cooks bustled back and forth, seemingly unperturbed by the regime change. No matter who was in charge, bread had to be baked and bellies had to be filled. Gwyn, accustomed to taking a soldier's due, grabbed a pair of oat cakes from a cooling tray and took a bite, suddenly sucking in breath against the heat as steam erupted from the cake's exposed interior. She looked at Brae a moment before leaving; he remained asleep despite the activity, and what little skin was visible through his great, bushy beard looked pale. Gwyn frowned and walked down the hallway to the main room. Dez was at the hearth, adding logs to the fire. "Sergeant," Gwyn greeted, "I've been ordered to the inn. If I'm not back in a couple of hours, can you see to my animals? Yourself, I mean, don't go delegating–"

"Yeah, I know the Atlund custom about strangers and your horses. Wait, what do you mean 'ordered' to the inn? Who by?"

"The innkeeper," Gwyn answered, not breaking her stride toward the front door. "I stopped there last night."

"Don't go getting yourself into more trouble than you already are, Captain," Dez called after her.

CHAPTER X

Gwyn didn't ignore Dez's remark but didn't respond to it as she closed the door behind her. The eastern sky was just graying, so at least she wouldn't further offend Nedris by tardiness. If her sense was right, the day would be warmer than yesterday but not enough to melt much, save to transform some of the roof-bound snow into icicles on the overhangs. She hastened down the main road, finishing her oat cakes that cooled rapidly in the chill air, and presented herself at the inn's front door, knocking loudly.

"Who the– Oh," came a voice from within. Someone hollered for Nedris, and in a moment the proprietor stood framed in the dim doorway, backlit from the fire in the hearth as the sun was only now breaking over the horizon and still well below the top of the stockade.

"Go around the back," the man ordered. "The gate's unlocked, so you won't have to jump the fence this time."

Gwyn grimaced at the reminder of her crime as she obeyed, already growing accustomed to Nedris' attitude. Taking the shorter route through the building, the man stood waiting for her when she opened the gate. Snow had been piled against the far fence to clear a path to a chicken coop and covered well, and toward this bank Nedris pointed. "Your victims are buried in there. Yesterday some of the men managed to dig enough to get one side of the east gate open. Take the bodies through the wall and put them somewhere north of the road. If you're still around when the snow melts, you can bury them. Come back when you're done."

A wooden shovel stuck out from the drift's sloped front, and near that point she could just make out a few small patches of earthy colors through the white. She picked up the crude tool and set to her grim work, and Nedris returned to the kitchen door. Before he entered, he clarified, "When I say, 'Come back,' I mean come back *here*." He pointed to the threshold. "The front door is for customers."

Gritting her teeth, Gwyn nodded her understanding and returned her attention to the snowbank. She'd uncovered a shoulder and part of an arm when her motion was arrested by a sudden realization. "For Terillah's sake," she growled. "All this on my damn birthday."

Dismissing the thought, she began digging and, in only a few minutes, had unearthed the first body and part of the second. Their clothes were drenched in blood, and she chose not to check if either had voided any other bodily contents; everything was frozen solid and gave no smell, so she cared little. Gwyn decided then to go back to the house for her mule, as dragging a full grown corpse through the snow was, though not beyond her considerable strength, no way to spend the morning after a victory, much less a birthday. She knew bringing one of the horses as well would make her job easier, but she refused to dishonor a steed that had borne her in battle with the chore of transporting a frozen murderer from one temporary grave to another. While in the stable she ensured Flamewind and

Thunderhead had hay and water, rather than ice, and checked their blankets. For a moment she leaned against Thunderhead's sturdy neck, allowing herself a rare feeling of respite, and wished she could understand him as Drax did. She patted his withers, and he snuffed at her back. She smiled. "You don't need magic to know me, do you, boy?" Thunderhead stamped and bobbed his head, and she liked to think he was agreeing.

Satisfied the horses were in good order, she led the mule out of the stable and through the trampled snow path to the main road, then back to the inn. When she entered the yard through the gate, the innkeeper stood up from the side of the well, water still sloshing in the bucket he'd just filled. Gwyn couldn't read his expression. "What's wrong?" she asked, her voice deep.

"Wasn't sure you were coming back," Nedris replied as he hoisted his bucket.

"I just went to get some help. I'm a killer, not a fool."

Nedris actually chuckled. "That's fair. I'll be around somewhere when you've finished."

The bodies were frozen into awkward shapes, so it took Gwyn a share of digging and two trips on the mule to complete her work. She found the open gate guarded by two men she'd seen fighting for Dez. She nodded a greeting before continuing with her burdens, battling through the deep drifts to her goal. As Gwyn crested the snow ramp on the other side of the gate she saw a trampled path leading east. On its northern side, some ten or fifteen yards distant, were nine mounds where bodies had been lain in the snow and covered, enough to discourage scavengers when much easier pickings were nearby. Those enticements were another twenty yards farther east where bodies were thrown into a scornful heap. She assumed the last outlaw she'd executed in the cellar was in the pile somewhere. Gwyn dropped a corpse onto the edge of the mass at the end of each trip, leaving both Tira's killers to freeze and, eventually, rot, if they weren't eaten first.

Gwyn had walked only a few steps away from the charnel heap before cursing and turning back. She knew the bodies had likely already been searched, but she couldn't shake off the compulsion to check for herself. For a quarter of an hour she shoved and tugged at frozen arms and legs, groping ghoulishly over the slain. Leather pouches and belts were of general value and had all been stripped for spoils, but clothing damaged in the fighting, of unusual proportion, or simply too worn out to bother with, had been left as their owners lay. Gwyn searched every pocket and crease. None of Drax's rings turned up in the search, but tucked into a pocket inside a guard's vest, she was surprised to locate his spectacles. Both glass lenses were intact, but the contraption had snapped in half at the wire that connected them over the bridge of his nose. She wrapped the pieces in a clean cloth and placed them in her belt pouch.

Nedris was nowhere in sight when Gwyn returned to the inn. Since she was at the back door, she decided to enter without knocking. A towheaded boy about Karon's age sat at a table in the kitchen, eating porridge. He looked up at her with saucer-wide eyes. "Are you Gwyn the Savage?" he asked.

"Yes," Gwyn answered.

"Did you really kill a thousand orcs?"

"I doubt it. I never really counted."

"My big brother says Atlund women is allowed to fight because they ain't as pretty as Southern ones, but I think he only said that because he heard Banz say it first, then he saw you come into the fort day before yesterday and he said Banz must have turds for his brains 'cause–"

"Shut your mouth, Eldos," came a cracking voice from the kitchen stairway. Gwyn looked over to see a boy in his early teens descending the steps. He reached the landing and peered around a post at Gwyn, then cleared his throat. "Are you looking for my father?" he asked.

Gwyn only nodded.

"Pa!" he shouted back up the stairs.

Gwyn heard a reply, too muffled to make out, then the older boy said, "He says to wait in the main room and he'll fetch you directly."

"I'm sure he will," Gwyn grumbled, walking to the inner door. "Everybody's 'fetching' me places lately."

"Bye, Gwyn the Savage," the younger boy called out.

She ignored him and heard the brothers arguing as she took a seat at one of the long tables in the great room, which now stood empty. The sun was fully up, and the boarders had all gone about their daily business. After a few minutes, the older boy emerged from the kitchen and took a seat nearby. "Sorry about my brother," he said after a short silence.

"He didn't bother me," Gwyn muttered.

"He's always asking people questions when Father's not around, especially soldiers and guards. I think he does it just because he knows what I'm going to do. When I'm old enough I'm going to go south and be a hired sword."

Gwyn had barely been listening to the boy, but at that declaration she snorted, despite herself.

"I'm stronger than I look," the youth retorted, his voice sullen.

"Strong here?" Gwyn asked, pointing to her arm. As the boy nodded, she continued, "That kind of strength will come on its own if you practice. I'm stronger than I look too, a lot stronger. It helps in a fight. Some. Mostly the strength you need is *here*." She pointed to her eyes. "If you're strong enough to watch a horde of screaming enemies charging at you and not flinch, strong enough to watch your friends die around you, strong enough to watch the life flicker out of somebody's eyes while he claws at your blade in his guts and cries for his mother, to do all that and not care…or even enjoy it. If your eyes are that strong, then by all means, go off south." She stared at the boy's eyes, which now were as wide as his younger brother's had been.

"Eldan, what's the matter with you?" came Nedris' voice from the kitchen doorway. "You look like somebody dropped a spider down your shirt."

"Uh, nothing," the boy muttered, standing from the table and walking quickly back toward the kitchen.

"What did you say to him?" Nedris asked once Eldan was gone. His voice carried an edge of accusation.

"Do you know what your son plans on doing when he's old enough?"

Nedris gave a quick roll of his eyes. "He's still on about being a mercenary?"

"It seems."

"Did you speak against it, then?"

"No," Gwyn answered, "what do I care what he does?"

"Of course not. Why would your kind care about a young boy's life? Come on; the rest of your work is upstairs."

Nedris led Gwyn to the room where she had done her killings the night before last. The door stood ajar, and the innkeeper pushed it open. He didn't go inside but gestured for Gwyn to do so. The room was cold and dark, but even in the meager light Gwyn could see the beds on either side of the space thoroughly stained rust-red. A two-foot circle on the floor, likewise, was sticky with congealed blood, where she guessed one of her victims must have flopped down before bleeding to death. The room was otherwise unharmed, save that behind the door Gwyn could see the bracket for the bar hung half-broken from a single, bent nail.

"I want it all back like it was," Nedris declared without preamble. "Replace the bedclothes, the mattresses, too, if any blood soaked into them. Scrub the floor and get carpenter's tools to plane it down if the stain won't come out. Repair the bracket you broke."

Gwyn was stymied. Of course she could strip the beds and burn the ruined sheets, then ask after a weaver to replace them, though she didn't know what it would cost. She'd never scrubbed a floor in her life but didn't suppose it could be that hard. But as for planing the floor or repairing the bracket, she didn't even know where to begin. Nedris had already started to walk away. "How much do you want?" Gwyn challenged.

"What?" Nedris demanded, turning.

"How much money? I don't know how to do these things. If you want them properly fixed, let me pay a carpenter."

"You destroyed it," Nedris countered. "*You* fix it."

Gwyn snapped. "You just want me to look like a fool!"

"Why might that be?" The man's voice was cold, and Gwyn saw his sons had come up the stairs for something, now standing a few paces behind their father, their expressions fearful.

Gwyn kept her voice low. "I know what I took from you, but it isn't something I can give back."

Nedris walked back to stand before her, almost touching her. "I suppose you have to do for yourself on campaign, eh? Cook, see to animals, maybe some sewing, that kind of thing. Are you good enough at any of that to get paid for it, or to trade the work for food or clothes?"

"No," Gwyn admitted.

"So if there's nobody needs killing, you're not good for a damn thing, then, are you?"

Gwyn ground her teeth, her arm tensing with the desire to wrap her hand around the little man's throat. At the same time, something twinged inside her, an unthought realization that she'd never *made* anything, and maybe never would. Her anger flashed all the hotter to quiet her vulnerability. "Seems there's always *somebody* who needs killing," she growled. Over their father's shoulder she could see the two boys staring, probably afraid of what she might do. Nedris' eyes bore into hers. Unlike his sons, he showed no fear. She read his expression and found only disgust.

She saw the slap coming a mile away. She could have stopped it in a hundred ways, even having her dirk in the man's heart before he could land it. Instead she let it come. Her cheek stung for but a moment, it being the weakest strike she had ever suffered, but inside it burned longer.

"Pa," the boys gasped.

"Keep your blood money," Nedris spat. "I'll repair my own inn. Hired swords never care about cleaning up their messes. Get out, and don't come back."

Gwyn seethed for a few seconds, then turned toward the guest room and stomped inside.

"What are you doing?" Nedris demanded.

Gwyn reappeared in the doorway with an armload of bloody sheets. "Get out of my way," she growled. "I'm fixing your damn room."

Gwyn toiled until sundown and knew she looked a fool at every moment, just as she'd feared, though nobody watched her. With every mistake and curse she cast her gaze about for witnesses, but she was always alone. Despite submitting to perform the labor, many expenses could only be covered with coin: replacement bedclothes, the rental of a plane for the stubborn patches on the floor, a staggering expense for iron nails for the door bracket. Finn's extortionary prices should ease in time, but for now they were still in effect. While visiting the blacksmith to buy nails, she asked if he could fix Drax's broken spectacles. He laughed at the foolish suggestion that this might have anything to do with his craft and directed Gwyn, embarrassed at her ignorance, to a man who made leaded glass. This craftsman welcomed her more warmly and, once learning who the work was for, refused her payment and told her to return the next day.

At the end of every trip Gwyn made for tools or materials, so many she lost count, she returned through the back door as ordered. Sometimes she passed Nedris in the kitchen, but he never so much as looked in her direction. In the end, repairing the innkeeper's guest room cost her two smashed fingers and more than half her savings from the South. Even had she found a lord who could offer her better terms, the market value of her abilities came clear to her in a way it never had before, and it figured poorer than she had expected. Still, as she surveyed her work in the failing light before leaving the room, she felt a surprising flush of pride at its completion, crude as it was.

Gwyn hadn't stopped since her meager breakfast of oat cakes, and her stomach growled as she clomped down the stairs. Despite Nedris' order not to come and go by the front door, she suspected he would make an exception if she used it to leave forever. Gwyn was surprised to see the man himself standing at the bottom of the steps, on a line between her and the exit. "Please," he said, extending his arm toward the tables of the main room, "stay for a meal."

Gwyn turned slightly away, regarding him with suspicion.

"I'll serve you from the same pot as my boys, if you're afraid I'm holding a grudge," Nedris offered.

Still skeptical but hungry enough to ignore it, she nodded and moved toward the nearest table. It was late for a midday meal and early for supper, so the main room was mostly vacant, just a pair of men sitting in the far corner in quiet conversation. Gwyn sat at an empty dish, and the boys brought a pot of stew and board of fresh bread from the kitchen and sat down. Nedris put out additional dishes and poured small beer for Eldos and proper ale for the rest, then sat down.

"You told me to leave," Gwyn stated. "Why did you change your mind?"

"Why did *you*?" Nedris asked.

"I thought, when you hit me," Gwyn answered, "that would settle it. Dishonor for dishonor. After, though, and seeing you had the guts to do it, I don't know. It didn't feel like enough. Now you."

Eldan began dishing out stew as his father spoke. "I've had the day to think. Like you, I thought hitting you would matter. I thought I'd feel better, at least a bit. I just felt small. You came in here and did what you did because killing is who you are. Not me. Who *I* am, the example I want for my boys, is service. Meeting needs. You can't take that, and I hold it dearer than life. It just took me a moment to hold it dearer than my pride, too. If I can serve a meal to one who's wronged me, that's the kind of strength I want my sons to see."

Gwyn sat back, a bit unsettled. She could sense the forgiveness in Nedris, but she couldn't understand it. She wondered if she'd ever actually forgiven anyone and couldn't clearly remember. She'd done this work for Nedris on the expectation that he would drop his legal complaint, but not that he would set aside his anger for a legitimate wrong, to willfully bear no malice. The thought made her self-conscious in a way she couldn't articulate, but she could only accept it or run for the door, and her growling belly decided the issue.

Gwyn ate heartily, complimenting Nedris on the stew and bread, both of which were far better than Dez's or Finn's former cooks'. Nedris chatted with his sons while Gwyn downed her first helping in silence. As Eldan began refilling her dish, she finally announced in a glum voice, "I fear I've ruined your floor."

Nedris laughed. "I'm afraid you have, too. I looked in during one of your errands. By all accounts you're a far better swordswoman than you are a carpenter. I was better off with the blood stains."

Gwyn smiled. "If my friend Drax was here, he'd say that sounded more like philosophy than décor."

"Maybe he'd be right," Nedris remarked, still chuckling. "Maybe we've both learned a little philosophy from this adventure."

Gwyn started on her second helping. "I guess anything's possible."

Darkness had fallen by the time Gwyn returned to the main house. She sought Dez, hoping to report she'd done her part in squaring things with Nedris, but she found him in the kitchen stooping over Brae.

"What's wrong?" she asked.

"He's burning hot," Dez answered, looking up, his forehead lined with worry.

"Did Drax come look at him?"

Dez nodded. "He looked at the wounds, ordered the stitching in his belly reopened, and went poking around in the cut. I hope you trust that elf; it took three men to hold Brae down and two more to get his friends out of the room when Drax started digging at his guts. Anyway, after that he packed some kind of poultice in there and bandaged it but ordered nobody was to stitch it until he said so."

"Drax said maybe I overestimated him," Gwyn sighed. "Maybe I did. But he's no fool; he wouldn't have done anything if Brae was getting better on his own."

"That's as much as I figured, and that seemed to satisfy everybody at the time. Now Brae's getting worse, though, and..." He shook his head. "I don't know."

Gwyn left and went to Drax's room. She knocked, but there was no answer, so she lifted the latch and went inside. Drax bolted upright in bed and groaned as soon as the door opened. "Gwyn," he called, "is that you?"

"It is."

"Alright. Close the door when you leave."

"I need to know about Brae," Gwyn insisted.

The elf sighed, reclining again. "Can't this wait until morning? I'm mending, but I had to use some magic to get a better look into the wound, and with nothing at hand to use for a focus. It was taxing. I can barely stay awake."

"In the time it took you to complain, you could have just told me."

"Fine. The bolt was stout, not barbed, so it just kind of shoved his bowels out of the way rather than cutting them. That's good, but it means the hole in his skin and muscle is more like a tear than a clean cut. That's not so good. I pulled a couple splinters out of him that should have been caught yesterday, too. That's bad. I tried a poultice. If he's lucky it'll keep him from…getting…blood poisoning."

"He's got a bad fever, Drax."

Gwyn could tell the elf was drifting off as he replied. "Of course he…has a fever. No…stopping that. Check him…the morning…"

She closed the door and went to her own room. Since her stomach was full of stew and bread, and she had nothing else to do, she lay on her bed in the dark and thought, letting the warmth of her body heat the blankets before she stripped to her underclothes and climbed under them. Her day had been long enough, and she soon drifted off to sleep.

Gwyn awoke in the middle of the night, her room pitch black. Her mind wrestled with a sensation she couldn't account for, a feeling identical to when she used to sit in her bedroom as a child after some mischief, knowing her mother and stepfather were arguing about her in the next room. Strange flashes illuminated the ceiling above her, faint and erratic, and she wrapped her blankets around her as she rose and turned to the window to investigate. As her gaze moved toward the jagged shadow of the mountains against the western sky, she started at what she saw there. In the far peaks and valleys a terrific storm raged, greater than any she could remember. The clouds were so low that, from her vantage, she could even see lightning shooting upward from them toward the higher sky.

In time the storm began to break apart, finally separating into two vast masses of cloud. The greater, darker disturbance drifted briefly in her direction, then sped into the north as the lesser cloud remained, still roiling and flashing. After her previous dreams, Gwyn had no doubt this tumult somehow revealed Daruneh and her nameless foe striving over her, though whether this was some battle of magic or only a symbol shown to her mind which dreamed even now, she had no idea. A fear of these unfathomable beings, a feeling no foe, however mighty, had ever inspired, hung heavy upon her. Their battle was happening close, *awfully* close, in the truest sense of the word.

One other thought gripped her as she sank to the floor, still gazing out the window at the stars: Were either of these powers fighting *for* her, or did they both merely fight *over* her?

For the first time in as long as she could remember, the sun was already high when Gwyn opened her eyes. She didn't remember returning to her bed, if indeed she'd left it in truth, and she felt warm and secure under her blankets, content in a way which the warrior part of her spirit scoffed at as she delayed rising for a few, precious minutes to herself and her private thoughts. Slowly the memory of her vision of the prior night intruded on her consciousness, a doubting whether it had been real or even a true revelation as so many of her dreams had become. It had been less vivid somehow than she'd grown accustomed to, and the notion that such omens could come to feel like a typical part of her life was, in itself, unsettling. As the warrior part came more fully awake at last, she chided herself. Whatever the dream had meant, if it meant anything at all, what could she do about it now? She had allies beaten and probably dying, animals to feed and water, and preparations to make even now if she meant to be off for home as soon as the snow melted.

Since the morning was well underway, Gwyn readied herself and set out to see the window maker. He presented the repaired lenses with pride, showing how he had bound the broken pieces together with wire, then secured all by brazing with melted lead. The result was less graceful than the original, but Gwyn trusted Drax would be pleased. Taking her leave, she made her way back to the big house to return the elf's property. On the way through the main hall, though, she decided to check in on Brae and was only a little surprised to find Drax already there, bathing the farrier's brow as he slept fitfully. The cooks seemed to have finished their morning tasks and worked at a quieter pace on preparations for the rest of the day. Gwyn suspected a deeper cause for their sullen demeanor: the fear of death hung in the room. As she took a cool loaf from a basket to the left of the door, Drax looked up and nodded at her.

"Do you remember our conversation last night?" she asked

"Just," the elf replied. "I changed his dressing and the poultice I've packed in the wound. In a few hours I'll clean everything out and stitch him up again. Nothing else I can do."

"Maybe these will help," Gwyn announced, handing Drax his lenses.

He thanked her, then looked at the repair job critically and gave it an experimental tug. He tried them on at last, moved his head a bit, and took them back off, apparently satisfied.

"How are you faring?" Gwyn finally asked.

"Better than him," he replied with a nod toward Brae. "I'll be fine." Gwyn heard the exhaustion in his voice, but also the edge of self-reliance she'd come to expect from the elf before his recent ordeal had blunted it. Its return made her glad.

Gwyn looked at the three cooks, then motioned Drax toward the hallway. The elf rose and followed her back to the main room, which was empty at present. Still, Gwyn chose the farthest point from any entrance and sat, tearing a chunk off her loaf and handing it to the elf when he joined her across the table.

"Dez got a couple of my rings back," Drax stated before Gwyn could speak. He held up his left hand.

"That's the one for fire without light?" Gwyn asked, pointing to the blackened metal band with its ruby setting.

Drax nodded, then indicated the remaining ring of etched copper. "And this one I use to set wards on my camp when I'm traveling alone and have to sleep with nobody to keep watch."

Gwyn got the sense Drax was baiting her, hoping she would scoff at his wizardly ways or, better still, spark an argument over learning he had a resource they could have used to get more sleep at times they had desperately needed it. She sidestepped his conversational snare and made a direct attack. "Why can't you heal Brae, Drax?"

He hesitated, looking at the bread in his hand as though preparing to take a bite. Instead, he asked, "This is your price for telling the name of your sword?"

"No," Gwyn answered, "it's not like that. By now, you either trust me or you don't."

Drax nodded but ate instead of speaking, his eyes distant. Once he'd finished, he muttered, "It wasn't supposed to be this way." For the first time Gwyn heard something like real bitterness in his voice. "I was an artist, you know? Using magic and twine and patience to sculpt growing things into beautiful… It's a long story, and even now, there's a lot of pain in it. If I let myself remember…" He shook his head. "My tribe has rules, very strict. The most strict of all is about killing. We aren't to kill anything with a spirit."

"You mean people?"

"Not even animals," Drax clarified. "We see life in plants, but no awareness. Everything else with life seems to have at least some kind of will and knowledge of itself, and we're not to snuff that spirit out. No matter what."

"I've seen you eat plenty of meat, and I've seen you kill, sorry to say. So I guess you don't hold to those ideals anymore."

"Maybe I never did."

The thought of such pacifism drove Gwyn's mind inevitably to battle. "How do your people protect themselves? In Atlund we have to fight all the time. I know the nomads of the east, beyond the Qachar Range, have never shown much interest in land south of the Sharai, and maybe the Elven Forest doesn't have the kind of beasts we still see on the frontiers sometimes, but even regular wolves and panthers will kill a stray traveler if they're hungry enough."

"Doesn't matter. We don't kill, even at the cost of our lives. Even if the 'wolves' walk on two legs and come with fire and weapons and enchanted things that pierced the tricks and illusions we used to keep ourselves safe. Even when they threatened and hurt and took what they wanted.

And who." Drax had gone to staring out the windows as he spoke, but now he returned his eyes to Gwyn. "I'm not like you," he asserted. "I never had vengeance in my heart. But when they came the third time, I wouldn't let them hurt us again. I took my magic of growth and beauty and I turned it against those men. Brutally. I know your stories, and I've seen your necklace of fangs, and I know beyond doubt you've never done anything to a body that's worse than what I did." The sadness in his eyes was countered by the trembling of his clenched fists. "And I would do it again."

"Sounds to me like you did right," Gwyn assured.

Drax nodded. "My chief did not agree. Nobody in my whole tribe came to my defense. By their own law they could not kill me, but," he shuddered, "our shaman's magic was very strong. Strong enough to take mine from me. Rip it out of me. Then they sent me away."

"If they took your magic, then how–?"

"They couldn't take the potential, the same as what a few humans are born with. Losing that magic was like losing sight or hearing or legs. I could have sought another tribe, one with different rules, but with no magic I would always be a cripple in elf lands. I left all my people behind and started over. I found a wizard in the South to teach me his ways, taught myself a lot more. I studied, yes, but not the lore you asked after, only the magic I would need to thrive in the human world, alone. Now I'm as you see me. I can do much, but the magic of my people is forever denied me. Most of my kind that went south made themselves useful in a war-torn land by making harvests more bountiful or healing the wounds of battle, but I–"

"Became a killer." Gwyn finished.

"I was already a killer. I just," Drax made a mirthless snort, "took it up professionally."

Gwyn took another bite of bread and spoke around it. "Bet you got paid better than I did."

Whether by luck or the strange effect she was said to have on morale, Gwyn's quip seemed to succeed in bringing Drax back toward his more lighthearted self. "I definitely did," he agreed with a smirk.

"What happened to all your money, anyway?"

"That, I think, is a story for another time." Drax stood to leave.

"Wait a minute," Gwyn interjected. "You told me when we started out you could get me safe shortcuts through the Elven Forest, and now you're telling me you're in exile?"

"Ah, well," the elf answered, rubbing the back of his neck, "I've been gone a long time, and I thought, if I spoke well and made my case, maybe." He shrugged.

"You owe Flamewind an apology, riding him all this way under false pretenses. You'd better get out of my sight; I haven't threatened to kill you in days."

Drax was forced to do more work on Brae in the afternoon. The enchanter lauded the return of his spectacles, as the use of his familiar focus would help him work his sight-enhancing magic more easily. For Brae's sake, Gwyn was glad of Drax's renewed enthusiasm, but when he began rambling about 'adjusting thaumaturgical lines' to compensate for the addition of lead to the frames, she quickly lost interest. Nevertheless, the elf performed with greatly improved precision over his former attempts, finding a few more fibers left behind by the crossbow bolt as well as patches of dead flesh and tiny cysts of putrid color. With a small paring knife honed to razor sharpness, Drax cut out these harbors of corruption as precisely as he could, then used his ring of iron and topaz, with extreme care, to cauterize where he cut. Brae bore the pain with fortitude and a pair of leather straps between his teeth, but it took four men to hold him still until he mercifully passed out. Drax finished his work but only had time to ask someone else to stitch up the outer wound before collapsing into a boneless heap on the floor, leaving Gwyn to carry him up to his bed. She stayed by his side a couple of hours, but when his swoon seemed to transition to proper, restful sleep, she went about her business.

Such business was minimal, at least for a time. None had need of her sword, and Dez had his hands full establishing some sort of governance for the fort. He asked Gwyn's advice on a few points, since her homeland eschewed the strict hierarchy the Southerners had so learned to depend upon, but she could sense the splintering of factions in the absence of a common enemy and managed to sidestep the political quagmire, a feat achieved by bluntness and apathy rather than guile. Left to her own devices, she began picking through the main house in search of any records kept by Finn's majordomo, Roxen, but these, too, proved fruitless. Servants directed her to the right papers, but the steward must have had a prodigious memory for his illicit affairs, since his only notes were a sketchy shorthand of initials and brief comments which Gwyn could not decipher.

She could see nothing else to learn in Finn's station regarding the weapons and mounts supposedly sent to Atlund. The traders who took them had not returned, which implied nothing given the time of year, and no one still alive in the station seemed to know the particulars of where the caravan went or who was to receive it when it got there. Meanwhile, the movement of the dark cloud in Gwyn's dream inspired a foreboding that her enemy was somehow established in the north already, maybe as far as her homeland. Whatever that might mean, she redoubled her determination to be away from the fort as soon as Drax was fit to travel. To that end, she dipped into her dwindling savings once more to purchase fresh shoes for the mounts. She allowed the farrier to shoe the mule, but she trimmed

Thunderhead's and Flamewind's hooves and nailed the shoes on herself, allowing the stranger, professional though he may be, only enough interaction with the horses to ensure proper sizing of the iron.

While waiting for the elf to recover, Gwyn also penned the letter to Baraxis which she had promised Dez, hoping to bolster his legal situation and that of everyone in Finn's Station, or whatever the residents chose to rename it. To the end of the letter she added the simple note, "Karon is safe," in case the message Daruneh had pledged to send went awry or wasn't believed. She wanted to explain to Baraxis her reasons for leaving the boy at the abbey instead of bringing him back to Sutherset, but much of what she needed to say she dared not commit to paper, and she couldn't seem to find words for the rest. The dialectical differences between the Atlund and Southern languages were less striking in writing than in speech, but she had never learned to write in the Southern style at all. With Dez busy at politics, she approached Nedris for help in proofreading her draft, and the innkeeper proved his character in obliging her without mention of her prior offense.

This critical task completed, Gwyn began to consider the implications and risks of her ultimate return, especially if her instinct of the enemy's watchfulness was correct. One evening she approached Dez in the tavern to seek his knowledge.

"I finally got these bleating goats to set a council for themselves, no thanks to you," he hollered over the din of patrons as Gwyn approached. He slid a pewter mug of mead across the table to her, and she sat. "About a quarter of the freemen wanted to put me in charge, a quarter wanted somebody else, and half wanted nobody at all. Wound up with a half dozen men who can barely stand each other as a ruling panel. I figure if everybody's pissed off equally, we prob'ly done something right."

"If you're already sick of the whining and backstabbing in another week or so, you should sell your cottage and come north with me and Drax," Gwyn answered after a sip of her mead.

Dez chuckled as he pulled a pint for a patron who'd just come to the front table. "I think I'd rather face the treason charges," he quipped.

"Speaking of bloody coups," Gwyn segued, "I could use some information. There are only three crossings of the Sharai into Atlund, and I have to assume every one of them will be watched."

"Alright," Dez played along.

"With the price on my head, and not knowing how bad things are in Atlund, I'd rather get back home unseen. I don't suppose any of the traders you dealt with in your caravan days were, let's say, something other than legitimate."

"Now, Gwyn, trafficking in smuggled goods, that's *illegal.*"

"Fair enough. But over the years you must have heard some of the 'bad' caravan runners talking. Right?"

"Well, for the sake of argument," Dez relented, "let's say somebody wanted to get into Atlund without going past any border guards. That person might take the north fringes of the Elven Forest back toward the Tunaris, up through the foothills, but keep below the tree line. And if that person wasn't scared of bears or cougars or wolf packs and such, they might find a steep, narrow canyon that opens up to a high plateau where one of the headwaters of the Sharai dives underground for a few miles, and that person could just," Dez paused and made a crawling motion with his fingers on the bar, "walk right across."

The region Dez described was far south and west of the forests Gwyn knew firsthand, but she still regarded the information with skepticism. "And the Atlund border patrols don't know this place?" she pressed.

"Knowing and *watching*, all day every day, those are two different things."

"True enough," Gwyn agreed. "This canyon doesn't sound easy to find, though."

"I'll have Evix draw you a map. Not that he ever used to run with smugglers, mind."

"No, I'm sure he learned all those knife skills in the kitchen."

Gwyn carried her mead to a table to make space at the bar, taking her ease a bit before heading back to the big house. Brae had remained feverish, and she spent as much time as she could tending to him. She had no skill in it, but some compulsion wouldn't allow her to leave him lying alone when she had nothing else of use to do. Drax exerted himself in order to help, likely delaying his own healing, for while he could not work magic to cure or mend, there was much he could do to ease Brae's discomfort, clouding his sense of pain to help him rest and contribute to his recovery.

After four days the blacksmith's fever broke, and he woke the next morning cleareyed and alert, still weak but, they hoped, no longer at death's door. His leg wound had mended substantially, so with great help he was able to move from the kitchen to a proper bed the house servants had prepared in a screened-off corner of the main room. This would improve his situation, and silence the growing complaints of the cooks, without requiring him to brave the stairs yet.

Dez offered, perhaps, good news to his blacksmith friend after he was resettled. "As soon as you're well enough, Brae, you've been given a seat on the governing council. As the man who dealt the killing blow to Finn, you were the only unanimous nominee."

"I don't want a reward for that, Dez."

"I knew you wouldn't, but I'd value your voice. All the men on the receiving end of your lighter whippings insisted, too, and even the families of some of the ones you made an end as quick as you could. Sorry to bring it up."

"I'll be happy enough in my forge, Sergeant," Brae rebutted. "You lot can argue about feast days and road tolls all you want. Come get me if anything important comes up. If the council doesn't like that, well, they voted me on, so they can damn well vote me back off again."

Dez laughed. "I'm glad you're getting better, my friend. I lost too many as it is."

Brae closed his eyes and lay his head back on the mattress. "We all have."

CHAPTER XI

While Brae healed from his wounds, the snow had begun to melt, slowly and with cycles of freezing again every night, turning the station into a slushy, icy mess. After the first morning of heavy digging, moving about with the snow itself had been tolerable, but the thaw brought mud and the reek of a week's worth of manure warming in every spare corner. Even with the fort's position at the crest of the hill allowing snowmelt to drain away, mucking everything out took countless hours of labor. In return, the dozens of horses that had been crammed into the walls in every available space were finally able to return to the paddock on the north side of the station, granting at least the relief from crowding in exchange.

The evening after Brae was moved out of the kitchen, Gwyn and Drax discussed plans to resume their journey.

"I know you still need rest, and it would be safest to overwinter here," Gwyn admitted, "but I'm loathe to stay. Knowing what I do now about arms and mounts being driven to Atlund, I think I have to take the risk."

"I could use a couple more days to mend my wounds," Drax replied. "After that, I'm eager to be away as well. With this bounty on you, and it likely coming from that thing we faced outside the abbey, I'm not keen to stay in one place too long, myself."

Gwyn leaned back on the stool where she sat, across from what had become Drax's customary place on the window ledge. "I have a suspicion that bounty has been withdrawn."

Drax's face showed surprise in the dim light. "What makes you say that?"

Gwyn had felt a greater kinship with the elf since hearing his story, even a clearer understanding of his reluctance to shed blood. Nevertheless, she felt a compulsion to move her gaze from his eyes to the floorboards as she answered. "I, uh, have dreams some-times," she admitted. "Ever since Tira's husband died, and I vowed retribution on his killers. Like that woke something up inside me. And Daruneh and her enemy, whatever he is, they appear in them, or speak. At first I didn't know them, but there's no doubt about it now. I think that enemy is waiting for me in the north. He knows where Karon is, he's reckoned where I'm going, so what more need is there for knowledge about my location?"

Drax didn't answer for a few moments. Gwyn looked into his eyes in the rushlight and sensed the calculation inspired by her words, the sifting of thoughts. She hesitated to admit the elf was smarter than she was, but she couldn't deny his mind worked with a precision for which she had no patience. Finally he asked, simply, "What if he's not inclined to wait?"

The question filled Gwyn's heart with a double foreboding. The first was obvious: Since Gwyn couldn't face this being, without Daruneh nearby she had no defense if he did assail them. The second stirred more deeply, a belief that Daruneh knew the reason for her enemy's hesitation but refused to share it. "I cannot guess," Gwyn finally answered. "When the thing attacked us in the valley, I was ready to fight before Daruneh stopped me. You seemed afflicted somehow but recovered. If it came at us again, between my sword and your magic, would we have any chance?"

"I can't say," Drax replied after a time, gazing at his hands and, Gwyn thought, the places for his lost rings. "My enchantments on your blade should offer some help, and if I don't hold back, some of my magic could do great damage if the being is flesh."

"*If* it's flesh? You claim the dead don't walk about the Physical Realm in spirit, so what else is there?"

Drax shrugged. "I told you this was out of my reach. Exile or no, I'll feel safer when we're in the Forest."

"Strangely enough," Gwyn admitted, remembering her prior foreboding in the place, "so will I."

They waited the two days Drax needed but not a moment longer. They said their goodbyes to most of the station in the tavern that night, where Dez presented Gwyn with a new pair of boots on behalf of the fort's residents in appreciation for her help, as well as a fresh gambeson to replace hers that was worn and damaged by crossbow bolt and surgery. Brae's closest friends had pooled their resources to purchase a smaller saddle for Flamewind, one more suited to Drax's slight frame, and after trying to refuse the gift to the edge of graciousness, the elf finally accepted with a bow. Gwyn felt suddenly sentimental about her own saddle that Flamewind still wore, but knowing every pound of gear would be precious on the coming journey, she began taking bids for it immediately, making back some of what she'd lost since leaving gainful employment. Once the excitement had calmed, Evix took Gwyn aside to explain his map of the smuggling route, which was half sketch and half description.

The pair retired early and rose before the dawn to be on their way. Gwyn triple-checked their preparations, but at last she could tarry no longer, feeling more anxious than she would admit.

Dez waited for them at the open gate. "Sorry to see you go, both of you. But you gotta do what's right for you and yours."

"Honestly, Dez, if who put that bounty on me is who I think it is, it's better for all of you I don't stay too long."

"If you say so," the sergeant relented. "Since the thaw, nobody I *don't* trust has left the station, and the ones I *do* have all come back. We'll try to keep the word bottled up here as long as we can, buy you a few days at least."

"Thank you," Gwyn replied, doubting it would matter but grateful Dez would work to hedge her bet. "I know I'll be long weeks away, but if you do learn anything about who up in Atlund bought the weapons and horses, try to send word. You may even hear from me if the right side of this conflict back home needs equipment. Finn's Station might just be the armory of Atlund, in a pinch." She swung onto Thunderhead's saddle and reached her hand down to Dez. He nodded to her as he clasped her wrist, and Drax's in turn.

Just as the rim of the sun broke over the eastern plain, the pair turned onto the road and began their long ride to the north.

Gwyn saw no spies or brigands on the open roads. The weather turned cold again, enough to keep mortal enemies hunkered in their hideouts in the foothills, or so Drax's keen eyes assured her. They rode and walked always bundled in the warm clothes Daruneh had given them, so any glimpse caught from a great distance couldn't hope to reveal their identities.

Once they'd traveled a few days from the station, into the true wilds where there was no profit for even the most desperate highwaymen, Gwyn's concern shifted from the chance of being tracked to the possibility the prior blizzard hadn't been entirely natural in origin. If that was true, she had no reason to believe they couldn't be smothered by another snowfall at any time. Was her mysterious malefactor truly content to let her reach her destination, or only waiting to freeze her to death in some place with no shelter?

All apprehensions aside, Gwyn and Drax moved with incredible haste through the wilds, only climbing into the slower foothills when the winds blew fierce enough to demand they find shelter. She had allowed the animals to fatten up as much as they could in their week and a half in the station. Daruneh's provisions proved as durable as she promised. Losing half of them at the bandit town had been a heavy blow, but the chance to resupply at Finn's Station, which they hadn't anticipated at the outset, ameliorated that injury somewhat. They rationed parsimoniously and lost nothing to spoilage. Dry scrub was their fuel, and every occasional green plant or kernel of wild grain served as forage for the animals. Drax's powers of flame kept them warm and twice melted streams and pools that would otherwise have denied them water at a perilous moment.

Traveling through the wilds alone was a danger Gwyn had never experienced, one that so demanded her attention she scarcely had the capacity to yearn for battle. With caravans, the safety lay in numbers, but traveling with only what they could carry, any mistake or mischance could be disastrous. With but two people and three mounts, hope came not from mutual support but from speed, driving to remain in such scant surroundings as briefly as possible.

When the big moon was out, they rode in the dark, stopping only when they could move their legs no farther. They walked to save the horses and mule, and rode only to save themselves. When Bully, or even Flamewind, began to flag, Thunderhead drove them on, pushing them to tap the limits of their endurance.

By the time Drax declared one evening that the smudge on the northern horizon was not merely cloud, but the thick wall of redwood and yew, birch and ash of the Elven Forest, woman, elf, and beast were lean, hungry, and footsore. But they had crossed the wilds in a mere twenty-two days, a pace that nearly doubled Gwyn's southward speed with the caravan. She had heard tales of great overland races between Atlund and the Southern Kingdoms in which men on horseback had surely covered the distance more quickly, but aside from these professional riders she knew of none that had done so.

Passing into the Elven Forest the next day, they walked from the unrelenting grip of winter into the first breaths of spring, experiencing a warming that should have taken weeks over the span of just a few furlongs. Gwyn let the horses graze for an hour as she and Drax filled waterskins, then she pressed ahead, driving the party for two more days before leaving the main road to throw off any pursuit that may, by some miracle, still follow behind them; meanwhile, she sought to stymie any entity, of any description, that might await her on the north side of the forest and assume she would travel through it in a straight line. Two more days they wandered west until she stood convinced of Drax's insistence they weren't being, and could no longer be, followed. Only then did Gwyn allow time for rest, setting a camp in a sunlit clearing with a clear stream running along its southwestern edge.

For a day they did almost nothing: sleeping, barely talking, completing nonstrenuous tasks like mending clothing and tack while consuming the last of the supplies from the abbey. For three more days they gathered wild produce and snared small game, eating their fill. Determined to set out again the next morning, Gwyn finally asked the question she found she'd been dreading for the last twenty leagues. "Drax?" she asked over their crackling fire.

"Mm," the elf grunted in reply around a mouthful of roast squirrel.

"If your tribe agrees to commute your sentence, well, we'll be parting ways then?"

Drax swallowed his game and cleared his throat. "I… I loathe the thought of leaving you to face all this madness alone. A war or some unnatural enemy, either one would be enough, and you have both." He went quiet, starting to tear another bite from the squirrel meat spitted through by a greenwood stick, then paused, regarding the dead animal he'd been consuming. He looked back at Gwyn, meeting her gaze through the flames. "The chance to be home, though, to live in peace in the green." He took a deep breath of the forest's cool, night air. "To have family again." He looked away. "Either choice asks a terrible price."

Gwyn wrestled with her thoughts as she finished her meal, but as the minutes strung one to another she realized words had left her. She prepared her bedroll for sleep, and as she drifted away she could feel the spirit of life and renewal flowing into her from the forest, continuing to mend her weary body. Alas, her troubled spirit found no comfort.

Drax took the lead the next day, by unspoken agreement discerning a course that would take him back into his tribe's lands and, ultimately, to his village. Two full days they traveled, and Drax expressed concern that the forest may turn against them as they crossed the border, denying safe paths and forage. Gwyn, as all Atlunders, knew the forest to be a place of wonder and strange magic, but she asked for no details on how it, or some elven hand through it, may seek to thwart them. On the contrary, as they went forward the trees and brush remained as vibrant with edible flora and fauna as ever, and their paths ahead presented no obstacles. Gwyn could sense Drax's spirits lifting, and if she didn't miss her guess she thought he led the way just a bit quicker.

The third morning out from their temporary camp was hastening on toward noon when Drax led the pair into a broad valley. Trees clothed the hillsides, but they saw clear, broad swaths of sky for the first time since entering the forest a week before. A wide stream ran down the valley's trough, and the flat spaces on either side were tilled and, presumably, planted, though nothing had sprouted yet. Further up the valley, where the land sloped too steeply for planting, sheep grazed on the lush grass, though these appeared a wilder breed than any Gwyn knew. A few goats were scattered among them, and as her eyes roamed over a brood of ducks paddling in a pool sheltered from the main stream, she noticed a row of nearby hutches woven from flexible canes. All the land stood well-tended, yet Gwyn saw not a soul about. Were it not for Drax's lack of alarm, she would have supposed the place had been recently deserted in the face of some catastrophe. Drax, however, led Gwyn on a worn track above the fields on the valley's north side, moving with quiet surety. Gwyn could only wonder what years Drax had spent in this place, what memories may even now be flooding him from all approaches, but he turned his head neither left nor right as he rode. Indeed, unless she was mistaken, Gwyn didn't believe the elf saw anything but Flamewind's gray mane. He seemed to have shrunk into himself.

In time the valley widened to their right, the hillside

giving way to a level upland of perhaps two acres under the shelter of surrounding ridges. This open space was dotted with dwellings the likes of which Gwyn had never seen: circles of low, bushy trees growing so close together she could scarcely have passed her hand between them. The gaps were filled with leafy foliage, and at about the height of her head the trees branched out into interleaving boughs forming roofs for each space. Over all these, viny plants sported flowers of every color, open to the sun, and bees droned lazily from one to another before ascending and zipping off to their hives. Gwyn remembered Drax's tale of weaving plants together for sculpture and wondered if, in more utilitarian days, he had made any of these homes himself.

In the rough center of the dwellings lay a flat green, and a tall elf stood in its midst, wearing a simple beige tunic of wool and linen. His shoulder-length blond hair moved in a subtle, warm breeze. Two shorter elves, a man and a woman, stood behind him and to either side. "Why do you come here, Drach'ss?" the tall one called as soon as they were close enough for easy hearing.

Drax rode forward a few more yards before stopping and giving his reply. "I come to beg forgiveness and clemency. Why do you speak to me in human tongue?"

"Our words are for our own kind. Not for your human companion. Nor for you, any longer. We owe you no consideration."

Gwyn heard Drax's voice break as he replied. "What you took from me you can never return. After twenty harvests have come and gone, can I not rejoin my people, crippled as you have made me? What justice is there in this, Taekun?"

"The only justice we can offer without becoming as wicked as you," the tall elf, Taekun, replied. "We are, none of us, killers. You are."

"And since you cast me out, have I not been forced to kill all the more? The world outside this forest doesn't offer the luxury of our pacifism."

"It sounds to us," the female elf spoke up, "that we have only helped you to find a world to which you are better suited, Drach'ss."

"Is this your doing then, Mother?" Drax spat. "Taekun could have kept me out but didn't. Did you let me in only to rebuke me yet again, after what those men did to my sister, your own daughter–"

"No, I… I wanted to see you. Despite everything. Our ways have existed for as long as we know; we cannot set them aside even for you. But we do love you, son. Always."

"A mother may be forgiven for loving her child," Taekun pronounced, "but the tribe cannot abide you. I was swayed to allow you here, in the hopes there may be something worth redeeming in you, but the stink of human magic and blood is heavy on you. You have only reconfirmed your crimes. You have no part in us. We will no longer open the ways, whether forward or back. May the forest judge you."

Drax hesitated, as though he wished to say more, but after a few moments he turned Flamewind's head and rode back up the path the way he had come, passing Gwyn where Thunderhead stood and taking the mule's reins as he did. Gwyn didn't move, staring at the trio of elves standing motionless on the green. After Drax had gone a few yards he called to her, "Gwyn, come on. We should never have come here."

"He's right, human," Taekun called. "You should leave."

"You're all fools," Gwyn condemned them, taking Thunderhead a few steps toward the elves. "You hold up your precious morals, but you can't answer for the blood at your feet. You think you deserve praise for allowing your innocent children to be butchered? One man rises up in courage, and you have the gall to call him wicked and *yourselves* just? 'May the forest judge him.' You even deny him the safe passage you would offer a stranger, no matter how evil, and secretly hope the forest will do to him what you're too self-righteous to do yourselves. By Terillah, woman, he's your own son! You will all face a reckoning, in this world or the next.

"Drax of the Western Vale no longer needs your clan of pious sheep," Gwyn continued. "He is *my* clan now. Drax may carry the Candon name of Atlund, fly our tartan *and* the colors of Lord Major Baraxis of Sutherset, and *you*...you may all go to *hell!*" She wheeled Thunderhead, growled a *h'yaw* he didn't seem to need, and cantered up the road, now passing Drax in turn as he sat wide-eyed on his horse. She heard him follow. As they rode out of the valley the forest closed in around them, and she knew the way forward would be hard.

Drax resumed the lead and set the straightest course he could manage to the boundary of his former tribe's lands. The going was strenuous. Flamewind was forest-wise, and he and Drax managed to pick many concealed paths to make progress, however the will of the elves tried to deny them. When this proved impossible Gwyn took point, and Thunderhead's mighty thews could often plow a way through brush the leaner horse couldn't wend between. The further they traveled from the village, the less the forest seemed to willfully fight them, slowly yielding back to the simple wild of an untamed land. Birds went quiet at their approach, but Gwyn could hear them in the distance once more, and again the foliage twitched with small animals scurrying away. Drax had been silent all afternoon, and Gwyn was not inclined to question him, but after they found a sheltered clearing in which to make camp, the elf spoke as he went about his tasks. "You didn't have to stand up for me."

Gwyn snorted. "There isn't much in life I *have* to do."

"What I should have said," Drax clarified, "was that they don't listen to anyone else anyway."

"Well," Gwyn answered, choosing her words, "I may have talked *at* them, but it wasn't *for* them."

"I thought so. I'm just trying to understand. What you said at the end was… You meant that?"

Gwyn busied herself tending to Thunderhead and didn't look at Drax, but she could feel his eyes on her. She nodded. "Your people made their choice to cast you aside. Twice. So I made *my* choice. Mine was the better."

She felt as much as heard Drax approach her back, and when she turned to face him he threw his arms around her, his head pressing against her sternum. Setting aside her discomfiture for his sake, she returned his embrace for a pair of heartbeats, then pushed him back to arms' length. "That'll be enough of that, then," she cautioned.

Drax nodded. "Of course. But thank you."

After another moment, Gwyn asked, "Should I call you 'Drach'ss,' then?"

The elf shrugged. "Drax is fine. The Southerners didn't take to the gutturals well, and they love their 'x's, so I simplified it a bit for them. The Atlund dialect would handle it better, but it would still sound strange amidst human speech. I'm used to it."

"Speaking of the Atlund tongue," Gwyn considered, "if you're coming north with me, I'll have to start teaching you its differences from Southern speech." She kept technically to the Southern dialect, but she let her Atlund brogue sound through at the end.

Drax smiled at her. He went about his business for a few minutes, then asked, "When we go among your people, then, does all this mean I'll have a place there? The South wasn't unkind to me, but I was never really one of them."

"You'll have a place as long as I have anything to say

about it," Gwyn shot back. She paused then, considering. "Except, truthfully, I may *not* have anything to say about it," she realized aloud. "I left on bad terms, or at least not good ones, and I've been gone two years. I may not be all that well thought of back home."

"I'm sure your reception will be better than mine, at least," Drax countered as he settled down to sleep.

Gwyn would never be accused of optimism, but she had to admit the elf was probably right.

The warrior's need for haste was no less, but if any leg of their journey encouraged delay, the forest of the elves was such a place. Drax's guidance proved invaluable, allowing the pair to make excellent time even through the thick and untamed woodland, but Gwyn resisted her urge to continue the driving pace she had demanded in the open wilds. They foraged as they went, drawing renewal from the land's abundance. Hiking through all the daylight hours made for strenuous exercise, but their beasts added back their reserves over the following days, returning to healthy vigor from the rawboned paucity they had suffered on their northward race.

Gwyn's sleep was deep and untroubled throughout their journey through the forest. Two weeks after leaving Drax's village behind, the evening brought an end to their hike at the edge of a clearing formed of a nearly perfect circle of hadun trees. Gwyn stood just outside, eyeing the space dubiously as she struggled between the sense that haduns brought good fortune and her people's teaching that any kind of ring in a forest was a space to be avoided. Drax, already inside, beckoned her into the clearing and assured her it would be safe enough, his expression amused if a bit patronizing.

That night, Gwyn woke to the sound of gentle singing and softly-plucked strings. Looking to the east, she made out the silhouettes of a few slender beings resting on the grass and in the lower branches of trees at the edge of the clearing. A cloud of fireflies surrounded the group, layering a pulsing glow of green on the dim red of her fire's embers. Gwyn sat up, and the figures went suddenly silent, their eyes flashing with reflected light as they stared at her. One of the figures dropped from the lower branches of a broad hadun tree and approached her. Without thinking, she sprang up and grabbed her sword.

"Fear not," the advancing elf encouraged her. "We will not harm you. Any friend of Lady Daruneh is welcome here." He spoke the Atlund tongue with a strange, rolling accent.

Gwyn kept her sword before her, scanning the clearing for other threats. Drax sat near the dying fire, his head nodding on his chest. For all his lack of military discipline, it was unlike him to sleep while on watch.

"He is unhurt as well," the elf assured, coming to stand at a respectful distance, but still well within her lunging range. He showed no fear.

"What is this about?" Gwyn demanded. "How do you know of Daruneh?"

"The Lady has traveled broadly through these forests over many years. She is beloved by many elves. I bring a message from her."

"Why not speak to me herself? And why bewitch my friend?"

"We do not question her reasons. Her instructions did not mention the exile, so we give him rest while we speak. He has achieved great power, but the curse of his tribe leaves him weak to our ways."

Gwyn felt affronted this interloper would take advantage of Drax's sentence and wanted to threaten the elf with a reckoning if the wizard didn't recover, but the knowledge of elves' sovereign powers over strangers within their domain kept her silent. "How can you prove you really speak for Daruneh?"

"She said you were clever and suspicious enough to ask. I am to tell you that Karon has mountain crocuses growing in every stray corner."

Gwyn glanced to her saddlebags where she kept the blossom the boy had given her, pressed between parchment layers and tucked into the small box containing the letter from home.

"Go on," she allowed.

"Lady Daruneh says she knows of the enemy's intrusion in your dreams. She suspects he takes the opportunity for slander. She only wants you to know her silence is not lack of care. She fears if she communicates to you, the enemy will follow her mind to pierce the veil she maintains over you."

Gwyn considered this. It seemed reasonable, given what little she knew. She also knew, as did any adult who'd grown from such a petulant child, how thin was the margin between a reason and an excuse. "Is that all?" she asked.

The elf nodded. "Our task is done. Sleep now, both of you. We think you will need your rest, and no harm may find you here."

Gwyn focused her will, wary of an attack on her mind as zil'basts had tried in her past, but she felt no such coercion. The elf turned his back and paced silently away to the tress. His companions resumed their songs, and the warrior eased softly back into restful sleep.

Gwyn and Drax spent two more weeks in the Elven Forest, during which the enchanter spoke but little, usually offering only directions, reports, or an occasional jest. Nevertheless, Gwyn noted a change in her elven friend. Since the confrontation in his village, the last of the formality and bombast had dropped from his speech with her, unless he meant it for humor, and though he still granted her plenty of physical room, he no longer seemed subtly guarded when there was need to come near her. In time she grew to accept and even appreciate his familiarity, cementing her spoken vow that he become one of her own people.

They caught a few, fleeting glimpses of other elves through the trees, but none approached the pair. In the first week they heard calls from either side for a time, proving they were followed. Gwyn grew wary of an attack, though Drax assured they would be safe as long as they did no harm; after a few hours the calls always died away without incident. Still, Gwyn noted puzzlement crossing the elf's features on a few occasions, and at length she asked Drax what concerned him.

"Boundaries between our tribes aren't fixed on maps like your people's," he answered, "but I remember roughly whose regions I'm in, at least for now. I'm staying well clear of any permanent settlements, but we've been in *somebody's* foraging lands since we left my village, hunting, too, for the tribes whose beliefs allow it. We're crossing large swaths, though, where I don't see any sign of it."

"Isn't that the way of your people?" Gwyn asked.

"To a human, certainly, but *I* should be able to spot something. And in some tribes' lands I have, but others, nothing. Like they're hiding close to home, or migrated away."

"Why would they do that?"

"I don't know," Drax admitted. "It likely doesn't affect us either way, but it's puzzling."

Gwyn led Thunderhead and Bully across a narrow gully, carefully following in Drax's footsteps and appreciating the simpler answers she seemed to get in their new rapport. "Probably doesn't affect us," she agreed, "but trust your instincts. You're the expert in these parts."

Drax looked over his shoulder at Gwyn, his expression oddly sardonic, but he only nodded and continued leading the way.

Through the second week they began foraging more than they needed each day, putting aside what stores Drax believed would keep the best in security for their final leg of travel through the more rugged forests of Gwyn's homeland. In all, two months had passed since their departure from Finn's station when they passed into the western foothills and the trees began to thin out.

Summiting a particularly bald prominence, Gwyn surveyed the lands eastward to see the edge of the forest marching away like a dark green line, demarking a carpet of green to the south from a dun plain to the north only now beginning to thaw. They kept to the valleys where water was more plentiful and brush cover was thicker, ever watching the peaks for signs they might be surveilled, but they saw no one. Meanwhile, they sought landmarks from Evix's map to verify his instructions as they went. Within two days they could hear the mighty Sharai tumbling down slopes and cataracts onto the plain. Another day of picking through passes and draws, occasionally retracing their steps and reinterpreting Evix's meaning or artwork, and they had found the narrow, twisting canyon that led to their destination.

Gwyn observed the high plateau from cover for nearly an hour before feeling satisfied no guards of her people waited in hiding. At last she hastened with her charges across the five mile stretch at a trot, ever watchful, before finally descending a long slope down into the dark pine and poplar forests of Atlund.

In some ways this would be the riskiest leg of the journey. Though by now the cruel Wind had ceased and even the northern lands had begun their long, wide turn from winter into spring, and though true enemies should be nil, these woods would be thick with logging and hunting parties, any of whom were likely to approach and question two strangers traveling in secret through their lands. Gwyn knew any of these encounters would end peacefully with her allowed to go on her way, at least if Atlund remained as she remembered it. Nevertheless, Daruneh's enemy, which she still believed to be hers as well, seemed content to allow her return, and this seemed all the more reason to keep it secret while she could. She led Drax higher up the slopes, moving slowly with constant breaks to listen for others moving in the woods. They kept so far from civilized lands they were regularly followed by mountain lions and heard wolves ringing their camp more than once, but they kept the mounts close and stayed wary, and apart from one stubborn wolf that had to be chased away with thrown sticks and pinecones, they had no danger. Even so, a journey that would have taken ten or eleven days on the roads, five for a courier exchanging his horse at every post, stretched over two weeks before Gwyn realized she knew the forest around her and could guide Drax with the confidence of memory through the foothills toward the place of her birth.

An easy hour from her village, Gwyn called a halt near a path of hardpacked earth under trodden leaves and pine needles. This was one of Tehgil's patrol routes, showing signs of recent use, so there could be no doubt the old warrior would be along before the close of day. Actually, Gwyn had to admit, there was *some* doubt. By avoiding any contact with her people on the journey through the forest, she had insulated herself from any news of the goings-on in Atlund. If there was real trouble, Tehgil was sure to be in the thick of it, and since she'd seen no signs of battle nearby, that meant he could be far from home. Or lying dead in ditch or barrow. Nevertheless, Gwyn knew she had no hope of containing the news of her homecoming if she simply walked through the gates of her village; she hoped by crossing paths with Tehgil in the woods she might contrive a way to make her final approach inconspicuous, and this was worth the risk of losing a few hours if, by nightfall, her first mentor hadn't appeared.

An hour past noon Gwyn heard footsteps on the path to the north. It sounded like three men. Gwyn scowled. Still, in her absence it was natural Tehgil would take on other young warriors to train, and anyone with him would be trustworthy. Staying concealed as best she could in the early spring brush, she peered down the leafy aisle toward the sounds.

At last men came into view around a bend in the trail, and Gwyn immediately withdrew behind the bole of the nearest tree.

"What's wrong," Drax muttered, his voice barely audible, his Atlund dialect now passable if heavily accented.

"They're not my clan," Gwyn replied. "They're in Kart family tartan, days away from their holdings." She hazarded a glance back to the trail. The men were a furlong away and not particularly alert, but they were armed as for patrol. She ground her teeth at the sight of Kart warriors marching Candon lands, her ancestral home, as if they had the right. True, the clans were friendly, there hadn't been bloodshed on any greater scale than a family feud in a hundred years, but even if Kart had allied with Candon in some struggle, armed men should have a Candon warrior leading them in Candon lands, or at least wear sashes of Candon plaid to show allegiance. In particular, despite her ignorance of the nuances of interclan politics, she recalled Clan Kart was the wealthiest by far of the western clans, and Tehgil had always voiced suspicion of their leadership.

A few generations back the Kart chieftain had tried merely to send money in support of some martial cause instead of committing warriors, and some in the west still scorned them for it even though it had passed beyond the memory of anyone still living.

What could this intrusion mean? In light of what she already knew, her mind ran to a thousand possibilities, all of them bad. Through two hundred yards of brush the men had little chance of spotting her little band, but as they neared it would grow impossible to stay hidden. "Can you conceal us somehow?" she finally asked Drax, the hush of her voice doing nothing to diminish her urgency.

The elf shook his head. "Not enough time."

Gwyn's mind raced. The distance closed by the second. Whoever these Kart men were, she had competed against them every year at Clanmeet, or against their brothers at the very least, and she knew how they were trained. If she and Drax moved now, they might slip away undetected, but surrounded by brush and leaf litter, the horses and mule might as well be an army crashing through the forest; there was no way they wouldn't be heard, no way the noises of the massive Thunderhead or laden Bully would be mistaken for a deer or other wild animal.

Looking to Drax with something like genuine regret, an expression which seemed to confound the expectant wizard, Gwyn mouthed, "I'm sorry. Improvise." With that, she shoved the hapless elf out onto the trail.

Chapter XII

The patrolling men immediately cried out in consternation. "Stop! What's that? Who goes there?"

"Hahah…" Drax forced awkwardly. "Just a traveler, you know, no need for alarm," he called, holding still and keeping his hands in plain view as the Kart men dashed down the last hundred yards toward him. Gwyn heard them and used the noise of their rapid motion to cover her own steps as she crept to the north, positioning herself to line up at the guards' right flank once they drew near to Drax.

"Hold still there!" the lead patrolman called as he ran.

"Holding, holding," Drax assured, "don't want any trouble."

"Is that an elf?" one of the guards asked as they slowed to a walk seven or eight yards from Drax. "By all the hells, I think that *is* an elf! Never seen one before, have you?"

From her hiding place, Gwyn observed the guards. Two appeared fit, but the one bringing up the rear was puffing audibly.

Casting the last speaker an angry look, the patrol leader

turned back to Drax. "Where's your pass?"

"Pass? I didn't know I needed one," Drax stammered.

"You can't get across the Sharai without a pass," the third guard insisted through his heavy breathing. "Every bridge is guarded."

Gwyn watched through the brush as Drax glanced about, obviously expecting her to do something. Unfortunately, her armor, sword, and hammer still hung uselessly on Thunderhead's saddle, leaving only her dirk against the spears of the patrol. She could still see no way to subdue the men without both severe bloodshed of her own countrymen, Kart clan though they were, and revealing her identity, so she tensed her muscles and waited to see what the elf would come up with.

"Oh, *that* pass," Drax exclaimed with an affected palm to his forehead. "I've been on the roads so long without anyone asking, I forgot all about it. I think I left it in my saddlebags; right this way, gentlemen. So sorry for the confusion…"

Drax continued to mutter apologies and pleasantries as he led the men slowly down the path to the south, closer to the horses. Gwyn could see the wariness in the leader's stance, but his suspicion and gaze were locked on Drax. The other two didn't show much concern over the sudden encounter and followed only a couple paces behind. This seemed the best moment she would get.

Pulling her hood down as far as she dared without blocking her vision, Gwyn burst into the path behind the patrol, aiming a savage kick into the breathless man's crotch from behind. It connected, and he doubled over, dropping his spear and wheezing now for a more acute reason. "Nobody moves, everybody lives," she commanded, pitching her voice down as much as she could manage. "Eyes and weapons on the ground."

Drax ceased his bumbling pretense and took a defensive

stance, the amber and gold ring on his right hand sparking ominously.

"What is this?" the patrol leader demanded, his voice venomous, as Drax reached his left hand forward to claim the man's spear. Gwyn, meanwhile, moved toward the remaining guard's back and laid her dirk across his throat. "Drop that sp–"

Gwyn rarely underestimated an enemy. The wheezing guard was fast, and his ability to shrug off pain prodigious. Wasting no time to recover his spear and bring the larger weapon to bear, he whipped out his own dirk in a blink and leaped at Gwyn, the point flashing toward her right eye.

Gwyn barely ducked in time, the point driving back her hood to reveal her wild, red tresses and feminine facial features. The middle guard gasped at the revelation as he stepped back and brought the blade of his spear on line. The dirk-wielding guard, meanwhile, seemed to pay Gwyn's gender no heed as he pulled back his weapon with deftness, just enough to avoid entangling in Gwyn's hood, and drove into a reverse stab toward her collarbone. She rolled to the right as the spearpoint sought her, lashing out with her legs to trap the dirk guard's knees and ankles and send him hurtling face first to the ground. A thunderclap smote the air, followed by a scream, as the patrol leader felt the lethal consequence of lunging at the self-proclaimed world's greatest enchanter. Gwyn braced her fists on the ground and pulled her legs free from the guard she'd tripped, whipping them behind her to gain range on the last standing guard and his flicking spearpoint.

"Gwyn!" Drax shouted as Gwyn gathered her feet under her. She looked at the elf, as did the last guard, briefly, and saw the spear he tossed to her sail to within arm's reach. She dropped her dirk and caught the longer weapon, pointing it not toward her standing opponent but at the neck of the man on the ground. Her eyes did her talking, and the last guard standing could swear he saw a strange light sparking in them as he dropped his spear.

"They've seen your face," Drax stated, his tone both flat and heavy.

"You yelling out my name just now didn't help matters," Gwyn replied.

The elf grimaced. "Sorry. I didn't know what else—"

"It's done now," Gwyn interrupted. The guard on the ground seemed wise enough not to move with the spearpoint pricking his skin, and the other looked no more inclined to continue the fight. Gwyn motioned to the patrol leader with her head and pitched her voice to Drax without taking her eyes off the guards. "Will he live?"

With guarded motions, Drax knelt down and felt for breath and heartbeat. He shook his head. "Too late. I'm sorry. He went for the spear, and I knew I couldn't outmatch his strength."

"You'll hang for this," the prone guard growled, his words muffled by the loam in his face.

"Shut it, Deflin," the other patrolman urged. "I'd rather not join him." He paused. "Gwyn of Candon. I take it you don't remember me."

The warrior narrowed her eyes. "Should I?"

"I mustered in your village before the fight against Kellgore. We trained together some. Vigurd is my name."

Gwyn made a careful survey of his features, but no memory came to her. Still, if he knew her from that war, his memory would be of an even more reckless killer than the woman that stood before him now. "Then you know I'll kill you if I have to," she threatened.

Vigurd nodded. "You're still a hero to many here. I don't expect you came all the way back just looking to kill patrollers. If you'll give up the elf—"

Her growing bond with Drax notwithstanding, Gwyn was shocked at how strongly she had to fight the urge to run Vigurd through at the threat. Instead she proclaimed, "He is Clan Candon now. A threat to his life will cost both of you yours. You are armed for war and marching in lands that are not your own; we're well within our rights. I'll speak for the elf in clan council."

The prostrate guard, Deflin, started to laugh, so Gwyn leaned on the spear, just enough to convince him to silence. "Things have changed a lot since you left, Candon," Vigurd explained. "An appeal to law will get you killed."

"Why say so, then?" Drax questioned. "Why not let us bring you in and let Gwyn march to her death?"

Vigurd glanced at the elf. "Fear of my own life, for one," he admitted. "And...I don't like what's happened. Maybe I figure it's better for me and mine if Gwyn finds her way to the people trying to put things right."

"Traitor!" Deflin spat through the dirt. "You'll pay for this, Vigurd, I'll–"

Gwyn flipped the spear and brought the butt down on the back of Deflin's head, and he went quiet. She'd killed enough to know the man was alive, but she poked him with the spear haft a few times to ensure he was truly unconscious before turning her attention back to Vigurd. The only time she'd let men live whom it was in her better judgment to kill, her reward had been one poorly-aimed crossbow bolt away from death. Still, those had been known highwaymen while these were countrymen, and one a former ally if his claims were true. "Get us into my village without anyone knowing who I am," she offered, "and keep this one's mouth shut, no matter what it takes, and you get to live. Play us false, and you'd best be far away when you do, or no matter what happens to us, one of us will kill you first."

Vigurd nodded his understanding, then helped Drax to bind and gag Deflin while Gwyn kept her spearpoint on his back in case he came around prematurely. After that they moved him into the bushes in case anyone wandered by, then dragged the slain patrol leader into a deeper thicket where Drax cremated the body as only a skilled wizard could. The elf wept, briefly and silently, as he worked; Gwyn said nothing about it but felt a strange heartsickness over the death, something like regret, but more sorrowful somehow. She wondered if it could be remorse.

This grim task completed, they returned to Deflin's bound form, now stirring. "I know you ordered me to keep him from talking," Vigurd said, "but if we drag him into town like that he won't have to speak a word to get us executed."

Gwyn nodded. The Clan Kart man was right. His bound comrade came around enough to realize his predicament and rolled onto his back, glaring daggers at Gwyn. She couldn't trust him to be silent, even under pain of death. "Drax, what about that forgetting magic you prepared in the bandit town. Could you work it now?"

Drax looked upward, and she could tell by the twitching of his eyes and the tilting of his head he was calculating the possibilities. "I probably could," he replied, "but I don't think it will help us. Against those raiders, by the time their companions showed up to ask why two men were dead, we'd have been long gone, with nobody who *could* remember nearby to challenge their lack of a story. If I use it on Deflin, he'll be asked to corroborate whatever lies we tell, and all he'll have is a span of missing memory."

"You can't make a false memory, then?"

"With a month to research in a well-appointed Southern library, maybe, but today? No."

"We have legends of wizards putting people to sleep for years," Vigurd offered.

Drax began to protest, then paused. "Actually, that could work. Not for years; he'd die of starvation, but for a couple of days, maybe longer if someone forces water down his throat without choking him."

Gwyn sighed. This could only buy them a little time. Killing Deflin, on the other hand, and combining his death into whatever lie they concocted to cover up his sergeant's disappearance, was a permanent solution. Still, they'd already killed one man. How many lives was her secret worth? She looked to Drax and nodded.

"Does he carry anything personal to him?" Drax asked Vigurd. "Some token or talisman he doesn't go without, like it's part of who he is?"

"Uh, yes, I think he has a lock of his sweetheart's hair in his belt pouch." Deflin started to struggle and protest against the gag.

"Get it," Gwyn ordered.

Vigurd rifled Deflin's pouch and found the lock of hair, tied at either end with a narrow strip of lavender cloth. Drax took it and removed himself a few paces away, piled up some pine needles for a cushion, and sat with his head bowed over the lover's token.

While he worked, Gwyn and Vigurd discussed the more mundane aspects of their next move. "If your friend hides his ears well," Vigurd claimed, "I can get you both through the gates without any questions, but what am I supposed to say about one man missing and another brought in unconscious?"

"Suppose your friend had a fall and struck the back of his head on a rock or a hard tree root," Gwyn answered after a few moments thought. She hadn't had occasion to tell a barefaced lie in a surprising length of time, but in her younger years they had been her secondly-favored way out of trouble, right behind violence. She continued, "You stayed to guard him while your captain went for help. When Drax and I came through with horses it seemed better to let us carry Deflin back than to keep waiting."

"But nobody's seen the captain."

"Right, and you're more concerned than anyone. In fact you started to worry the closer we got to the village without crossing paths with him and the help he was supposed to be bringing back. You'll be frantic to find him as soon as Deflin is settled. Can you carry that lie?"

The young man hesitated. "I don't know. I'll try. Even if I can, it's just a matter of time before something goes wrong. Since you're not coming back as yourself, you'll be thought a stranger, and folk are likely to blame you for all this, just by coincidence."

"Let me worry about that," Gwyn rebutted. Her unvoiced thought was that whatever changes had befallen her homeland, the people in her village were not likely to show great enthusiasm for solving the disappearance of a Kart man in their lands in defiance of time-honored law and tradition. Of course, Vigurd might have given her a report to help confirm or deny that suspicion, but she only barely trusted his instinct at self-preservation, much less his perspective on the upheavals in her home.

"Fine," Vigurd replied, "but what about Deflin? If you aren't killing him now, then I assume you won't let him die under the elf's sleep magic either, so he has to wake up eventually. Then I'm as condemned as you are."

"I know," she snapped, exasperated. "Just give me a couple days to plan my next move. If you hold up your end, I won't leave you to the noose or the headsman." She could see Vigurd was not satisfied with this answer, but he had no more grounds to demand a better one than she had to give it. Drax continued his silent work, and Deflin had given up struggling against the ropes. Vigurd seemed eager to impress her, and her thoughts drifted back to Daruneh's words about her influence over fighters. She wondered if this might inspire him to honesty in some subtle way, but she couldn't be sure enough to risk opening her ears to potential lies, not with so much at stake. One question, though, she could no longer delay. "Do you know, or remember, a man called Tehgil?" she asked.

Vigurd gave a brief chuckle. "Between Clanmeets and the Forest Campaign I don't expect I'll ever forget him, but they aren't memories I need much yet. I see him about the village most days."

Gwyn's chest suddenly loosened, and it was her first realization it had been tight. Relief that Tehgil still lived, whatever else had befallen, spread through her, steadied her. She looked down the path, yearning to be home.

Drax took another hour to finish his spell, then asked Gwyn's help to close Deflin's obstinate fist over the lock of hair. As soon as she'd done it, the man's eyes rolled back in his head before the lids drooped closed and his muscles went slack. After that, Drax twined the tied lock through Deflin's fingers and ensured it was secure. "Don't let anyone take that from him," Drax ordered Vigurd. "He'll wake up within the hour if that happens, you understand?"

Vigurd nodded.

Gwyn thought Drax looked and sounded weary, but not utterly spent as she'd seen him before. She recalled the importance of a deep connection to the talisman he'd enchanted to render her invisible to orcs during the siege of the Capital and his remaining capacity to launch a full magical assault on zil'basts after doing it. Maybe one day she'd muster her patience and ask the enchanter to explain this pattern.

They tied Deflin to Flamewind and hid Gwyn's sword as best they could. The rest of her gear was new or nondescript enough not to be noticed. She and Drax both donned their hoods, and in less than an hour the western gate of Gwyn's village was in view. Her breath caught for a moment in her throat. Two years ago, when she turned her back on those timber walls in the predawn gray, she'd neither known nor cared if she would see the place, or anyone in it, ever again. Now, the realization that the old village still stood in one piece, with the buds of its central hadun tree showing like a breath of green above the houses, nearly brought tears to her eyes. It took immense effort to let Vigurd lead the band forward as though she'd never been there, to keep herself from spurring Thunderhead to a gallop straight back to her home.

Vigurd vouched for Gwyn and Drax and claimed to have examined their travel passes in the woods. Gwyn ground her teeth at the thought of needing permission to go about freely in her own home but remained silent out of pure necessity. Vigurd plied the gate guards with the deception Gwyn had lined out earlier; he could have been more convincing, but it would serve. One of the guards, in Kart tartan, scurried off to organize a search for the captain, but the other, in proper Candon plaid, remained behind. Gwyn recognized the man and turned away from him before her face might betray her. She hoped the men of her clan were innocent of whatever madness had gripped her home, but she couldn't know for sure.

Vigurd then led them to an abandoned house, which during Gwyn's residence had been used by the clan to store shared tools and other oddments. Now it had, apparently, been converted to a sort of barracks. They dropped Deflin in his bunk; Vigurd stayed to pretend ministering to his head wound for a time before joining the search for the dead captain. No obstacle now stood between Gwyn and her home.

Lischa sat at the heavy table in her great room, sewing a patch onto the knee of Adric's favorite work trousers. Since Lirisch had grown big enough to help his father in the fields, the house had grown deafeningly quiet during the day. Even Tehgil visited only occasionally once Gwyn had left for good. Sometimes she considered taking her work to the common house where the widows and women with grown children tended to gather, but she didn't know how to relate to them. She'd first been widowed at such an early age that her peers hadn't known quite what to do with her, and, in hindsight, she had to admit her obsession with getting retribution for her dead husband hadn't helped. That attitude hadn't changed even after she remarried, and over the years the distance had only grown. She couldn't help but think of Gwyn and how her insistence that the girl be trained as a warrior had isolated her from the other girls of the village in a similar way. Now Gwyn had gone off to fight as though the whole weight of the world was hers to bear, not unlike her father. The sins of the parents always devolved to their children.

Despite her solitude, Lischa was only a little surprised to hear a knock at her door. Probably any of a handful of neighbors wanting to borrow or trade something, or one of the town gossips desperate to share news of the commotion a few minutes ago at the west gate and finding no closer intimate about. She was much surprised, however, to see a stranger when she opened the door, a small man in a blue robe of heavy silk, a fabric rarely seen in these parts. His face was shadowed by a hood, his stance uneasy. The knife tucked into Lischa's sash was more tool than weapon, but her hand strayed to it as she asked, "Who are you?"

"I'm sorry to startle you, woman," the man answered, his voice clear but soft. "I have news of your daughter, Gwyn."

Lischa's breath caught in her throat. "My Gwyn?" she heard herself say. Her heart pounded with a flood of emotion. Was Gwyn alive? Where was she? If she was dead, would Lischa be relieved to at least know? What if she lived but was ill or injured, or in some other plight? Did she need her mother? How far might Lischa have to go?

The notion that the stranger before her was sure to answer these questions commanded her mind but made no impression on her tumultuous heart. The feelings rushed so fast she felt tears burn her eyes.

"Yes," the man answered into her uncertainty. "It's good news, I swear, but whatever happens I beg you to keep calm and quiet. May my friend and I enter?"

"Yes, of– Friend?" Lischa could see no one else.

The man motioned to his left, and a cloaked figure stepped into view, its hood reaching nearly to the lintel of the doorway. Lischa gave back a step in alarm, a layer of fear now covering her shifting emotions. Her hand gripped her knife. The figure raised a finger to its lips as it stepped across the threshold. The small man followed and shut the door behind him. The tall figure drew back its hood, revealing fine features framed by wild red tresses, all dominated by the most piercing green eyes Lischa had ever seen, and ones she knew for twenty years.

Lischa threw open her arms, tears flowing down her cheeks. "Gw–!"

Gwyn clapped her hand across Lischa's mouth. "Half the village probably saw us come to the door," she cautioned. "I can't afford anyone to hear you shouting my name."

Only then did Lischa note the changes in her daughter. The brash defiance in her expression hadn't departed, but it was tempered somehow, married to an implacable confidence that showed in her face and posture. It was subtle; many people would not have noticed, but she had lived among warriors all her life, and she knew her daughter: the child she had birthed, the youth she had made, and the woman who stood now before her. Lischa nodded as her tears continued to run over her daughter's hand still covering her mouth.

Gwyn lowered that hand, and as soon as it had moved

out of the way, Lischa wrapped her arms around Gwyn, gripping her with every ounce of her might, pressing her head into her eldest's collarbone. Even if Gwyn turned away, never to return, Lischa would pour every embrace, every affection she had denied the child during her harsh upbringing into this moment. Though she had always been a woman of few words, and even now those sounds refused to force their way past her tears, Gwyn would know how dearly Lischa loved her, whether she wanted to or not. Her joy nearly overcame her senses when she felt Gwyn's arms wrap around her in return, the earthy and acrid odors of long travel washing over her, piquing her nostrils, though she did not care, any more than she did for Gwyn's urgent secrecy or the stranger she had brought to the door. Her wayward daughter had come home, and nothing else mattered.

"Mother," Gwyn said, only slightly easing her embrace, "I'll explain everything, I promise, but I need you to open the stable door and lead my animals in, then close the shutters so I can get them settled without being seen."

Gwyn's voice carried no tone of disrespect, but Lischa couldn't help hearing the note of command, the assumption that her words would be obeyed. What had befallen her daughter in these two years? Lischa smiled as she finally stepped back from Gwyn and wiped the tears from her face, realizing this was the wrong question. Short of death itself, nothing would "befall" her Gwyn; *she* did the befalling. Finding her voice at last, she replied, "Of course, anything you need," before walking toward the back of the house and its exit to the stables. Before turning out of sight, she couldn't help looking back at her daughter, a long-lost smile still established on her lips.

"Shall I go help her?" Drax asked.

Gwyn stared down the hallway where her mother had

gone. Her heart roiled with emotions, some that seemed to hail from years long past. Trying to think through them, she looked down at the elf. "Not just now," she answered. "Once Mother has everything closed up, you can help me unload our beasts. Then I'll make proper introductions."

Drax wore a wry expression. "How do you feel?"

Gwyn scowled. "Your face says you knew I wouldn't like that question, so why ask it?"

"That was reason enough," the elf quipped with a grin, but then his expression grew serious. "Honestly, you haven't said much about your home or your leaving it, but enough to say it was difficult. Coming home can be hard."

Gwyn nodded at the obvious pain and irony in Drax's words. "We knew my homecoming would be more welcome than yours, and my leaving was easier, too. At the time I didn't think I had any choice, but I've heard enough stories now to see how much choice I really had." She took a deep breath, filling her nose with the familiar scents of her childhood home. "Maybe I should have thought more carefully."

Drax laughed nearly out loud. "Story of your life, Gwyn the Savage."

"Do I need to go back to threatening to kill you?" She immediately regretted the jest, as the mention of death, even in this context, bludgeoned the elf's expression with guilt over the patrol captain. In all their battles together, this was the first time Drax took more blood on his own hands than Gwyn did. She started to apologize, but Lischa's return cut her off.

"It's all ready for you," the older woman announced. "Hurry back. And take care to snuff the lantern when you're done." Gwyn smiled at the motherly instruction as she led Drax through the house to the stables.

As the preeminent warrior in the village, Girahl's house, while not so lavishly appointed as merchants' or the most successful farmers', had been one of the larger in the village in the hopes that he would fill it with strong offspring, and against the west side was built a stable of half a dozen stalls for his own horses and those of his children who still lived at home. Adric had taken down the northmost partition to make one larger stall for his plow horse, and occasionally Tehgil had boarded extra mounts in the other stalls for warriors on his patrols that didn't have their own homes yet, but Gwyn's horses had been the only other permanent residents. Now, as expected, the space stood empty until Adric returned from the fields. The southern stall was crammed with wood scraps and tools, but the remaining three took only a few minutes to clear. Upon seeing how cramped for space Thunderhead would be in a regular stall, built for the smaller Atlund breeds, Gwyn felt tempted to commandeer the plow horse's double slot, then chided herself for considering such an offense. Old habits died hard.

The horses and mule had remained in fine condition since leaving the Elven Forest. The mountain trails through the Atlund woods had been difficult at times, but nothing compared to the grueling pace Gwyn had forced northward across the plains, and she and Drax had walked much of the time, as much out of the necessity of carefully picking their paths as for the horses' sake, so the beasts were well rested. Even Bully's load had lightened considerably as their supplies steadily dwindled. Gwyn and Drax unsaddled and unloaded the animals with the unconscious movements born of endless repetition, then spared only a few minutes to briefly rub them down before ensuring their food and water troughs were full, snuffing the lantern, and returning to the house and Lischa sitting at the main table. Gwyn laid her great sword on the heavy planks, the one piece of her gear too noble to be left in the stable.

"So who is your friend?" Lischa asked as the pair took

seats on the surrounding benches.

"Mother, this is Drax. He's an elf. We've fought together, and he's… I…" She glanced at Drax. "I take him as my oath-brother."

Drax, unfamiliar with Atlund customs, showed only little surprise given Gwyn's vows to his tribe in the Forest, but Lischa's eyes widened. Drax doffed his hood and tucked back his hair so his pointed ears were no longer hidden, and with the shadows fully dispelled from his face Lischa gazed pointedly at the tint of violet to his gray eyes. "Swearing such oaths across clans would raise eyebrows enough to some," Lischa remarked. "An elf? The elders will balk."

"Let them," Gwyn rebutted. "He–"

"Yes," Lischa agreed, "let them. I didn't mean… I was just caught by surprise." She turned to Drax. "You helped Gwyn get home to me. For that, everything I have is yours; you could be king of all the South or the lowest worm of the dirt for all I care."

Drax appeared to want to say something, but he simply nodded his thanks and took Lischa's hand as she offered it across the table.

"Now," Lischa continued, turning back to Gwyn, "tell me everything."

Gwyn shook her head, then saw a hurt expression cowl her mother's eyes. Gwyn remembered her blunt refusals to speak to anyone about the brutalities of her time in the woods when she fled her home on her sixteenth birthday and the concern her willful isolation had caused her family. "I will," Gwyn said, reassuring, "but first I need *you* to tell *me* everything. I got your letter some five months ago. I came back as quick as I could, never mind some trouble along the way. With what little I've seen, I can tell a lot has gone wrong since you wrote it. Vassin must be dead."

Lischa nodded, her face sad. "Only a couple of weeks

after we wrote to you. Things fell apart after that. The Kingmoot was little better than a riot, it's said. The king had been in fine health, and many suspected poison when he fell ill so suddenly, but nobody could guess who would do such a thing, or why. Any clan that put forth their chieftain as a candidate for the crown came under immediate suspicion; people began throwing accusations, the ones accused would storm out over the offense. Every time a king passes, some in the Conclave argue we don't need the monarchy anymore, and with all the chaos, their voices were stronger. But this time some of the elders claimed if Atlund no longer needs a king, maybe it no longer needs a Conclave. Some saw the threat to dissolve the Conclave as more than harsh words and mustered for war, angling to besiege the Citadel to force the outcome they wanted. Flaring tempers reignited ages-old clan feuds, and renegades started raids for livestock against their adversaries. Some skirmishes broke out, and the bloodshed only made the factions in the Kingmoot dig in harder."

"By Terillah," Drax muttered.

"We're an honorable people," Gwyn offered, "but proud and headstrong. I should know."

"Weeks went by with no progress," Lischa continued. "As members of Vassin's clan, our warriors helped hold the roads to the Citadel, and no other clan was reckless enough to strike the first blow. Everything was a stalemate until Clan Kart put forth a candidate and demanded another vote. Somehow, he got the support he needed and squeaked onto the throne."

"Who?" Gwyn asked.

"Haric of Kart."

"Haric? Why do I know that name?"

Lischa made a mirthless chuckle. "You bloodied his nose when you were eight."

Gwyn quickly searched her memory. Within the span of

a whole year of her childhood, the hint that she'd punched him in the nose wasn't nearly specific enough for recollection, but along with the victim being from Clan Kart, her mind snapped to the Clanmeet festival and a boy a couple of years her senior crawling under the feast table trying to look up skirts. "That scrawny, little pervert?" Gwyn exploded. "How in all the hells did he sway the elders of the Conclave?"

Lischa scowled with a shrug. "Nobody knows for sure. Those against the monarchy altogether seemed to think Haric a fair compromise, since they expected him to be weak enough to control, but the votes that put him over the top were the eastern clan elders. They backed him almost unanimously, for no reason. Early on people whispered about some secret deal, but once Haric and Kart took the Citadel it wasn't long before the whispering stopped. One way or another."

Gwyn's eyes narrowed. "What do you mean 'one way or another'?"

"Most stopped talking on their own…after the loudest ones disappeared. Or had accidents."

"Madness," Gwyn spat and grabbed her sword, standing from the bench and turning toward the stable.

"Gwyn, where are you going?" Drax questioned.

"I'm riding to the Citadel, raising the hue and cry all the way. I should be able to raise a couple brigades worth of decent warriors between here and there. We don't have to stand for this!"

"It won't work, Gwyn," Lischa cautioned, her voice urgent. "Haric keeps the Citadel locked up tight, and he has defenses I haven't told you about."

"Like Clan Kart patrols watching the woods and roads?" Drax hazarded.

"That's only the beginning," Lischa confirmed. Gwyn

turned back and sat down at the bench, leaning her back against the table's edge. "We know your war in the Southern Kingdoms came to an end," Lischa went on, "or at least to a major pause. I guess some men didn't have anything left to go home to; we've had mercenary companies crossing the bridges for the last couple of months. Every one that came in, we hoped to see you among them, but… Anyway, Haric has hardly turned any of them away. He's opened the coffers of Atlund to keep them here, under his command. He sends them wherever he wants a heavy hand, and that frees him to send his own clan's warriors or other loyalists to keep an eye on places where he needs to be more subtle."

"So they're funding their own jailers," Drax uttered, echoing his assessment of Finn's Station. He fixed Gwyn with a hard look. "Little bit different when it's your own people, huh?"

"Not for you, apparently," Gwyn growled.

Drax shrugged.

"I still say we just deal with this treasonous king now," Gwyn insisted. "I have even better reputation with the Southerners than I do with Atlunders. I can talk those mercenaries into backing me over Haric, or at least getting out of my way. If the eastern clans don't like it, they know where to find me." The thought of winning the men over to her cause had started from a mundane enough strategy, but in saying it Gwyn once again remembered Daruneh's words. The image of leading all the armies of Atlund came unbidden to her mind, but she thrust the thought aside.

Lischa shook her head. "You've changed, Gwyn, but not enough. You think no Atlunder would have spine or rage enough to try that until you came back? I still haven't finished. Haric has a wizard, too."

"What?" Gwyn exclaimed, sitting up. "From where?

No wizard from the South left before I did; one of us would have heard of it," she concluded, turning to Drax, who nodded agreement.

Lischa was slow to answer. "If you'd stayed a bit longer after the Forest Campaign, you *would* have heard of it. Kellgore had an apprentice."

Gwyn leaped to her feet again, her heart hammering with ire. "I'll gut him right now, I swear I will, I'll–"

"No, Gwyn," Lischa insisted. "It isn't what you think. Kellgore held the boy against his will. He tried to keep his master's madness in check as he could, worked in secret trying to find a way to turn the minions back to their prior selves."

"You believe this? From Haric!?"

"It's not Haric's story," Lischa argued. "It's Vassin's. The king didn't trust him either, at first. He had him brought back secretly, in chains, to the Citadel, to test his claims."

"Vassin wouldn't have kept that from me." Gwyn grumbled.

"He wouldn't? Gwyn, you were the *first* person he thought of hiding it from. He knew what you'd do if you found out, and since he'd granted this apprentice his life, Vassin would have had to kill you over it if you came with blood on your mind."

Gwyn sighed, then squinted in puzzlement. "How do *you* know what the king was thinking?"

Lischa winced. "Curse my wagging tongue," she muttered. "Tehgil knew," she admitted, finally.

Gwyn felt a lance of pain that her oath-father would keep such a secret, but she knew he and Vassin had been right. Nothing would have stopped her from spilling this new wizard's blood if she had known. Just as nothing would stop her now. "Makes no difference," she vowed. "Haric has a wizard, well so have I."

"No no no," Drax shot back, putting up his hands. "I just got here, and I've already stumbled into more trouble than I can afford. I'm not going to war with you against people I don't even know, definitely not until we learn more."

"Learn more? What more is there? Strange wizard brought back to the Citadel in disgrace wins the king's trust and the next thing anybody knows he gets poisoned to death? How is that not enough?"

"It isn't that simple, Gwyn," Lischa cautioned. "Of course everyone suspected Dahaer when the king took ill, but he hadn't been around the king for weeks before that; he'd been back in the western mountains still trying to cure minions Kellgore left behind."

Gwyn looked at Drax, raising one eyebrow.

The elf shrugged. "I'm not saying it's impossible, but he can't be in two places at once."

"Or move from one place to another without crossing the space in between," Gwyn concluded.

"Anyway, Dahaer seemed loyal to the crown by all estimates. There's no proof he played Vassin false. He kept out of the Kingmoot altogether, and since Haric was appointed he's been just as loyal to the office."

"I still don't like it," Gwyn argued. "The whole thing stinks."

Before the debate could continue, the front door to the longhouse boomed open.

CHAPTER XIII

Gwyn readied her sword and bounded over the table, placing herself between her mother and the open doorway with the bulky silhouette now framed in its light. A band of golden sun shining through the west-facing shutters glinted on a short sword held forward, and Gwyn's gaze tunneled down to it, her mind alert for any ruse as she prepared to thwart the attack from the undersized weapon. She was vaguely aware of her mother calling something from behind her, and this distraction only increased her confusion to see the short blade tumble unexpectedly to the ground. The figure rushed her, but the arms spread wide, dropping all defense, and only at the last second did she smile and avert her guard. The arms wrapped around her, crushing her ribs, and heaved her off the ground. Pain shot through her scalp as it smacked into an overhead joist with a *thunk*.

"Dammit, Tehgil," Gwyn gasped. "That was my *head*."

"Sorry, sorry," the older warrior replied, setting Gwyn back down as Drax shut the door behind him. Tehgil stepped back, keeping his hands on Gwyn's shoulders and looking her up and down. "Little Gwyn," he sighed. "You're home. I'm so glad to see you again, I don't even know what to say."

"You said enough already," Gwyn quipped, rubbing the back of her skull. She set her sword back on the table and embraced Tehgil, firmly if less violently than he had bearhugged her. She rested her chin on his shoulder and let his familiar scent wash over her, sweat and leather and metal, not unlike her own and yet wholly different. A thousand memories flashed through her mind too quickly for any one to find purchase. "I missed you, Tehgil," she whispered.

"I'd bet we missed you more," he answered, not unkindly. He let her go and stepped back again. "You've grown, Little Gwyn. Not taller. Stronger, though. Tougher. Up here." He tapped her forehead.

"I've learned a lot. And they're things I know you and Nafar tried to teach me, but…" She shrugged. "I'm sorry," she finally admitted.

"You've learned, and you're home," Tehgil replied as he collected his dropped sword and sat at the table next to Drax, seemingly unabashed by his presence. "I won't promise not to scold you sometime for the way you left and the hurt you caused your mother, but that can wait. Today is for joy."

"I'm glad you came, Tehgil," Lischa finally spoke, "but why did you, and with your sword in your hand?"

Tehgil's smile weakened. "You should know there's no secrets around here. I heard strangers had gone into your house and that you'd closed up all the shutters. With everything going on, I had to make sure you weren't under duress."

"I'm glad you're still taking care of the house," Gwyn said in thanks.

"I've learned not to step on Adric's toes quite so much since you left," Tehgil answered, "but with him out in the fields I know he's glad of me, too, especially during planting and reaping when his days are longer than the sun's."

"I was just telling Gwyn about 'everything going on,'" Lischa said.

Tehgil nodded, his face now serious.

"Mother and my friend, Drax, here–"

"Oath-brother," Drax corrected, sitting up a bit straighter.

Tehgil turned to the elf, his eyes widening, then looked back to Gwyn. She nodded, and between two warriors, her eyes said all. "Welcome, and thank you," Tehgil said to the wizard, extending his hand. Drax clasped it.

"As I was saying," Gwyn continued, "these two had just managed to talk me out of storming the Citadel and bringing about a change in leadership. Mother hadn't got so far as explaining why *you* stood by for any of this."

"What should I have done?" Tehgil objected. "Haric's selection kept the whole nation from boiling over, and at first he didn't do anything worth fighting against. Lots of us were suspicious, but there was no proof to act on. You can't go killing people just because you don't like them."

Drax pointed to himself as he looked at Tehgil. "See? That's what *I* tell her. All the time."

Gwyn scowled at Drax. "I've killed lots of people for lots of reasons, but never *just* because I didn't like them." She paused. "What about Nafar? I can't believe his loyalty to the crown would push him to sit still for silencing critics or letting Kart warriors patrol wherever they please."

Even before Gwyn finished speaking, Tehgil and Lischa traded significant looks. Drax, despite his unfamiliarity with the pair, seemed to notice and sat up, furrowing his brow toward Gwyn. "What was that?" Gwyn demanded. "What was that look?"

"Nafar resigned from the guard as soon as Haric was crowned," Lischa explained.

"Fine," Gwyn pressed, her eyes still focused on Tehgil. "What else?"

Tehgil and Lischa looked at each other once more, then the older man turned his thick neck to gaze about the room as if the very walls might be listening. Finally, he replied, "Nafar has been gathering…how to put it?"

"Quiet dissenters," Lischa provided. "Those too honorable to be cowed but too clever to start a battle they can't win."

Tehgil nodded. "Lots of warriors from the western and central clans; others, too. Farmers, traders, a few loremasters and scholarly types, you know, men good with words."

"And women," Lischa added.

"Some," he acknowledged. "So far Nafar's cadre is trying to find out why the eastern clans were so eager to declare for Haric. I'm sort of in charge of the northwestern villages hereabout."

"Do you know a Kart man called Vigurd?" Drax interjected.

"I do," Tehgil answered.

"Can he be trusted?"

"Farther than most. *Why*?"

Drax hesitated, and Gwyn related, in succinct terms, their confrontation with the Kart patrol in the woods and Drax's short term solution.

Lischa was aghast, Tehgil merely grim. "That explains the commotion outside the western gate," the older man sighed. "Vigurd is no fool, and he agreed to tell the first lie. If he hasn't recanted it by now, he's bound to stay the course, or else his own neck is on the block.

"Deflin is a problem. He's loyal to Haric right down the line." Tehgil scowled. "I hate to say it, but things would probably be better if you'd killed him."

"Tehgil," Lischa protested.

"It crossed my mind," Gwyn agreed. She flexed her right hand, her gaze unfocused. "I don't know if I'll ever shed my fill of blood. And I can't say a man being unarmed and helpless has always stopped me. Most people would say that's wrong, but I know what I believe, and if I kill a man in cold blood, I know *why*. Just saving my own skin has never been reason enough."

A pall fell over the room at Gwyn's spoken reverie as Lischa and Tehgil remembered the girl that had left them and regarded the woman that had returned.

"Why were you coming down from the uplands anyway?" Tehgil finally asked. "How'd you get across the Sharai without getting a pass?"

If Tehgil's opinion of Vigurd and Drax's enchantment on Deflin could be trusted, Gwyn reasoned, they should be safe enough for at least the rest of the day and night. Settling in, Gwyn announced, "I guess I should start at the beginning."

Gwyn shared most of her tale forthrightly, but she didn't reveal how specific were her dreams of the condemned, nor disclose the intrusions of Daruneh and her adversary into her sleeping mind. When the time came to relate Daruneh's appearance and direction to the abbey, Gwyn found herself unwilling to admit the preternatural quality of the web into which she'd stumbled, instead portraying the woman in the cottage and the refuge of the abbey as mundane, chance occurrences. The call for information about her she was forced to tell, as it explained her desire to enter Atlund unseen, but she claimed not to have any guess as to who may have placed the bounty save the political enemies she had made in the South, and with Southern mercenaries now resident in Atlund, this explanation satisfied Tehgil and Lischa.

Both listeners had reacted predictably throughout the tale, with Tehgil showing the most interest in Gwyn's actions and training while Lischa teared occasionally at the knowledge of her daughter's pain and asked questions about her emotions during critical moments. To these inquiries Gwyn held back nothing, speaking of her thrill in battle and blood even when she knew Lischa expected fear or regret. The woman had pushed her daughter unashamedly into the warrior's life for sixteen years, and Gwyn would not shield her from the result even though she had since repented of it.

Lischa gasped aloud when Gwyn narrated her slaughter of the two outlaws in the inn, but Gwyn held her mother's gaze. "It had to be done," she averred. "I know you regret making me into the Hand of Vengeance, but I still don't. I hope you can understand that."

Lischa swallowed hard and nodded.

At last, with occasional additions from Drax, Gwyn arrived at the path in the woods west of the village, the tale of ill-fated battle she had already told.

"At least now we know where the weapons and horses from Finn's station wound up," Drax added at the end.

"What do you mean?" Tehgil asked.

"When I heard about them," Gwyn answered, "I was afraid Atlund must be in open war, but at least *that* never happened, and thanks to Terillah for small favors. So that shipment must be outfitting Haric's new mercenary friends," she finished with a sigh.

Lischa and Tehgil both shook their heads. "They came armed and armored themselves, and not with new gear," Tehgil stated. "Some had mounts, but those they did have were already well broke, and not enough to make up a herd like what you say left the South."

"It would be nice to have *one* question answered for our trouble, wouldn't it?" Drax griped.

"I have a question of my own," Lischa stated. "How long ago did you say Finn started putting together this cargo to send northward?"

"Dez didn't say precisely," Gwyn answered, looking upward as she added her time in travel to what she remembered of Dez's report. "Finn would have showed up there and started making his orders, what, a year ago, now. Does that sound right to you?" she asked Drax.

The elf nodded. "The way Dez told it, he came up to the fort with a purpose, so he may have started plans sooner, talking with contacts further in the South."

"And from your tone, it seems like you don't think Finn was in earnest when he originally said he was gathering it all for the orc wars. You think he wanted to send it up here all along."

"Yes," Gwyn answered, not seeing her mother's point. Then suddenly she sat up, her back rigid. "Finn started calling for smiths and horses at least two months before Vassin died," she realized.

"So if you're sure these supplies are related to the king's death and Haric's rise to the throne," Lischa began.

"Then it proves somebody, at the very least, *knew* the crown was going to change clans long before it happened," Tehgil concluded.

"We have to prove it, though," Drax reminded the group. "We still don't know where the shipments went or who asked for them. Without that, it's all speculation."

As Gwyn's story had ended, Lischa had cracked the shutters to check the sun and begun heating water over the hearth in large kettles before returning to the table. "The boys will be home soon," she announced. "I need to meet them on the road so they aren't too taken aback by your beasts when they stable the plow horse, and I suspect you both would have rather cleaned up from your travels before telling your stories." She pointed to the kettles over the fire.

"There won't be enough to fill the washtub for a soak of your muscles, but it will get the cleaning job done. I'll find fresh clothes for you both."

Gwyn claimed the liberty of the first bath and carried the hot kettles to the back of the house where a small washroom held a sizable copper tub and a small basin in the corner that provided for life's necessities when the Wind prevented a walk to the outhouse. As Gwyn poured the hot water into the bottom of the tub and located the rough soap and towels in their familiar places, Lischa came through the doorway, which Gwyn hadn't yet closed, with an armload of clothes that she set on top of a low cabinet.

"I don't think you've outgrown any of your old things, and some of Aldrin's clothes should fit Drax well enough. I'll just leave them here." She didn't look up, and Gwyn thought the woman seemed smaller, somehow. At last she stopped and raised her eyes to meet Gwyn's as though forcing herself. "You can't stay, can you?" she asked, her voice laden with dejection.

"Not for long," Gwyn admitted, her tone soft. "At least not yet. I'm sorry."

"Don't be," Lischa answered through misty eyes and a taut smile. "You're here now, and at least this time, when you go, I'll know… I'll know it's really your choice, and not because of my failure." She wiped her eyes and bolstered her smile. "And I know you'll come back if you can."

Gwyn set down the soap and towels on the pile of clothes and stepped toward her mother, wrapping her arms around the smaller woman. "I will," she promised. "I love you, Mama."

Lischa laughed through tears too complex to call "happy" or "sad" and finally stepped out of Gwyn's embrace. "I'd best be off to meet the boys," she said and was gone.

~ * ~

Gwyn could feel herself withdrawing as soon as Adric and her half-brothers, Aldrin and Lirisch, entered the house. All were welcoming, but despite living with Adric and Aldrin as long as she could remember, and Lirisch only a few years less, she had never bothered really knowing them. In what little attention she'd paid them at all she had been a condescending bully, and while she could now recognize how unwarranted her behavior had been, she didn't have it in her heart to build bridges in what little time she had in her childhood home.

Nevertheless, Lischa and Adric turned out the larders to celebrate Gwyn's return after Tehgil made the rounds to the village gossips to quiet them with some dissimulation. Spring always proved lean in the far north as the winter stockpiles had been consumed and the new harvest hadn't yet come in even of early crops, but they had salt pork and potatoes enough for twice their number, supplemented with a couple brook trout Lirisch had managed to catch that day, a contribution in which the youth took great and obvious pride. Adric had offered to have a goat or pig slaughtered by another villager who still owed him for some of last year's grain, but Gwyn insisted this would draw too much attention.

The family ate and talked well into the evening until Adric, sensing Gwyn's inhibition with characteristic sensitivity, insisted he and his sons needed to retire to their beds, as the morning and fields would wait for no man. He brought fresh mugs of tea to the women and whispered something in Lischa's ear before retreating; she smiled and patted his hand as he moved away. Tehgil and Drax, likewise, said their partings, man retiring to his own home and elf to Gwyn's old room. At last Gwyn sat alone at the table with her mother.

For several minutes neither spoke, drinking in the silent togetherness as the firelight pulsed through the room, it's crackling occasionally punctuated by the lowing or bleat of neighbors' animals. Even as one inured to the discomforts of long travel, the special contentment of a full belly and a solid roof came over Gwyn, a restfulness that fended off the oblivion of sleep in which such rare advantages could no longer be savored. Gwyn's mind wandered, and in time she picked up her mug and crossed to one of the cushioned chairs near the hearth, Lischa following soon after.

Gwyn was accustomed to facing an uncertain future, but her presence in the place of her rearing sent her thoughts into the past. With Daruneh's cryptic statements, their utterance now months gone, even that foundation seemed a mystery; Drax could insist that even magic couldn't alter events already passed, but merely a word could cast them into doubt. Every event of her childhood, every choice she'd made, now rested in the shadow of the forces that had observed her entire life. She pondered her flight to the South, her thirst for war, the friends she had made there. The hollowness left by leaving Ardos, Baraxis, and all the Sutherese felt as powerful as the comfort in reuniting with the family of her childhood. Shon and Rak, both dead, neither leaving enough behind even to bury – she had avenged them, but had she really mourned them? Had any of these choices, any of these kinships, really been her own, or was her trail blazed for her by the supposed power handed down the generations? "Mother," she finally asked, "what was Father really like? What did other people think of him?"

Lischa's tone was wistful, leading Gwyn to wonder if she would really get an answer of the kind she needed. "Your father was," Lischa began, but then she paused and took a deep breath. "He was a hero. All the girls loved him, and all the men followed him. When his eye settled on me,

I thought I was the luckiest girl in the world." She closed her eyes, the firelight flickering over her face and highlighting the lines around her eyes. "When I remember when we were together, and force my memory through the pain of losing him…" She squinted hard, then opened her eyes again. "When I can make myself do that, I *still* feel like the luckiest girl in the world. Girahl did have a few rivals when he was your age, and they hated him at first, to be sure, but they all came around. That's just how he was; nobody could resist his character for long." Lischa's eyes became dark then, just for a moment. "That's why I still get so angry at him sometimes, for going into those woods alone. He could have snapped his fingers and had a dozen warriors with him, not just Tehgil. I don't know why he did it. I just try to believe he must have had a good reason. He was too good a man not to."

Gwyn remembered her strange feelings toward Shon, their conversation describing one another as people of special influence, the adulation she couldn't deny seeing in the eyes of soldiers she led. Did Lischa's description of her father carry some confirmation he'd held a similar power? Perhaps her words represented only the halcyon memories of past love, but Gwyn doubted it. She gazed into the fire and said simply, "I wish I could have known him." She realized she had never spoken those plain words aloud, and a sudden feeling of loss welled up within her. For all her obsession with avenging Girahl, all her venom toward Vassin when she lost the chance, her father's place in her life had never been more than a sort of icon. She hadn't really envisioned him as a real, living person before this moment. She suddenly felt the reality of his absence from her life, one she could never truly grieve, having never known otherwise, but one she could imagine her mother battling with the same blinding rage Gwyn knew so well from her own heart. Gwyn looked back to Lischa and imagined her as a young woman not much older than herself, her heart in tatters and facing the world with no one but a hungry, Windborne babe for family. With the weight of everything Girahl's survival might have meant for them both, she repeated, "I wish I could have known him."

Lischa reached across the space between them to put her hand over Gwyn's on the chair arm. "I wish that, too, Gwyn. Maybe even more, I wish *he* could have known *you*."

Gwyn rose before the dawn, awakening on a pile of furs before the banked embers of the fire. Realizing she must be the first one up, she fed and stoked the coals to a little flame before quickly performing her ablutions and dressing. The comfort of the house already began to feel restrictive with the knowledge that she still couldn't chance showing her face, so it was some relief when Tehgil came to call not long after the men had breakfasted on leftovers from the night before and departed for the fields and Lischa, rising late, had begun work on a proper meal.

"I've eaten," Tehgil assured the lady of the house as he sat. "How did you sleep, Gwyn?"

"Well enough," she replied. "I've been glad for the chance to rest and spend time with everyone, but there's still no end of trouble, and I need to know what can be done about it."

"Right to business, then," Tehgil sighed, though he did it with a smile. "Who does that remind you of?" he called to Lischa by the fire.

"Just like her father," she replied without looking up as she cracked eggs into a skillet on the grate. "The quickest and loudest with a jest, but best not waste time with idle talk once his mind was set on something."

"Fine, Gwyn," Tehgil agreed. "Vigurd actually came to call last night, late, after the other Kart men were asleep.

All he's worried about is getting out of town before the truth comes out. I told him to be ready. What else do you want to know?"

"You've started with the lay of the land as it is," she began, "so let's stick with that. I know you've kept your ears open. What did you hear of Deflin or the spread of news Drax and I are here?"

"I've got the town gossips convinced, for now, that you two are scouting out contracts for grain to ship to the war-ravaged South, and got Adric's name from other villages along the roads up from the Sharai. I changed the story just enough each time to keep them arguing over the details instead of picking at the main lie."

"Should hold them another couple days alright," Gwyn said. "What about Deflin?"

"Still asleep."

"Of course he is," Drax called from the hallway, half-stumbling from Gwyn's room, Aldrin's clothes a decent fit on him but rumpled from his sleep. "I told you he'd be out as long as that lock of hair was on him, didn't I?"

"Behave yourself," Gwyn ordered the elf. "Is the physician getting frustrated yet? Planning to do anything we need to know about?" she asked Tehgil.

"Not sure," he admitted. "I wandered by the barracks this morning, but there was nothing going on yet. If I know Durell, though, he won't wait much past noon today before trying something. Maybe nothing too drastic, but maybe enough to learn it isn't a natural sleep. Some of the more superstitious tongues are already starting to wag."

"I had an idea about that," Drax spoke up as he sat. "What if we could take Deflin out of town somewhere? You wanted to see a loremaster, Gwyn. Would someone like that ever weigh in on a mysterious case?"

"A loremaster?" Tehgil questioned. "What for? You

never sat still for lessons as a lass, and now probably isn't the time to get caught up."

Gwyn glared at Drax for his indiscretion, then simply replied, "I'd rather not say." Tehgil's expression forced her to wonder if some of the holes in her story had become more apparent after the shock and joy of her return had worn off. "He's right, though. That idea might work, buy us a couple more days to rest and plan our moves."

"Not worth the risk, I think," Tehgil countered. "Durell would want to go along, and trying to talk him out of it would tip our hand." The older man's face grew sad. "If there's a way to keep you safe here for more than another day, two at the most, I can't think of it."

"It doesn't matter much," she answered. "I need to be on my way as soon as I can."

"Where?" Tehgil asked. Gwyn could see from Drax's expression he was just as curious, and Lischa looked up at her from the fire.

"I need to get to Nafar," Gwyn revealed. "You said he's gathering some kind of opposition. In his days as captain of King Vassin's guard, he traveled everywhere and made allies all over, and he's already on the hunt for evidence against Haric. If anybody knows about our mystery wagon trains, it's him, and if we can add what Mother worked out last night, it may be enough to move with."

Tehgil's face was more serious than Gwyn was used to, but he nodded his acceptance of the plan. "You spit two hares with one arrow, then. I should have had some news from the captain by now, but his messenger is overdue. You can take my report back with you."

"You can't come along to show me the way, then?" Gwyn was disappointed but not surprised.

"No, I'm sort of the central hub of news around here, for exactly the reason that I don't travel around much. If I leave, it throws everything into confusion and backup plans, and that's not good for anybody. I can give you directions well enough to where he's hiding out."

"He may not like that," Gwyn commented. "He never trusted me."

"Only because he thought you were a rabid dog," Tehgil said with a chuckle. "That's a different kind of mistrust than thinking you'd ever betray him to an enemy. He'll understand. I'll tell you, along with the news I'm supposed to send back. You'll have to memorize it, though; nothing can be written down."

"And, ah, the nearest loremaster?" Drax asked.

Tehgil gave them both a suspicious look but didn't argue. Without delay he began teaching them the recitation to take to Nafar.

Gwyn only remained in the village until midday. Her time in the home was quiet; neither she, nor Lischa, was one to waste words, and both had said the most important things first. While the younger women of the village took food out to their men in the fields and many of the older folks took the luxury of afternoon naps, Gwyn gave her mother a final embrace at the stable door. Drax did the same while Gwyn clasped wrists with Tehgil. "In another day," she told him, "make an excuse to get near Deflin and take the lock of hair out of his hand. Just leave it there so it looks like he worked it off in his sleep."

"I will," her oath-father and first mentor promised.

With that, she led Thunderhead out with Bully's reins looped about her saddle horn. Drax was only a moment behind with Flamewind. Lischa's eyes were bright with tears when Gwyn looked back. She felt tempted to tarry, but Vigurd waited for them on his own horse at the front of the house, and shows of emotion out here in the open would destroy Tehgil's ruse about them. Drax used the rail of the stable to reach the saddle so he didn't have to display his ability to make Flamewind bow for him, Gwyn mounted Thunderhead, and the pair walked their horses toward the eastern gate.

On Tehgil's advice to prepare for a quick flight from the village, Vigurd had begged his way out of the search for the "missing" patrol leader, claiming exhaustion after completing his full day's patrol the day before only to go scouring the woods for tracks until after dark. He then "escorted" the "strangers" out of town and up the north road, supplying both Gwyn and Drax with passes he'd taken from the barracks in case they ran afoul of patrols.

"You're in this thing, now, Vigurd," Gwyn cautioned. "All the way."

"I know," he answered with a grim nod. "I hoped it wouldn't come to this, for any Atlunder, but that hope is gone."

"The only hope we have now is outrunning the news of our treason against the new monarch," Gwyn said. "I do have one detour to make first."

With that, the trio headed north. In less than an hour a track split off from the main road, heading west into the forest. Following Tehgil's directions, Gwyn took it, winding through the dense woods as birdsong filled the air, the trees closing in around them still nearly bare in the cold spring.

After half a meandering mile the path began to ascend, then entered a cutting between two hills. Knowing her destination should be near, Gwyn bade Drax and Vigurd to wait and urged Thunderhead up the slope. Finally the track turned again as the trees thinned, opening into a sheltered dell. In the center of the acre-wide space stood a stone cottage, quite unlike the log longhouses so typical in Atlund. The thatch on the roof looked new, the stones scrubbed clean of moss and lichen. So maintained, such a place may have sat there, unminding, for centuries, and maybe it had. A man stood before the door, a man of Tehgil's size sporting a bushy, orange beard. He swung a heavy ax, splitting thick logs in one pile into firewood in another. Gwyn saw his eyes scan over her, noted the subtle hitch in his motion that proved he marked her approach, but he did not speak or pause in his task.

At last she drew near enough for a respectful hail. "Are you the loremaster?" she asked dubiously.

The man grunted a laugh as he placed another log. "Not hardly. She's inside."

Gwyn dismounted but hesitated as she reached for her sword. The ax fell with a *thunk*, and the split pieces clattered away. "Are you not from these parts?" the man questioned. "Carry what you wish."

Gwyn freed the blade and approached the cottage, her very muscles wary. Opening the door, she peered inside, unsure what to expect.

Light streamed through the windows, and a small fire warmed the space. A woman sat at the far window, her mouth moving silently as she worked at a jumble of knitting that tumbled across her lap. Her face was finely lined, her light hair turning to gray, showing her a decade older than Gwyn's mother. She glanced up at Gwyn, but for several long moments the only sound was the fall of the ax, the hollow percussion of dry wood.

"Come in and sit, Gwyn of Candon," the woman finally said, motioning with her still-working needles to an empty chair across from her.

"How do you know me? Gwyn asked as she took the offered seat, laying her blade across her lap.

"Oh, I could scarcely forget you," the woman answered. "I tried to assist my predecessor in the teaching of your village, but you were always too busy picking fights and causing trouble to learn anything. I cuffed your head and tweaked your ear more than once, but since your mother showed no interest in your learning of history, I gave up and let you wander off instead of ruining the lessons for all the other children."

Gwyn had no clear recollection of this, but she had to admit the tale fit with the pattern she knew of her childhood.

"What brings so recalcitrant a student now to my door?" she prodded.

Gwyn searched for words. "My life has become strange," she said at last. "Maybe it always has been. A wise woman in the South says I have some legacy bound up with ancient legends. If I knew them better, maybe I could suss out my place in it all."

The woman gave a wan smile. "Wishing to know history in order to learn one's own present. How novel a concept," she said, her tone leaning to the sardonic. "Still, to tell all the legends of our people would take many days, *Gwyn et Sheevasa*. You'll have to tell me more of what you want." Gwyn hesitated. "Your secrets are safe here," the woman urged. "Some of my kind participate in the struggle of their day, whatever that may be, offering their wisdom of the past to guide their neighbors. Others, then, must withdraw, safeguard the knowledge we possess lest all be lost in one catastrophe. I do not get involved."

Reluctantly Gwyn proceeded. "In the South I was confronted by two beings. One seemed human, but I don't believe she was. The other seemed monstrous, but that may not have been any more true. The first, a woman, or appearing to be, told me the other wanted to kill or control me because I had some power I inherited from down the centuries, going to the firstborn in each generation. She said it gave me influence to inspire others to great deeds and might accomplish more if brought out fully. She would say nothing else, for fear of inciting me to do something rash, I think."

The loremaster continued with her knitting as she

smiled and replied, "And if so wise a creature counsels silence, why should I speak?"

"I don't ask for secret revelation, only the knowledge I might have already if I showed more interest as a child."

"Very well," the woman assented, at last setting her needles and yarn aside. "You seem to speak of a time when the clans of Atlund were young, when man did well even to work stone tools and hides. The dragons were in the world then, and they protected man in his primitive fear, but in time they went away or died. No one really knows.

"Other beings came among the people then, human in form but wielding great power and magic. The legends of different clans call them by their own names: the Elders, the Sages, the Supernals," her voice trailed off in a way that Gwyn took to mean there were other names besides, but the loremaster didn't list them. "Some," the woman continued, "even forsook the revelation of Terillah and worshiped them as gods, and to those primitive hunters, gods they were, or might as well have been. These beings showed favor to their chosen among the peoples and taught them many things, elevating them to the first Great Chieftains of the clans. Their peoples followed these empowered leaders without question, but the Supernals offered constant shepherding as well, training man to work metal, to cultivate the land, to create art and song, and even to command the forces of magic, at least for those few born with the gift."

Gwyn gripped her sword as she listened. Was Daruneh one of these ancient beings? Was her enemy? "What happened to them?" Gwyn found herself asking into a pause in the loremaster's tale.

"As time passed, something changed. The Chieftains' descendants rejected the teaching of their great mentors, and some sought to lord their power over their subjects. Inevitably these paragons of men came into conflict with one another over lands or resources or simple pride, and whole clans would rally to the slaughter. Some say the Supernals tried to take their power back to stem the tide of blood but found that they could not. Like all creations, they had eventually broken free from their creators. Aghast at what they had wrought, the Supernals fled far away, and no tale tells of them thereafter."

"Then those Great Chieftains, or their descendants," Gwyn asked, "what became of them?"

"Not many had been made, and fewer still had turned to wickedness. The rest banded together with their clans and destroyed the oppressors, and in that alliance, the seeds of the nation of Atlund as we know it today were first planted. The great powers waned with each generation, until they, too, disappeared from history." The loremaster regarded Gwyn with a curl to her lip and a gleam in her eye. "Of course," she went on, "this is only one of our people's creation legends. I'm told the elves have their own, and I little doubt the orcs have as well. As for Atlunders, we teach them as our heritage, but only a superstitious few see any truth in them these days. Certainly nothing I would expect a woman of the world, such as yourself, one who has seen the great, wide South and returned to our rustic land, to take much interest in, mystic counsellors notwithstanding."

"Mock me all you want," Gwyn shot back, seething. "Only tell me plainly: do you think this legend could be real, and if not, then what else am I in the middle of?"

"Forgive me," the woman replied gently. "I should not have doubted your sincerity. You would be the oldest former student to return for payback at their old teacher with some tall tale, but not, by far, the first. I will answer as clearly as I can.

"Do I believe this legend could be real? I can't say for certain. Some clans in the northeast say their people were taught by a race of bird-men who hatched from giant eggs. Those bordering the Sharai claim they learned the ways of battle from the ogres before their extinction. Perhaps all are true, or none. But in any case where history has shone light on legend, we always see in the latter some seed of truth. If the myth of the Supernals isn't the explanation you seek, I don't have a better one."

Gwyn nodded. "What would you counsel me to do?"

The loremaster was quick and confident in her response. "If you wish to see your story writ large on the pages of history, pick a side and pray to Terillah you have chosen the winner. On the other hand, if you wish to lead a long and happy life, if it were me, I would stay as far away from this conflict as possible. I fear it will come to a tragic end."

Gwyn sat for a moment in reflection. She had certainly never thought much of being remembered as anything but a great warrior, and her reputation in that regard seemed already assured, at least in the South. She had never put any effort toward securing a long or happy life, either, she had to admit. The loremaster gazed at her as though searching her thoughts. Finally Gwyn stood. "You seem less personally interested in my story than I would expect for one of your profession," she remarked.

"You'll notice I haven't resumed my knitting. Rest assured I will set quill to parchment as soon as you are gone, to record your report and pen letters to my nearest associates."

"Please," Gwyn pressed, "write down what you must, but hide it well, and tell no others yet. If you fear tragedy, stave off what you can by keeping this secret, and tell no one I was here. I don't know if your woodsman recognized me, but I hope he is trusty as well."

The woman nodded. "He is. We will stay silent for now. Fare you well, Gwyn of Candon."

A payment of two silver coins was customary for a

loremaster's advice. Gwyn left four on the table, offered her thanks, and quickly departed.

CHAPTER XIV

Once again Gwyn drove her party to travel more quickly than was reasonable, but compared to her grueling sprint through the wilds in winter, Atlund in spring was no great challenge. She couldn't be sure when Deflin would awaken and sound the alarm, but after he did the odds were good a courier would be sent to the Citadel. That would take a day. Word would spread then, if the king willed it, along with warrants for Gwyn's arrest or summary execution, but even the fastest riders would be ordered to stop at key towns to post bills and inform criers, and they wouldn't know where she was going in order to target their announcement. If Gwyn moved quickly and followed Tehgil's directions without fail, she could reach Nafar's secret camp before word of her return or supposed crime caught up to her.

This task proved easier than even Gwyn had expected, and she was grateful for a change in her luck. Drax's magic, even after losing some of his tools in Finn's Station, helped them to camp with stealth so they could avoid the inns and taverns, and though Vigurd, as a westerner like Gwyn, had only occasionally traveled into the central regions of Atlund, he did at least know the major roads and towns, the better to parallel and avoid them, which was more knowledge than Gwyn could boast. In only two days they left lands where Vigurd could be recognized, and in the current state of affairs his Kart clan tartan and guard's sigil allowed him passage without challenge anywhere they chose to risk the roads. Gwyn wrapped *Tyralist* and stowed it in Bully's baggage to conceal it as best she could, only because the great, two-handed weapons were less common the farther they traveled from the northern Tunaris with their traditions of battling giant beasts in the forests. She considered shearing off her hair to be less recognizable but couldn't bear the thought, wrapping it instead in a scarf and binding it as closely as she could, though locks were forever slipping out in their usual rebellious manner. Fortunately, wild red tresses were rather more common in Atlund than in the South. Drax kept his hood up to hide his ears and eschewed his dark lenses; they drew too much attention, and the pale northern sun would remain tolerable until the height of summer. Thus disguised, they used the roads for a week, passing quickly through towns and camping in gullies and copses to avoid crowds.

As they traveled eastward, the forests gave way to broad, dry plains checkered with fields along irrigation ditches that had taken generations to dig. Many of these lay dry for now, but soon the snow on the lower slopes would begin its yearly melt in earnest, watering the plots of amaranth and beans. Elsewhere cattle lowed as they grazed on the wild grasses, their shaggy hides protecting them from evening chills. Trees only grew near the banks of larger streams or in low pockets that collected the infrequent rains. The few clouds were high and thin, and though the farmsteads and crofts gave the region a wholesome feeling, Gwyn felt exposed as she had crossing the wilds, naked before the watching eyes of her enemies. Though Daruneh's great adversary had kept his promise to relent, so far she had no words from the mysterious sage either, whether in dream or waking, and after pondering the loremaster's advice she began to think that was for the best. As long as Karon was safe and Daruneh's magic forced the enemy to leave her alone, perhaps she really could avoid further entanglements. Still, the sun and moons no longer felt friendly, peering down at her world and illuminating that which she needed to keep secret.

With each passing day Gwyn's apprehension increased, sure the demands for her capture must be nipping at her heels. After their eighth day out from her village she insisted they leave the roads, though Drax would sneak back into the villages they passed when he could, watching and listening for news. On the night of the tenth day he returned with a report.

"I overheard two people talking," he explained to Gwyn and Vigurd as they chewed their supper of jerky and oat porridge, "two people who seemed to be deputized into the king's patrol force, though they weren't wearing his clan plaid. It seems the king hasn't put out a general call for your arrest. He may be as eager to keep your return a secret as you are."

"That's probably wise," Vigurd mused. "You may have lost some favor when you left, but not all, and now that the Southern mercenaries are bringing tales of your heroism up here, you've likely gained back even more."

"Whatever the reason," Drax continued, "the news has only been passed amongst the king's loyal watchers. Their orders are not to approach you without support; if any make a sighting they're to raise a proper posse before giving pursuit. 'Alive if possible, dead if necessary,' was the phrase I heard."

"That plays in our favor," Gwyn replied. "Fewer people

looking for us, and off the main roads we aren't likely to run into the king's patrols. We should make our destination in ten more days." Silently Gwyn pondered the larger implication, that King Haric feared her, and smiled.

The next day, in the afternoon, Gwyn asked suddenly, "Drax, what do you see on the northern horizon?"

The elf had been lost in his own thoughts and occasionally scanning their south flank. He turned his head to follow Gwyn's gaze and immediately saw the dust cloud on the northern road that had caught his oath-sister's attention. "A few dozen men," the elf stated, "maybe a quarter on horseback. All Southerners, for sure."

"Armed?"

"Naturally. What do you want to do?"

Gwyn looked about on the flat plain. They were south of an east-west road, moving parallel, but a north-south thoroughfare lay ahead. She could just make out a signpost a few miles away, where the crossroads should be. If the mercenary band continued straight through the intersection, they'd pass each other within easy hailing distance. Gwyn doubted any Southerners were within the circle Haric entrusted with orders for her capture, given her exceptional reputation within their homeland, but any of his hirelings were likely to question strangers traveling off the roads if it didn't take them out of their way. "I think Bully's pack is rubbing him wrong," Gwyn stated. "Best make some adjustments."

"He's fine," Vigurd assured.

"I know that, but *they* don't," she explained, nodding her head toward the approaching Southerners as she dismounted Thunderhead. "I just want to stall until they reach the crossroads, and if any of them are watching, I don't want to look too suspicious." Gwyn busied herself for a few long moments.

"More company," Vigurd announced then, staring into the northwest as Drax continued his surveillance of the mercenaries to the northeast. "Wagon coming over the hill, looks like fur traders, maybe."

Gwyn sighed in frustration. If the fighting company continued south, she'd meant to turn north to avoid them, a response she suspected was common enough not to attract attention. Now that course would bring her into contact with the traders who, while less threatening in the moment, were likely westerners, folk who might recognize her and whose loyalties she couldn't guess. The minutes dragged on as Gwyn gave the impression of adjusting Bully's pack and waited to see where everyone would go.

Finally the mercenary company reached the crossroads, and to Gwyn's relief they turned to the west. She waited a few more moments for effect before mounting Thunderhead, watching the soldiers and wagon move toward one another to the north. She continued to watch as she started her band moving again, but in only a few minutes four riders galloped forward from the Southern troop, coming to surround the approaching wagon. "What's this?" she said aloud. The wagon's driver, now close enough to be seen as a man just entering his middle years, his hair thinning and beard short, seemed to be arguing with the mercenary riders, but their words died on the wind long before they reached Gwyn. Next to him, a woman a few years younger with full, dark tresses pressed close as for protection. In another moment two of the riders dismounted and began rifling through the couple's goods. A few pelts they threw over their shoulder as they worked, others they tossed to the ground.

"Worthless curs," Vigurd spat.

The woman reached back over the wagon's seat to pull one of the choice furs from the pile, seeking to save it from theft or mishandling, but as soon as she moved, an adjacent rider struck her face with a riding crop.

Gwyn lamented not freeing her sword while tarrying at Bully's pack, but she reached for her hammer and turned Thunderhead toward the north.

"Gwyn, you can't," Drax cautioned, suddenly spurring Flamewind into her path.

"Like hell," she growled, checking Thunderhead but pulling the hammer from its loop on the saddle.

"We can't fight fifty armed men, Gwyn. Even if we could, they're a league away. By the time we get there, it will all be over."

Gwyn felt the weight of her weapon, the need to swing it. Her breath was ragged, her glare boring into Drax's violet-washed irises.

"I'm not saying you shouldn't, Gwyn, or even that I don't want you to. But right now, you truly can't."

She stared for another moment, then straightened and urged Thunderhead back to the east, turning her face away from whatever would befall on the north road. Part of her felt compelled to watch, but she didn't know how to bear the weight of such images pressing down on her sense of helplessness.

Drax rode at her stirrup for a while, saying nothing.

"We have to stop this, Drax," she insisted.

"We will, Gwyn. You know Nafar is our best chance." He looked toward her, searching her expression. "Are you alright?" he asked.

Gwyn shook her head. "No. But I will be."

The next evening Vigurd sauntered into a tavern in a quiet hamlet a mile from the band's campsite. Though a modest place, it seemed to draw farmers from the surrounding countryside as nearly a dozen men sat at tables eating and drinking. All cast their glances to the door with expectancy when he entered, expressions that turned to suspicion when they didn't recognize the newcomer. He looked about in turn, surveying whether any of the customers bore the king's badges.

"What brings you here, stranger?" the barman asked from behind his counter.

"Bad decisions and a footsore horse," Vigurd answered with an easy sigh. "I was pointed to a shortcut at the last crossroads, but the only thing it's shortened is my patience. Do any of you know a good way back to the main road?"

"If you head north out of town, across the fields, you'll find a ford across the stream. That'll put you on the right track," the barman replied, relaxing. "You might as well settle for a drink and a billet, though. The ford's easy to miss in the dark, and the banks are steep in some places."

"I'll have the drink at least," Vigurd answered, sitting at a stool and setting a coin on the counter. The barman set down a tankard of ale, which seemed the only thing on offer, and went about his business. Vigurd listened to the conversation start up again in hushed tones, the patrons uneasy discussing their personal business with a stranger present. Some occasionally looked meaningfully in his direction. In such out-of-the-way places, a traveler might be expected to provide news or an amusing tale in exchange for the social imposition of his presence. He waited until most of his drink was gone before calling to the audience in general, "Any of you fellows heard the big news from the eastern clans?"

The room went quiet. "What news is that?" called a voice in return.

"They're saying *Gwyn et Sheevasa* has come back," he answered.

"Who says?" demanded another voice.

"Just a merchant I spoke to from back that way."

"You vouch for him?" asked a third.

"Not at all. Just telling you what I heard."

"Bah, that's nonsense," said the barman. "Why go there, all the way across the country from her own clan?"

Vigurd shrugged. "Claimed she'd heard about the change in leadership and didn't want to be where she was expected. Used some of her big mercenary money from the South to broker passage with one of the nomad bands that isn't raiding right now and came through the passes in the Qachar range. Said some of the men that way saw her big as life, red hair, giant sword, and all."

"Do you think it could be?" another man hazarded to his companion.

"Sounds like rubbish to me," called one from another table.

"Well, you know the saying," the barman added, scratching his chin. "The only difference between a rumor and a fact? About a week."

A few in the room chuckled at the saying which, though common, was used in sincerity and cynicism with equal frequency. Vigurd finished his ale and took his leave.

Thirty minutes later the clan Kart man returned to Gwyn's campsite.

"You're sure you weren't followed?" Gwyn demanded.

"I'm sure," Vigurd assured her with a sigh. "What are you trying to accomplish with this?"

"I have to do *something*," Gwyn answered. "We already know Haric has learned I'm back, but the only others with the truth are the ones *he* wants. If he thinks it serves his interest to keep the secret, then I want the opposite. As long as nobody knows where I really am, maybe the idea I've come back will have his loyalists and hired swords looking over their backs a bit, wondering if any atrocities they're considering will really go unpunished. It isn't much, but it's all I can think of until we join up with Nafar. And it might even work to our advantage for folks to have a seed of hope, maybe even enough to think they've seen me this place or that, and to be ready when I do come calling."

Drax opened his mouth to speak, then glanced at Vigurd. He paused an extra moment before saying, "That's stepping into your 'influence' a bit more than you have in the past, Gwyn. Are you sure that's such a good idea?"

"If it weren't for bad ideas I'd have none at all, Drax," she answered. "It's gotten me this far."

"Only because I'm here to rescue you," the elf insisted, pointing his camp knife at Gwyn's left arm, then to her sword wrapped and stowed on Bully.

"Only in your twisted imagination," Gwyn rebutted.

"You two are going to get me killed," Vigurd grumbled.

Later, Vigurd slept as Drax shook Gwyn to raise her for her turn on watch. After she had made ready, Drax remained sitting next to her. "You aren't tired?" Gwyn asked. It wouldn't be the first time the elf had passed a nearly sleepless night in her company. "If you aren't going to sleep then take my watch so I can."

"No, I just wanted to speak a bit more openly." He paused and listened to Vigurd's breath, then leaned closer to Gwyn to murmur in her ear. "You said your dreams of Daruneh's enemy started after you swore vengeance on the orcs that killed your friend Shon. Then we came face to face with him not long after you did the same against Tira's killers. What if your vow lights some kind of beacon, and what if your power to inspire does, too? I know it happens on its own, but if you try to really use it, aren't you afraid you'll reveal yourself again, somehow?"

"I hadn't thought about it," Gwyn answered, running her fingers through her hair. She considered for a moment, weighing her own ideas against Drax's counsel. "It's just rumors, for now," she decided. "Maybe benefiting from my reputation a little. Nothing supernatural about that. If the time comes that I do need to help raise an army, I suspect we'll have to say 'damn the risks' anyway. But we'll cross that bridge when we get to it."

Drax was silent for a few moments. "It's one thing to rally fighting men to fight more bravely. Calling them away from home and safety for your own agenda, though, that feels like something else."

"Is that what you're really worried about? Not that I'll expose my presence, but that I'll get people killed?"

"They aren't wholly separate. I'm worried about *you*, about what may happen when all this catches up to you. One way or the other."

Drax's moralizing frustrated Gwyn, and her only answer was a low grunt. She knew he didn't mean to judge her, though. When she said nothing, Drax stood to go to his bedroll. Gwyn grabbed his sleeve. Drax jerked his arm away in aggravation but turned back to her nevertheless. "You're a good oath-brother, Drax," she whispered.

Two nights later Vigurd repeated his performance in another village, this time claiming to have heard news of Gwyn's return from a trapper coming out of the southwestern Tunaris. Three nights later she had paid a fisherman to paddle her across the Sharai on a moonless night. The next she was to have sneaked across the bridge with one of the mercenary bands from the South, but this claim was countered by a farmer who swore he had a reliable source placing her in the northern forests where she spent her days training a cadre of female warriors she'd helped escape from the harems of the eastern nomads. Whatever the ultimate effect of Gwyn's plan might be, her rumor was surely spreading.

The spring rains had come to central Atlund when Gwyn led the party into a region of forested hills, low but rugged. Constant drizzle reminded Gwyn of the night she'd met Daruneh in the lonely cottage, and the fog clinging in the draws and hollows threatened her visibility as she struggled to follow the last of Tehgil's directions to Nafar's secret camp. The rain seemed to keep the birds hunkered in their nests, so the shrill whistle that pierced the sky on their second day in the hills betrayed a watcher up ahead. Halting, Gwyn unbound her hair, wet and tangled, and freed her sword from Bully's pack. Blade in hand, she rode forward through the looming defile.

A screening thicket took shape in the fog, and Gwyn dismounted to lead Thunderhead, with Drax and Vigurd doing likewise. Picking carefully through the ten yards of brush, Gwyn emerged on the other side in a narrow valley that stretched farther than she could make out in the mist. Shadowy trees thrust up on either side, and she espied the silhouette of a tent at the edge of her vision to the right, across the loamy floor from a picket line of a dozen horses. She continued just far enough for her companions to exit the thicket behind her, then stopped, waiting for a challenge. Her muscles tensed with the knowledge that her armor would not stop a well-placed arrow.

A form stepped out from behind a tree some twenty yards away, a lean man with more salt in his beard than Gwyn had remembered. "Nafar of Hradash," Gwyn called.

"*Gwyn et Sheevasa,*" Gwyn's old teacher replied, pacing closer. I heard rumors you'd returned, but I didn't believe a one of them. After what happened in the Forest Campaign, I was sure you'd got yourself killed down there in the orc wars, no matter what Tehgil or those Southern sellswords said. Even wondered if that was your aim sometimes."

"Maybe at first," she admitted, "but I got better."

"Better teachers, eh?" Nafar asked, now standing within arms' reach of Gwyn.

"Better student," she replied.

Nafar stared at her for a moment. "You've changed, Gwyn. Much."

"That's the general consensus," she answered. She hadn't had a decent fight since she left Finn's Station, and seeing Nafar again made her itch for battle, her memories resurrecting a measure of the haughty overconfidence she'd left dead on some Southern battlefield. "Maybe when you're armed I can show you just *how* much."

Nafar chuckled. "Maybe less than I thought. I wouldn't mind seeing what you could teach me from the Southern fighters, but not now. First I need you to vouch for your companions." Nafar's glance flicked left and right, and Gwyn followed it to spot the archers who stood from behind shoulders of rock on either side of the thicket.

"I vouch for the elf. He's called Drax, a mercenary like me." Gwyn caught Nafar's dubious expression. "Same ends, different means," she clarified. "The other man is Vigurd. Tehgil vouches for him, at least enough not to get an arrow in his throat."

"Fair enough," Nafar said with a nod. Motioning with his arm, he led the party away from the thicket, deeper into the canyon. Sounds began to waft to Gwyn's ears, voices and ringing steel and axes falling on wood. As they advanced, Gwyn began to see forms, then features of people setting about their tasks or moving from one place to another. Nafar showed Gwyn and her companions to the picket line to tether their horses, then to a ring of stumps about the ashes of a campfire. "Why are you here, Gwyn?" Nafar asked as they sat.

Gwyn wanted to launch into the tale of Finn's station, the shipment of weapons and horses, and the discrepancy of timing Lischa had realized, but after seeing the discipline in Nafar's camp she felt a knot in her gut over the other reason for her visit. "I have much news," she answered at last. "Most urgent, I think, is to tell you that your courier to Tehgil didn't appear as expected. At best, he was overdue."

"What?" Nafar asked, sitting straighter. "How long?"

"Tehgil said a week," Gwyn answered.

"Damn. He left a day early and couldn't have been that long delayed. Something's happened. Wait here." Nafar stood and hustled deeper into the valley, leaving the three newcomers to stunned silence. Gwyn noticed a few armed men move in their direction and stand nearby, unwavering. They made no threat but showed clearly Gwyn and her allies didn't yet have liberty to move about the camp. She didn't know these guards, so she felt reluctant to have any open conversation with Drax and Vigurd in their presence. Somewhat frustrated, she settled in to wait.

Nafar returned in a quarter of an hour, his face difficult to read. He shared nothing of his plans regarding the missing courier before sitting down once more. "You said you had 'much' news," he prompted Gwyn.

In response she first relayed Tehgil's report, news of the movements of Haric loyalists, Clan Kart guards, and the mercenary forces, seemingly gleaned from several other agents who reported to Tehgil as a primary contact. Concluding, she added, "I brought news of my own to Atlund, and my mother used it to draw some interesting conclusions." At last Gwyn was able to relay their suspicions based on the weapon purchase preceding Vassin's poisoning.

Nafar stroked his beard, and Gwyn thought she noted a glimmer in his stony, pockmarked face. "Interesting," he mused. "Useless without more proof, of course, confirmation of who made the order. We had reports of a trade caravan heading east just north of the Sharai. That's common enough; the only reason any took notice at all is the large herd of Southern-bred horses they drove with them. We assumed there was a surplus after the orc war ended and didn't give it much more thought."

"And *I* assumed Atlund had broken out into open warfare, but that hasn't happened, either. So who in Atlund would pay for Southern steel and mounts without cause?"

"Maybe the eastern clans?" Vigurd piped up. "They go through munitions more quickly in their skirmishes with raiders from over the mountains. Maybe Haric promised them the delivery in exchange for their support in the Kingmoot."

"Possible," Nafar allowed, "but not very likely. I know the east's warriors better than most westerners. They aren't so proud as to spurn the help, but they wouldn't be bought so cheap."

"You don't know why they threw in with him, though?" Gwyn asked.

"No. We have a long list of the elders that voted for him, but none of my people have been able to get close enough to any of them for a straight answer. The general rumor is that Haric promised them peace with the raiders, but that's all."

"All our answers seem to lie in the east," Drax concluded.

"To the east, and on the other side of at least one decent meal and decent night's sleep," Nafar insisted. "We aren't as well-appointed as even the rudest tavern, but we can provide better than you've had since you left the roads, at least." He started to walk away, then turned back to Gwyn. "After we've eaten maybe I'll accept the match you offered. The men would appreciate the sport." Gwyn grinned a wolfish grin at Nafar's retreating back.

Supper was an informal affair, Nafar's four dozen partisans clustering around a handful of campfires and freely sharing what was cooked on each. Several warriors approached Gwyn in turn, attempting to renew acquaintances from the forest campaign, but she remembered none of them, able to offer nothing but her sincere apologies. Each campfire had a woman or two, most accompanying a beau in the camp and providing for everyone's daily needs much as they would have at home. Three were younger than Gwyn and dressed as fighters. They eyed her from afar but didn't approach. She knew they followed her example, at least in part, and wasn't sure how to feel about it. She couldn't deny a love for her warrior's life, but Drax's words about luring people away from the safety of their homes, even unintentionally, nagged at her more than she would admit.

"What you see here is maybe a third of those who have signed on," Nafar explained between bites at a joint of meat. "The ones who've done something to run afoul of the pretender on the throne, a few who are just of an age to leave home and would rather live here than bow to Clan Kart rule."

"Why hasn't anybody in the Conclave challenged Haric since he hired the mercenaries or installed his warriors across the land?" Gwyn asked. "It's a flagrant defiance of our law against the king standing an army in peacetime."

"The deaths of some early dissenters certainly had a chilling effect," Nafar answered. "Those with influence are watched the most closely, and some fear his wizard."

"Tehgil said you vouch for him," Gwyn challenged.

"I vouch for his loyalty to the *throne*," Nafar replied, "which is why I don't think he did any harm to Vassin. But if the one sitting in that throne is a tyrant, then the wizard becomes an enemy to the clans. That's where we are now."

Gwyn looked at Drax. "I know what you're thinking," he said, "and I need to know a lot more before I guess whether I can take him."

Nafar caught the implication and looked at Drax with fresh, wide eyes. "You travel with a wizard?" he gasped to Gwyn.

"*He* travels with *me*," Gwyn insisted as Drax, speaking at once, replied, "An enchanter by trade. Care for a demonstration?"

"No no," Gwyn refused, keeping Drax on his seat with an outstretched arm. "Nafar still owes *me* a demonstration, so to speak."

The older warrior stood and tossed the bone of his supper into a stock pot near the fire. "It's time, I suppose." He motioned to a young, fair-haired lad passing by. "Fetch my sword and shield."

By the time the boy returned with Nafar's arms, word of the imminent contest had spread through the camp, causing a crowd to gather in the open space west of the campfires. Gwyn hefted her sword and walked to stand before them, waiting for Nafar to follow. The older man took his place a dozen feet away from her, prompting the gathered crowd to spread around the combatants in an informal ring. After a few perfunctory stretches, Nafar dropped into guard, shielded side forward and blade high with the point toward Gwyn, and waited.

Gwyn did not attack. She circled a bit, keeping Nafar at the very edge of her longer blade's range, meaning she was out of his. "I can't believe what I'm seeing," Nafar declared. "When did you–"

As Nafar was speaking, Gwyn lunged. She made no feint but went straight at his front leg. Nafar dropped his shield in time, but only just, and only by yielding a step which prevented him from working inside Gwyn's reach before she could recover and adjust. She brought her sword back into guard and waited again. In the briefest moment after her attack she saw Nafar's surprise at her quickness, a product both of training and of Drax's enchantment on her heavy blade. But only for a moment. Now Nafar's jaw was set, his eyes focused. He held his shield slightly lower and his weight a bit less forward. Gwyn knew another strike at his legs would not go so clearly in her favor.

She faked to the left with a sudden shift of her weight, but Nafar didn't take the bait. A flurry of possibilities flashed through her mind in the space of an eyeblink. Gwyn swung her sword in a fast chop at Nafar's head. He raised his shield at an angle, letting Gwyn's blade crash flat against it, and took his opportunity. Keeping his shield overhead like a roof, he lunged forward with his blade. Gwyn stepped offline to the right, then flicked her sword downward toward her opponent's extended hand. Nafar withdrew his thrust in time and brought his shield back to guard his chest. They squared off again, and the dance continued.

For five minutes they battled back and forth, the crowd responding with cheers and shouts as the spectacle drew them further and further into the world of the two fighters before them. Sweat stood on Nafar's forehead, but two years in the south had acclimated Gwyn to greater heat, so the cool air of the northern spring felt refreshing. On the other hand, the air here was thinner, and she found herself breathing harder than she would have expected. Neither fighter wore armor, so their endurance was yet untested. Gwyn saw something in Nafar's eyes, then, as though he found the duel tedious. For an instant Gwyn feared he even now toyed with her as he had more than three years before, but his exertion suggested otherwise. He had wanted to see how Gwyn could fight now, and he had. By some of his wordless noises and expressions, she believed he approved of her skill. But now he was ready to end the game and go about his evening. He could be lured into an attempt at a decisive strike.

Gwyn went for Nafar's leg again. This time he dodged diagonally to Gwyn's right, putting his blade cleanly on line with her chest. Having not committed to the attack, she whipped her blade in his direction, ready to bat his point aside and thrust forward toward *his* chest. But his blade wasn't there. Nafar had pivoted at the last moment and bashed Gwyn off-balance with his shield. Now his blade came back, whistling at her throat. He had opened her up so expertly she couldn't hope to parry; she tried to duck as she swung her blade up at Nafar, who had failed to close off all lines of attack, but too late. He stopped his blade an inch from her eyes at the exact moment Gwyn ended her own slash a hairsbreadth from the veins of his neck.

After a momentary gasp, the crowd erupted in applause. Gwyn cursed herself at falling for the deception in Nafar's final riposte, but after a heartbeat she felt happy to accept the draw. Gwyn relaxed as Nafar did and extended her arm. Nafar transferred his sword to his shield hand so he could clasp her wrist in congratulation. "You haven't lost a step," Gwyn conceded.

"And you've found a few," Nafar admitted.

Gwyn nodded her thanks for the compliment as a man from the crowd handed both fighters clay tumblers of water, which they gratefully drank.

"Tehgil was right about you," Nafar allowed. "I told him he was a damn fool to hope you'd survive down there, much less come back, and in so many words, too. But he was right." Nafar took a renewing breath and nodded as if to himself. "I'm glad you're here." The erstwhile royal guard turned and walked back to his tent.

Gwyn inspected the edges of her sword in the failing light as she returned to the spot where she'd dropped her gear to prepare for camp. A sense of pride welled up from deep within her. She'd trained with several peerless soldiers and skilled tacticians in her time away, and fought beside many more, but in pure skill, Nafar was, to the best of her knowledge, the greatest warrior in the world. *I just fought to a draw*, she realized, *against the greatest warrior in the world.*

CHAPTER XV

Gwyn woke before dawn. She had been tempted to celebrate too heartily, both by the other warriors in the camp and her own self-congratulatory pride, but she had managed to refrain. Not far from the relative safety of Nafar's sanctum, she knew foes still abounded, and she needed to keep her senses sharp. Rising, she walked to the canvas-screened corner of the camp set aside for women and made herself ready for the day, then returned to her billet to check on her companions. Drax snored softly, apparently feeling quite safe in his present environs. Next to the unconscious elf lay an empty bedroll.

Gwyn's muscles tensed. She cast her wary gaze about the camp; she hadn't noticed Vigurd as she made her way to or from the other side of the camp, nor could she see him now. Hardly anyone was up and about. She looked to the men's corner and the place where the latrines had been dug, waiting and watching for anyone to emerge. After a couple of minutes she knelt and shook her oath-brother awake. "Drax," she hissed. "Drax, wake up! Where's Vigurd?"

"How should I know?" Drax croaked, groggy and indignant. "I'm not his keeper." The elf sat up, squinting and rubbing sleep out of one eye as he took in Gwyn's urgent expression. "What's wrong?"

"I have a bad feeling," Gwyn murmured, standing. "Vigurd!" she shouted. "Vigurd, where are you?" She felt her heart beating in her throat as the seconds stretched on. The Clan Kart warrior did not appear nor call back.

Nafar emerged from his tent wearing only a long shift but with his sword in his hand. "Gwyn," he called more softly than she'd been shouting, "what's the matter?"

"Vigurd is missing," she stated, walking toward the captain.

"Hells," he growled. By now many in the camp were stirring, and Nafar began barking orders. "Vastil, take two men and scout the east end. Ganlin, your squad takes the near end, and fan out to canvas the approach."

"Where can I be useful?" Drax asked, fastening his robes as he drew near.

"Mithna," Nafar continued, "take the elf with you and scout the northern cleft, but don't leave the hills until the other scouts report back."

A lithe woman just tying her blonde hair back nodded once to Drax before starting up the slope on the north side of the camp.

Nafar scowled. "You don't think he just wandered off."

"No," Gwyn confirmed. "I hope I'm wrong."

Minutes stretched by, the sounds of Nafar's people moving through the woods drifting back to Gwyn's ears. Suddenly those rustling noises were rent by a startled cry. Moments later Mithna and Drax came bounding back down the slope. "Gwyn," Drax called, "we are betrayed!"

"It's Gorran," Mithna added to Nafar. "His throat's been cut."

"Damn," Gwyn hissed, suddenly aghast. "Nafar, I'm

sorry. I shouldn't have brought him here." Her heart felt sick. She'd come home to help and all she'd accomplished so far was to get two of her countrymen killed.

Nafar shook his head, his face a picture of self-recrimination. "I blame myself. It isn't as though I've ever trusted *your* judgment. I should have had him watched. He fooled Tehgil, and that was enough to fool us both."

"I did trust Tehgil," Gwyn continued, "but I sent Vigurd away from our camp unwatched, thinking if he planned to betray me I could at least force it to a time of my own choosing. He was too clever to take the bait."

"His only priority must have been finding this place," Nafar surmised. "Haric knows the western clans and their influential warriors well; he must have suspected Tehgil would ally with me. Vigurd was probably ordered to keep watch on your oath-father months ago. He likely found and killed my courier in the hopes of forcing Tehgil into a hasty move."

"Why not just follow the courier?" Drax asked.

Nafar looked at him sidelong. "He may have tried, but nothing alive could track my man through the woods."

"This bodes poorly for Tehgil," Gwyn stated, her tone dark. "If his value was in leading Vigurd here, then now he's outlived his usefulness." She clenched her fist. Once again, she was too far away to protect those who needed her.

"What do we do now?" asked one of Nafar's men. Others had taken the initiative to call back the scouts. "Do we go after him?"

Gwyn was about to answer in the affirmative, but Nafar spoke first and as decisively as always. "No. He could have hours of lead, and he knows where he intends to go while we can only follow at tracking speed. He's sure to reach reinforcements before he's overtaken, and that means death for anyone following him."

Gwyn realized Nafar was right. All Vigurd had to do was strike the nearest road, then tracking him would become impossible anyway. He could travel freely on the king's authority while Gwyn, Nafar, and most of his band were wanted by the law.

"We're prepared for this," Nafar continued. "Strike the camp and scatter back to your own homes and hideouts. Pass information to your direct contacts until you hear differently. The fight isn't over, it's just changing."

Gwyn was sure emotions must be rioting for all the men and women who had taken to calling this camp home, who had made this struggle their life's purpose and ordered their daily routines around it, but none of these emotions showed on the surface. They set about their tasks with stern discipline; some of the lightest packers were hiking out of the valley within minutes. Nafar had trained them well, which surprised Gwyn not at all.

Before Nafar could walk away to gather his gear, Gwyn asked, "Where are *you* going, Hradash?"

"Oh, I'm going with you, Candon. We've got caravans to track and elders to question. Unless you'd rather just go home."

Gwyn shook her head. She knew Nafar's comment was in jest, but indeed the fresh concern for her family did ignite the desire to abandon the mission and return to her village. Nevertheless, her course had not changed. "But before we go," she said, "I'll help you bury Gorran."

In Nafar's role as King Vassin's bodyguard he went wherever the king went. This, combined with Vassin's proclivity for going out among his people, made Nafar, quite possibly, the most broadly-traveled Atlunder alive. Gwyn was amused, however, to realize that a life of traveling with royal retinue had left him less inured to the rigors of rugged camp life than Gwyn or Drax. His one consolation in this was the presence of his page, Mithna, a relationship Gwyn and Drax only discovered upon setting out. At first Gwyn chafed at having another member added unbidden to her company, but Mithna only spoke when her duties required it, and having her at hand seemed to satisfy Nafar's propensity for giving orders. Between Nafar's knowledge of the layout of roads and towns and Drax's elvish instincts for woods and dales and all the wild places in between, they made good time bearing southeast while avoiding detection.

"Where are we heading?" Gwyn asked after they'd gone only a little distance. The general direction led them toward the eastern clan elders and likely caravan path, but she knew Nafar was sure to have a sharper goal in view.

"Only one of the chieftains on the easternmost border broke with his neighbors and voted against Haric in the Kingmoot," Nafar explained. "He must either know something the rest didn't, or have drawn a conclusion they couldn't, and I want to know what that is. My efforts haven't been able to break into the border clans much, and rumor says the man has been practically in seclusion for months, so I prioritized other things. But adding your suspicions about this wagon train and herd, if they kept on the road where my people last spotted them, they'd have gone straight to his lands. That's too great a coincidence to ignore."

"Which clan is it?" Gwyn queried.

"At the very southern end of our eastern border. Clan Baldor."

Had Gwyn been on foot, the rest of the party might have noticed the hitch in her step at the mention of the name. Sudro was from Baldor, the boy she'd briefly befriended during the Forest Campaign, the first boy she'd ever kissed. He'd died saving her life. Most of the eastern border clans hadn't sent warriors to those battles in the western forests, since the threat of attack from their own enemies in the east prevented it, but she recalled hearing that the only pass into Baldor lands was small and guarded by a stone fortress, so they had sent a small company to show support to the crown. Sudro, already accustomed to traveling far with his merchant father, had been among them. With the wizard Kellgore killed while she lay injured, she had seen no way to repay the debt she owed Sudro's people and had been too bitter to care. Perhaps now she could find a way to make good.

Nafar checked in with what contacts he could as they progressed. Given his fame, it was impossible for him to appear in person; instead, he sent Mithna. Trading her rough traveler's garb or armor for the dress of a young maid, she could travel with relative impunity. A large basket of linens, as though for washing, added authenticity if her route was near enough to water. Of course, apart from a short belt knife that no Atlunder would travel without, a mere tool of daily life and no proper weapon, she had to go unarmed.

Gwyn looked across the campfire at her newest acquaintance after the younger woman had returned from one such errand. At last she was forced to break her virtual silence toward the taciturn page. "Doesn't it bother you to go about without weapons? What if you were recognized, or attacked for any other reason?"

Mithna shrugged, her blonde hair, which she'd just unbound, slipping off her rising shoulders. "When I'm out of the camp, my mission is not to draw attention. If I had to fight, the mission has already failed. I bend all my skill toward not failing."

Gwyn shook her head. "I haven't gone more than five feet from a weapon since I was ten. At least, not when I could help it."

Mithna didn't reply, and Gwyn realized she hadn't asked another question. She had always considered herself a quiet person, or at least disinclined to idle conversation, but if Mithna spoke any less she would have been functionally mute.

"Can I ask you something?" Drax piped up.

Mithna hesitated. "Go ahead," she finally answered as she unfurled her bedroll.

"How did you end up as Nafar's page? That seems like a high honor for one so young."

"She volunteered," Nafar answered, returning to the camp from a brief patrol, his words saving the girl from the need for further speech. "My prior page didn't agree with my 'treasonous' ideas and stayed on with Haric when I left. Mithna's father is an old friend, and when he heard what I was up to, she sought me out."

"Why, though?" Drax pressed after a moment's pause.

Nafar stayed silent and looked at Mithna. "My brothers died in the Forest Campaign," she finally said. "Someone has to fight for my family."

"Your father put you up to it, then?" Drax asked.

Mithna fixed the elf with a glare of such venom as Gwyn wouldn't have thought the girl capable until that moment. "Nobody put me up to anything," the blonde snapped. "Haric is a tyrant. *Every* house owes its blood to his defeat."

"Apologies," Drax muttered. "I shouldn't have assumed."

Mithna slid under her blankets with no further comments.

The next morning the band set out later than usual, waiting for a line of merchant wagons to pass on a road they were bound to cross. Traffic would likely diminish as spring wore on, but with Atlunders confined largely to their own homes throughout the winter, the movement of goods was always heavy after the thaw.

"We've had a winter and half a spring's worth of snow and rains since your caravan came through, Gwyn," Nafar observed. "I can take us to the last place any of my people saw it, but tracking it from there will be as good as impossible. If they turned northward before reaching Baldor lands, we won't know it."

"You said the Baldor chieftain might have useful knowledge, regardless. All we can do is stay the course and hope for the best."

"Because you're such an optimist?" Drax scoffed.

"When left with no other choice," Gwyn answered. This inspired a chuckle from Mithna, which took Gwyn by surprise.

That night, the fair-haired page returned from another clandestine meeting with one of Nafar's contacts. "Interesting news," she announced.

"Interesting how?" Nafar questioned.

"I asked your man the usual questions about Haric's patrols, whether Clan Kart or mercenary. Then I asked if he overheard anything from the caravan that passed through here, and he asked, 'Which one?'"

Gwyn sat up straighter on the fallen log she used as a seat. "Which one?" she echoed.

Mithna nodded. "He said he saw the one in the fall, then another right after the thaw, and a third a fortnight after that."

"Do you think Dez went ahead with the next shipments?" Drax asked.

"Even if he did," Gwyn answered, shaking her head, "they couldn't have gotten here in time. The second group had to have camped just south of the Sharai and crossed as soon as the Winds stopped."

"Just a coincidence?" the elf hazarded. "You've said trade is the busiest just after winter."

"Possible," Mithna spoke up again, "but I don't think likely. I bade the man describe what he saw, and he was sure the horses were of Southern stock, and the guards weren't Atlunders."

"So whether they have the same destination or not," Nafar concluded, "nobody on *our* side is importing weapons or mounts from the South."

"Bad news regardless, then," Drax sighed. "Why should I be surprised?"

The band was silent for the remainder of the evening, none voicing the obvious implications. Whatever this conspiracy meant, it reached even farther than Gwyn had realized. Moreover, the first shipment was thought to contain weapons and horses enough for a mixed force of some hundreds. Tripling that meant the enemy was preparing to field an army of well over a thousand. And there could be more.

For another week Gwyn and her companions traveled toward the east, finally slowing as the last of their provisions ran out and they were forced to forage for provender along the way. Mithna volunteered to take the additional risk of going into villages and towns to purchase fresh supplies, but what little was left of Nafar's silver didn't stretch far, and in the unexpected chaos of her return Gwyn had neglected to exchange her coins from the South; passing Southern currency was deemed to draw more attention than the group could afford.

Meanwhile, the page's reports from Nafar's allies, while growing more infrequent, confirmed the passage of the two additional shipments and seemed to suggest a fourth, though the relative timing of the sightings left this inconclusive.

The sun was at its zenith when the band approached the most dangerous moments of their journey. They had finally come far enough south to parallel the great River Road, running along the Sharai's northern bank. Now the easternmost major crossing of that great river lay just to the south, and the road running northward from it saw constant traffic. Long stretches of this thoroughfare ran between high banks, limiting opportunities to cross it away from major intersections. Gwyn and her companions would have no choice but to attempt a passage under the cover of darkness, but if they happened to be spotted by a patrol, there was no way they could hope to talk their way out of the confrontation.

Drax scouted the area near the road and located a thicket where the group could rest, unseen, until nightfall. Gwyn kept her mail on, as she had during much of the ride across her homeland, fearing an attack at any moment ever since the debacle in the forest outside her village. The band was obliged to remain silent as noises from the road drifted clearly to their ears. They picketed the horses at the western edge of the thicket and let them graze on whatever tender shoots and leaves they could reach. Gwyn was eager to reach some stable where they could rest them with proper feed, but that time still lay in a future without any guarantee.

The creaking of wagon wheels and jingling of tack and harness mixed with the spring breeze to build a soothing undercurrent to the otherwise fraught afternoon. No one slept, but all sat or reclined as best they could on the uneven turf and rested their eyes in turns. The sun hung an hour above the horizon, and Gwyn sat on the ground, hunched to let some of her mail's weight rest on the loamy soil. Her eyelids sank to narrow her vision into a blurry slit of yellow light.

"Stop!" came the terrified shriek from the direction of the road.

A horse in the distance gave a panicked whinny, then a chorus of shouts erupted, all from the same direction. Gwyn leaped to her feet and charged from the thicket, her sword in hand.

"Gwyn, don't!" Drax called.

"Not again, Drax!" she shouted back as she ran. She heard crashing through the brush behind her and to the right, looked to see Mithna hard on her heels with a spear held parallel to the ground in her right hand. From noises farther behind, she knew Nafar or Drax were following, maybe both.

Mithna's strides were shorter than Gwyn's, but she was unarmored; she caught up quickly to the more experienced warrior and kept pace. They reached the road in less than half a minute, and before covering the whole distance Gwyn could see at least some of what had transpired.

A squad of four armed men, Southerners, stood blocking the road, one of them on horseback. Opposed to them were some twenty travelers, mostly women and children on foot, led by an older man that struggled to stay in the saddle as one of the Southern mercenaries took his horse's bridle and tried to haul him to the ground with his other hand. The older man was coughing as the woman behind him, also mounted, continued to scream for the soldiers to leave them alone and let them pass.

Gwyn's anger burned hot within her. She had no idea what had started this altercation, and she didn't care. "Stand down, you filthy dogs!" she ordered, now just ten yards away.

With a final, mighty tug, the mercenary managed to haul the old man from his horse. He tipped sideways, hitting the ground with a heavy *thud*. A second mercenary laid a quarrel across his spanned crossbow. Gwyn shouted, "Mithna!" and pointed. The younger fighter braced her feet and hurled her spear. This man wore only a padded jack, and the heavy spear point tore through it, impaling him. Mithna drew a short sword from her belt and continued her charge.

The mercenary leader on horseback turned toward the new threat. His shield was lashed to his horse's tack, but his sword was in his hand. Gwyn continued her sprint and flew from the elevated bank, thrusting her point as she sailed through the air. The mounted man turned his helmeted head to the side and moved his sword into guard, but neither quite quick enough; Gwyn's point punched into his face below his left cheekbone and ripped through the other side. Blood poured from the man's mangled jaws as he screamed in agony and terror. Gwyn landed behind the mercenary at the old man's horse as Mithna half dropped-half slid down the embankment to the road.

The fourth sellsword, standing somewhat farther back, babbled, "Gw…Gwyn the Savage!" He turned to flee, and Mithna charged after him.

The soldier in front of Gwyn had turned shoulders and head back toward her, barely able to react to the sudden chaos, but his hips still pointed squarely away. Gwyn kicked the back of his right knee, dropping him to it. He'd had no time to draw his blade. She grabbed the back of his tunic and laid her edge across his throat.

Before Mithna could catch up to the fleeing mercenary, Nafar had mounted his white stallion and galloped to the north, finding a section of embankment shallow enough to be negotiated by his surefooted warhorse. He brandished his sword and turned his mount, showing fiery in the evening sun, to block the fleeing fighter's escape.

"Gwyn," Drax shouted as he closed on the scene with the remainder of the animals in tow, "don't kill him."

"Why not?" she growled back. The man babbled and sobbed before her, probably begging for mercy, fueling her desire to scourge his weakness and villainy from her land.

"Father, are you alright?" the mounted woman called, choking down her hysteria over the surge of blood and death that had just consumed her world.

The older man stirred. "Just knocked my wits about a bit," he replied as he pushed himself to a sitting posture. "It'll take more than this mewling pup to put an end to me."

Gwyn noted the children looking on. Nafar drove his prisoner back toward the scene of action. Mithna stood over the dead mercenary with her spear through his chest. Her eyes were wide, her face ashen, and Gwyn knew she had never killed before. Her hostage's captain no longer screamed, but he clung to consciousness, whimpering and leaning over his horse's mane. He'd have to be dealt with, for there could be no recovery from such a wound. Gwyn ground her teeth and pressed her edge into the kneeling soldier's throat, which put a stop to his whining. "Grandfather," she asked the older man, "what would you have us do with them?"

"What did they want?" Drax asked the question Gwyn hadn't cared to.

"They stopped us and asked our business," the woman on horseback answered. "I don't know why. My father said it was none of *their* damn business, and that's when they set upon us."

"Beating old men and terrorizing women and children," Gwyn growled out through clenched teeth. "You're no soldier. I'll wager you never did your duty in your own home, either, just stood guard over the lands of nobles too cowardly to fight."

"Disarm them," the old man answered, standing up with a groan. "Strip them. Bind their hands and send them back to their masters."

Gwyn nodded and shoved her charge onto his face. With a sudden shift she thrust her blade into the horseman's exposed neck, silencing him forever. "If they live to tell their tale," she warned the old man, "it could mean trouble for you down the road."

"Less than for you, I think," he answered with a grim smile.

"You're right about that, father," Nafar interjected. "We need to be gone from here. Mithna," he added with a turn of his head toward the page, "are you planning on keeping that spear?"

The girl nodded, then flipped the dead man onto his side, set her foot against his back, and pulled the spear the rest of the way through him. She promptly retched, and Nafar looked away as he tossed a rag down to her to wipe the worst of the blood and gore off the weapon.

Gwyn and Nafar held the two surviving mercenaries at bay while Drax, Mithna, and the old man relieved them of first their weapons and armor, then their clothing. The old man's daughter, from her mounted height, acted as lookout, but as the sun continued to lower, most traffic had already staked out their campsites or lodgings.

After the prisoners' hands had been bound, Gwyn added to their sentence. "Tie the dead men to them. Let them be dragged back to their camp or barracks. Tell them this is the closest Gwyn the Savage knows to mercy. Tell them Atlund does not belong to them, and she never will."

Drax and Nafar did as Gwyn bid them. Once the mercenaries had started off to the south with their gruesome burdens, Nafar said to Gwyn, "This isn't mere resistance anymore, Gwyn." He pointed toward the struggling men. "That's a declaration of war."

She looked at the blood soaking the road, the innocent family led to the north by their battered patriarch, Mithna with her disillusioned conviction, and Drax in his grim acceptance. "Let it stand," she nodded. The four mounted their horses and found a slope out of the road, driving to the east to be far away before more enemies could appear.

~ * ~

The band was forced to camp in the open that night, so they made no fire. There was hardly any moon, so Drax with his sharper night vision took a double watch, but he woke Gwyn after midnight to take her turn. With no light to speak of, she could only strain her ears to hear any danger approaching over the chirping of night insects and frogs. After an hour, she was startled to hear a rustling of fabric against grass behind her. She turned, brandishing her sword and preparing to shout the alarm, but the figure she saw demanded silence. "I thought you might not speak to me again," she muttered.

"Thought, or hoped?" Daruneh replied.

"Why come to me now, then, after all this time?" Gwyn asked, ignoring the woman's question.

"As my friends told you in the forest, I was reluctant to take such a risk all this time. Now, though, it seems everyone knows where you are, or close enough as to make no difference."

"Is Karon well?" Gwyn knew this visitation would end on Daruneh's terms and not her own, so she wanted to learn of the boy while she had the chance. Moreover, she felt a foreboding over whatever business brought Daruneh here and wished to delay it, certain it would be as dire as it was undaunted by her swordsmanship.

"The abbey suits him," she answered, "and increasingly he suits the abbey. He's had a growth spurt. The horses are all enamored of him, but that should be no surprise. He takes after his father in that way. I think his true power lays in the gardens, though."

"The gardens? You said his power was like mine and Shon's, inspiring mighty deeds, or however you said it."

Daruneh hesitated. "All your kind had that aptitude. Each also had a realm of special dominion governed by their deepest passion. You once believed Karon's father gave special power to the horse he rode on his ill-fated attempt to lift the siege of Roon. You were not wrong."

"Shon was a master of horse, Karon of growing things." Gwyn looked to the stars before returning her gaze to Daruneh's silhouette, the faint glint of her eyes. "What was my father?"

"A protector."

Gwyn did not ask what she was, herself. She already knew the answer. "I learned more of the source of this power, or tried to."

"Yes, I know," Daruneh admitted. "I listen more than I speak."

"Is it the truth?"

"The realities of the present are never as simple as the histories they become. But your loremaster was correct in the sense of it."

"Why not simply tell me that yourself? It seems harmless enough," Gwyn challenged.

Gwyn barely saw Daruneh's ironic smile in the darkness. "Many things may *seem* harmless. I don't doubt some of your early opponents made the same assumption of you and greatly erred. You are right, though, I little feared that tale would cause trouble on its own. Still, knowledge is the only real coin I have, and I spend it sparingly. Might you have done anything differently between our last meeting and your gaining of that knowledge?"

Gwyn considered briefly. "Not that I could say," she admitted.

"So why tell you?" Daruneh asked rhetorically.

"Perhaps so I would have less cause to think you hide things from me."

Daruneh's eyes narrowed. "The words come from your lips, but I sense they were put there by another will."

"No one has mastery over my thoughts," Gwyn shot back.

"Not mastery, but influence can be subtle. Beware the honeyed tongue; the sweetness may hide its fork."

"At least he doesn't speak in riddles. Don't fret. I trust him no more now than I did in the canyon. But even a liar may say the sky is blue, as you might put it."

Daruneh nodded, her lips tight. "I will not use his own tactics to poison you against him, as I'm sure he has attempted against me. Let that stand as evidence of our differences."

Finally Gwyn could delay no longer. "Why are you here? What need brought you?"

"Only to give special warning," Daruneh answered. "Your lineage offers you many protections, but others of humankind are susceptible to temptations, to whispers in the dark. Not that a man can be made to do that which he doesn't desire, but those of weak or wicked hearts might be swayed to succumb to ambitions they might otherwise have resisted. I sense the enemy's inky fingerprints in the thoughts of many on your path ahead. Take care not to be drawn into their nets."

Gwyn shook her head, starting suddenly, to find herself sitting once more on the ground, and Daruneh was gone.

Once again Gwyn chose speed over stealth, outrunning the reliable witnesses of her location. The deeper they traveled into danger, the more even Nafar took his lead from her, following her instincts and boldness where a calculated strategy would never dare tread. Mithna and Drax only occasionally went into towns for news, but when they did they found the rumors of Gwyn's return had continued to spread. The reports from the surviving mercenaries would lend credence to some and not quite dispel the fog of war from any others, creating a haze of paranoia for Haric's loyalists, or at least that was Gwyn's hope.

Another week brought them to the edge of Clan Baldor's territory. Gwyn was surprised to find the land nearly deserted. They still avoided the villages, but they saw few people in the distance even in the fields and forests. Nafar explained that much of Clan Baldor's income came from trade, so once planting time had ended, many of its men, even whole families, took to the roads. More troubling, most of the single company Clan Baldor had sent to the effort against Kellgore had not returned, and in some smaller villages, it was said, the toll on their young men was plainly visible in the surviving population. Gwyn thought of Sudro again. The three years that had passed might as well have been a lifetime.

In the east, the threat of raids from the nomads on the other side of the Qachar range drove heavier fortifications for the larger towns. The seat of Clan Baldor was such a place, with a hedge of upright logs a hundred yards from the village wall. These were spaced a little over a foot apart; archers could shoot between them easily, and skirmishers on foot could even slip in and out at will, but the nomads' notorious light cavalry could not ride through except at the gaps for the main roads, which were easily barricaded. Against the foothills of the mountains, quarries were abundant, so the main village wall was made of stone as a protection against fire. The span between the fortifications was scattered with ditches and stake barriers, forming a respectable killing field. To call the town unassailable would be untrue, but it could be easily held by a small number of capable archers, too tough a nut to crack for all but the largest and most determined raiding parties.

For a small band of skilled infiltrators, on the other hand, the fortifications presented less challenge. The night patrols were spaced and trained to raise the alarm against massed enemies; there was little motive for anyone to sneak over the walls except to open the gate in advance of an attack, and fortifying the gatehouse against such sabotage was more feasible than guarding every foot of parapet.

A mile to the south the foothills thrust out a protruding horn of rock, screening the town from view, and here they left Mithna to guard the horses and extra gear. Drax, having exchanged his robes for a tunic and breeches, led Gwyn and Nafar toward the town between sundown and moonrise, feeling their way forward with the benefit of the elf's night-tuned eyes in the lead, fixing on the glow of lantern and firelight ahead. In an hour they reached the base of the wall. Drax removed his boots and replaced them with a pair of light sandals he had prepared the night before. He checked the coil of rope wound crosswise over his chest, then looked up, eyeing the top of the wall. *Aridan's* crescent, if he yet rose, stayed hidden behind the town, but *Bia Creg* stared down, unblinking and ominous. Gwyn and Nafar looked either way, watching for the silhouettes of guards against the stars.

Gwyn was sure the coast was clear, but Drax hesitated. "Go," she hissed.

"It's just, I haven't really practiced this, and–"

"Go, dammit!" she insisted.

Drax let out a frustrated sigh, bent his knees, and leaped.

The magic of his enchanted sandals shot him into the air, catapulting him the twenty feet to the top of the wall. For a moment his jump looked perfect, then he started to slow. Head and shoulders crested the top, but his upward speed failed entirely before his feet came close. He continued forward at the peak of his jump, nearly slamming into the wall; Drax reached with both arms, just managed to hook his right elbow around a merlon, and hung there.

Gwyn looked on in dread, her eyes flicking left and right to look for guards. Whether any came or not, there was nothing she could do, for Drax was too far away now to sound a warning without being overheard. The elf caught the edge of the wall with his left hand, adding to his grip, then swung sideways once, twice, and at last managed to force his right knee over the edge of an embrasure, flopping over the battlement onto the wall walk.

Just then, Gwyn saw a guard make the turn at the left corner. She and Nafar pressed themselves against the base of the wall, holding their breath and waiting for Drax to lower the rope to them. If he didn't he would be completely alone. Seconds passed, but the rope never came. The guard's boots made no noise loud enough to reach them on the ground, so Gwyn gauged his speed in her mind, knowing his shouts of alarm must ring out at any moment. She knew Drax wouldn't kill the man, which was just as well, since they had no idea whose forces manned the town walls, but how else could he silence him?

No yells or commotion sounded from above, and after another minute the rope finally snaked down before their wary eyes. Gwyn looked to see Drax at the wall top, urgently waving them up. She grabbed the rope and began pulling herself off the ground, the weight of her sword her only burden as she had left her armor back with the horses, a choice she hoped she didn't come to regret. Halfway up, she felt tension on the rope below her hands as Nafar likewise began his ascent.

Gwyn hauled herself over the top, then began hoisting the rope upward to speed Nafar's climb. The captain made the top, then Drax un-looped the rope from the merlon before following the pair to the steps at the corner of the wall, dropping down into their shadow just as another guard made his turn. Once again they waited, scarcely daring to breathe, and once again the watchman passed without spotting them. In another moment they were on the ground, and once past the perimeter they could move more freely. The town was under no curfew, and a few people could be seen moving between buildings in the distance.

"How did you miss being spotted by that guard?" Gwyn asked, her voice barely over a whisper. "I didn't think you could go invisible that fast."

"I can't," the elf replied. "The other side of the wall was dark there, so I just hung down over the far edge until he was gone. Thank Terillah he didn't spot my fingers."

"He's very capable," Nafar observed.

Gwyn was about to admonish Nafar for complimenting the self-assured elf, but before she could speak Drax answered, "Thank you. Now who has my boots?" Only then did she notice his sandals held in his hand. She looked at Nafar, who looked back at her.

"What's wrong with those?" Gwyn asked, pointing to the shoes in his hand.

"I'd rather not go bounding five feet in the air with every step. I explained this to you this afternoon."

Gwyn had a vague recollection of Drax's lecture, but once he explained he'd be able to leap to the top of the wall, she'd stopped listening. As they continued through the alleys, she tried to think of an apology that would satisfy the aggrieved enchanter.

"Fantastic," he grunted. "Now I'm barefoot until this enchantment wears off, by which time my feet will be too covered in muck to put them back into clean shoes. On the off chance we even make it out of here alive, you owe me a pair of boots. Comfortable, durable, *magic* boots, I might add."

"Add it to the tally," Gwyn answered, keeping her hand on her dirk as she took point. Their work was far from over; Envil, Clan Baldor's chieftain, was likely to be guarded. Getting past those wardens without bloodshed would fall

to Nafar, but until they got there she wanted to be in front
if they ran into trouble.

CHAPTER XVI

Clan Baldor's main longhouse stood on a raised platform in the rough center of the town, so navigating there was easy, even for Gwyn who was unfamiliar with nearly every community other than her own. *Bia Creg* had disappeared on her wandering way by the time they reached the log steps set into the earthen mound, and here Nafar took the lead, his sword sheathed and shield strapped to his back.

The guards at the door to the longhouse wore Baldor tartan, which Gwyn took to be a good sign. The captain mounted the first step, lit dimly by lanterns flanking the door above, when the guards called out, "Who goes there?"

"I'm a friend," Nafar responded, his empty hands held before him. "At least, I once was." He took another step, inclining his face upward to catch more of the light from the guards' lanterns. "I remain a friend to all who are loyal to their clans and to what our nation has been, not this horror it's quickly becoming."

"Captain Nafar," the guard on the left exclaimed. "Captain, you can't be here."

"By whose order?" Nafar pressed. "The pretender king who breaks our ancient law?" He continued up the steps. The guards were no more than ten yards away now.

"Stop there!" the guard on the right ordered, lowering his spear.

"Arland, I don't know…" the guard on the left cautioned.

"Gwyn, do something," Drax muttered.

Gwyn knew what he meant. He wanted her to step forward, to somehow use her sway over the hearts of fighting men to calm the situation, but she didn't know how. She had never really tried to tap this ability of her own will, and even when she had envisioned doing so it was always to enflame warriors' will to fight. The notion of influencing an appeal to calmer heads was foreign to her. Already she chided her decision to approach without her sword in her hand and itched to draw her dirk.

"I have business with your chieftain," Nafar continued, neither stopping nor speeding his approach, though now he angled directly toward Arland, the guard that had challenged him. "I come in peace and good faith."

"Drop your sword belt," the guard demanded.

"Yes, I come armed," the captain replied in an even voice. "That's a warrior's right. My companions and I will remain outside while you–"

"Stop!" Arland ordered. Then he thrust his spear.

Nafar spun to the left like lightning, turning fully around and driving the shield on his back into the point of the striking spear. Without any pause he continued his turn, driving his left arm into the weapon's haft and wrapping it in the crook of his elbow. The guard, to his credit, couched the spear well and kept his grip, but the speed and shock of Nafar's maneuver pulled the man off balance. By the time the captain's right arm whipped toward the guard, his sword was in hand, the point slipping past Arland's shield and kissing his throat with the lethal cold of steel. The other guard, on the left, barely had time to point his spear before realizing any further move would cost his comrade his life.

Best in the world, Gwyn thought as she rushed forward and relieved Arland of his weapon. His expression flashed between shock, anger, and shame.

"We're going inside now," Nafar stated, returning his sword to its scabbard. Gwyn handed the spear off to Drax, then, expecting more guards in the chieftain's immediate presence, lifted her sword sling over her head and hung it over one shoulder, offering her quicker access if something went wrong.

The other guard raised his spear and pushed the door open before them, nodding as they passed, whether out of general respect or thanks for not killing his friend, Gwyn couldn't tell.

Gwyn's village was not the seat of her clan chieftain, so she hadn't often been in a hall as large as this one. The main space was at least sixty feet deep and maybe half as wide. Two campfires burned in stone circles set at even intervals between the door and the far end, where a raised dais held a small table and handful of chairs, one of which was larger and better carved than the others. In the far wall were two doors that led to other chambers taking up the remainder of the structure. If Baldor arranged its buildings as the western clans did, these would be smaller rooms for private discussions or rest by those who spent long hours in the hall, but no proper residence.

A few clan officials had drawn to the side walls at the commotion outside while the chieftain's bodyguard had begun to move from the dais toward the door. When they saw Nafar's face they stopped, unsure what to do. These men were older, old enough to be well aware not only of

Nafar's honor but his capability. Here was a man they didn't want to kill and deeply doubted they could, a mix of emotions writ clearly on their faces.

"Clan Baldor is the only clan in the east holding onto anything like courage," Nafar called. "I'm here to test the weight of it."

"If we wanted to harm your master," Gwyn added, trusting herself at last not to make things worse by speaking, "you don't have enough men here to stop any two of us, and we are three. Tomorrow your captain should begin training you harder or recruiting more men. Both, if he can manage it. But tonight you can only thank Terillah we come in friendship and let us speak our peace."

"That was well said," Drax murmured, a note of surprise in his voice.

"She speaks true," the chieftain called from the table where he sat, eating a late supper of roast mutton. "Let them approach."

The guards withdrew to the sides, allowing the trio to walk to the platform, though Gwyn noticed that, in so doing, the men now effectively surrounded them while protecting the few other civilians in the hall. She still had no reason to believe they could best her, but they knew their duty.

"I've tried at whiles to send someone to speak to you for months, Envil," Nafar began when they were close enough, "but you refused every messenger. Why?"

Clan Baldor's chieftain, Envil, was a stocky man, short for an Atlunder, but the padding of age about his middle did nothing to conceal his barrel chest or massive arms. If she had to fight him, Gwyn considered, she would have to take care not to let him inside her reach. The man's hair was more gray than black, and he kept his beard shaved. A sash of Baldor plaid crossed his light green tunic. He didn't answer Nafar's question immediately, waving the trio up onto the platform.

"Damage done now," he grumbled. "You might as well sit and eat. I can at least offer some kind of hospitality, and I have little enough appetite these days."

Drax hesitated, but Gwyn and Nafar accepted the invitation, at which the elf followed. Gwyn could see the piece of roast Envil ate was cut from the same shank that rested on the table, and there was but one pitcher of mead as well. Even if poison was tolerated in Atlund, which it wasn't, there would have been no time to adulterate anything Envil offered.

Nafar only ate a single bite, proving his willingness to share Envil's table, before pressing, "I know it wouldn't be true to say we've been friends; Hradash and Baldor are long weeks of travel separated, but you always had respect for Vassin and treated my men and me as honored guests. Alone of the eastern clans, you had courage enough to vote against Haric, but you were shouted down in the Kingmoot when you tried to explain why. Tell me what's going on."

Envil stayed silent, and Gwyn saw despair in his eyes, and resignation. He looked then to one of his bodyguard, the captain she supposed, fixing him with that same look of pained hopelessness.

"Everyone out," the lead bodyguard ordered, ushering his own men from the hall. They protested, but only weakly, also motioning the few clan officials to exit before them as they left. At last the guard captain closed the doors behind the others and barred them, finally returning to the dais.

Envil took a long draught of mead before beginning his answer. "After the Kingmoot, the other eastern chieftains...*encouraged* me to keep my mouth shut, even before my party had left the Citadel. They warned me my vote wouldn't be forgotten. The journey home was long, and by the time I got here, my wife and daughters were gone. In their place was a letter left by one of Haric's ambassadors, a man called Rossaen, explaining that due to a threat of raids from the north, my family had been taken to the fortress that guards the South Pass through the Qachar range. I was assured they would be quite safe, as those of my warriors found to be the most 'loyal' would accompany them, along with reinforcements from Clan Kart. I was encouraged to commit myself to the administration of my lands and promised they would be returned to me when Rossaen deemed the danger had passed."

Gwyn found her hands had clenched into fists, her nails biting into her palms. Taking innocents hostage was galling enough, but the obvious duplicity in the message, so intentionally obvious, in fact, that it seemed driven as much by smugness as any real desire for deniability, was detestable to everything an Atlund warrior stood for. Where had Haric found so many poor excuses for her countrymen? She wouldn't have thought enough men so worthless and craven lived in her entire nation as to fill a feasting hall, yet Haric seemed to have recruited them all.

"Haric could have held your family anywhere," Drax observed, "even back in the Citadel where he enjoys ultimate control. What's so special about that keep, or that pass? Special enough to force you to avoid it under pain of their death?"

Envil's expression didn't change to one of consideration or bewilderment; it remained a mixture of disgust and misery. Gwyn sussed by the chieftain's reaction that he knew well the answer to Drax's question, and by his confidence a picture began to form in her mind, a scenario that tied the eastern clans' support for Haric, the strange orders of weapons and horses, and the South Pass together in treason. She felt no surprise when Envil gave his answer.

"Haven't you guessed? The South Pass is the most remote of all the ways through the Qachar range. A careful party could cross the Sharai at the eastern bridge, head east to the crossroads, leave the main road when most traffic heads north, and not meet another person all the way to the pass itself. What better place to deliver aid and support to your mortal enemies without arousing suspicion?"

Nafar shook his head in disbelief. Drax narrowed his eyes in confusion, his quick mind gathering threads but, lacking a deep grounding in Atlund history, finding no warp through which to weave them. "We knew Haric had somehow gained the support of the eastern clans by promising them peace," Gwyn explained to her oath-brother. "He used the Clan Kart treasury to purchase the weapons and horses as a tribute to the nomads east of the Qachars, money he had no motive to spend without knowing Vassin, a young and healthy king, would soon die."

"How could he be such a fool?" Nafar wondered, aghast. "There's nothing to keep them from turning and attacking us at a whim, now armed with Southern steel and armor."

"That's actually the *best* we can hope for," Envil added. "The last explanations I heard, before my obstinance saw me forced out of the negotiations, were that the nomads to our immediate east would be encouraged to turn their new armaments on their neighbors to the south and unite all the tribes under their own banner. I refused to buy peace in my own time by forcing my grandchildren to face such a unified horde."

"Why would anyone else?" Nafar asked. "Why were you the only one to resist?"

"Somehow Haric's men, this Rossaen the wiliest amongst them, convinced my fellow chieftains we wouldn't be the eventual target. He was certain that with the orcs now withdrawing deeper into their own territory to lick their wounds, perhaps forever, the nomads would push south, where the Qachars are lower and more easily crossed, and drive the war-weary Southerners off their best lands."

Gwyn pounded the table, setting the plates and cups to rattling. "Damned if I'll sit by for treason in my homeland

and invasion for my Southern comrades, be it in a year or a generation. I've had enough of this underhanded dealing and poisoning in the dark. Somebody show me who to stab to put an end to this madness."

"You don't understand," Envil replied. "If I could have just cut Rossaen's throat and taken back my fort and family I'd have done it by now. Haric has eyes and ears everywhere. By morning someone will have made their way out of this town and taken to the roads, using writ or reputation to gain a fresh horse at every post. Your coming here has signed my family's death warrant. Mine, too, once they no longer have anything over me to keep me silent."

Gwyn jumped to her feet, shaking with the urge to strike the chieftain. "What kind of Atlunder are you?" she demanded. "What kind of man? What sort of coward would take such threats unanswered, just lay down and quit? If *I* was your daughter, I'd rather die at my captor's hand with you fighting to reach me than live with such a father." Gwyn watched Envil's eyes smolder with rage at her accusations, held his gaze as she willed his ire to burst into open flame.

Envil left his chair, staring Gwyn down though he had to look half a foot upward to do it. "You dare call me a coward in my own hall?"

Drax, Nafar, and the guard captain started forward, but each belligerent waved their supporters back.

"I so dare," Gwyn confirmed, "and feel safe enough in the doing. You deny you're a coward, then prove it with more than words."

"You would fight me?" the chieftain challenged.

Gwyn scoffed. "I would *kill* you." She suddenly realized her temper was besting her aim and eased her posture. "But I would not have you test your courage against *me*." She pointed toward the south. "Go get them back, dammit!"

The mention of Envil's failed duty seemed to bring back his helpless shame, but something new remained in his expression, and Gwyn dared to think it was hope. "How?" Envil demanded. "They could kill any of my family the moment I show my face."

Gwyn looked over her shoulder at Drax and Nafar, hoping either of the clever warriors would break in with their own brilliant plan. Neither offered help, both looking expectantly back at her. With a note of dread at her own stratagem, she turned toward Envil once more. "Simple," she answered. "You're going to turn us in."

The Clan Baldor fortress in the South Pass was an austere, solid structure, built against the north wall of the pass at a place where the cliffs were steep. It consisted of a hall keep of three stories, a small bailey holding stables and assorted outbuildings, and a three-sided curtain wall which enclosed them, the mountain itself serving as the north wall. The three sides were also defended by a wide moat, though it remained dry except after heavy rains. In the east and west sides of the curtain wall stood great drawbridges and portcullises to allow passage. Both of these portals were protected by gate houses built around and over them; to the east, from whence attack was expected, the gatehouse was large, blocked by narrow bastions thrusting forward on either side and with murder holes set in the roof through which to attack any enemies who breached the outer defenses and passed below. The western guard house, facing friendly lands, was a smaller, less threatening structure built mostly to house the mechanisms controlling the drawbridge and portcullis and shield them from the weather. In the southern wall, at roughly the center, stood a square mural tower, and from its southern side projected a thick barrier wall stretching the sixty yards to the southern cliff of the pass. This wall was built as a pure obstacle, bearing neither gate nor portal.

Luvo stood watch on the barrier wall, the early sun at his back as he gazed off into the west, toward home. He wished he knew which of his Clan Kart relatives he had offended to find himself cast to the other side of the nation, there to be implicated in the scheme to arm the eastern nomads, a secret held so closely he feared what might be done to ensure his silence once his duty here had been fulfilled. Perhaps a quick death by his own people was the best he could hope for, certainly better than what he might expect if he fell into the hands of Clan Baldor's remaining loyal warriors. Haric had made many promises, and with the Clan Kart *and* royal treasuries and years of political maneuvering at his back, he seemed well-positioned to fulfill them. Now Luvo was forced to admit he would likely have been better off with less ambition and more bravery. Plenty of Atlund women respected scars more than money, anyway.

One of the Baldor chief's minders had arrived on a courier horse just yesterday, bringing bad news. Nafar, the former royal guard captain, and Gwyn of Clan Candon had met with the chieftain two nights before. None could say for sure what that would mean, since the agent had felt it best to bring his report as soon as the wanted traitors appeared, but it couldn't be anything good. Luvo had overheard the argument between the Clan Kart captain and Rossaen, Haric's ambassador, after the courier spoke. The captain insisted they should kill one of Envil's daughters and send her head back in a basket merely for speaking to the criminals, as a warning to Envil and anyone else who might learn of it. Rossaen insisted this would be overly rash, as their keeping of the hostages wasn't meant to be widely known just yet, and such a gesture could never remain secret. The eastern clans may be cowed by their complicity in this scheme, which most Atlunders would find shameful, but if word reached the central clans, they might rise up as a unified body before King Haric was ready, especially in light of the rumors of *Gwyn et Sheevasa's* return, rumors now confirmed as fact. Better to bide their time, for now. They could always kill one of Envil's women at any later point, after all, but they couldn't very well *unkill* anyone once the deed was done.

Luvo feared men like Rossaen and Haric. In his experience, those seeking to lord power over others were simple bullies with simple motivations, men easy to predict and quick to shrink from opposition. Haric and the people in his circle were different. Most were cowards, at least with regard to physical risk, but they were clever, patient, and ruthless, and that combination made them dangerous.

The guard was roused from his grim reflection by movement at the far horizon of his vision. The last of the wagon trains of arms and mounts was supposed to have been diverted farther to the south, to the new staging area; they had sent messages to that effect, but it was possible those had gone awry. He waited to sound the alarm until he had some idea who was coming. As the minutes passed, Luvo could see the approaching group was too small to be the merchants, but too many to be another messenger from Baldor with a follow-on report. "Sergeant," he called. "Riders coming in from the west." His direct superior exited the mural tower and joined him in surveilling the approaching group.

In only a few more minutes the approaching party came near enough to be counted, numbering a dozen, all on horseback, but the best part of an hour had passed before any certain identification could be made. When no room was left for doubt, the sergeant said, "Go. Get Rossaen, bring him here now." Luvo sprinted off to follow his superior's order.

Running through the tower at the north end of the

barrier wall, Luvo passed onto the alure of the fort's curtain wall. Not slowing, he sprinted to the east corner steps and bounded down them, crossing the gravel bailey and presenting himself to the guards at the great, iron-banded doors of the keep. "The sergeant requests Rossaen's presence on the wall immediately," Luvo relayed. One of the guards opened the doors and hustled off inside.

"Trouble?" the remaining guard asked.

Luvo shrugged. "Not enough to reach us in here." He was sure his sergeant would berate him later if he revealed any more without permission. In barely a minute the absent guard returned with Ambassador Rossaen, his black mustache freshly trimmed, his blue outer robes embroidered with gold thread and slit up the back to permit easy movement and even riding, if the need arose. He acknowledged Luvo with a nod then showed himself to the barrier wall, forcing the guard to step quickly to keep up with his long strides.

"What have you to report, Sergeant?" Rossaen asked in his smooth voice as he crested the wall.

The sergeant pointed. "The Baldor chieftain approaches, Ambassador, along with eight of his warriors. He also appears to have the traitors Nafar and Gwyn, along with the elf that's said to travel with them. But, sir, it appears they're bound."

"Interesting," Rossaen mused, drawing out each syllable. He squinted at the approaching party, able to make a general count of the shapes, but his nearsighted eyes revealed no more. "What of the girl that was spotted with the traitors on the trade road?"

"No sign of her, sir."

"And the condition of Baldor's warriors?"

"Well armed, but somewhat the worse for battle. Bandages on nearly all of them. One man has his arm in a sling."

"Interesting," Rossaen repeated. "Envil was said to have true love for his family, I suppose. Summon archers," he ordered Luvo. "I little doubt they'll stop before they're in range, but I'll take no chances."

In short order the barrier wall bristled with ten bowmen, all waiting to see what would befall. At last the approaching party reached the edge of shouting distance and stopped.

"Men of the keep," the voice of Baldor's chieftain lofted to the wall, echoing off the surrounding stone, "I have prisoners. These traitors came to me in the night. I knew what report would be made against me, so I apprehended them and brought them here immediately."

"Send them forward," Rossaen called back. "We will hold them and make report to the king on your behalf."

"I will not. You and your king think me an obstacle, some of my own people think me a coward. Maybe you're all right, but I'm no fool. I hold valuable prizes, dearly bought. They killed seven of my best men and wounded most of the rest. I mean to trade them for my wife and children."

Rossaen pondered this unsurprising proposal. He had intended to hold Baldor's women indefinitely as leverage, at least until Haric ordered them moved to the Citadel or killed, but this was an unforeseeable turn. By seizing such heroes of the people, Envil made himself complicit in Clan Kart's activities in the east, a fact which might be enough to ensure his cooperation. If so, he may be of more use in the future if his family was returned to him unharmed, perhaps buying greater loyalty than mere compliance. This was not a decision he was prepared to make without time to consider. "I will not send them out," Rossaen shouted, "but you may accompany the prisoners inside to see your women before we continue our negotiations. I will send guards for escort. Order the prisoners to dismount." The ambassador turned to the sergeant. "Go and make inspection of the prisoners and chieftain, then disarm him. If you're satisfied there is no deceit, march them in. Take five men with you."

Luvo had already hoisted his shield before the sergeant pointed to him, knowing full well he would be chosen. The sergeant motioned to four of the archers, two of whom were obliged to exchange their bows for spears and shields before joining the detail. In a few moments the half-dozen men stood waiting at the western gate as the portcullis was raised into its enclosure by men in the guardhouse. Slowly the drawbridge lowered over the dry moat on the far side, allowing the guards to exit. Luvo stood just behind and to the right of his sergeant. An archer marched to his right and the two other spearmen to his left, with the final archer on the far left flank.

The walk to the Baldor delegation seemed to take forever, Luvo's boots crunching on the sand and loose stone of the pass as wind whistled about the cliffs. He swept his eyes over the Clan Baldor group, noting the warriors had withdrawn far enough not to appear threatening, though they had also spread out somewhat to avoid presenting a single, massed target for the archers on the wall. Envil still sat on his sorrel mare, his sword and dagger already handed off to his guards in anticipation of the terms to enter the keep, their deviation from Atlund custom notwithstanding. The prisoners had dismounted as ordered, their horses held by a nearby Baldor warrior. He saw the massive black steed Gwyn was rumored to be riding since her return, it's mane and tail stirring in the breeze; the glorious white stallion Nafar famously rode, and which Luvo had seen firsthand at parade more than once, looking travelworn and unkempt at present; and the gray forest horse the elf had been riding on the approach. At last he stood not five yards from the foursome, his spear readied, as the sergeant went forward to search the band for anything suspicious. Luvo had never met the famed *Gwyn et Sheevasa* before, nor any elf, nor had he stood so close to Nafar. He had no idea about elves but thought the other two would be taller, especially Gwyn. He guessed that was always the way when meeting one's heroes. He never imagined it would be like this.

The sergeant searched the prisoners for weapons or other concealed objects. Gwyn visibly seethed at the man's touch, but he did his duty quickly and dispassionately, moving to the elf without testing the limit of her forbearance. He checked their bonds next with a quick tug on each, then secured the chieftain's oath that he hid no weapons on himself or his animal. Finally the sergeant ordered the spearmen to surround the party, one at each side, and the archers to trail behind on either flank with arrows nocked. Taking point, the sergeant began the march back to the keep.

Luvo was stationed behind the prisoners, and despite initial distraction by the lovely Gwyn, he found himself staring at the back of the elf's head more than either of the bound Atlunders. He'd long been fascinated by the creatures but always seemed to miss opportunities to meet one; he supposed the Baldor men, being from a merchant clan, had the chance to trade with them all the time, but hailing from so far to the north, Luvo wasn't so fortunate. A sudden gust forced him to raise his shield to block dust blowing into his eyes, and as he lowered it again he saw the elf's odd, blue skullcap had been lifted off his head and blown into Luvo's path. The elf turned and grabbed at it with his bound hands but hadn't the reach. The archers tensed.

"It's alright," Luvo called, "everybody be calm." Transferring his spear to his shield hand for a moment, he stooped and picked up the blue cloth, knocking the dust off against his knee before placing it back on the elf's head. As he withdrew his hand, it brushed the tip of the elf's pointed ear. He began to apologize, having no idea if this was a sensitive matter, but was distracted by how soft the ear tip was, folding over easily like a dog's. Then it fell off.

Luvo's eyes widened as he looked to the ground to see a part of the elf's ear lying there, a piece of carefully painted deerskin gathering dust on a strip of hide glue at one edge. "You're no elf!" he shouted.

Suddenly the Baldor chieftain reared his horse, the mare lashing out with her forehooves to hammer savagely at the back of the sergeant's head. Nafar yelled a word in a language Luvo didn't recognize, and at that the ropes binding the prisoners incinerated in a sudden flash. The darkhaired youth, for so Luvo now realized the "elf" to be, ducked around Envil's horse and sprinted toward the cover of boulders at the cliff face. Gwyn turned toward him, using the momentum of her spin to add force to a devastating left cross to his jaw, whipping his head like a ragdoll's. Luvo's vision went fuzzy around the edges, but he clung to consciousness like a drowning man to driftwood. Before he could even transfer his spear back to his right hand, though, Gwyn was on him, driving him to the ground with her hands around his throat. He heard shouts and the pounding of hooves as he fell, his world spinning. His head smashed into the stone, and he remembered no more.

Gwyn and Drax stood just across the moat from the western drawbridge, waiting for Envil to appear with Nafar, Mithna, and the rest of his men. In this rare instance she was glad of a moment to be still, adjusting to the strangeness of her current perceptions and reflect on the decisions that had wrought them.

"You can't go in there alone," Gwyn had insisted to

Drax back in the Baldor feasting hall. "It's too dangerous, and besides, the last time you went in by yourself, you got beat half to death and imprisoned in Finn's cellar."

"Well, I can only work magic to make sure they can't see *me*," he countered.

Gwyn paused in thought. "When we talked about this outside the bandit town, you said I'd be 'practically blind.'"

"Right."

"Define 'practically.'"

Drax shook his head. "Gwyn, this is a bad idea."

"Could we at least test it?" she asked. "I mean, it wouldn't do anything…permanent?"

Then it was Drax's turn to pause. "I can't think of any reason it should."

"Let's do it, then," Gwyn insisted, handing Drax her claw necklace, just as she had in the Southern Capital the year before.

Drax gave up arguing with his oath-sister. "I'll be back in half an hour," he said with a sigh.

In the meantime, Nafar had returned with Mithna and their animals, now that Envil's cooperation was secured. All sat at the table awaiting the enchanter's report. Nafar even had the elf's boots on the floor beside him, a bit damp with dew but otherwise none the worse for their temporary abandonment.

A few minutes ahead of schedule Drax returned with the necklace, it showing no sign of changes, and handed it back to Gwyn. "I don't know *exactly* what your vision will be like once you put this on. I'd close my eyes first if I were you. Might be a little less disorienting, at least give you a second to prepare."

Gwyn had closed her eyes as suggested, then slipped the necklace back on. Nafar and Mithna both gasped aloud. Eyes still closed, Gwyn remarked, "Alright, I guess it works. I don't feel any different."

"That's normal," Drax reminded her. "You didn't feel any different when we did this at the Capital."

She nodded. "Here goes." She opened her eyes.

Gwyn's breath caught in her throat. She hadn't known quite what to expect. Total blackness. Shapes and movement, light and shadow? Whatever she might have expected, it hadn't been *this*.

"Well?" Drax questioned, able to see plainly she'd opened her eyes as his spell did nothing against the sight of elves. "What can you see?"

Gwyn was at a complete loss for words. Her vision was changed, to be sure, but it fit no definition of 'practically blind' she could imagine. The walls, the furniture, she was aware of them, but only as darkness blocking other sight. To her left, the lodge fires glowed astoundingly bright, the oranges and yellows vibrant, the white-hot heart of the flame scintillating like sunlight through a thousand prisms. Every living thing stood out in brilliant contrast to the umbral shapes: a fly buzzed from the nearer fire to the back of a chair, it's buggy features clear details in a dull, red glow; Mithna, Nafar, and Drax, before her, emanated color and brightness everywhere their clothing didn't block, like vessels of lightning wrapped in the starry night sky and shining like sunlight all at once, their eyes opalescent spheres that told all their secrets in a tongue Gwyn could never hope to understand and didn't want to, seeing them as totally ethereal and yet more real than she had ever realized a living entity could be, even herself. She raised her hands before her face, gazing at the light of them, reading every scar and bloodstain in the pattern of their stars without judgment. A wondering gasp escaped her throat, and she felt tears running down her cheeks.

"Gwyn, are you alright?" Nafar asked.

"It's… Everyone's…*shining*!" she gasped.

"Take it off!" Drax ordered. "Take it off right now!"

"But–"

Drax reached forward and grabbed the necklace, reaching to the limit of his height to pull it over her head. Gwyn was too fascinated to stop him, and the fangs caught in her hair and pulled it down over her face. When she lifted her head and brushed the unruly locks back from her eyes, everything was back to normal. Drax's expression showed concern as he ran his fingers over each piece of the necklace, sensing his work with narrowed eyes.

"Does everything look normal again?" he asked.

Gwyn nodded.

"Here," he said, thrusting the necklace toward Mithna. "Put that on."

"Hey," Gwyn protested the handing over of her property, but Mithna followed Drax's instructions and faded from Gwyn's sight, though she still appeared as a strange apparition that twitched and flashed when she moved.

"It doesn't work as well because the amulet isn't hers," Drax explained to Nafar's puzzled expression. "Well," he asked, looking plainly at Mithna's form, "what do you see?"

"Uh," Mithna hesitated, "nothing. Wait, no, I can make out the fire, barely, and if I move my head I can see shadows passing in front of it." She was silent another moment. "Yes, that's all." She reappeared as she pulled the necklace off and handed it back to Gwyn.

"I don't... Oh," Drax had said, elongating the word in his dawning realization. "We'll talk about this later."

Gwyn had been frustrated but trusted the finality of Drax's tone. Later they sealed themselves in one of the Baldor hall's private meeting rooms.

"It's this power you have from your ancestors, or whatever Daruneh and the loremaster are calling them."

"Descendants of the first Great Chieftains, 'paragons of men,' the loremaster said," Gwyn clarified.

"Alright, Paragons, then. I think you, or your senses, at

least, are not entirely what a scholar would call human."

"That's impossible," Gwyn countered. "My mother and father were human, what else could I be?"

"Yes, anatomically, but metaphysically speaking your father was partially something…else. Something more. Didn't Daruneh say it was passed to the firstborn? So it isn't a matter of breeding, exactly, or it would go to all the children, and it would weaken over generations with the bloodline. So your blood is human, your body is human, but *you* are partly of these 'Paragons.'"

"So…when you cast your spell that fools human eyes…?"

"It dims your human sight, as it did to Mithna, but that lets this other sense, the not-human part, show through."

"You think Daruneh sees like that?" Gwyn asked.

"I wouldn't presume to guess," Drax replied, "but I would have wagered my profits from the war she didn't see the world quite as we do, and this seems to prove I'm right."

For the first time since knowing him, Gwyn was genuinely interested in the workings of Drax's magic, but she feared any questions she might ask would encourage him to experiment, and they both had work to do and preparations to make. "All that matters now," she said, "is that, strange as it is, I can see well enough to get past the outer gates and into the main keep. This is going to work."

Now at the fortress in the South Pass, Gwyn marveled once more at the world of light and shadow she inhabited. On the alure of the barrier wall, a guard stood looking into the west, his glow indistinct through the stone but visible nonetheless. The wood of the drawbridge and portcullis showed dark in her vision, but through the thicker stone of the gatehouse she could just make out the sparks of another pair of men, perhaps sitting but ready at a moment's notice to work the levers and winches of the portal. Drax's face and hands glowed and shone as bright as noontime next to her. Slowly overcoming the distraction of her altered vision, she began to feel once again exposed to the eyes of the enemy as she had when crossing the battlefield against the orcs, but she knew, with greater confidence than she had then, that Drax's magic would hold. As long as Envil and his party of warriors and imposters appeared before the sun rose above the barrier wall they would cast no shadows. Nothing would betray their presence.

From the start it was planned that Nafar would accompany Envil and the diversionary party. While Gwyn was widely known by reputation, her face was recognizable to comparatively few, especially as years and war had changed it. Nafar, on the other hand, had served two kings, traveling throughout all the nation with both, and was likely to be known by any Atlund warrior upon close inspection. Envil had sent his trusted guard captain to a troupe of players based in the town to obtain a red wig that would serve as Mithna's disguise. Their false elf ears were altogether inferior to the challenge before them, being meant only to give an impression on stage and not to actually fool anyone, but Drax had worked extensively with the troupe's makeup artist to form them into a convincing accoutrement. Or so they hoped. Gwyn felt this to be the weakest part of the plan and tried to convince Drax to do something magical about it, but when he insisted he had only so much time and energy to work with and forced her to choose between convincing ears and rope bindings that could disintegrate on command, she reluctantly chose the latter.

Gwyn peered into the west, an image of darkness swimming with the motes of a thousand tiny creatures flying through the morning air or skittering along the translucent cliff walls. Lichen glowed on invisible boulders, and small plants shone a dim green and moved in the wind, like tiny fountains hanging in the air. The better part of an hour crawled by as the pair watched and waited, unable to make the slightest sound lest they alert the guards to some mischief afoot. Finally Gwyn saw the sparking glow of a dozen men and horses at the edge of her vision, though the darkness and indistinction of the surrounding world deprived her of any sense of distance. Another hour passed before Envil and his party stopped and began their shouted parlay with Haric's men at the top of the wall.

Gwyn and her companions had believed the defenders of the keep would either permit entrance for Envil and his supposed captives or, better yet, send someone out to escort them in. The latter would require the gate to be opened that much sooner, buying Gwyn and Drax more time. If neither proved true, then they would be forced to improvise some means over the wall.

As Gwyn listened to Envil and Haric's ambassador shout back and forth, she believed the clan chieftain to be playing his part well. Soon the rattle of chains and grinding of capstans signaled the raising of the portcullis and lowering of the drawbridge. Gwyn watched as the shimmering figures of half a dozen guards marched out, then she and the being of light that was Drax moved across the drawbridge as quickly as the need for silence would allow. Even disciplined guards were likely to leave the gates open in the absence of any other threat, given how quickly the escort was meant to return with their charges, and in this the infiltrators were not disappointed, allowing them time to go quietly. Likewise, the gatehouse door was left unbarred. Drax and Gwyn entered and made quick, silent work of the gate operators within. From there the duo moved to the steps leading up to the doors of the hall keep. Two guards stood ready, and there was no way to bypass them. Gwyn drew near the one on the right, pausing once within striking distance and looking over at Drax. The scintillating elf stood directly before the other guard, holding his lightning ring over the man's heart, only inches away. When Gwyn lunged, Drax spoke his magical command. Blood sprayed the wall to the right of the door, and a crackling buzz sounded from the left as both guards fell, clutching throat and chest. Before Gwyn could worry if their work had been quiet enough she heard shouting from the pass outside and from the barrier wall above. Something had gone wrong. Still, they could do nothing for their comrades and had their own mission to execute. They pushed the doors open and slipped inside.

Immediately Gwyn felt disoriented. Lanterns, still burning to aid the early sun, glowed brightly in her view but gave no illumination to their surroundings. Wood paneling and fabric tapestries showed heavy and black, blocking her sight, but living people glowed through stone barriers or scintillated brokenly through walls of wattle and daub. Continuing to pass invisibly would be an asset, but in this environment, the effect on her vision was too high a price. Gwyn drew the necklace from under her armor and removed it.

Nothing changed. She cried out in shock.

"What?" Drax hissed. "Are you wounded?"

"Drax," Gwyn muttered, feeling for the wall to her right. "Drax, my sight isn't changing back."

"You'll be fine. Just blink a few times; it'll pass."

She did. It didn't. "It isn't working." Panic edged her tone.

"Damn," Drax cursed. "Put the necklace back on. At least then nobody can see you, either."

Gwyn frantically sought her memory for where she had put the grim ornament before realizing it was still in her hand. She placed the leather thong over her head and opened her eyes, which she hadn't remembered closing. She peered at her surroundings, trying to make sense of the dim shapes and textures around her. It was confusing but better than nothing, and they had no time to lose. "I can manage. Take the lead and don't move too quickly."

Gwyn followed Drax to the left wall of the large space in which they stood, then along the stones toward the back of the room.

A voice sounded faintly from outside. "Guards! Guards, we're– No! They're inside. Someone's inside! Search the keep, I'm going for Rossaen."

"We're not spotted," Drax assured Gwyn. "They've just found the door guards."

More soldiers came rushing from the farther recesses of the keep. Gwyn watched the shining forms of some rush outside while others fanned out to search hiding places. She and Drax slipped quietly between them, past the line of their search, and rested against a pillar. Gwyn's heart filled with dread. As the guards hustled about, she could see the wooden hafts of their spears and the planks of their round shields as deeper blackness that obscured whatever lay behind it, but the metal parts, the spear points and the shields' central bosses and the swords of those that carried them, were completely invisible. Her dirk felt so natural in her hand, the position of the blade so instinctive to her, when dispatching the guards minutes before she hadn't noticed, as she did now, that the metal of it, too, was absent from her vision. Invisible or not, how could she fight against weapons she couldn't see?

CHAPTER XVII

Mithna took the spear from her fallen enemy. She couldn't tell if he was unconscious or dead, and she couldn't afford to think about it. The contorted face of the man she had slain on the road still plagued her thoughts. Worse was the sensation she could still feel in her palms, the strange shaking of the spear as she pulled it from the man's body, movement caused by his subtle twitching. He hadn't quite been dead, and she'd brutally retrieved her weapon and left him bleeding in the dirt. She forced the memories away. She knew this fight was just, and just things always had a price. Nafar had trained her well; she had only to keep moving, to trust her instincts.

She tugged once at the fallen guard's shield, but it was strapped well to his arm. No time for that. The Clan Baldor man holding her horse rode close. Arrows began to fall. She kept one eye on the wall as she put her left foot into the huge, black horse's stirrup. She'd feared the great stallion wouldn't permit any rider but Gwyn, but the elf had laughed at her concern and said, "It's fine. He likes you."

He'd had a strange confidence in his voice when he said it. She braced the spear on the ground to help vault into the high saddle, then spurred the horse toward the gate. Had Gwyn and Drax dealt with the men at the controls? Would the drawbridge start rising at any moment? She urged more speed from her mount, the gait jarring her bones.

A Baldor man next to her ducked behind his shield. She just heard the *thud* of the arrow over the hammering of hooves. Somewhere to her right another warrior was less wary or lucky, and she heard him cry out. A horse screamed, and she thanked Terillah it wasn't hers, immediately guilty for valuing her own life more highly than her comrades'. The elf's horse, carrying one of Envil's nephews disguised as Drax, was first across the bridge, but Mithna was only a few strides behind, then the rest of the troop, horseshoes thundering on the heavy planks. They took only an instant to dismount and regroup, their horses a liability in such tight quarters. Fortunately for the attackers, the keep had been built to repel raids from the east, so the defenses on the western gate were minimal, the sight lines into the entryway poor. Envil made a quick check of the gatehouse, then ushered his nephew inside and ordered him to bar the door.

Mithna took stock of their casualties as she pulled off her red wig and dropped it to the ground, exposing her straight, blonde hair tied in a tight bun at the back of her head. The last horse through the gate had an arrow stuck in his shoulder. His rider snapped it off at the skin and tossed the shaft to the ground in anger. They had lost one man to the barrage, and a second pulled a shaft from his right arm; it bled, though his mail had weakened the impact and kept it from going too deep. Her own mail, of course, was stowed away back at camp since she had to play the role of a prisoner. She looked to Nafar, likewise unarmored. He had a cut above his eye from the scuffle with the spearmen and three arrows stuck in his shield. He smashed them off against the nearest wall.

"Take Rossaen alive, keep anyone from getting to the keep with orders to kill hostages, buy time for Gwyn and Drax," Nafar ordered. "Shields up, spears out, form square on me."

Mithna finally had a moment to retrieve a spare shield picked up by one of the Baldor men. She forced her arm through the straps and hefted her spear, taking point in front of her master.

Gwyn shadowed Drax to the back of the hall, toward the stairs into the lower levels of the keep. The squat building boasted no corner towers, and the upper story was occupied by a large strategy hall, so Envil had predicted his family would be held below. The structure had no dungeons, either, but it would require little ingenuity to secure any of the private rooms of the lower floor for holding prisoners.

Before entering the stairwell, Gwyn sheathed her dirk and unstrapped the great sword from her back. As she drew it from its sheath, she was shocked to realize she could see it, the blade glowing with a faint, purple light hanging ethereally in the air below her hand. She remembered the dim illumination of the runes Drax had etched into the ricasso to bind his enchantments two years before. The characters were hidden now beneath the leather wrapping of the foregrip, but their hue was identical to the radiance she now saw. She glanced at Drax's boots and thought she saw the same faint glow limning the edges of the leather's abyssal opacity. Would she see that signature color in his enchanted rings if the starry glow of his hands didn't shine through the metal and gems? Her eyes were brought back to the sword in her hand as other shades flashed suddenly through it, scarlet and icy blue. What did *that* mean?

Suddenly overwhelmed by the mysteries of her life, she cast the sword's sling to the floor at the base of the wall. There was work to be done, and Drax was staring at her, waiting, his shining eyes shouting curiosity he didn't dare voice. Wrapping her hands on the familiar hilt and foregrip, she briefly considered the irony that the only sword she could see was her own, and it had become such an extension of her body she didn't need to. She gave Drax a nod, and again he took point. She kept her weapon in her right hand and placed her left on his shoulder for guidance as they descended the first flight.

The pair made a turn in the stairs and stopped at a broad landing. The steps continued downward to root cellars and other storage. If the king's ambassador desired the women's incarceration to be particularly unpleasant, he might have locked them up there. On this level, though, the hallway stretched in two directions, forward and to the right. All this Gwyn knew from Envil's sketches of the building's architecture, but the combination of living things and building materials still made a wreck of her vision. At least she had worked out the pattern: light, heat, living things, and, apparently, magic glowed in various ways; things formerly alive showed black and opaque; and things never alive appeared transparent or, in enough layers, translucent. She squinted into the interminable darkness, hoping to see living shapes in a pattern that would suggest Envil's family, but between woven wall hangings or other coverings she could only guess at, nothing showed. They needed to find the hostages quickly; in the cramped quarters of the lower chambers, any guards that set upon Gwyn would almost certainly wield swords instead of spears, showing nothing to her altered sight.

Envil had been unable to offer any prediction of which room might contain his family, so Gwyn assumed Drax's choice to be arbitrary when he led them forward down that hall. They had only gone a few paces when a commotion sounded from the stairway. Gwyn looked over her shoulder, craning her neck to see around what she thought was a wall banner in the hopes of providing Drax with advance detail on what was coming.

"Two dozen could hold this place against an army," a shouting voice echoed from the stairwell, "but not, it seems, against some red-headed western bitch and an elf. Come on; I need leverage."

"Drax," Gwyn whispered, "seven men are coming down the stairs. I think the third one is unarmed; that's got to be Rossaen. I'm going to hit his guards, then he'll probably run. Can you slip through the melee and follow him?" The glowing forms continued down the stairs.

"Can you handle so many?" Drax asked. "I mean, as you are?"

"I'll have to. Just shadow him to the hostages and keep them safe. Only don't kill him."

"*You're* telling *me?*"

Gwyn meant to tell him to shut up, but by then the enemy had reached the stairway landing. They went to the right. Gwyn sprinted toward them, Drax just a step behind and to her left. As quietly as she could move, the rearmost guard still heard her footfalls and began to turn, but too late. Her sword's point burst through him, splattering blood on the wall, a dull, red glow hanging in nothingness to Gwyn's sight. The guard to his left turned toward his ally's screaming and gurgling, then raised his hands toward his face by instinct. Gwyn saw his eyes then, as only she now could. The confusion and terror were written there, expressions she had watched countless times with relish as she extinguished them. Now, somehow the colors shifting in the orbs of his eyes showed the reality and humanity she had always ignored, showed her beyond the armed enemy to the frightened boy, uncomprehending how his friend had suddenly been slaughtered and afraid this sudden, bloody fate would also be his.

She hesitated, only for an instant, and if she made some sound apart from her ragged breath she could never know, but the guard shoved forward in panic with one hand, pushing Gwyn's shoulders back to arm's length, and moved his other toward his belt for sword or dagger. Gwyn reacted by instinct, moving her right hand to her sword's foregrip and punching a foot of blade into the enemy's throat, unable to tell if he might be wearing metal armor. His eyes dimmed, and he sank toward her, clawing and grasping for anything to keep from falling. Before Gwyn fully realized what was happening, his dying hand had gripped her fang necklace, all his weight hanging on it as he collapsed. The worn leather thong arrested his fall for only an instant before giving way, and he took it with him to the ground.

The remaining guards had looked back toward the bloody disturbance, and now they cried out in alarm at Gwyn's sudden appearance before them. She realized they could see her, but her vision remained unchanged. Rossaen slipped between the two guards who had preceded him into the narrow hallway and bolted.

"Come on!" Gwyn challenged, taking a step back, drawing the guards toward her to open a slim path for Drax. She saw the elf's expressive, glowing eyes shoot her one last look of heavy concern, then he ran after Rossaen as fast as his shorter strides could take him.

The constricted space of the lower keep cramped the sweeping reach of Gwyn's great sword, and now the advancing guards drew their own blades, weapons she couldn't see. She guessed their attacks by the movements of their arms and footwork, but the precise angles of their grip and wrists were invisible to her, and the inches thus concealed were the only distance between life and death in battle. She thrust and swept her blade at the enemy almost blindly, knowing she had handled the weapon better the first day she'd wielded it than she did now. Her erratic flurry of motion at least gave the guards pause, and she took another step back, her mind racing.

Mithna now stood side by side with Nafar, fighting in the broad doorway of the keep. Envil had taken two of his men to the top of the wall to deal with the archers. So far they had not returned, and it seemed too long. The remainder of the enemy guard, these in Baldor tartan, had barred the doors, but they had no means to deter the attackers from within, so the Baldor men had torn a heavy timber from a nearby scaffolding and smashed through the barrier in only a few charges.

For long moments the two sides squared against one another, each trying to find gaps in the shield wall, then attempting to shove the other back, determined to gain ground or bear an opponent to the floor to open a hole in the formation. Nafar tolerated this only briefly before the guards immediately in front of him slackened their pressure just slightly to breathe, and in that instant he was upon them. Dropping his spear, he slipped between the enemy's hafts like water flowing between rocks, drawing his sword in the same motion and severing the neck of one enemy. The second died only a moment later.

Mithna followed him through, carefully disengaging as he had taught her so as not to give her enemy too great an opening, and between the two of them they flanked the opposing shield wall, forcing the next few foes to turn and draw shorter weapons. The Baldor men pressed the advantage, and the shoving formations dissolved into a general melee.

Nafar and Mithna fought dispassionately, ready to disarm, wound, or kill only as the tactics best warranted, but the warriors from Baldor showed no quarter. True enough, these were former friends, or even relatives, but this was a battle between loyalist and traitor, and they inflicted the known penalty for such betrayal. Quickly the Baldor enemies realized their only hope of survival lay in victory, and their defense became desperate.

Mithna's spear had broken, so she fought on with an ax taken from a fallen enemy. Or ally. In the chaos of blood-covered faces and matching colors it was difficult to tell. A fighter thrust his spear at her. She drove her shield into the attack, hoping to bind the blade in the wood planks. Her eyes went wide as the point protruded before them, but it missed her shield arm. Before the attacker could withdraw she swung her weapon at the spear haft. The agile war ax failed to cleave through the heavy shaft, but the cut scored deeply. She allowed her opponent to withdraw; his spear wrenched free of her shield, and she leaned backward as if the sudden loss of tension had thrown her balance. This left her front leg exposed, baiting the man into a low thrust. Mithna raised her foot and drove forward, then quickly dropped her weight back onto the front foot, trapping the spearpoint against the flagstones and splintering the weakened haft. Her foe kept the broken end in his left hand and pulled a dagger from his belt with his right.

She heard Nafar cry out to her left and hazarded a quick glance over her shoulder. His right side now bled from a ragged wound below his ribs, but the guard who had inflicted it was already spitted on the captain's blade. Her own enemy leapt forward in her moment of distraction, but she turned behind her shield. The dagger struck the wood, but her own shield blocked her vision, hiding the quick movement of the enemy's left hand until the last moment. The broken spear shaft struck Mithna in the temple, stunning her. She swung her axe and felt it bite flesh, not armor, and knew she had been lucky. He recoiled, yelling in pain, and before she knew what she was doing she had taken the opening, burying her weapon in his stunned face.

The left guard lunged at Gwyn. She sidestepped his thrust, but to ensure a margin of safety she was forced to move too early and too far, allowing the enemy to recover to a guard stance long before she could attempt any counter. Perhaps sensing her disorientation, the right guard made a hasty, low thrust. She pivoted, striking down at the forward arm, felt the bloody edge of her sword open the veins of his forearm, but she'd given too little room, and his blade twitched toward her, slicing a nasty draw cut into her thigh as they both withdrew.

The first attacker made a hasty slash, forcing her back in a desperate retreat, whipping her sword to clear what she hoped was his line of attack. The sudden move threw yet more droplets from her blooded blade to spatter against the invisible wall, and finally she saw it. The blood. Running down her leg, pouring out of her enemy's arm, painting the edge of the second guard's blade, glowing red and angry. The edge of his blade.

She lunged for him, taking her out of line with the swordsman who had thrust at her first. Now aware of the exact position of his weapon, knowing he would be distracted by the wound in his arm, she easily avoided his late counterattack. He tried to give ground to buy more time but was hemmed in by the guard behind him, and Gwyn's point flashed into his opalescent eye. The second guard made a slash for her neck, but she raised her left arm to catch it on her mail sleeve, accepting the raw impact and knowing it couldn't cut through. As her attacker withdrew, she dropped her forearm along the edge of his blade, letting it slice into her, watching it take on the reddish hue as she stepped back. She couldn't miss the flash of confusion in the swordsman's eyes, for her motion in taking the cut had been too bold to be accidental.

She moved to the left, stacking the two guards on that side so one was blocked by the other, forcing the precious heartbeats it would cost the last enemy to maneuver over his dead companion. They all hesitated, and she let them, drawing out the seconds for Drax to find the women, or for Nafar and the Baldor men to subdue the keep.

Drax darted down the hallway after Rossaen. He heard the sounds of the scuffle begin behind him and forced himself to ignore them. Gwyn would be alright. She always was. Cut, battered, but alive. There were innocents ahead who needed him, and not only that, if Rossaen managed to put them at bay, the odds of keeping the ambassador alive, along with the consequential knowledge in his head, dwindled markedly.

Still, the more quickly he could complete this immediate task, the sooner he could return to Gwyn and the others who might need his help in the battle. He continued following the ambassador, wishing the man wasn't so tall and quick; until he laid eyes on him Drax had pictured him as old and not so hale. The elf had not slept enough since weaving the enchantments needed for the ruse, and his endurance flagged. He began to lose ground.

Fortunately, Rossaen was forced to stop to unlock the door at his destination, and this allowed Drax to close the distance. Less fortunately, his breathing by this point had become clearly audible once his quarry stopped his own mad dash. Before opening the door Rossaen turned back into the hallway, his eyes wide.

"Who's there?" he demanded, pulling a dagger from his belt and slashing the air.

Drax was taken by surprise and jumped back. His feet

slid as he landed, their scrape sounding frighteningly loud to his ears, and the light of Rossaen's lantern shone brightly in his face; he knew he cast a bold shadow. He braced his feet and raised his hands, prepared to dodge the enemy's dagger strike and begin the grapple, his mind racing for some way to subdue the larger man without killing him. Then Rossaen spun the other direction and flung his lantern at the elf's invisible form.

Gwyn sparred for a few heartbeats with her foe, waiting for an opportunity. The rightmost guard had stepped over the dead one and threatened to engage her two-to-one; the last enemy still stood back, blocked by his comrades in the narrow hallway.

Both her forward foes attacked at once. The one on the left, his sword still painted with her blood, swung at her neck again; the other thrust for her belly. If the latter blade was stiff and well-pointed, it threatened to pierce her mail, but she couldn't see it. She threw up a block against the edge coming at her neck and followed the line of the lunger's arm to predict the location of the point, then took a bold risk. Keeping hold of her sword's foregrip in her right hand, she let go with her left and reached down to the blade that had just thrust past her dodging midsection. She had to move quickly, as the foe on her left might easily crash through her weakened guard if he pressed. Blood from the cut on her forearm flowed down onto her hand, and she slipped her palm downward to smear some on the stabber's blade. Reacting quickly, the man forced his weapon upward as he withdrew from the missed thrust, and Gwyn felt the edge tear deeply into her left palm. She screamed at the sudden pain. This was a crippling wound. She could hesitate no longer.

Taking advantage, the foe on the left shoved against her guard, throwing his whole body forward in the hope of moving her sword just far enough to allow him to slide his edge through the bind for a stab at her face. Gwyn stepped back and left, leaving the clash so quickly her enemy came forward, off balance. Before he could capitalize on the opening, she pivoted right and wrapped her bleeding arm around his forward hand, pulling him sideways. Now he served as a shield against his compatriots, and his own weapon was under her control. She punched forward with her right hand, ramming her sword's stiff guard into the man's face, stunning him and opening a gushing cut over his left eye. Her own blood continued to flow, and the fingers of her left hand felt cold.

Drax knew he should roll on the ground to extinguish the flames, but if he did that Rossaen would certainly get inside the prisoner's room and bar the door behind him. Instead, Drax lunged at the ambassador, catching him in the sternum with his shoulder. He felt the man's dagger punch into the meat behind his shoulder, but the administrator lacked the strength to force it through the bone. It would heal. Before he could attempt another stab, the pair had crashed through the unlatched door and slammed onto the stone floor. He heard women's screams from ahead of him. Before Rossaen could recover, Drax placed his right hand in the man's dense, black mane, his ruby ring flashed, and Rossaen's hair began to crackle and burn with invisible flame.

As the man slapped at his head in pained confusion and the hostages looked on in utter bewilderment, Drax rolled off Rossaen and removed his bracelet of simple leather and glass beads, the one he'd managed to secret away from Finn's men before losing consciousness. The women in the room gasped at his sudden appearance, and he looked up to see the foremost was in her early middle years, gold of hair and shapely. Next to her was a young maid, of solid build like her father but sharing her mother's flaxen locks. Behind them crouched two younger girls he couldn't clearly see. "I'm here to rescue you," he announced. "Please help me."

Roused from their shock, the women jumped to action. "The pitcher," called the matron to the two younger girls, pointing to a sideboard across the room. Meanwhile, she fell upon Rossaen, pinning his arms while her eldest daughter kicked him squarely in the head.

"We need him alive," Drax begged as the younger girls doused the flames on his clothes. The bottoms of his trousers, where the oil had run most heavily, still burned with tiny tongues of flame, and the middle daughter grabbed a blanket to finish extinguishing him. As she patted his shins, Drax knew he had burns there but didn't think them too severe. The eldest daughter moved from Rossaen's head and relieved him of his dagger, throwing another kick into his ribs for good measure.

"I won't fight, just put me out!" the ambassador screamed, his hair nearly consumed and the skin of his forehead blistering. Drax pushed himself off the ground and took the blanket from his legs, wrapping it around Rossaen's head to smother the flames, his left shoulder throbbing with every move.

"Are you alright?" the matriarch asked him, confusion over many points still clear on her features.

"I will be," he answered, still holding the blanket over Rossaen's face. *But what about Gwyn?* he wondered, looking toward the door.

Gwyn still grappled with the bludgeoned guard. He fought against her, but the more he struggled the more difficulty his allies had in getting an attack past him and into Gwyn. He clawed at her right arm, trying to slow her movement, but relentlessly she brought her edge to his neck. She saw his desperate determination dissolve into horror just as her steel opened flesh. With a final pull she cut his throat and finally let go of his arm, leaving him to crumple to the floor. She brought her left hand back to her sword's hilt for a proper grip and realized how weak it now felt. The last two fingers on her sliced hand seemed not to be working at all.

Two foes remained. One had her hand's blood illuminating his sword, and she brought her own weapon to guard against him. The other had barely engaged so far, and Gwyn saw panic glowing in his eyes. For a bare moment she ignored the fighting enemy and lunged at the frightened one, bellowing rage. His attention scanning briefly over his dead companions, he turned and fled as the final fighter screamed and cursed him for a coward. She turned to the man, bloody but unbeaten, the hellish battle light flashing hot in her eyes. The man's face went slack, but he drove in, pulling a dagger from his belt. He kept his sword in guard, trying to ward off Gwyn's blade as he worked inside her reach for a knife strike. Instead of forcing him back, Gwyn maintained her own guard and stepped off line to the left as he advanced. Taking him completely by surprise, she reached her longer arms past his weapon and fed him a face-full of *Tyralist's* pommel. He reeled for a moment, and she gutted him before he could recover. Her fervor dissipating, the pain of her wounds flamed anew, and she grunted against the agony. Pressing her left hand against her chest, she limped off in the direction Rossaen and Drax had gone.

Mithna heard footsteps from the back of the hall and brought her shield and ax back up before her, but only one man in Kart plaid appeared. When he laid eyes on the scene before him he dropped his sword and collapsed to the floor. The blonde page, likewise, turned to survey the aftermath.

The fight had been all but won when Envil returned with his two men, leaning heavily on his spear as blood poured from his right hip. Only two of the Baldor traitors were left then, fighting desperately in a corner, and when they saw the expression of their chieftain, one not of wrath or vengeance but of deep pain and sorrow, at last they laid down arms. Envil did not promise them their lives, but at least safe conduct back to the clan seat for the elders to hear them and decide their fate. Clan Baldor had lost two more of her loyal warriors, and everyone was wounded. One more was unlikely to live the night, so far from real help.

"Lie down," Mithna told her master.

"I don't take orders from you, lass," Nafar grunted back, blood oozing through the fingers of the hand he held over his side. Nevertheless, he levered himself to the ground and stretched out.

"Go get my saddle bags off Gwyn's horse," Mithna shouted to one of the least injured of the Baldor men. He nodded and ran off. She unbelted her outer tunic and pulled it over her head, balling it up and pressing it onto Nafar's wound. He hissed in pain. "You need to be sewn up," she announced."

"You say that like I didn't know," Nafar answered, hissing again in a rhythm like a chuckle. "Are there others worse off than me?"

Mithna looked around. "Two. One, I don't think anyone can help. The Baldor men are seeing to the other."

"Any sign of Gwyn?"

She shook her head.

The runner appeared with Mithna's saddlebags, and she removed more bandages, needle, and thread. She pulled away the bloody wad of her tunic and spread the wound open for a moment, which caused Nafar to growl. "Bleeding's slowing. It's a bit jagged, but it didn't get into the muscle much. Your guts are intact. Hold that there."

She pressed Nafar's hand back onto the bloody tunic, and he did as she bid. His expression showed this was only the most recent of many such surgeries. Mithna wiped her bloody hands on her breeches and proceeded to thread a needle.

Nafar's stoic expression took on a curious note, then dismayed. "Do you hear that?"

A different Baldor man, his belt converted to a sling for his right arm, entered the doorway, breathing heavily. He presented himself to Envil who limped toward the stairs at the back of the hall, where he believed his family to be, while his men tried to convince him to wait for help. "Chieftain," the breathless man gasped, "we're in trouble."

Drax stood by the door in hesitation, reluctant to leave the rescued hostages alone with their former captor for a host of reasons. He turned toward the Baldor matriarch to ask her condition when suddenly the girls screamed once again. Drax turned and prepared to defend himself before seeing Gwyn standing in the doorway. Blood ran from her left arm and right leg, but the way she cradled her bloody hand gave him the most concern. She pointed her sword at his charred clothes. "What the hell happened to you?"

"I could ask you the same. Are we clear?"

"I think so." Drax saw Gwyn's gaze fall to Rossaen's covered face. "He's not dead," the elf clarified.

"I know," she replied. "Best get his hands bound."

Drax took the meaning of Gwyn's supernatural observation. "Your eyes?"

"The same."

Rossaen showed no contrition as they tied him. They hauled him to his feet and forced him to march toward the stairs. "Fools," he spat. "What do you think you've gained by this? Were your death warrants not signed boldly enough already?"

"You're going before the Conclave," Gwyn growled. "You'll tell what you know of Haric's moves before Vassin's death."

"And after it," the eldest woman added.

"You won't live to get me there," Rossaen swore.

"Then neither will you," Gwyn promised. "None of us will lose any sleep slaying a traitor, especially Envil after you abducted his family and armed his enemies."

"*His* enemies?" Rossaen laughed. "More like *his*." He gestured with his elbow toward Drax.

"What are you talking about?" the elf demanded.

"We tried to ply the northern nomads with dreams of conquest over their brothers, or even the battered Southerners. They seemed amenable at first, but in the end they demanded a more pristine jewel."

"What do you mean?" Drax repeated, stepping in front of Rossaen and stopping him with a shove.

"The Elven Forest, of course," the ambassador replied. "The nomads have lived for generations on nothing but scrub brush and rock. They're ready for a change to something greener."

"You lie," Gwyn accused.

"Why lie?" Rossaen laughed. "The damage is done. We waited here for one more wagon train and some dozens of final stragglers from the east. Most of the tribes are already through and well on their way."

Drax's eyes went wide as he looked to Gwyn. "No!" he shouted. "You can't–"

By now they had turned the corner bringing the stairs in sight, and Mithna came barreling down them, shouting, "Gwyn! Gwyn!"

"We're over here," she called back, stopping the younger fighter short as she nearly went past the landing into the cellars.

Reversing her momentum, Mithna leaned her head out

into the hallway, quickly seeing that Envil's family was now safe. "Gwyn, come quick!" With that she turned from the landing and charged back up the stairs.

Gwyn hesitated. "Can you handle him?" she asked Drax.

The elf showed a malice in his eyes she had scarcely seen outside a mirror, and as she glanced to Envil's wife and eldest daughter, their own glowing expressions and eyes suggested Rossaen had only ever entered their presence under heavy guard. Satisfied, she ran after Mithna.

She had begun to acclimate to her altered vision, but the stone steps gave her considerable trouble. She was embarrassed to hear Drax lead his charges onto the bottom of the stairs by the time she cleared the top. Once on the main floor with its fabric hangings and wood paneling, she could at least suss out the walls and floor, finally managing a proper sprint across the open hall. Mithna stood in the doorway, beckoning her outside. As soon as she cleared the threshold, Mithna now a few steps ahead, her eyes were drawn toward a glowing mass to the east, dim and hazy through the thick stone of the fort's curtain wall. The unmistakable sound of many mounted men moving together echoed up to her. "What's that?" she asked, pointing at the stone.

Mithna understood little of what Drax's magic had done to Gwyn's sight, but she had enough awareness not to question it. "A nomad raiding party, nearly two hundred men ahorse. They'll be here in a quarter of an hour."

"They're not well armored…" called a Baldor man from the walls.

"Not yet," Rossaen snickered as Drax hustled him forward.

"We have enough men and bows to hold them," the sentry finished.

Gwyn shook her head. "Not as torn up as we are, and Haric's spies will know we came here soon, if they don't already. They'll trap us from both sides and starve us out." Drax approached holding something dark in his hands. As he reached toward her sword she realized it must be the sling she'd discarded. She wanted to take the sling from him instead, but with a pang of worry she kept her left hand still and handed the blade off to her oath-brother.

"Clean it first," she heard Envil's wife instruct, confident with the wisdom of a warrior clan's matriarch. Her eldest daughter drew up beside Gwyn, and the warrior gingerly allowed the young lady to take her hand and begin wrapping it in a bandage.

Nafar hobbled up, still favoring his wounded side. "What do we do now, Candon?"

Gwyn ground her teeth at the gall of it. "You know there's only one answer to that, Hradash. We run."

The beleaguered Atlunders finished patching up their walking wounded and saddled the horses left by the fort's defenders. The dying Baldor man, still conscious, refused to be brought along, lest he slow down the rest. They strove with him, but he threatened to kill himself at the first opportunity if they took him by force, and none would dishonor him by taking away his weapons. Envil's wife prayed with him, then they left him where he lay.

Rossaen and the surviving Baldor and Kart traitors were tied on their saddles and kept at the center of the group along with the horses captured from the fort's stables, watched over by Envil's nephew with a long spear. By the time the troop was prepared to set out, the advancing nomads had given up shouting to be let in, as they'd expected to be, and started arguing amongst themselves whether to begin filling the eastern moat with rubble to make a causeway and force their way through the gates or to simply go back to their homes and miss out on the promise of elven plunder.

Gwyn paused at the back of their party, turning in the saddle to look at the fortress but seeing only the spark-filled blackness. For the first time she had a moment to consider the possibility that her vision might never return to normal and choked down the rare sensation of fear. She turned forward to see Nafar looking back at her. She nodded once, and the loyal Atlunders, broken and bleeding, set spurs to their mounts and fled.

EPILOGUE

Gwyn sat on the ground on the night of their first camp away from the pass, staring into the fire. Drax came and sat next to her.

"How's your hand?" he asked.

"Stopped bleeding, but otherwise the same," Gwyn grumbled.

"And your eyes?"

"Starting to improve, I think. It's hard to tell in the dark, but the campfire seems less…unreal, and when I look away from it, the glow of the plants and night bugs is less bright."

"I'm sorry," Drax offered. "I've never had an enchantment with side effects like yours, so I never guessed they could persist if you wore the amulet too long. Which reminds me, I picked this up for you." Drax pressed the crude fetish of fangs into her hands.

Gwyn couldn't believe she had forgotten it. She stretched the necklace out and felt the ends of the leather, then realized she couldn't retie it without sight. "I can't lay the blame on you," she told Drax. "You didn't want to do it in the first place." She balled the necklace back up and placed it into her pouch.

"Still, if it had gotten you killed…"

Gwyn stayed quiet in case Drax wanted to finish his sentence, but she knew he wouldn't.

"Gwyn," he finally continued, "you know I have to head south from here. It's probably too late to warn my people, but I have to try, or at least do something. Their magic is strong, but they know nothing of war. I can't just let so many die without even trying."

She nodded. "I'd do the same."

"I don't have to take Flamewind. I can go on foot, or take one of the horses from the fort if Envil will permit me."

Gwyn had known this moment would come, and she'd pondered it as carefully as she did anything. "I think," she replied slowly, "Flamewind should go with you. I think…*I* should go with you."

Drax leaned back in surprise. "What about your home? Your family?"

"I have family in the west, in the south, and I have family sitting right here. It will take weeks to move Rossaen to the Conclave, and there's no guarantee of the outcome. Atlund may need my sword soon, but my oath-brother needs it now. I won't withhold it."

For the third time Drax embraced Gwyn, and she squeezed him briefly with her right arm. "I should try to insist you stay here," Drax admitted, "but I don't have the will."

Gwyn thought of the thousands of innocent elves soon fated to learn the horror of war, a horror she could call by that name even while reveling in it. She imagined their eyes, naïve and afraid, facing steel and flame and death, contrasted with the wickedness in the souls of some of her own people that had supported this invasion, and she knew that no matter what it might cost Atlund, she could not abandon the elves. More powerful still, she felt the muster of forces in Atlund, the quickening desire to lead armies in her name, the temptation of what Daruneh had called the "inky fingerprints" of her great adversary, and reckoned wisdom might lie in being elsewhere. "Neither do I," she finally replied.

Gwyn gazed into the flames, resolved for the second time in three years to turn toward the south and ride to war.

APPENDIX A
DRAMATIS PERSONAE

Adezavax, Sergeant – (a-DEZ-a-vax) – also known as Dez, leader of the fighters guarding the merchant caravan that Gwyn accompanied to the Southern Kingdoms after leaving Atlund

Adric – (ADD-rick) – Gwyn's stepfather

Aldrin – (AL-drin) – Gwyn's elder stepbrother

Ardos – (ARE-dose) – a middle-aged Sutherese sergeant, friend to Gwyn, husband of Mona, father of Daramis, also of two older sons who were killed in action against invading orcs

Baraxis, Lord Major – (buh-RAX-iss) – also, briefly, Lord General, lord of the fief of Sutherset in the Southern Kingdoms, major of the Storn River Bridge Battalion, patron and later liege of Gwyn, her mentor in combat, tactics, and leadership

Dahaer – (duh-HAIR) – a wizard

Daruneh – (DAH-roo-nay) – mysterious observer and apparent benefactor

Drax – (DRAX) – elven enchanter, wizard-for-hire in the Southern Kingdoms, instrumental to the breaking of the orcish siege on the Capital

Girahl – (gir-RAWL) – father of Gwyn, renowned warrior of Clan Candon of Atlund, often courted (unsuccessfully) to join the king's bodyguard, oath-brother to Tehgil, first husband of Lischa, killed before Gwyn's birth by the wizard Kellgore in the forests west of his home

Gwyn et Sheevasa – (GWIN et shee-VOSS-uh) – literally "Hand of Vengeance," also known as Gwyn the Savage, especially in the Southern Kingdoms, and Gwyn of Candon in Atlund, and simply as Gwyn to acquaintances (and elsewhere herein); only daughter of Girahl and Lischa; mercenary

Haric – (HARR-ick) – young politician from Clan Kart, in his early twenties

Karon – (CAR-un) – boy of five years, son of Shon and Tira

Kellgore – (KELL-gore) – evil wizard taking up residence in Atlund's western forests in the decades prior to Gwyn's birth, responsible for the transformation of lost and abducted Atlunders into beastlike creatures known as Minions of Kellgore (or, colloquially, simply "minions"), slain by King Vassin V in Gwyn's sixteenth year

Lirisch – (LEER-ish) – Gwyn's younger stepbrother

Lischa – (LI-shuh) – mother of Gwyn, wife of Girahl until widowed by him prior to Gwyn's birth, later remarried to Adric, subsequently mother of Aldrin and Lirisch

Mithna – (MYTH-nuh) – page to Captain Nafar

Nafar, Captain – (nuh-FAR) – captain of King Vassin's bodyguard, reluctant mentor to Gwyn during the muster leading up to the Forest Campaign

Rossaen – (ROSS-ay-en) – Recently appointed liaison between the Atlund Citadel and the eastern clan chieftains

Shon, Captain – (SHON) – second-in-command to Lord Major Baraxis, Gwyn's direct superior upon her initial hiring in Sutherset, later her close friend and confidante, slain at the siege of Roon in Baraxis' eastern campaign against the orcs, wife of Tira, father of Karon

Sudro – (SOO-dro) – young warrior from Clan Baldor in eastern Atlund, briefly confidante to Gwyn during the Forest Campaign, in which he was killed in action

Tehgil – (TAY-gul) – oath-father of Gwyn, oath-brother of Girahl, widower at an early age (wife and son died in childbirth)

Tira – (TIR-uh) – wife of Shon, steward of his lands and herds in his absence, mother of Karon, now widowed

Vassin V, King – (VASS-in) – Gwyn's second cousin, once removed, king of Atlund during the Forest Campaign against Kellgore launched in Gwyn's sixteenth year, slayed Kellgore at the culmination of that campaign, known to Gwyn to be in ill health at the start of her return home from the Southern Kingdoms

Vigurd – (VIH-gurd) – An Atlund warrior from Clan Kart

APPENDIX B
GLOSSARY OF FICTIONAL AND MEDIEVAL TERMS

Alure – the top, flat surface of a fortified wall on which guards could walk, especially when granting access to towers built into or adjoining the wall; also called a "wall walk"

Baldor – (BAL-dur) – A clan inhabiting Atlund's farthest southeastern corner, bounded by the Sharai on the south and the Qachars in the east

Battlement – the top courses of stones of a fortification wall, often crenellated, meaning the profile alternates between raised sections (merlons), which provide cover, and lowered sections (embrasures or crenets), which provide visibility and clear lines of attack

Candon – (CAN-dun) – Atlund clan to which Gwyn belongs, a small clan informally subordinate to the larger Vassin Clan, their close kin

Demesne – the portion of a noble's holdings used as his personal lands and residence

Embrasure – in a crenellated battlement, any of the alternating lower sections which provide visibility for defenders and allow attack with ranged weaponry; also called a crenet

Faithful One, the – called *Aridan* (ARE-i-dan) in the Atlund tongue, a moon of predictable phases and good light

Fief – the lands of a noble, held from a more powerful noble or royal in exchange for an oath of fealty

Forest Campaign – term used to refer to the military action against the evil wizard Kellgore that took place during Gwyn's sixteenth year in the forested western frontier of Atlund

Gambeson – a garment of quilted cloth comprised of many layers of linen or wool, worn to provide padding under mail or as armor in its own right

Halberd – a weapon consisting of an ax head with a top spike fixed to a long pole, usually five to six feet in overall length

Kart – a wealthy Atlund clan situated in the northwestern regions, near the Citadel

Little Wanderer, the – called *Bia Creg* (BEE-uh CREG) in the Atlund tongue, a strange, tiny moon that moves backwards through the sky and sometimes winks in and out of visibility, too small to provide illumination

Mail – metal armor composed of interlocking rings, providing flexible protection, especially against cuts (sometimes referred to as "chainmail," a term disfavored by historians)

Merlon – in a crenellated battlement, any of the alternating raised sections which provide cover to defenders

Minion – in Atlund, usually an abbreviated term for "Minions of Kellgore," humans transformed into beasts by an evil wizard, along with their progeny which were caused to multiply by unnatural means; see "Kellgore" in Appendix A

Mural tower – a tower built within a fortification wall

Padded jack – similar to gambeson (see above) but often with an outer layer of leather and more likely to be worn as primary armor (rather than as a padding layer under mail)

Parapet – the top portion of a fortification wall where defenders are stationed

Pillory – an instrument of corporal punishment in which a victim was bound by trapping their wrists and neck in holes through a split, wooden board, forcing them to stand in a hunched position for a period of beating or ridicule; sometimes confused with "stocks" which were for the feet

Qachars – (ka-HARS) – alternately Qachar Range or Qachar Mountains; mountain range on Atlund's eastern border, running southeast to border the Elven Forest and Southern Kingdoms as well; rugged and sheer in the north with relatively few navigable passes; lands east are dry and often desolate, believed by most Atlunders to be scourged by chaotic magics

Ricasso – the unsharpened section of a sword blade, just above the guard

Rushlight – a primitive and inexpensive form of lighting made by soaking the pith of plants from the rush family in leftover fat or grease, then mounting them in iron clips secured to metal legs or wood blocks; their quality and duration of light varied greatly

Sally port – a small, secured opening in a fortification wall, meant to allow defenders inside to exit and attack a besieging force without opening the larger, main gates

Sharai – (shuh-RYE) – mighty river flowing from the northern Tunaris in an east-southeasterly direction, forming Atlund's southern border, until it reaches nearly the foothills of the Qachar range where it turns and runs nearly due south for hundreds of leagues

Sippet – small piece of dry or toasted bread served with spreads or stews

Small beer – beer brewed with just enough alcohol to render water safe to drink, given to small children or those whose constitutions won't tolerate a stronger brew

Storn – (STORN) – river in the west of the Southern Kingdoms, flowing down from the Tunaris before joining greater waters; lands south stood contested by the orcs for generations, making the Storn the effective southern border of the nation along its length

Sutherese – residents of Sutherset, a moniker given by themselves which they carry with pride

Sutherset – fief of Lord Major Baraxis, in the west of the Southern Kingdoms

Terillah – (TERR-i-law) – creator deity worshipped by most humans and elves (with the rare exceptions being atheist or agnostic; worship of other gods is unknown in the current era), believed to provide providential protection and blessing to just and innocent adherents

Tunaris – (too-NAR-ees) – alternately Tunari Range or Tunari Mountains, mountain range forming Atlund's western border, running nearly due south for hundreds of leagues to form the western border of the Elven Forest and a substantial barrier in the west of the Southern Kingdoms; west of the mountains lies the western sea, from whence explorers have never returned; in the south a narrow strip of fertile, sparsely populated land does exist between the mountains and the sea

Warded lock – a mechanical lock in which the lever or bolt is blocked by a series of obstructions (wards) that can be bypassed using a key cut with the correct pattern; keys usually take the form of cylindrical shank with a ring or flat disc for holding at one end and a flat metal plate cut to engage with the lock's ward pattern on the other end – the overall silhouette of the iconic "old fashioned" key

Wind, the – called *tyralist* (TEER-a-list) in the old Atlund language, an enchanted gale that blows out of the north from dusk to dawn during the winter, from the icy northern wastes of Atlund to the River Sharai in the south, which causes homicidal madness upon brief exposure; prolonged exposure is fatal

Zil'bast – a rough transliteration of an orcish word meaning, approximately, "death powered," orcs twisted by unknown forces to grant them magical abilities; as these abilities were not natural to the orcish race, their magical power is volatile, susceptible to violent disruption by certain wizards

About the Author

Shane L. Coffey lives in Missouri with his wife and the multitude of characters trying to fight their way from his brain to his computer screen. He is a man of simple tastes, inexpensive hobbies, and little travel…but if any organization starts making plans for an expedition to Chulak or Rivendell, he'll be very interested to know whether they require any skillsets he possesses (or could convincingly fake).

To read more of the author's work, visit burnthemap.com